RANDOM
HOUSE

LARGE
PRINT

THE ENEMY
OF MY ENEMY

THE ENEMY
OF MY ENEMY

Also by W.E.B. Griffin and
William E. Butterworth IV
Available from Random House Large Print

Death at Nuremberg

W.E.B. GRIFFIN
and William E. Butterworth IV

★
THE ENEMY
OF MY ENEMY
★

A Clandestine Operations Novel
Book V

RANDOM HOUSE
LARGE PRINT

Published in the United States of America by Random House Large Print in association with G. P. Putnam's Sons, an imprint of Penguin Random House LLC.

Penguin supports copyright. Copyright fuels creativity, encourages diverse voices, promotes free speech, and creates a vibrant culture. Thank you for buying an authorized edition of this book and for complying with copyright laws by not reproducing, scanning, or distributing any part of it in any form without permission. You are supporting writers and allowing Penguin to continue to publish books for every reader.

Cover design: Eric Fuentecilla
Cover images: (officer) Stephen Mulcahey / Arcangel; (buildings) ALE_ES0 / Shutterstock
Photograph of the authors by Tom Clancy

The Library of Congress has established a Cataloging-in-Publication record for this title.

ISBN: 978-1-9848-2758-6

www.randomhouse.com/largeprint

FIRST LARGE PRINT EDITION

Printed in the United States of America

10 9 8 7 6 5 4 3 2 1

This Large Print edition published in accord with the standards of the N.A.V.H.

26 July 1777

"The necessity of procuring good intelligence is apparent and need not be further urged."

George Washington
General and Commander in Chief
The Continental Army

FOR THE LATE

WILLIAM E. COLBY
An OSS Jedburgh First Lieutenant who became director of the Central Intelligence Agency.

AARON BANK
An OSS Jedburgh First Lieutenant who became a colonel and the father of Special Forces.

WILLIAM R. CORSON
A legendary Marine intelligence officer whom the KGB hated more than any other U.S. intelligence officer—and not only because he wrote the definitive work on them.

RENÉ J. DÉFOURNEAUX
A U.S. Army OSS Second Lieutenant attached to the British SOE who jumped into Occupied France alone and later became a legendary U.S. Army intelligence officer.

FOR THE LIVING

BILLY WAUGH
A legendary Special Forces Command Sergeant Major who retired and then went on to hunt down the infamous Carlos the Jackal. Billy could have terminated Osama bin Laden in the early 1990s but could not get permission to do so. After fifty years in the business, Billy is still going after the bad guys.

JOHNNY REITZEL
An Army Special Operations officer who could have terminated the head terrorist of the seized cruise ship **Achille Lauro** but could not get permission to do so.

RALPH PETERS
An Army intelligence officer who has written the best analysis of our war against terrorists and of our enemy that I have ever seen.

And for the New Breed

MARC L
A senior intelligence officer who, despite his youth, reminds me of Bill Colby more and more each day.

FRANK L
A legendary Defense Intelligence Agency officer who retired and now follows in Billy Waugh's footsteps.

OUR NATION OWES THESE PATRIOTS
A DEBT BEYOND REPAYMENT.

AND
In Loving Memory Of
Colonel José Manuel Menéndez
Cavalry, Argentine Army, Retired

THE ENEMY
OF MY ENEMY

PREFACE

In the late afternoon of April 12, 1945, a Secret Service agent on Vice President Harry S Truman's protection detail informed him he was urgently needed at the White House. Truman was surprised. Since their inauguration in January, the sixty-one-year-old Vice President had seen President Franklin Delano Roosevelt only twice, and had never been alone with him.

The story went around that Truman was closer to FDR's wife, Eleanor, than he was to the ailing sixty-three-year-old.

When Truman got to the White House, he in fact was greeted by Mrs. Roosevelt.

"Harry," she said. "The President is dead."

Roosevelt had died hours before in Warm Springs, Georgia, in the company of his mistress, Lucy Mercer.

It has been reliably reported that immediately after Truman was sworn in by Chief Justice

Harlan Stone as the thirty-third President of the United States, his first order was: "Get Justice Jackson and Captain Souers over here right now."

Captain Sidney W. Souers, United States Navy Reserve, and Colonel Harry S Truman, Missouri National Guard, were old and close "Weekend Warrior" buddies from Missouri.

When Souers, at the time the chairman of the board of a large insurance company, was called to active duty in Washington, he moved into the small apartment in which then–U.S. Senator Truman lived. There was room because Mrs. Bess Truman hated Washington and was seldom in the city.

Truman and Supreme Court Associate Justice Robert H. Jackson had become friends when the latter had advised the Truman Committee on how to deal with war profiteers.

The three frequently dined and had a couple of drinks together in the Truman apartment.

Truman neither liked nor trusted the people close to President Roosevelt, and knew he needed the advice of friends whom he could trust without reservation.

The next day, April 13th, there was proof that Roosevelt and the people around him didn't like or trust Truman either.

U.S. Army Major General Leslie Groves—whom Truman had never met—was shown into the Oval Office by a visibly nervous Secretary of State Edward Stettinius Jr. Then Stettinius left the President alone with General Groves.

Groves told Truman America's greatest secret: The United States had developed the most powerful weapon the world had ever known: the atomic bomb.

Truman was furious that he had been kept in the dark by Roosevelt, almost certainly at the advice of those around him.

A month after General Alfred Jodl, the chief of staff of the German Armed Forces High Command, had signed on May 7th the unconditional surrender documents ending the war in Europe, the first of Roosevelt's cronies to go was Stettinius. Truman fired him on June 27, 1945, replacing him on July 3rd—some said at the recommendation of Justice Jackson—with James F. Byrnes.

On August 6, 1945, an American B-29 bomber dropped the world's first deployed atomic bomb over the Japanese city of Hiroshima.

Three days later, a second B-29 dropped another A-bomb on Nagasaki.

In a radio address on August 15th, citing the devastating power of "a new and most cruel bomb," Japanese Emperor Hirohito announced his country's unconditional surrender.

Almost immediately after the formal surrender ceremonies aboard the battleship USS **Missouri** in Tokyo Bay, Truman came under enormous pressure from the Army, the Navy, the State Department, and the Federal Bureau of Investigation. They demanded, for their own interagency rivalry reasons, that he disestablish the Office of Strategic Services—the OSS—America's first centralized intelligence agency, which FDR had created around the start of World War II.

Reasoning that the war was over, and the OSS no longer needed, Truman did as requested.

He soon realized that that had been a serious mistake, as all the agencies that had cried for the death of the OSS now were fighting one another to take over its functions.

Truman reacted in Trumanesque fashion.

By executive order, he established the Directorate of Central Intelligence, answerable only to him, and named his crony Sid Souers, whom he promoted to rear admiral, as its director.

I

[ONE]
The White House
1600 Pennsylvania Avenue, N.W.
Washington, D.C.
1415 8 April 1946

A Secret Service agent in suit and tie opened the door to the Oval Office and announced, "Mr. President, Admiral Souers."

"Show him in, then close the door," President Harry S Truman ordered. "No interruptions."

Admiral Sidney W. Souers entered the room and stopped short of the coffee table in front of a couch. The stocky fifty-four-year-old was in his Navy Service Dress Blue woolen uniform, its sleeves near the cuffs bristling with gold braid. He had an intelligent face, with warm, inquisitive eyes, a headful of closely cropped graying hair, and a neatly trimmed mustache.

"Mr. President."

"You took your sweet time getting here, Sid."

"Harry, I hung up the phone and walked out of my office. What's so urgent?"

Truman picked up a sheet of paper from his desk and waved it angrily.

Souers recognized it as the SIGABA message he had sent over hours earlier. He saw that the paper had his handwritten note at the top, which read "There's more to this. Let me know when you want to discuss— SWS."

"These Nazi bastards escaping in Nuremberg," Truman blurted. "That's urgent and goddamn unacceptable."

Truman's eyes went to the paper, scanning it:

TOP SECRET

URGENT
DUPLICATION FORBIDDEN
FROM: DIRECTOR DCI GERMANY
0010 GREENWICH 8 APR 1946
TO: DIRECTOR WASH DC
1—COL M COHEN, CHIEF NUREMBERG TRIBUNAL CIC, INFORMS THAT BURGDORF AND VON DIETELBURG ESCAPED TRIBUNAL PRISON INFIRMARY 5 APR. COHEN SUSPECTS ODESSA INVOLVEMENT. ESCAPE HAS NOT, REPEAT, NOT BEEN MADE PUBLIC.
2—COL WASSERMAN, CHIEF CIC VIENNA, REPORTS

WALTER WANGERMANN, VIENNA POLICE CHIEF
OF INTELLIGENCE, HAS INFORMED HIM BRUNO
HOLZKNECHT, CHIEF OF POLICE SURVEILLANCE, IS
MISSING AS OF 5 APR. WANGERMANN SUSPECTS
DCI INVOLVEMENT. WASSERMAN SUSPECTS NKGB,
MOSSAD, OR AVO INVOLVEMENT.
3—CONSIDERING RECENT ACTIVITIES OF CRONLEY
ET AL, UNDERSIGNED CONSIDERS DCI INVOLVE-
MENT IN NUREMBERG AND VIENNA INCIDENTS. AN
INVESTIGATION WOULD BE ILL-ADVISED AND NO
ACTION IN THAT REGARD HAS BEEN UNDERTAKEN.
4—FURTHER DEVELOPMENTS WILL BE REPORTED
AS THEY OCCUR.
WALLACE, COL, DIRECTOR DCI GERMANY
END

TOP SECRET

"And you say there's more?" Truman said, toss-
ing the sheet back to the desktop. "Jesus! It's bad
enough that this Odessa organization has been
smuggling SS bastards out of Europe—and out of
our grasp so we can't prosecute them—but now,
when we finally grab two of Odessa's top leaders,
they somehow snatch the sons of bitches from our
prison? It's outrageous!"

The President came out from behind his desk
and walked to the couch.

"Pour yourself a drink, Sid. While you're at it, pour one for me."

"It's two o'clock in the afternoon."

"Pour the drinks. You're going to need it," the President said, then sat down, and while Souers was retrieving a bottle of Haig & Haig scotch from the credenza, where it was concealed from public view, he picked up the telephone. "Get Justice Jackson for me," he ordered, then pushed the SPEAKER button and put the telephone handset back in its cradle.

When Truman had been a United States senator from Missouri, Supreme Court Justice Robert H. Jackson would join him and Captain Souers, USNR, for dinner and drinks in Truman's apartment—away from the prying eyes, and ears, of the Washington establishment.

Now, Truman had recently named the fifty-four-year-old Jackson—who had been FDR's attorney general before nominating him to serve on the Supreme Court—as chief U.S. prosecutor for the Nuremberg trials.

Voices from the telephone speaker immediately began to be heard.

"Vint Hill, Presidential priority. Justice Jackson in Nuremberg on a secure line. Conversation will not, repeat, not be transcribed."

"White House, hold one," another voice said,

then, "Fulda, Presidential priority. Justice Jackson in Nuremberg. Secure line, no transcription."

"White House, hold one."

"Justice Jackson's chambers."

"This is the White House calling. The President for Justice Jackson. The line is secure."

"One moment, please."

"Robert Jackson."

"Hello, Bob."

"Mr. President."

"Hey, Bob," Souers called out.

"Anchors aweigh, Sid."

"Bob," the President said, "Sid and I were sitting around having a little nip, and we figured, what the hell, let's call Bob and have a little chat."

"That's flattering, Mr. President. What would you two like to chat about?"

"How about those Nazi bastards who escaped the Tribunal Prison? We've got to get them back and make damn sure it never happens again."

"Harry, everybody's working on it. Just a few minutes ago, I had Colonel Cohen in my office."

"He's the counterintelligence guy in Nuremberg?" Truman said, glancing at the SIGABA message.

"Right. Smart as they come. The only thing he had new for me was that he added the AVO to the list of suspects."

"And what the hell is that?"

"It stands for 'Államvedélmi Osztálya.' It's the Russian-controlled Secret Police in Hungary. It's headed by a chap named Gábor Péter, who Cohen says is a real sonofabitch."

"That's all this Colonel Cohen had to say?" the President asked, almost incredulously, staring at the telephone.

"He said Super Spook might have some ideas. And should be involved, and I heartily agree."

"Who the hell is Super Spook? More important, why isn't he involved?"

"Captain Jim Cronley. The man you chose to be my bodyguard. He ran the operation in Vienna that bagged Burgdorf and von Dietelburg. I started calling him Super Spook when he figured out how Odessa managed to smuggle cyanide capsules into the Tribunal Prison."

"I know who Cronley is, Bob. I promoted him to captain. And gave him the Distinguished Service Medal for what he did in Argentina with that half ton of uranium oxide some other Nazi bastard was about to sell to the goddamn Russians. And now you call him Super Spook? A twenty-two-year-old?"

"He's that good, Harry. Young, yes, but remarkably good. You just said so yourself, in so many words."

"Then why the hell isn't he involved? Jesus H. Christ!"

"He's in Argentina," Souers put in.

Truman's eyes went to Souers.

"Okay, and what the hell is he doing in Argentina? Actually, strike that. I don't give a damn what he's doing in Argentina. Get him back to Germany. As soon as possible. By that I mean yesterday."

"Oh, shit," Souers said. There was a tone of resignation when he said it.

"Oh, shit what, Sid?"

"Harry, the truth is, I didn't tell you . . ."

"I advised Sid not to tell you," Justice Jackson interjected.

"Tell me what, damn it?"

Souers pointed at the SIGABA message.

"It is alluded to in that," he said. "Cronley's op in Vienna that bagged Burgdorf and von Dietelburg. It didn't go smoothly. One Austrian was killed and another wounded as they were arresting Burgdorf and von Dietelburg."

"So what?" the President said, then asked, "Cronley shot them?"

"No," Souers said, "the shooter was a lieutenant named Spurgeon. Of the Vienna CIC." He sighed audibly. "Harry, can you hold your questions until I'm finished telling what went down?"

"Probably not, but let's see."

"Cronley was working pretty closely with the Austrians when he realized what they were up to, that when they captured von Dietelburg he would be an Austrian prisoner, not ours. They intended to put him on trial themselves. Cronley decided this was a bad idea."

"Why?"

"There you go, Harry. Let me finish."

"Make it quick."

The sound of Justice Jackson chuckling came over the phone speaker.

Truman glared at the telephone.

"Okay," Souers began, "I don't know how much Cronley considered your belief that these people should be tried, and hanged, with as much publicity as possible as common criminals so that the Germans would not regard them as martyrs to Nazism, murdered by the vindictive victors. But every time I decide he's too young and inexperienced to understand such and such, he's proved me dead wrong."

"Go on."

"Anyway, he concluded that the solution to the problem was to keep the Austrians out of the actual arrest—"

"He decided this on his own?" the President interrupted, his tone again incredulous. "Without checking with his superiors?"

"And there you go again, Harry," Justice Jackson said, followed by an audible grunt. "Let Sid finish."

Truman impatiently gestured for Souers to go on.

Souers continued. "That's why I wrote on the message that there was more. Including that Cronley's relations with his immediate superior, Colonel Wallace, who sent that SIGABA message to me, are not cordial. Cronley also believes that if you think your superior is going to say no when you ask permission to do something and you know you're right, don't ask, just do it."

"And beg forgiveness afterward," the President added. "I'm familiar with it."

"The justification that Cronley offered," Souers went on, "for arresting Burgdorf and von Dietelburg on his own was that they wouldn't live long in an Austrian prison—"

Justice Jackson interjected: "And he could then fly them directly to Nuremberg, on illegal airplanes, without the hassle of going through border control authorities."

"Illegal airplanes?" Truman parroted.

"Two Fieseler Storches," Jackson answered. "Sort of German Piper Cubs, but much better. Three-place, not just two-place. The Air Force ordered their destruction. Cronley appeared not to know about this order."

Jackson laughed, then went on. "In his 'innocence,' he kept his two in a well-guarded hangar in Nuremberg. The aircraft were thus available to fly to the Compound in Munich, first with one of General Gehlen's assets in Russia, one Rachel Bischoff—"

"Whom the Austrians wanted very much to interrogate," Souers interjected.

"—and later Burgdorf and von Dietelburg to the same place," Jackson finished.

"At this point, the Austrians went ballistic," Souers said. "They issued arrest warrants. For murder, in the case of Lieutenant Spurgeon, and for various crimes and misdemeanors for Cronley, Winters, and everybody else concerned. OMGUS has issued a 'detainer' on everybody for illegally leaving and then entering Germany without passing through an entry point. And the Air Force is demanding that the Army bring charges: one, against Cronley for not destroying the Storches, and, two, against Cronley and Winter for flying them after the Air Force declared them unsafe. And also charges against Cronley for flying at all, because he is neither an Army aviator nor an AAF pilot."

"Lawyer that I am," Jackson said, "I'm finding it hard to understand the legal ramifications of a nonpilot illegally flying an ostensibly nonexistent airplane, but that's where we are, Harry."

"Jesus H. Christ," the President said.

"Oscar Schultz," Souers then said, "on learning what had happened, decided the solution to the problem was to get everybody the hell out of Dodge while he, quote, poured money on the Austrian volcano, unquote. So, everybody went to Argentina just about a month ago. Cletus Frade is hiding them in Mendoza, on one of his estancias."

After a moment, President Truman, his tone unpleasant, said, "Is that all?"

"More or less," Souers said. "For now."

"I was annoyed with this situation when I first got wind of it today," Truman went on, his voice rising. "Now that I've learned all this—and, more important, that both of you bastards kept it from me—I am what is known as royally pissed off."

"Harry," Jackson said, "both Sid and I felt that it would die down."

"But it hasn't, has it?" Truman snapped. "Even worse, Burgdorf and von Dietelburg, those despicable Nazi bastards, are now on the loose, goddamn it!"

"Harry, Bob and I decided that you had more important things on your plate—"

"Well, Sid," Truman interrupted, "you were wrong. The most important thing on my plate at this time is getting those two SS sons of bitches back behind bars so we can try them and then hang them. If this Colonel Cohen thinks Captain

Cronley can help him, you get Cronley out of goddamn Argentina and to goddamn Germany as soon as humanly possible. Got it?"

Admiral Souers said, "Yes, Mr. President."

"And you, Bob, you start right now on getting OMGUS and the Air Force and anybody else off Cronley's back—and Cronley's people's backs—and keep them off. They deserve medals and they damn sure shouldn't have to be running from the law like John Dillinger's gang of bank robbers. Got it?"

Justice Jackson said, "Yes, Mr. President."

[TWO]
The Polo Field
Estancia Don Guillermo
Kilometer 40.4, Provincial Route 60
Mendoza Province, Argentina
1345 9 April 1946

Polo was the oldest equestrian sport in the world. It featured opposing four-man teams attempting to strike with long-handled mallets a ball between twelve and a half and fifteen inches in circumference into the other team's goal.

The players on the Mendoza estancia's polo field were expert horsemen mounted on superbly trained Arabian ponies. But they were not dressed in the usual manner—boots, white trousers, and colored cotton short-sleeved shirts—with seven of the eight wearing the outfits of working gauchos, the Argentine version of American cowboys. It included a wide-brimmed black leather hat, a white shirt with billowing sleeves, tucked into equally billowing black trousers tucked into knee-length soft black leather boots. Around their waists, they wore wide leather belts decorated with silver studs, inserted into the back of which were silver-handled knives with blades at least twelve inches long.

The hatless eighth player wore a gray sweatshirt emblazoned with the logo of the Agriculture and Mechanical College of Texas—commonly called Texas A&M—blue jeans, and what were properly termed Western or cowboy boots.

He was a tall, muscular, blond twenty-two-year-old. On the list—classified Secret—of "Detached Officers" maintained in the Pentagon, he was listed as: Cronley, James D. Jr., Captain, Cavalry, AUS O-396754. Permanently detached to Directorate of Central Intelligence.

After wresting control of the ball from an opposing gaucho about to score a goal, Cronley then drove it at a full gallop toward the other end of the field. As he did, he saw a man waving a sheet of paper near the goal.

The man's name was Maximillian Ostrowski. He had spent World War II as an intelligence officer with the Free Polish Army and was now a DCI special agent.

Cronley smacked the ball a final time, scoring.

But instead of returning to the field, he reined in the jet-black Arabian and dismounted.

"This just came," Ostrowski said, handing him the sheet of paper.

Cronley's eyes went to it:

TOP SECRET–LINDBERGH

URGENT

DUPLICATION FORBIDDEN

FROM: DIRECTOR SOUTHERN CONE

1945 GREENWICH 9 APR 1946

TO: ALTAR BOY MENDOZA

PASS TO GEN MARTIN

1—LODESTAR WILL PICK UP YOU, WINTERS, SPURGEON, PULASKI, AND OSTROWSKI ASAP TODAY. TRY TO STAY OUT OF SIGHT IN BUENOS AIRES.

2—I WILL SEND MY PRECISE ETA PISTARINI TOMORROW ASAP. HAVE EVERYBODY THERE.

TEX

END

TOP SECRET–LINDBERGH

"I wonder if we're about to be let out of jail," Cronley said.

"Either that or be flown in chains to Vienna to face the wrath of the Angry Austrians," Ostrowski replied.

"Wallace would love that."

"Yes, he would. What happens now?"

"We finish the last chucker, Max, and then it's off to Uncle Willy's guesthouse."

Cronley nimbly mounted the Arabian and returned to the field.

[THREE]
Ministro Pistarini Airport
Buenos Aires, Argentina
1115 10 April 1946

The Lockheed Constellation came in low over the passenger terminal, and the hangars beside it, touching down smoothly on Pistarini's north-south runway. When the Connie finished rolling to the end of the runway, it turned and started taxiing toward the terminal, where two other Constellations were parked on the tarmac.

The Model L-049, featuring a sleek fuselage and distinctive triple-tail vertical stabilizers, was the finest transport aircraft in the world. It was capable of flying forty passengers in its pressurized cabin higher (at an altitude of 35,000 feet) and faster (cruising at better than 300 knots) and for a longer distance (up to 4,300 miles) than any other transport aircraft in the world.

The Constellations at the terminal bore the insignia of South American Airways, Argentina's national airline. The one that had just landed read HOWELL PETROLEUM INTERNATIONAL along its fuselage. On both sides of its nose, there was lettered DOROTEA.

That referred to Doña Dorotea Mallin de Frade, who was the granddaughter-in-law of Cletus Marcus Howell, president and chairman of the board of Howell Petroleum International and by far its largest stockholder.

Howell had ordered DOROTEA lettered on the aircraft the day after Doña Dorotea had given birth to Cletus Howell Frade Jr., his first great-grandson.

Doña Dorotea came out of the terminal as the aircraft approached and then stopped. She was a tall, long-legged, blond twenty-five-year-old, with blue eyes and a marvelous milky complexion. She was what came to mind when one heard the phrase "classic English beauty."

She saw frenzied activity around a pair of half-ton trucks mounted with stairways. While the stairs would permit the **Dorotea**'s passengers to deplane, she saw, however, that no one seemed to have the keys to the vehicles.

Oh, bloody hell! she thought. **Without keys, the stairs cannot be driven to the aircraft's door.**

Then, in Spanish, she exploded: "If you can't find the goddamn keys, get the old goddamn stairs out of the goddamn hangar!"

Those who knew Doña Dorotea knew that she got her Buckingham Palace accent and profane vocabulary from her mother, an English aristocrat who had met and married an Italo-Argentine oligarch while both were studying at the London School of Economics. And Doña Dorotea had acquired her ferocious temper and profane Spanish vocabulary from her father. That vocabulary—in both tongues—had been augmented by her marriage to Cletus Frade, who not only cursed like the U.S. Marine that he was but could and often did curse fluently in the Spanish-based patois known as Texican.

The workers a minute or so later came out of one of the hangars pushing an old set of metal stairs. It was a fragile-looking contraption, one mounted on small wheels that rattled and squeaked with such volume that it appeared one or more would fall off at any moment. The stairs themselves were steep, quite narrow, and, instead of a substantial handrail, had a flimsy rope.

While this was happening, other members of the welcoming party came out of the terminal. The crowd, led by Jim Cronley, included those who had flown up from Mendoza, plus a very beautiful, stylishly dressed brunette with dark eyes in her twenties who, like Doña Dorotea, also had marvelously long legs. This was Alicia Carzino-Cormano de von Wachtstein.

She was followed out of the terminal by two nannies, one of whom held the hands of Alicia's two children, and the other the hands of Doña Dorotea's two children.

The passenger door of the **Dorotea** opened, and Cletus Frade started quickly down the dangerous-looking stairs.

Cronley looked over and saw the disappointment in Alicia's eyes.

Sorry, Alicia. Hansel is shutting the airplane down. He'll get off in a minute.

Cletus Frade embraced his wife, lifting her off the ground in the process, and then started to offer his hand to Cronley. He then changed his mind, wrapped his arms around him, and also lifted him off his feet.

"What the hell is going on, Clete?" Cronley asked, after breaking free of the embrace.

Frade simply pointed up to the aircraft's door.

Jim Cronley's mother, elegant and trim, had come out of the aircraft and was very carefully making her way down the steep, narrow stairway. Cronley's throat tightened and his eyes watered. He could not immediately recall that last time he had seen his mother. He walked quickly over to meet her.

His mother finally made it to the foot of the stairs, then raised her eyes from the steps and saw him.

"**Mein Liebchen, mein Liebchen!**" she cried, and threw herself into his arms.

He picked her up and carried her to one side of the stairs.

Maybe thirty seconds later, he freed himself from her barrage of kisses.

He looked up the stairway, expecting to see his father. Instead, he found himself looking up the skirt of an adult female who was holding an infant while slowly descending the steps. He saw far enough up her skirt, before he averted his eyes, to note that she was wearing blue-lace panties.

Who the hell is that?

And why were you looking at some strange female's crotch while hugging your mother?

His mother continued kissing and crying.

The next thing he was aware of was a hand on his shoulder, then his father's voice.

"How are you, son?"

Cronley freed himself enough from his mother's embrace to get his arm around his father. The three of them hugged one another, Cronley hoping no one saw the tears running down his cheeks.

When he opened his eyes again, there was a familiar face looking at him curiously.

Jesus Christ. Unless I'm losing my mind, that's Ginger!

That was her blue-lace crotch I was just looking at!

What the hell is she doing here?

With her months-old baby?

Dumb question. Babies are usually with their mothers, stupid!

"Hello, Jimmy," Ginger said.

"Hey, Ginger."

Cronley's history with twenty-two-year-old Virginia Moriarty went back to their growing up together in the Texas Panhandle.

"Sorry to interrupt," Cletus Frade announced as he held up a SIGABA printout, "but this is important. It came in when we were an hour out."

"What?" Cronley said, stepping closer to him.

He took the sheet and read it.

Top Secret–Lindbergh? he thought. **So Oscar Shultz forwarded Wallace's message about Burgdorf and von Dietelburg escaping the Tribunal Prison, with Wallace saying Cohen blames**

Odessa. And that Wasserman says the Vienna police intel chief suspects DCI's hand in his surveillance chief's disappearance?

He looked at Frade. "Jesus H. Christ!"

"Yeah," Frade said. "Initial reaction?"

"Wallace, especially with this 'no action undertaken' bullshit, is covering his ass again."

"Okay, aside from that obvious part . . . ?"

"Well, for starters, the Tribunal Prison escape? With Cohen and the Twenty-sixth Infantry sitting on it? I would have said impossible."

Frade nodded. "All right, give it some more thought on your way to the guesthouse. When you get there, get everybody lunch and start saying your good-byes."

"While you . . . ?"

"While I'm in the Bunker talking to El Jefe on the SIGABA. When I'm finished, then I'll come."

"You got it."

Cronley saw Ginger Moriarty being escorted with her infant to one of the vehicles that had just pulled up. He motioned his parents toward the second from the front of the line.

Cronley was glad to be able to get away from Ginger. The last time he had seen her, she had called him—with more, he believed, than a little justification—a bastard and a miserable son of a bitch, and told him to get the hell out of her house.

[FOUR]
4730 Avenida del Libertador General
San Martín
Buenos Aires, Argentina
1355 10 April 1946

The master bedroom, what Cletus Frade called Uncle Willy's bedroom, had been built by his grand-uncle Guillermo at the turn of the century. It had a mirrored ceiling and life-size marble statuary showing two couples, and one trio, engaged in the reproductive act.

Jim Cronley had just started shaving when he heard a familiar female voice outside the bathroom door.

"What is this place, a brothel?" Ginger Moriarty asked.

"Noticed the statues, have you?"

"Well, I'm glad I asked Father McGrath to give me a minute alone with you before he came in. I wouldn't want it getting around that I led a priest into your private whorehouse."

Cronley, using a thick cotton towel, wiped the soap from his face and went into the bedroom, where he grandly swept his hand around the room.

"This is all Clete's grand-uncle's doings. Personally, I am as pure as the driven snow."

She grunted.

"So, what's on your mind, Ginger?"

"Actually, I came up here to apologize. I'm just not sure if I came to Argentina only to do that. I think there may be another reason, besides me getting away from my parents."

"Then what the hell are you doing in Argentina?"

"It's sort of complicated."

"Give it a shot."

"I don't know . . . Well, okay, what the hell. I was having supper with your folks and Clete's at your spread in Midland when Admiral Souers called and told Clete to pick you and the others up down here and take you all to Germany. Immediately. Which meant the next morning."

"And . . . ?"

"And Clete told everybody. Then your mother said she hadn't seen you since you left for Germany and asked Clete if there was any reason why she and your dad couldn't ride down here with him to see you. He couldn't think of any reason, and then Clete's folks said they thought they'd ride along, too, so they could see their grandchildren. And then they could all go back to Texas together. So I got in on the act and asked him if there was any reason I couldn't go, not only down here but to Germany as well—"

"Why the hell do you want to go back to Germany for?" Cronley interrupted.

"Because after what happened to . . . my husband . . . all of our stuff, including our car, was put in storage by the Army when they sent me back to the States. There's a lot of stuff of Bruce's I want Little Bruce to have when he's grown, and a lot of stuff I never want to see again, so I'm going to Munich to sort through everything. Understood?"

"I suppose."

"And then I wanted to apologize to you."

"I have no idea what you're talking about."

"Listen. Pay attention. I apologize for what I said—screamed—at you in my house at the Compound. I was out of my mind—"

"You don't owe me any kind of an apology," Cronley put in. "You were justified."

"—and I'm really sorry for screaming at your parents at Bruce's funeral," she finished. "You heard about that?"

He nodded.

"So when I came to my senses and realized they had nothing to do with what happened, I went to them—actually, to your mother—and apologized. She was, no surprise, very gracious. She asked me how I was doing. I told her that before Bruce's casket touched the bottom of his grave, my parents had started to search for a new husband for their widowed daughter and her fatherless child and that it was driving me bonkers.

"Your mother told me very kindly—again, no surprise—that they meant well. When I started to leave, I asked her if she ever saw you again to please tell you I was sorry. Shortly after that, when Clete announced he was headed here and then on to Germany, she caught my eye and nodded. So here I am. And I have just apologized."

"Ginger, at least once a day I think that if I hadn't had Bone . . . **Bruce** . . . transferred to DCI, he'd still be alive. You really don't owe me an apology."

"Well, you've got one. Mission accomplished."

She turned and walked out of the bedroom.

Cronley, watching the door close behind her, thought, **She never got to whatever reason it was besides the apology.**

If there ever was anything other than the apology . . .

Finished with his shave, Cronley began drying his face with a thick towel. He heard a tap on the outer door, then saw in the mirror that a tall, muscular, gray-haired man in his fifties, wearing a clerical collar, had entered Uncle Willy's bedroom.

Has to be that Catholic priest, Cronley thought.

What's this all about?

Cronley, watching the priest take more than an idle interest in the life-size marble statuary, said in a raised voice, "What can I do for you, Father?"

The priest moved to the bathroom door, stopped, and announced, "I'm very happy to meet you, Super Spook, for reasons I'll explain in a bit. I thought you might be a little uncomfortable downstairs with a priest in the room you don't know, so I came up to put your mind at rest."

"I don't like being called Super Spook—let's start with that."

"Really? When I heard that, it was applied to you in a manner suggesting admiration. Let me start this interesting, and somewhat amusing, tale from the beginning. Admiral Souers was fascinated with something you'd been working on—Himmler's new religion—and wanted an outside opinion of heretical religions.

"His people came up with the name of a professor at the University of the South who had written several books on the subject and who was regarded by some people as an expert on the subject.

"Admiral Souers told Oscar Schultz . . ." He paused and raised his eyebrows in question.

"I'm familiar with El Jefe," Cronley said.

". . . to go talk to this man and see if he would come to Washington to talk to the admiral. Your friend Cletus was in town in connection with your difficulties in Vienna and was free pending decisions being made in connection with that. So, El Jefe prevailed upon the Air Force to loan the DCI a P-51, which had been fitted with a second seat, telling them the DCI had a fully qualified pilot to fly it.

"This was not entirely true. But as with many, perhaps most, Marine Corps fighter pilots, Cletus shares the belief that he can fly anything. With El Jefe in the backseat, Cletus made his first flight in a P-51, to Tennessee, to talk to the professor. En route, El Jefe told Cletus they had lucked out, that he had checked further and learned the professor held a commission as a commander in the Naval Reserve.

"At the university, they were directed to the professor's office door. Above which was a little sign reading FATHER MCGRATH.

"This caused an outburst of profanity on Cletus's part, one loud enough for the professor to hear it all on the far side of the closed door. If memory serves, he said, 'I'll be damned! If this priest is my Father McGrath, we've hit the fucking payload!'

"At that point, I opened the door, whereupon Cletus wrapped his arms around me and, after kissing me on the forehead, inquired, 'How the hell are you?'"

Cronley grinned. "I take it, Father, that you two were previously acquainted."

"You could say that, and that would be somewhat of an understatement. Cletus's announcements caused some consternation on the part of my secretary, even after I told her the last time the colonel and I had seen each other was on Guadalcanal, where I had been chaplain to VMF 226 and he had been a lieutenant flying F4F Wildcats."

"Jesus Christ!" Cronley said, quickly adding, "Sorry, Father."

"Watch your mouth or I'll think you're a heathen."

"I'm not a heathen, I'm Episcopalian. And now that I think about it, so is the University of the South. And isn't McGrath . . . ?"

"'Grath' is a translation of 'craith,'" the priest said, nodding, "which means 'grace,' while 'mac' means 'son of'—"

"I'll be damned," Cronley interrupted. "The literal translation becomes 'son of divine grace.'"

"Keep keeping company with the likes of Cletus, my son, and you may well be damned," the priest said, smiling broadly and offering his hand. "J-for-Jack McGrath. Pleasure to finally meet you, Super Spook."

Cronley took the hand. "And you, Father. Any friend of Cletus, et cetera, et cetera . . ."

"It's Jack, please."

"How about Father Jack?"

"Deal. You must be wondering what is an Irish priest named McGrath doing there on Guadalcanal."

"Yeah, I guess."

"It **is** Episcopalian, as am I. The Pope doesn't have a copyright on 'Father.'"

"And you're a commander in the Chaplain Corps of the Naval Reserve?"

"Deduced that, did you? No wonder they call you Super Spook."

"Very funny."

"So eventually, over dinner, we got to the purpose of El Jefe's visit. And to anticipate your next question, 'Why couldn't El Jefe deduce from my books on religious heresy that I was a priest?' In other words, why did they say 'By J. R. McGrath, Ph.D.' rather than 'By Reverend J. R. McGrath, D.D.'?"

"I have the feeling you're going to tell me."

"I am. Because I learned with my early books that maybe five or six thousand devout people will buy a book by a priest so that they can advertise their own piety by displaying them, usually without having read them, on their coffee tables. When I published my first book on religious heresy, I dropped the 'Reverend' and the 'D.D.' and substituted 'Ph.D.' for the latter. That book sold thirty-five thousand copies, and subsequent books have done even better.

"At that point, I introduced into the conversation that my present interest was looking into rumors I had heard that the late, unlamented Heinrich Himmler had been trying to launch a Nazi-based religion and asked if, perchance, either of them, as intelligence officers, had heard anything about it.

"Cletus chuckled, and said, 'Oh, boy, have we ever!' and El Jefe added, 'And one of our guys, Super Spook, is an expert on that subject.'

"So naturally I asked, 'Super Spook?' And Cletus told me all about your lifelong relationship. He said you had been dubbed Super Spook because you were very good at finding and arresting some really evil Nazis. And that your 'ass was in a deep crack at the moment' because your latest exploit resulted in the Austrian government calling for your scalp. As were the Air Force and most of the European intelligence establishment.

"I said, 'Nevertheless, I'd really like to meet him.'

"He gave me a strange look and asked if I was open to a wild offer, presuming I could get away from the university for a couple of months, maybe longer.

"I told him not only was I a tenured professor, meaning I couldn't be fired, but that I was anxious to escape the world of academia for a while. So what was the wild offer? I asked. He told me and here I am."

"That's a helluva story."

"Which I thought I should tell you. Now that I have, may I suggest we go downstairs for our lunch?"

"You may. But please tell them I said to start without me, Father Jack. I'll join you after I gather some things for the trip."

"Will do."

[FIVE]
4730 Avenida del Libertador General San Martín
Buenos Aires, Argentina
2030 10 April 1946

Cronley drained the last of the bottle of '41 Estancia Don Guillermo Cabernet Sauvignon into the crystal stem that sat on the massive marble sink of Uncle Willy's bathroom. He both felt and heard his stomach growl. Not only had they started lunch without him, it had ended in his absence, too. All he managed to scrounge after the table had been cleared was the makings for a small lomo sandwich—sliced rare filet mignon with horseradish on a hard-crusted baguette.

The blame for his having missed the meal rested with Cletus Frade.

Frade had called while Cronley was packing his suitcase, announcing that the **Dorotea** would be wheels-up for Germany at first light and that Cronley was being summoned to the Bunker to answer, over the SIGABA, El Jefe's questions—which Frade said meant DCI Souers's questions—concerning Wallace's last communiqué.

That had consumed, it turned out, the remainder of the afternoon and into the early evening.

When Cronley had finally returned to Uncle Willy's bedroom to finish packing and get dressed for dinner, it had been with a bottle of the fine Cab they had flown in by the caseload in the Lodestar from Frade's estancia in Mendoza.

Cronley came out of the bathroom, showered and smelling of the eau de cologne he had found in a cardboard box in one of the closets. He had helped himself to one of the remaining half dozen liter bottles. He suspected the cologne had been in the closet since Uncle Willy had lived there himself a generation or two before.

Cronley had a bath towel tucked around his waist. On his way out of the bathroom, the towel slipped off and he stumbled over it, nearly falling to the marble floor.

"Shit!"

He looked down at the towel on the floor, then kicked it. It flew into the bedroom, coming to rest on the lamp shade of a wall fixture. The wet cotton touched the hot lightbulb, causing it to explode.

If I go over there, I'll cut my feet on the glass.

So, fuck it, I'll get it later.

Stark naked, he walked over to the bed, where he had left his clothes.

He felt the damp towel being draped over his shoulder.

A female voice said, "You dropped something. Don't turn around until you put it on."

Ginger!

What the hell is she doing up here again?

When, towel in place, he turned around, she was standing there, arms crossed over her ample bosom. She was dressed for dinner in a fancy black dress that, he could not help but notice, not only did little to conceal her curves, it very nicely accentuated them.

What the hell do they call those?

Cocktail dresses.

Jesus, she is one attractive broad, especially in that tiny outfit.

It was cut so low in front that he could see where the bottom of the double string of pearls around her neck disappeared between her breasts.

"You were missed at lunch," she said.

"It was not my decision, Ginger . . . What the hell are you doing up here again?"

"I had to come up to check on the baby. On the way, I realized that I have some more things to say to you. And I decided they couldn't wait."

"Your timing is lousy. And what if somebody comes through that door looking for me?"

"This won't take long, Jimmy. I'll take my chances."

Jesus Christ, her eyes are blue—a beautiful blue.

"Okay, then, spit it out."

"I heard what was said in the library."

"Heard what?"

"That we're off to Germany first thing in the morning, and that as soon as we land, you're back in your Super Spook role, and that means that once again you are about to disappear from my life."

"You know what I do for a living. It's what got Bonehead—"

"Shut up!" she snapped. "Let me finish what I didn't finish before!"

So there actually was something else, he thought.

He shrugged. "So, finish."

"I was pissed at you because you were stupid—"

"I'm often accused of that."

"Goddamn you, please shut up!"

There's tears glistening . . . She's about to start crying.

What the hell is going on?

"And it was your stupidity, and mine, that had suddenly turned me into the widow of Bruce Moriarty, with a child to raise all by myself."

"Ginger, I've been kicking myself, just about daily, for taking Bone—**Bruce**—out of the Constabulary and into the DCI."

"You did that to be a nice guy. More than that, you did it because you loved him and were taking care of him, as you always did. And because he loved you, you made him as happy as a pig in mud to be in the DCI with you."

"I don't understand where you're going with this."

"That's what I mean about you being stupid."

He threw both hands up in frustration. "Tell me!"

"You ever wonder why I married Bruce in the first place?"

I know why Bonehead married you. He told me.

Do I tell her he did?

What the hell . . .

"He . . . uh . . . told me you were in the family way."

"I was. The way that happened was that Bruce asked me if it was all right if he brought you along with him to the Kappa Delta Sigma New Year's Eve party. I was surprised, mostly because Jimmy Cronley made no secret of the fact that he thought sororities and their social events were bullshit.

"I also was excited. I told him sure. And I gussied myself up real nice. New dress, new shoes, hours in the beauty parlor, and plenty of Chanel No. 5 behind my ears and between my boobs. Tonight was the night I would snare Jimmy Cronley in my web."

Jesus Christ!

"So, the two of you show up. Bruce heads right for me. You head right for Candice Howard."

"Why not? You were Bruce's girl."

"That's what I mean about you being stupid. Anyway, an hour later, during which you finally said something to me . . . You remember what you said?"

"No."

" 'Be gentle with Bonehead, Ginger' is what you said. 'He's not experienced with sorority girls like you.' "

"Ginger, the reason I never made a pass at you was because Bruce was nuts about you."

"And that's precisely what I mean about you being stupid. That wasn't a two-way street, and you should have seen that. Anyway, about an hour later all the girls were whispering to each other that the prize for first score of the evening went to Candice Howard. She had Jimmy Cronley upstairs, where he was screwing her brains out.

"I figured, what the hell, and took Bruce upstairs. He got my pearl of great price. And in the process, lucky me, I got knocked up. He did the gentlemanly thing, of course. And in June we graduated, and then Bruce—after following you into the cavalry instead of the engineers, which he really wanted—and his pregnant wife wound up at Fort Knox with you. Where you used to visit us in that ugly apartment and talk about you being godfather to the baby. And then Bruce came home one night and said that you were gone, that you were now in the Counterintelligence Corps, whatever the hell that was."

Cronley shrugged. "They needed German-speaking officers in the CIC in Germany," he said.

"Anyway, at that time I decided my life had been decided. It was my destiny to be an Army wife. Our baby would be an Army brat. Bruce was a genuine good guy, smart, and he'd probably get to be a colonel, maybe even a general. It would be a pretty good life, and I was just going to have to forget my schoolgirl crush on Jimmy Cronley. He was out of our life forever."

"And then I showed up in Fritzlar?" Cronley asked, softly.

"And then **Captain** Cronley showed up in Fritzlar. Flying a mysterious secret airplane across the East German border to rescue a Russian woman and her children. And with enough clout to get Bruce out of the Constabulary and into the DCI.

"I didn't want to leave Fritzlar. I didn't want to be around you. Women about to have a baby shouldn't be thinking about a man who is not the father of that baby."

"Ginger—"

"Shut up, Jimmy, let me finish. So off we go to Munich, and the Compound, because I can't think of any way not to go. And I have the baby. And we're back to you being the godfather. And right after you gave us thirty minutes of your valuable time to show up for the christening, you were off again, this time to Nuremberg.

"That really decided it for me. I was going to be a good mother and a good wife. And you were out of my life. Period. End of story.

"And then the chaplain comes to call. 'There has been an accident. Your husband was cleaning a pistol and it went off.'

"And you showed up to offer your condolences.

And I was thinking that if you weren't so stupid, you'd have seen how I felt about you, that if you hadn't taken Candice Howard upstairs at the Kappa Delta Sigma house and screwed her brains out, maybe I would have become Mrs. Cronley instead of the Widow Moriarty.

"So I told you get the hell out of my house.

"And when they handed me the flag after we lowered Bruce's casket into the ground, and I saw your mother and father, I lost it and gave her hell, too, just because she was your mother."

She paused, cleared her throat, then went on. "I told you I came to my senses and went to your mother and apologized. And that she said maybe I should come down here. So I came. As much to get away from my mother, and her parade of nice, young, unmarried men, as anything else. But also to apologize."

"No apology is necessary. How many times do I have to tell you that?"

Ginger ignored him and went on.

"And on the **Dorotea**, on the way down, I half decided to take a chance and tell you the reasons behind me being Ginger the Bitch to you."

"Half decided? You just did."

"The final decision was made when I was coming down the stairs from the airplane. When I saw you with your mother, my girlish heart nearly jumped out of my chest. Then I saw that you were looking up my dress. I thought, he hasn't changed. But then I finally decided to take a chance."

There was a long silence, then Cronley said, "And you did. Why?"

"I just told you. It was my attempt to make a Hail Mary pass."

"About what?"

"You're so damn smart, Super Spook, figure it out yourself. Let me know when you have and what you want to do because—"

She stopped when she heard the baby wailing.

"Don't go anywhere, Jimmy."

A minute or so later, she returned with the softly sobbing infant, rocking him in the crook of her arm.

"Here," she said, now holding Baby Bruce out toward him, "hold him while I get his bottle ready."

"What the hell?" Cronley said. "I don't know how to do that."

"It's simple. Just make sure you support his head. Hold your arm this way."

She moved Cronley's right arm as hers had been, cradling the infant in it with his head resting against Cronley's chest.

"Good. See, Jimmy? Not so mysterious."

Cronley, with a look that was equal parts terror and awe, glanced from her to the infant.

Baby Bruce, blinking, stared back at him.

He has his mother's amazing blue eyes.

"I'll be right back," she said, then touched his cheek and hurried out of the bedroom and down the hall.

"Hurry, damn it!"

A few minutes later—what seemed an eternity to Cronley—she returned with a baby bottle. She held it out to Cronley.

"Oh, not no," he said. "**Hell** no."

"Oh, hell yes."

As Cronley met her eyes, she slipped the bottle's nipple between the infant's lips. She moved Cronley's free hand to hold the bottle.

There then came the sound of a contented gurgle from Baby Bruce, and when Cronley looked down, he grinned around the bottle's nipple and blinked his blue eyes.

"He's beautiful, Ginger. Peaceful."

"Uh-huh."

Cronley felt something warm growing inside his gut.

Jesus, is this little creature making me melt or is that wretched fear?

Next, he felt the infant's torso begin twisting in his arm. And then Baby Bruce loudly expelled a burst of flatulence.

[SIX]
4730 Avenida del Libertador General
San Martín
Buenos Aires, Argentina
0230 11 April 1946

Cronley turned in the bed to switch off the bedside lamp.

Ginger was standing halfway between the bed and the door. She was wearing a dressing gown and, under it, pajamas. She had Baby Bruce in her arms.

When she saw that he had seen her, she walked over to the bed.

She thrust the sleeping infant toward Cronley.

"Take him," she said. "You know he doesn't bite. Breaks wind with wild abandon, yes, but no bite."

He had no choice but to take the child.

"What the hell are you up to?" Cronley asked.

"When I went to check on him, I had an epiphany. He's another of your goddamn problems. Being a father scares you to death."

Cronley didn't reply.

"So," she went on, "tell me what you want me to do with him. I'm open to anything but putting him up for adoption or drowning him."

"You're crazy . . . drunk . . ."

"Probably. You make me crazy and drive me to drink."

The infant made a sound.

Cronley saw that the baby's blanket was covering his mouth and that he was trying to push it away.

Very carefully, using his index finger, Cronley moved the blanket away. Baby Bruce smiled and then reached for and grabbed Cronley's finger.

"Christ, he's beautiful! And I think he really likes me!"

"So do I—**we** do. What the hell else do you need?"

He looked up from the baby's blue eyes and saw that Ginger had slipped out of the dressing gown and was unbuttoning her pajama top.

"What the hell else do you need?" she repeated.

When he didn't reply, she put her fingers in the hem of her pajama bottoms and slid them off her hips.

"For Christ's sake," she said, her voice breaking, "what the hell else do you need?"

"Right now, I can't think of a thing. But what we do with what's his name?"

"We put a pacifier in his mouth and put him on the couch."

She slipped out of her pajama top and came to the bed and reached for the child.

"And his name is Bruce. Try to remember that."

"Jesus Christ!" Cronley wheezed, out of breath, when he rolled off Ginger five minutes later.

"Yeah, Jesus Christ. Can I assume that I passed the test?"

"You get both ears and the tail."

He spread his arms, and she crawled into them.

"I always knew I loved you, Jimmy. But until just now, when I felt you in me, I really didn't know how much."

After perhaps sixty seconds of the only sound being Jimmy's labored breathing, she said, "It's now your turn to say something. Preferably, something nice."

"I was wondering what to say."

" 'I love you, too,' would be nice."

"I mean to our parents, to Clete—to everybody. Last night, you had barely forgiven me for getting Bonehead whacked, and, at breakfast, we're a couple of lovebirds. They're going to know something happened. I don't give a damn what they think, but you?"

"I don't give a damn either. But you're right. So, during the day you will slowly discover that I am an attractive, unattached woman, and I will slowly stop resisting your unwanted attentions.

And at night I will sneak into your bedroom, and we will screw the brains out of each other."

"That'll probably work."

"Are you going to say it now?"

"You mean say that I love you? Why? I think you've known that all along."

"Say it, damn you, Jimmy!"

He did.

And then she rolled onto her back and pulled him to her.

II

**4730 Avenida del Libertador General
San Martín
Buenos Aires, Argentina
0315 11 April 1946**

Cletus Frade opened the door to Uncle Willy's bedroom, flipped on the lights, and shouted, "Drop your cock and pick up your socks—we've gotta go!"

Startled awake, the baby started to howl.

Ginger, naked, jumped out of bed to comfort him.

Cronley said, "Oh, shit!"

"Just to clear the air," Frade announced, his back now turned to them, "I have just been stricken by temporary blindness. When you get your pants on, Romeo, have a look at these."

He tossed two teletypewriter printouts on the floor and then went back out the door.

Cronley, in his birthday suit, went to the printouts and picked them up.

The first was a NOTAM—Notice to Airmen—from the U.S. Army Air Force field at Puerto Allegre, Brazil, which was just across the border. Airmen bound for Europe were warned to expect "significant headwinds within five hundred miles of the South American continent from oh-six-hundred hours." Cronley did the mental arithmetic and concluded they had to get as far away from the South American continent as soon as possible.

The second sheet of paper was a SIGABA message:

TOP SECRET–LINDBERGH

URGENT
DUPLICATION FORBIDDEN
FROM: ASST DIRECTOR
TO: TEX
1—AS SOON AS EN ROUTE SIGABA CONTACT CAN BE ESTABLISHED WITH DCI-EUROPE FURNISH ETA RHINE-MAIN.
2—YOU WILL BE MET BY LTCOL WILSON WHO WILL TAKE YOUR PASSENGERS TO NUREMBERG.

3—ASAP AFTER PASSENGER TRANSFER RETURN
TO WASHINGTON. ADVISE ETA.
SCHULTZ
END

TOP SECRET–LINDBERGH

Cronley looked across the room to Ginger. She was bouncing the baby against her naked bosom and looking at Cronley as tears flowed down her cheeks.

"Hey, not to worry," he said with conviction, something he did not feel at all, as he went to her. "Clete's a good guy. He's not going to say anything."

She nodded, and handed him the baby. She walked to her discarded clothing, quickly slipped into the dressing gown, and then motioned for him to give her the infant.

She met his eyes, shrugged, leaned up, and kissed him on the cheek.

She then chuckled, and said, "Is this the wages of sin that everybody's talking about?"

She walked out of the room.

He hurriedly dressed, finished packing, and then went in search of Ginger.

As he and she started down the wide main stairs together, they immediately saw by everyone's expression—particularly that of his mother, who glared at him, and that of Max Ostrowski, who was grinning broadly—that their secret was out.

"It wasn't Clete," Ginger said. "Dorotea went to my room, and I wasn't there."

"Well, let's get loaded," Cletus Frade said as they reached the bottom stair. "We have a headwind to dodge."

As Cronley's mother kissed him good-bye, she whispered, "How could you? What in God's name were you thinking?"

[TWO]
Rhine-Main Airfield
Frankfurt am Main, American Zone of
Occupation, Germany
2305 12 April 1946

The Beechcraft C-45—General I. D. White's personal aircraft—that Cronley expected to see was nowhere in sight as the **Dorotea** taxied up to the transient tarmac. The only other aircraft there was a Gooney Bird, an Air Force C-47.

But when Cronley saw Lieutenant Colonel

William "Hotshot Billy" Wilson walking out onto the tarmac, he decided he had the C-45 hidden somewhere.

Rhine-Main was an Air Force base, and the "Fly Boys" didn't like the "Ground Pounders" to have aircraft larger than two-seater Piper Cubs. It was said that General White got to keep his small, twin-engine C-45 only because his U.S. Constabulary patrolled all the highways in Germany, especially the Autobahn. How long it took them to "inspect" Air Force trucks on the highways was entirely up to them.

Wilson was waiting for them at the foot of the stairway on wheels.

"Welcome to Deutschland," he said, shaking hands with Cronley.

Cletus Frade, Max Ostrowski, and Tom Winters arrived as Wilson pointed to the Gooney Bird, and said, "Your chariot awaits."

Cronley noticed for the first time that it had the Constabulary's Circle C insignia painted both on the nose and on the vertical stabilizer.

Wilson added, "You should feel honored to fly on the first C-47 aircraft to appear on any U.S. Army Table of Organization and Equipment."

"How the hell did you pull that off?" Cronley said.

Wilson didn't reply but instead nodded toward Ginger, who was coming down the stairs. "Is somebody going to explain to me how the Widow Moriarty is involved in this?"

"Officially," Frade said, "she is here to gather up her household goods. She had to leave them here when they flew her to the States with Bone-head's corpse."

"And unofficially?"

"You don't want to know," Frade said, "does he, Super Spook?"

"Fuck you, Clete."

Wilson thought about it and decided not to pursue the question.

"You're going right back?" he asked Frade. "Are you all right to fly?"

"Against my better judgment, I let Super Spook and Winters watch the fuel gauge needles drop as we flew across the ocean while Hansel and I slept. I'm all right."

"Good luck, then," Wilson said, shaking his hand.

Wilson then looked at Cronley.

"Come on, Super Spook, off to Nuremberg and the Farber Palast. You have—everybody has—an appointment with Justice Jackson at oh-eight-hundred tomorrow." He glanced at his watch and corrected himself. "Eight hundred today!"

[THREE]
Flughafen
Nuremberg, American Zone of
Occupation, Germany
0120 13 April 1946

Captain Chauncey "Tiny" Dunwiddie, who was six foot four and weighed close to three hundred pounds, was waiting for Cronley and the others when they landed at the airfield seven kilometers north of Nuremberg.

He was leaning on the fender of the enormous Horch Sport Cabriolet touring car that Cronley had inherited from Colonel Robert Mattingly when Cronley had gotten the kidnapped officer back from the NKGB. It was parked behind a Chevrolet staff car, and two other Chevrolets were parked behind it.

The drivers of the cars hurried to relieve the incomers of their luggage and usher them into the cars. Ginger and her baby and Father McGrath were put into the one immediately behind the Horch.

Dunwiddie got behind the steering wheel of the Horch, and Cronley got in beside him. Max Ostrowski and Tom Winters got in the backseat. Dunwiddie blew the horn, and the convoy got under way.

"What's with Bonehead's widow and the Catholic priest?" Dunwiddie asked.

"He's an Episcopal priest," Cronley said. "And he's an expert on heretical religions, like the Church of Saint Heinrich the Divine. Schultz—or maybe the admiral—found him at the University of the South."

"And what's with Ginger Moriarty?"

"She got Clete to bring her with us so that she can get her household goods out of the quarter-master's warehouse in Munich. She didn't have time to do that when they sent her to the States with Bonehead's corpse right after he got whacked."

"Oh. And how's she going to get to Munich?"

"As soon as I can find the time, I'll take her. So, leave the Horch at the palast."

"You're going to have a hard time finding time."

"So far as Father McGrath is concerned . . ."

"Oh, yeah. Tell me about him."

Cronley thought, **He swallowed that household goods bullshit whole.**

While it is true that to be a good intelligence officer you have to be able to lie convincingly through your teeth, it hurts when you have to lie to your friends.

And Tiny certainly is in that small and ever-diminishing category.

Cronley began: "After El Jefe found this heretical religions expert at the University of the South, the admiral sent El Jefe and Clete to talk to him. They found out that he knew Clete from his days as the chaplain of Clete's fighter squadron on Guadalcanal. He still has his commission as a commander in the Navy Chaplain Corps. The admiral called the Pentagon and they called him up for active duty, assigned to DCI. He's a nice— and very interesting—guy. And I think he's going be quite useful."

"Well, the DCI can certainly use some moral guidance," Dunwiddie said, chuckling.

[FOUR]
Farber Palast
Stein, near Nuremberg, American
Zone of Occupation, Germany
1330 14 April 1946

"Madame, my entire staff stands ready at your service," the elegantly dressed palace manager said, greeting Ginger. "Mr. Brewster of Mr. Justice Jackson's office was kind enough to call and announce your pending arrival."

"Excellent," Cronley said. "Well then, where can you put Mrs. Moriarty and her child?"

"Correct me if I'm wrong," Ginger said, shifting the sleeping infant to her other shoulder, "but doesn't Captain Cronley have a room here?"

"Yes, madame," the manager said, smiling. "The Duchess Suite. It's splendid."

"I'm sure it is. Can you have someone take me—and my luggage—there, please?"

The manager looked to Cronley, who, after a moment's hesitation, nodded.

"My pleasure, madame," the manager said, grandly gesturing for the bellman to come to them.

Ginger turned to Cronley, said, "Don't be too long," and walked to the elevator bank.

The awkward silence between everyone wasn't broken until the elevator door closed on Ginger, the baby, and the bellman with her luggage.

"Jimmy, what the hell is that all about?" Dunwiddie demanded.

Father McGrath cleared his throat, and said, "Since Jim, judging by the look on his face, appears as surprised as the rest of you, I'd better take that question."

Now everybody looked at him.

"Ginger and I had a long chat across the ocean," McGrath began, "while Super Spook and Tom were flying the airplane and Clete and von Wachtstein were snoring in their seats. Cutting to the chase, she confirmed what most of us suspected when she and Jim came down the staircase in Buenos Aires together. Specifically, that a substantial change had occurred in the nature of their relationship."

Dunwiddie turned to Cronley, who arched his eyebrows.

McGrath went on. "I first thought that she had concluded what had happened was a mistake and that she had come to me for advice on how to get out of a difficult relationship. She quickly disabused me of that notion. She said she had been in love with Jim since their college days and now intends to marry him as soon as possible and doesn't care at all what anyone—her family, Jim's family, or anyone else—thinks about it."

"Jesus!" Winters said.

"You want to **marry** her?" Dunwiddie asked.

"As soon as possible," Cronley said, nodding. "And anyone who doesn't like it can take a flying fuck at a rolling doughnut."

"She next said that as they began their new life together," McGrath went on, "and until they married, she had no intention of pretending she was, quote, a born-again virgin saving her virtue for wedlock, sneaking into his bedroom like a fräulein trying to earn a box of Hershey bars, unquote."

"Colorful!" Winters said.

"Good for her," Max Ostrowski said.

"There are some problems that I can see," Dunwiddie announced.

"Why am I not surprised?" Cronley said.

"For one thing, I don't think Justice Jackson is going to like this at all."

"Fuck him," Cronley snapped. "It's none of his business."

"That's so stupid, I won't dignify it with a reply," Dunwiddie said. "The other problem is, getting married. This isn't the States, where you give them two bucks for a license and then get married."

"I don't think I understand, Captain Dunwiddie," Father McGrath said. "I don't see where there's any impediment to their marriage."

"The Army is nobly protecting its members from wicked women," Dunwiddie said.

"Please elaborate," Father McGrath said.

"I got this story from Fat Freddy," Dunwiddie said.

"And Fat Freddy is?"

"Hessinger, Friedrich, DCI senior special agent," Cronley offered. "He's a bit on the chubby side, thus A/K/A Fat Freddy."

"He's also one of many American-German Jews in the CIC who are chasing Nazis," Dunwiddie went on. "One of them was at Harvard with Fat Freddy. Both of them got out of Germany just in time to not get fed into the ovens.

"Freddy's friend was engaged when he fled Germany. She, however, didn't get out. The friend figured she had been murdered. Her father was a rabbi. The SS especially did not like rabbis or their families.

"Fast-forward to Freddy's friend coming to Germany as a CIC special agent, which means he had all the clearances to get into all the records. He starts looking for references to his fiancée. He hoped he could at least find out where she had been gassed and incinerated. Then find in which mass grave her ashes had been dumped, so he could lay a rose on it.

"But he finds her—alive—in a Displaced Persons camp outside Hannover. She had somehow come up with a Polish passport that said she was a Catholic and she had been able to dodge the ovens.

"First, he has trouble with the Office of Military Government getting her out of the DP camp. He was working for Colonel Mortimer Cohen of the CIC, who lost most of his family to the ovens. Colonel Cohen—this was long before I met Mort—used all of his considerable clout to get her out of the DP camp, then to get her a new **Kennkarte** in her real name, and then to run her through the De-Nazification Court, which made her a certified non-Nazi.

"So, this guy has the love of his life installed in an apartment in Nuremberg and the obvious next step is to get married and live happily ever after. He asks how he can do that, and they tell him. It required an investigation of the lady and a bunch of other crap, including getting a letter from the German government stating she wasn't a prostitute. Even with Cohen's clout, he had a hard time speeding things up. In the end, it took six months to get final permission."

"I remember that now," Cronley said. "And I also remember you had a hell of a lot to do with that, Tiny, even more than Cohen."

"I was pissed at the stupidity of the U.S. Army."

"Well, I need you to get pissed again and do the same thing for Ginger and me. Quickly and quietly."

Dunwiddie shook his head. "Would that I could, Jimmy, but the way that works is, the American male who wants to get married has to go through a lot of bullshit—counseling by his immediate commander and then a chaplain, for example—and only after he gets through that can he apply for permission to get married. Then the bullshit starts for the bride-to-be. I can't imagine that the widow of a recently deceased officer is going to need a letter from the German government stating she's not a prostitute, but the man has to go through the bullshit first."

Cronley looked at his feet while shaking his head angrily, then looked up, and said, "That poses a number of problems, starting with my immediate commanding officer. I damn sure don't want to start this process by having to ask Wallace, 'Please, Colonel, sir, I'm in love and want to get married.'"

Dunwiddie grunted. "That wouldn't do you any good anyway. He's not your commanding officer anymore. There was a DP—"

"A what?" Ostrowski interrupted.

Dunwiddie did not answer directly and instead handed Cronley a SIGABA printout.

"I wasn't going to give you this, knowing what it will do to your already out-of-control ego, but I seem to have no choice. That's a DP message"—he looked at Ostrowski—"a message from the President. DP means 'By Direction of the President.'"

Cronley read the brief message, which was addressed to General Lucius Clay—the military governor of Germany and the commander in chief of U.S. forces in Germany—with a copy to Justice Jackson, and classified Top Secret–Presidential: "To facilitate Captain James D. Cronley Jr.'s search for Burgdorf and von Dietelburg, he and such other personnel as he may select are placed under the command, responsibility, and authority of Mr. Justice Jackson with immediate effect. —Harry S Truman, Commander in Chief."

Cronley looked up from the sheet as Dunwiddie said, "That was to cover your asses for your escapades in Vienna. But don't get the idea it will have any effect on your plans to get married."

"Why not?"

"Well, for one thing, you certainly can't go to Justice Jackson with your romantic intentions. He's now your commanding officer."

"Why not?" Cronley repeated. "I can see a lot of my problems going away once he meets the love of my life."

"That's just not going to happen. Or, to rephrase it: Over my dead body."

"Have it your way, Tiny. I'll deliver your eulogy."

"Goddamn it, Jimmy, I'm serious!"

Cronley just stared at him, then glanced at the others, and said, "As much as I hate to leave such charming company, my intended awaits. Breakfast at oh-six-hundred, gentlemen. We have an appointment with Mr. Justice Jackson at oh-eight-hundred, and I certainly don't want to be late."

He turned and walked quickly to the elevator bank.

[FIVE]
The Dining Room
Farber Palast
Stein, near Nuremberg, American
Zone of Occupation, Germany
0635 15 April 1946

"You sonofabitch," Ginger said as she and Cronley walked into the enormous, busy room. "You knew he was going to be here!"

She had made it clear—before and after they made love, and then upon wakening—that she had absolutely no intention of meeting with Mr. Justice Jackson, there would be no fallen woman pleading for forgiveness and compassion.

Cronley, who was occupied with not dropping Baby Bruce squirming in his arms, at first had no idea what she was talking about. But then, glancing around the room, he saw Father McGrath sitting at a table with Kenneth Brewster, Justice Jackson's law clerk at the Supreme Court and now his deputy at the Tribunal, and, finally, Jackson himself.

When McGrath saw Cronley and Ginger, he rose to his feet and waved them over.

"Give me Bruce!" Ginger snapped. "We're out of here!"

"No," Cronley replied. "Master Bruce and I are

going to make our manners known to Mr. Justice Jackson."

He walked to the table.

Ginger, hands on her hips, watched. White-faced with anger, she followed.

Jackson stood up, and, after a moment, Brewster rose.

"Long time, no see, Super Spook," Jackson said. "How's Argentina?"

"Mr. Justice," Cronley said. "Father, Brewster."

"Why don't you sit down, Jim," Jackson said, "before you drop that precious child and make his mother even more angry than she apparently already is."

Jackson moved around the table and pulled out a chair first for Cronley and then for Ginger.

"I'm Robert Jackson, Mrs. Moriarty, and this is my deputy, Ken Brewster."

Ginger, who had no choice but to take the offered chair, politely replied, "How do you do?"

"You and I have something in common, Mrs. Moriarty," Jackson said.

"Excuse me?"

"From time to time, we really want to throttle Super Spook. He can be infuriating, can't he?"

Ginger felt herself automatically nodding.

"This morning, for example, when Ken woke me to tell me that Super Spook had returned from Argentina with a woman and her baby, I wondered if I could find some statute that would permit me to have him hanged, and then drawn and quartered, before mounting his severed head atop the nearest lamp pole."

Despite herself, Ginger could not keep from smiling.

Jackson went on. "The reason I was so annoyed, Ginger . . . May I call you Ginger? I am old enough to be your father."

"Please do."

"Thank you. The reason I was so angry with him, Ginger, is that he has been charged by President Truman with recapturing two really evil men who have broken out of the Tribunal Prison."

As Jackson returned to his chair, he gestured to the coffee service on the table.

"May I offer you some coffee, perhaps tea?"

"No, thank you," she replied, and glanced at Cronley. "We won't be staying that long."

Jackson nodded, then continued. "I'm old school, Ginger. I believe that when the President of the United States asks you to do something, you have the duty to do it. Thus when Ken gave me the news, my first thought was how in hell—excuse me—how in the world does Jim expect to carry out this duty while dragging some South American señorita and her child—who, as far as I know, is not even his—along with him?

"I had no one to turn to for advice—that is,

until I remembered Father McGrath. I woke him and explained the situation. He, of course, then explained to me that you were not some Argentine tootsie but rather the widow of an officer who had been killed in action—indeed, possibly murdered at the orders of the very men the President has ordered Jim to recapture."

Justice Jackson paused to let that sink in, took another sip of his coffee, then continued. "Father McGrath also told me that he had had a long talk with you while you were crossing the South Atlantic and had been completely unsuccessful in trying to convince you that the only logical thing for you to do was to return to the United States with Colonel Frade and put your romantic plans, your intended marriage, on hold until Jim has von Dietelburg and Burgdorf back in the Tribunal Prison. He let me know, in other words, that I was stuck with you and Jim being together.

"So as much as this discomfits Ken, a calm analysis of the situation makes it clear that you two lovebirds have me in a very difficult position. The President wants, immediately, a detailed report of the escape and of our—which is to say, Jim's—plans for their recapture. As we speak, the major players are gathering in my conference room, with the obvious exception of Jim. Since the President sent Jim here to supervise the recapture of von Dietelburg and Burgdorf, he will absolutely want to hear what he has to say.

"I certainly am not going to call the President of the United States and tell him that Jim Cronley is too busy to even think about making any plans since he is too busy with his romantic problems.

"And I don't want any questions about you, Ginger, making their way around the gossip circuit. What I have decided to do is hide you in plain sight. The President has authorized Jim to recruit into the inner circle such persons as he feels necessary. In the report we are going to send to the President this morning, we will make you one of those persons. I don't think he'll question the names on the list. And if he doesn't, it can be presumed that the President knows Mrs. Virginia Moriarty is a member of the Recapture Team."

"What do I do?" she asked.

"You will participate in this morning's meeting. Which raises the problem of the baby—what to do with him? I have made arrangements for you to place him in the care of a nurse from the Field Hospital during the meeting and at such times, as a member of the team, when you can't be seen carrying a baby in your arms. Understand? Is that all right with you?"

"This is a lot to consider, out of the blue," she said.

"I need a yes or no, please. Time is of the essence."

"Okay," she said after a moment. "I mean, yes."

"Thank you," Jackson said, and made eye contact with Cronley. "You have any problems with any of this, Jim?"

"No, sir. Thank you, sir."

"Okay. Hand the baby to Father Jack. Then eat your breakfast. Quickly."

Jackson looked at his wristwatch.

"A car will be at the door in eighteen minutes. Let's go, Ken."

[SIX]
Justizpalast
Nuremberg, American Zone of
Occupation, Germany
0735 15 April 1946

The Palace of Justice, which housed the War Crimes Tribunal, didn't look at all like the palaces on picture postcards. It was a collection of plain four-story stucco buildings with two-story-high red-roofed attics.

The Compound was surrounded by fences topped with concertina barbed wire and guarded by soldiers wearing shoulder insignias of the 1st

Infantry Division. The guards' web belts and the leather pistol holsters attached to them were white. They wore white plastic helmet liners and highly polished combat boots, into which their trousers were "bloused."

Cronley's car was passed into the Compound without trouble after Max Ostrowski, who was driving, flashed his credentials at the sergeant in charge of the striped-pole barrier across the road.

And then they reached the building that housed the Office of the Chief United States Prosecutor. Getting into the building required that they each show identification. There, the trouble began.

Ginger had no identification besides her passport. She had thrown her Military Dependent identification card atop her husband's casket as it was lowered into the ground.

After a good fifteen minutes, Kenneth Brewster marched out of the building. Following him was a motherly looking woman in her thirties, a nurse, upon whose uniform gleamed the silver oak leaves of a lieutenant colonel.

"What's the holdup?" Brewster demanded, somewhat imperiously, and then without waiting for a reply gestured for the nurse to go to Ginger, who now was holding the baby.

She handed over Baby Bruce more than a little reluctantly, then everyone walked into the building, where they found Justice Jackson waiting for them.

Jackson led them to his conference room door, then said, "Ken, put someone on your desk to make sure we're not disturbed for any, repeat, any reason."

"Yes, Mr. Justice."

"Pencil sharpened, Mrs. Rogers?" Jackson asked.

Mrs. Lorraine Rogers, a widow in her early fifties, wore a conservative gray sweater and dark woolen skirt. Her shoulder-length red hair, brushed tight against the scalp, had been pulled into a ponytail.

"Yes, Mr. Justice," she said as she uncovered her Stenotype machine.

"Okay, let's get started. This meeting of the Tribunal Prison Escape Committee is convened as of seven forty-five on the morning of April fifteenth, 1946, in the office of the U.S. Prosecutor in the International Tribunal Compound in Nuremberg, Germany. All proceedings, including the transcript of proceedings, will be classified Top Secret–Presidential.

"Present are the undersigned: Mr. Kenneth Brewster of my office; Colonel Mortimer S. Cohen, chief of U.S. Counterintelligence for the Tribunal; Colonel James T. Rasberry, commanding officer of the Twenty-sixth Infantry Regiment; and Captains James D. Cronley Jr., Thomas Winters, and Chauncey Dunwiddie of the Directorate of Central Intelligence. Also present are: Father Jack McGrath, Max Ostrowski of the DCI, Mrs. Virginia Moriarty, and others selected by Captain Cronley to assist in the recapture of the escaped prisoners—to wit, former SS-Brigadeführer Franz von Dietelburg and SS-Generalmajor Wilhelm Burgdorf.

"Colonel Cohen, will you please recount what happened here on or about April fifth of this year?"

"Yes, sir," Cohen said, cleared his throat, then began. "At approximately oh-six-ten on the sixth, I received a telephone call from Lieutenant Lewis J. Feller, telling me there had possibly been an escape from the Tribunal Prison."

"Who is Lieutenant Feller?" Jackson said.

"An officer of the Twenty-sixth Infantry, which is charged with guarding the Tribunal Prison. He had, he said, just come on duty as officer of the day when he found the on-duty OD, the sergeant of the guard, and maybe seven soldiers, sprawled unconscious in the guard shack just outside the prison cellblock. I asked him if he had notified Colonel Rasberry. He said he had.

"So, I put my pants on and went to the prison. When I got there, Rasberry told me he had run a bed check and found more soldiers unconscious—

and that Burgdorf and von Dietelburg were missing."

"These were prisoners awaiting trial?"

"Yes, sir," Colonel Cohen said.

"Do you know, from personal knowledge, how they came to be incarcerated in the Tribunal Prison?"

"Yes, sir. Super Spook and company arrested them in Vienna and flew them to Nuremberg."

"And, for the record, Super Spook is?"

"Captain Cronley, sir."

"Let the record show," Jackson said, "that I started calling Captain Cronley Super Spook following his outstanding intelligence efforts in the past. The fact that other intelligence officers have taken up referring to him by that nickname shows they share my admiration of his performance." He paused to allow Mrs. Rogers time to record all that, then went on. "Now, from your personal knowledge, Colonel Cohen, was Cronley made aware of these events at the prison?"

"No, sir, he was not."

"Again, from your personal knowledge, Colonel, why wasn't he?"

"He was in Argentina, sir. I had heard that as rumor, and you later confirmed it."

"Had Captain Cronley not been in Argentina, would he have been notified, and would he have participated in your subsequent investigation?"

"Absolutely. He's thoroughly familiar with the prison. Not only that, but with the assistance of Super Spook Junior—"

"Does Super Spook Junior have a name?"

"Yes, sir. Captain Cronley calls him Casey— initial **K**, initial **C**—Wagner."

"And Casey Wagner is?"

"A DCI agent, sir."

"And he is called Super Spook Junior why?"

"Well," Colonel Cohen said, "he works with Captain Cronley. He's also very young."

"How young?"

"I believe he's eighteen, sir."

"And he's an agent of DCI? Isn't that a little unusual?"

"Yes, sir, it is. But he is a very unusual young man. Cronley took him into the DCI after Wagner had determined how Odessa was getting Nazis on the run over the Franco–German border and then to Spain. We bagged two really bad Odessa Nazis—"

"For the record, would you please define 'Odessa'?"

"Organisation Der Ehemaligen SS-Angehörigen. In English, that's Organization of Former SS Personnel. I think it's forty percent probable that they're involved in this prison break."

"And the Odessa Nazis bagged because of this young man Wagner were whom?"

"Former SS-Brigadeführer Ulrich Heimstadter and his former deputy, Standartenführer Oskar Müller. Among other things, what we wanted them for was the massacre of slave laborers at Peenemünde, the German rocket laboratories."

"Colonel Cohen," Cronley said, "you said it was forty percent probable that Odessa was involved in this break. Who else is suspect?"

"Let's not go down that road right now," Jackson said.

Cohen ignored him, and said, "The NKGB. That's obvious. But I have a gut feeling that the AVO may be involved. That's the—"

"Államvédelmi Osztálya, acronym AVO," Cronley provided. "The Russian-controlled Secret Police in Hungary. Its chief is a real sonofabitch, Gábor Péter. He murdered Niedermeyer's wife, Karol—"

"This escape was a professional operation," Cohen interrupted Cronley while looking at Justice Jackson. "The AVO is very professional. Many of its members—including Gábor Péter—go back to the Nazi Arrow organization, which was run by the SS. My scenario here is that if the NKGB wanted people out of the Tribunal Prison, (a) they have been planning this for some time, (b) Cronley's pal Ivan Serov figured that not only is the AVO very good but if something went wrong, better the AVO take the rap, not the NKGB, and

(c) that the operation was designed to spring somebody else—that somebody-else list is long— not Burgdorf and von Dietelburg, who had been there only a short time. But when they learned that those two were in the prison, they decided they wanted them more than anyone on the somebody-else list."

There was a lot to consider, and no one said anything. It was Cronley who broke the silence.

"That scenario makes a lot of sense."

"Cronley's pal Ivan Serov?" Jackson asked of Cohen.

"Colonel of State Security Ivan Serov, first deputy to Commissar of State Security Nikolaevich Merkulov. Super Spook dealt with him when the NKGB had Colonel Mattingly and wanted to swap him for Polkóvnik Sergei Likharev and family."

"Identify those people, please," Jackson said.

"Super Spook turned Colonel Likharev—who we caught trying to sneak out of the DCI Pullach Compound—by promising to get his family out of Russia and then did. The Likharevs went to Argentina."

"Where," Cronley put in, "he has proved to be a very good asset regarding the NKGB. He used to work as Ivan's deputy."

"Let's get back to what happened here," Jackson said. "You said when you went to the prison you found the guards were unconscious?"

"Yes, sir," Colonel Cohen said. "They'd been gassed."

"How do you know that? With what?"

"My people found a little puddle of brown liquid outside the entrance to the prison. It had solidified. They think that it's leakage from a gas tank. Their scenario is, the tank possibly was put on the ground, with a tube to carry the gas between the door and its sill, or maybe some kind of device to spray it in the air. Then its valve was opened. When enough time had passed to knock out the guards on the other side of the door, they entered the prison cellblock itself and knocked out the guards there, who are unarmed, by spraying the gas directly in their faces.

"Sort of strengthening this scenario is the fact that the main I.G. Farben gas plant in Hungary, which made the Zyklon B that was used in the death camps, and where they still manufacture various gases and probably still does Zyklon B, had a laboratory in which other gases were developed.

"They were tested at Treblinka, as well as other concentration camps, including those in Hungary. When the Germans were first allied with Hungary, and later took it over completely, the Arrow organization got access to and used Zyklon B and other gases to murder maybe a half-million people.

"Rephrasing it, my scenario, which may be far-fetched, is (a) that the AVO staged the prison break, (b) that it was intended to free somebody other than Burgdorf and von Dietelburg, and (c) that they used some kind of gas—something pretty sophisticated—to knock out, but intentionally not kill, the guards. Thirty-odd dead Americans would have caused an outrage that they didn't need."

"I don't think it's far-fetched," Colonel Rasberry said. "What impressed me was the professionalism of the break. I don't think Serov has the capability to do what was done."

"Can you amplify that, Colonel?" Jackson asked.

"They entered the Tribunal Compound in an Army ambulance," Rasberry said. "We finally found out that it was stolen six weeks before the escape from the Fifty-seventh Field Hospital in Giessen, which is a long way from here. They were wearing U.S. Army uniforms and they spoke English. They left the Compound the same way—I mean, they had a Trip Ticket to show my people.

"The ambulance was found in the Rhine-Main–Danube Canal five days after the break, which suggests they drove directly there, where others must've waited, probably with clothing and counterfeit **Kennkarten** for Burgdorf and von

Dietelburg. The ambulance was in a sort of pool, a lake, on the canal, twenty feet under. It was found by accident—something fell off a barge and the crew was looking for it. If that hadn't happened, we'd probably never have learned what happened to the ambulance."

"For the record, please define **Kennkarten**," Jackson said.

"German identity documents."

"Any questions, Super Spook?" Jackson asked.

"No, sir."

"Any suggestions on what we should do next?"

"Colonel Cohen," Cronley asked, "was Casey Wagner involved in your interrogations of the people, German and American?"

"Yes, of course."

"And?"

"He came up with the scenario that they had driven the ambulance to a rendezvous point somewhere, either in a forest or near water, and that we should start by finding the ambulance. So, we asked General White to have the Constabulary start looking for it. Which they did, and they came up with nothing."

"I suggest, sir," Cronley said, looking at Justice Jackson, "that our only option is to re-interrogate the guards, the German personnel in the prison, and the prisoners. Maybe if we can determine who the AVO was originally intending to break out—"

"You think it was the AVO?" Jackson interrupted.

"Yes, sir. Because of their skill, and because Ivan Serov is a master of covering his ass . . . Sorry . . . And I'd like Wagner to be there. Where is he?"

"In Sonthofen with General White," Cohen said, then chuckled. "General White is serving as the ad hoc chairman of the German branch of Norwich University's Scholarship Committee."

"What's that all about?"

"The general thinks that Sergeant—excuse me, Special Agent—Wagner would make a fine career officer and the way to do that is for him to graduate from Norwich."

"And Norwich is the one in Vermont?" Jackson asked.

"Yes, sir, the oldest private military academy. Its graduates are commissioned into the Regular Army the same day as West Point graduates, so they start off with the same date of rank. By coincidence, I'm sure, General White is a 1920 graduate of Norwich. I'll call over there and let them know we need Wagner here."

"Are there any objections to Cronley's ideas how we should proceed?" Jackson asked.

There were none.

"So ordered. This meeting of the Prison Escape Committee is concluded at eight fifty-three on the morning of April fourteenth, 1946," Jackson said, and then went on. "Mrs. Rogers, as your first priority please type up your notes in disposition form, then have Ken look at them, and, when he has, get on the SIGABA and send it 'Eyes Only the President' to the White House."

"Yes, sir. Shall I copy to Admiral Souers?"

"No. I know the President well enough to know that as soon as he reads the SIGABA, he'll send for the admiral to get his take on it."

"Yes, sir," Mrs. Rodgers said, and left the conference room.

"I would like to make amends to Mrs. Moriarty," Justice Jackson said.

"Sir?" Cohen asked.

"Ginger, I gave you ten minutes to eat your breakfast and then I took your baby away from you. So, what I'm going to suggest is that you, your baby, and Father McGrath be my guests for lunch. Give us a little break, so to speak. And I really want to hear what Father McGrath thinks of Himmler's new religion. How about twelve-thirty hours at the Farber Palast? Can you arrange that, Jim?"

"Consider it done, sir," Cronley said.

"You are also invited, of course. You, Dunwiddie, and Ostrowski."

III

[ONE]
**The Dining Room, Farber Palast
Stein, near Nuremberg, American
Zone of Occupation, Germany
1330 15 April 1946**

A waiter delivered two bottles of Veuve Clicquot champagne to the table.

"With the compliments, **meine Dame und Herren**, of Oberst Serov."

As a second waiter placed champagne flutes before everybody, Cronley saw Serov sitting at the bar, raising a flute toward their table.

Cronley gestured to him to come over.

"What are you up to, Jim?" Justice Jackson asked.

"I respectfully suggest, sir," Cronley said, "that the question is, what is Serov up to?"

"Point taken," Jackson said, smiling.

Serov, wearing the dress uniform of an infantry colonel, approached the table.

"Mr. Justice," he said. "How nice to see you again, sir."

"Colonel," Jackson said.

"Pull up a chair, Ivan," Cronley said, "and tell us what you expect to get for your bottles of bubbly."

"A moment of your time," Serov replied. "First, to welcome you back from Argentina. And, second, to ask how the inquiry into the escape is going."

So, Serov knows where I was?

No surprise.

"I don't know how that Argentina rumor got started," Cronley said. "And this is not the place to discuss the escape."

Serov didn't reply, instead turning to the waiter and telling him to bring his open bottle of champagne to the table.

"Someone once said, 'There is no such thing as too much money or champagne,'" Serov said. "Are you going to introduce me to your friends?"

"Ginger, Father McGrath, when you get home you can dazzle people by reporting that you met a very senior officer of the NKGB. This is Colonel Ivan Serov, first deputy to Commissar of State Security Nikolaevich Merkulov."

"I thought I told you, James, that is in the past.

I am now back in my beloved infantry, serving as adviser to the Soviet chief prosecutor to the Tribunal. I speak English, he doesn't."

Serov turned to McGrath.

"Father, it is a pleasure to meet you. But James hasn't given me the proper name of this lovely lady."

"This is Mrs. Moriarty," McGrath said, "a friend of the family."

"And the widow of the late Lieutenant Bruce Moriarty," Cronley said, an edge to his tone.

Serov turned to Ginger.

"I heard, of course, about your husband, Mrs. Moriarty. A tragedy. My condolences."

It wasn't a tragedy, Ivan, Cronley thought. It was an assassination.

And I'm just about convinced—not sure, but just about convinced—that you were behind it.

"I know how it is to lose someone," Serov went on, "to lose one's life companion . . ."

And where are you going now with this, you bastard?

". . . I recently lost my Rozalina. On March seventeen. Not quite a month ago."

"I'm very sorry to hear that," Jackson said.

"I didn't know about your wife, Ivan," Cronley said. "I'm sorry."

Serov nodded solemnly.

Cronley was not surprised to realize that he

really did feel badly for the Russian, that it wasn't just the expected thing to say. In late October—not quite six months earlier—the drunk driver of a big rig had killed his bride, Marjorie Howell Cronley, as she drove her Buick into Washington on U.S. 1. They had been married the day before by a justice of the peace.

Serov went on. "Rozalina died of breast cancer at the Tomsk cancer hospital. We'd met there—the hospital is part of Tomsk National Research Medical Center—and were married there and then gone away, only to return for Rozalina to die there. We'd been married not quite twenty years."

Twenty years? Cronley thought.

Jesus, I didn't have twenty hours.

Serov paused as the waiter delivered the open champagne bottle, put it before Serov, then filled the others' flutes with a fresh bottle.

Cronley lifted his flute.

"May I propose we toast your bride?"

"Thank you, James," Serov said, clearly moved by the gesture.

He picked up his champagne flute, and when everyone else had raised theirs, he said, "To my beautiful Rozalina, now blessed with eternal peace."

After everyone took a sip, Serov continued. "She married me against the wishes of her family. At the time, I thought it was because I was then an NKGB officer. But over the years, I came to understand it was because they thought I was a heathen. They were wrong. While I certainly wasn't a devout, go to mass every day Christian—which is hardly the path to promotion within the NKGB—neither was I an atheist.

"The issue of religion—I suppose I should say Christianity—arose when Rozalina became seriously ill. We returned to Tomsk not for sentimental reasons but rather because it's the best cancer facility in the Soviet Union, and I had by then risen sufficiently in rank so that I could get her admitted."

Risen to general. What's this colonel bullshit?
And to me? I know better.

When I first met you, you made it clear that dealing with a captain was beneath the dignity of a general.

"I could also arrange accommodations for her family in Tomsk—her father, a brother, and two sisters; her mother was dead—and did so. And they prayed, on their knees, every day at her bedside. I remember thinking, when she was gone, that maybe if I had dropped to my knees beside them, Rozalina would still be alive."

He paused, cleared his throat, and went on. "I then did what any man alone in the world—"

"What do you mean alone?" Cronley interrupted.

"Well, my relationship with Rozalina's family ended with her death. Mutually."

"And you'd had no children?" Ginger asked.

Serov, his tone bitter and sarcastic, said, "God, despite the long hours Rozalina had spent praying on her knees, asking Him for children, had chosen not to bless us with even one. So, I was alone and did what any reasonable man would do, given the circumstances: I came back to Nuremberg and threw myself into my work. Life goes on."

"Yes, it does," Ginger said. "At first, you don't think it will, but then something happens."

She means me, Cronley thought.

Confirmation of that speculation came when he looked at her and she met his eyes and gave him a soft smile.

"I apologize for troubling you with my troubles," Serov said. "I don't know what came over me."

"No apologies are necessary, Colonel," Jackson said.

Serov raised his champagne flute.

"**Za to, chtoby sbyvalus mechty!**" he said.

"Well, I'll drink to that, whatever it means," Ginger said.

"You were expecting **Nostrovia!** perhaps?"

"That's what I've heard at the movies."

"I understand," Serov said. "Somebody should tell Hollywood that **Nostrovia!** as a toast is meaningless, and also that all Russians are not monsters. What I propose as a toast—**Za to, chtoby sbyva-lus mechty**—means 'Let our dreams come true.'"

"Well, I'll drink to that," Justice Jackson said.

"So will I," Ginger said, and again met Cronley's eyes and smiled at him.

Oh, Jesus! Cronley thought.

"Would it be impolitic of me to ask again how your investigation into the escape of Burgdorf and von Dietelburg is progressing?" Serov asked. "We're all wondering how that could have happened."

Talk about brass balls!

The odds are ninety-nine to one that you arranged it!

"I'll let Jim answer that, Colonel," Jackson said. "He's in charge of the investigation."

"Well, Ivan—"

"Excuse me, Jim," Serov interrupted him and snapped his fingers to attract the attention of a waiter hovering nearby.

"**Herr Oberst?**" the waiter said.

Serov pointed to the table where Tiny Dunwiddie and Max Ostrowski were sitting with the nurse and the baby.

"Send a bottle of the champagne to that table with my compliments," he said.

"**Jawohl, Herr Oberst.**"

"Curiosity overwhelms me," Serov said. "Who

is the infant whose protection requires the services of two of DCI's best agents? And the attention of a very senior Army nurse?"

"That's John Jay McCloy's love child, Ivan," Cronley said. "I suppose that now that you've spotted them, that secret's no longer so secret."

"My God, Jim," Jackson said. His tone suggested he was more amused at the injecting of the assistant secretary of war than shocked.

"That is my son," Ginger said, evenly.

Cronley was not finished.

"We're all friends here, Ivan. So, tell me—what's the gossip on Lubyanka Square? Does Nikolaevich Merkulov go home to Mrs. Merkulov every night? Or does he have a little something on the side? Maybe a ballet dancer?"

Serov's face went white and his eyes flashed. He stood up.

"Sometimes, Cronley, you go too far," he said, angrily. He nodded his head toward Jackson. "You'll have to excuse me, Mr. Justice. I just remembered an appointment."

He stormed out of the dining room.

Everyone at the table exchanged glances.

"Was that wise, Jim?" Jackson asked.

"It was stupid," Ginger snapped.

"Oh, good ol' Ivan'll be back," Cronley replied. "He wants something. I told him the escape is off-limits here."

"What?" Jackson asked.

"I haven't figured that out yet. But I will."

"To change the subject, where are you going to start?" Jackson asked.

"Specifically?"

Jackson nodded.

"You remember when Colonel Cohen said that if Odessa was behind the break, he thought they were trying to free somebody besides von Dietelburg and Burgdorf?"

"I do."

"Well, I think I know who they were after."

"Who?"

"Standartenführer Oskar Müller and SS-Brigadeführer Ulrich Heimstadter. I'm going to start with them."

"Who are they?" Ginger asked.

Cronley flashed her an impatient look.

Jackson picked up on it.

"Get used to that, Cronley. If we're going to hide Ginger in plain sight, the more she knows about everything, the better. I suggest you take that to heart."

Ginger looked very pleased.

Cronley had a look of resignation, then nodded.

"Toward the end of the war, my love," he said, "when it looked as if the German rocket facility at Peenemünde was about to be captured by either the Russians or the Americans—we ultimately took it—Brigadeführer Heimstadter and Standartenführer Müller decided the best way to make sure that the thousand-odd slave workers there didn't tell either the Reds or the Amis what Wernher von Braun and his friends had been up to was to kill them. First, they made the slave workers dig an enormous hole—a mass grave. Then, until the bullets ran out, the Germans lined them up at the edge of the grave and shot them in the back of the head. They fell into the hole. When bullets ran out, the Germans pushed them into the grave alive, then buried them with a bulldozer."

"My God!" Ginger said.

"Really bad Nazis. Presuming the break was staged by Odessa, what Cohen thinks—and I agree—is that Odessa wanted Heimstadter and Müller but then learned that von Dietelburg and Burgdorf were in the prison and sprung those two bastards instead. Which confirms that von Dietelburg and Burgdorf are more important to Odessa than just about anyone else."

Cronley looked around the table, then added, "This afternoon, I'm going to the prison and shake up Heimstadter and Müller a little before I really start talking to them, which I will do immediately on my return from Strasbourg tomorrow."

"You're going where?" Ginger asked.

"We are going to Strasbourg to see what Colonel Jean-Paul Fortin knows, or has heard, or can find out for me, about the prison break. We'll take Father McGrath and, of course, the baby and the nurse."

"And bodyguards?" Jackson asked.

"Yes, sir. We'll need another car. Everyone won't fit in the Horch. Max Ostrowski will drive the other car. That's enough security."

"Okay," Jackson said. "Let me know what Fortin comes up with. And now I'm going to have to leave you."

[TWO]
Farber Palast
Stein, near Nuremberg, American
Zone of Occupation, Germany
1505 15 April 1946

There were three U.S. Army staff cars parked in a line at the stairs to the palace when Cronley drove up in the Horch convertible sedan.

Ginger Moriarty, who was holding Baby Bruce, stood on the steps with Father J-for-Jack McGrath and Tiny Dunwiddie.

On the right of the steps were five men wearing U.S. Army uniforms. The lapels of their Ike jackets had blue-and-white patches reading U.S. that identified them as civilian employees of the Army.

They were, in fact, DCI agents.

Cronley got out of the car and went to Dunwiddie.

"What's going on, Tiny?"

"Mr. Justice Jackson called and told me to make sure you didn't go off to Strasbourg alone."

"You mean, without bodyguards? Guess he didn't agree with me that Max was enough."

"Precisely. So here we are."

"Fortin will think we're invading."

"Give the commandant my regards, Jim," Dunwiddie said. "And now I will return to my duties. Any orders, **mon chef**?"

"Get on the horn to your godfather and make sure Casey is here when we get back."

"I hear and obey, **mon chef**," Dunwiddie replied. He turned to the others. "Have a nice trip."

Dunwiddie walked to the row of staff cars, got in the first one, and drove away. As he did, one of the DCI agents left the others, went to a second staff car, and got in behind the wheel. The remaining agents walked to Cronley and the others.

"Interesting man," Father McGrath said. "I couldn't tell if he dislikes you intensely or if you're friends."

"A little of both, but mostly very good friends."

"What was that about his godfather?"

"Tiny's Norwich. So was his father, class of '20. And so was General White. He's Tiny's godfather."

Max Ostrowski walked up to Cronley.

"Tiny said a lead staff car and a trail car, with the Horch in the middle. That okay with you? And who sits where?"

"I suppose that's better than using M8 armored cars."

"Is all this security really necessary?" Father McGrath asked.

"Jackson wants to keep you all alive," Ostrowski said. "And he's not been unreasonable."

Ostrowski then pointed to the door of the Horch. There were four indentions in it, covered with fresh paint.

"Those look like bullet holes," Father McGrath said, making it a question.

Ginger's eyes grew wide. "Bullet holes?"

"Repaired bullet holes," Ostrowski said.

Oh, goddamn you, Max, Cronley thought.

Ginger didn't have to hear this!

Wait . . .

"Actually," Cronley said, "a couple months back, at the end of February, Tom Winters and I were ambushed while taking a shortcut from the airport to here. Turned into a Wild West gunfight.

We got the bad guys—they were Odessa—who had Schmeissers. One of them was an eighteen-year-old girl. I shot her in the forehead."

Cronley felt Ginger's horrified eyes on him.

If that doesn't buttress my argument that Ginger had better find some nice insurance salesman instead of a guy who people are trying to whack—and, sooner or later, will succeed—I'll have to think of something else.

There was silence, which was then broken by Ostrowski: "We're back to who sits where?"

[THREE]
Hôtel Maison Rouge
Rue des Francs-Bourgeois 101
Strasbourg, France
2005 15 April 1946

Colonel Jean-Paul Fortin, a trim forty-year-old, marched purposely into the hotel dining room and up toward the table where Cronley and the others were sitting. He was wearing a U.S. Army olive-drab Ike jacket and trousers, and had removed his kepi from his head. Shoulder boards identified him as colonel. He was accompanied by a similarly uniformed officer whose boards identified him as a captain.

Cronley stood up as the officers approached the table. Fortin wrapped his arms around him affectionately.

"Dunwiddie telephoned to say you were coming," he greeted Cronley. "I expected you at the office, but then DuPres spotted your Nazimobile parked outside."

"We're having dinner. There was no place to eat on the way over. Join us?"

"I'll join you, but Pierre and I have had our dinner."

He motioned for the other officer to bring them chairs. When he had, they sat down. Fortin signaled for a waiter.

"Bring cognac," he ordered.

"Everybody," Cronley then announced, "this is Colonel Jean-Paul Fortin, who tries but usually fails to maintain the peace in Strasbourg. And this is Capitaine Pierre DuPres. I don't know what he did wrong, but as punishment Pierre was assigned to Jean-Paul as his deputy."

DuPres laughed.

"Jean-Paul, this is Mrs. Virginia Moriarty and Father Jack McGrath. You know Max."

"**Enchanté**," Fortin said, taking Ginger's hand and kissing it. "And you are here why, madame?"

Cronley said, "Ginger, who is the widow of Lieutenant Moriarty, is with me."

"The gentleman who made the mistake of taking a nap in your bed?"

"Uh-huh. End of the interrogation, **mon colonel**. And before you say something—or, worse, do something stupid—be advised that Father McGrath is Anglican, Church of England, not Roman Catholic."

"Isn't that a meaningless distinction, James?" Fortin said.

"Your ignorance is showing again, Jean-Paul," Cronley replied.

"You may find this hard to believe," DuPres said to no one in particular, "but they're really quite fond of each other."

"Well, you could have fooled me," Ginger said.

"There's a rumor going around," Cronley said, "that when a Catholic priest says something that annoys Colonel Fortin, next thing you know the priest is trying to swim in the Rhine."

"Which is hard to do," Max Ostrowski added, "after someone has shot you in the elbows and knees with a .22."

Cronley saw Ginger was looking at Ostrowski with disbelief that turned into horrified realization Fortin was not denying the implied accusation.

She shouldn't be hearing this.

She shouldn't be here.

Which means I shouldn't have brought her.

Which is yet another indication that we

shouldn't be together—that she'd be far better off with any of the nice, safe guys her parents are trying to match her with.

Mother asked what I was thinking. And the truth is—pardon my French—I was thinking with the head of my dick.

And, wow, I've really fucked this up . . .

"Dunwiddie didn't say why you were coming," Fortin said, and added, "with a priest."

"I like to think of myself as a scholar/priest, Colonel," McGrath said. "My specialty is heretical religions. I'm in Germany looking into the one that Heinrich Himmler started."

"Am I supposed to believe that you and James are simply friends? And that you have no connection with the DCI?"

McGrath shrugged, then said, "Let me throw this up for your edification. I trust you're familiar with Colonel Cletus Frade of the DCI?"

Fortin nodded.

"When Colonel Frade was a fighter pilot on Guadalcanal," McGrath went on, "I was the fighter group's chaplain. Cletus asked me to help him find out more about Himmler's heretical religion. I'm happy to do so."

"And that's what you're doing in Strasbourg?" Fortin pursued.

"You must be the very good—relentless— intelligence officer Jimmy tells me you are,"

McGrath said. "Actually, I'm in Strasbourg for several reasons. First, on the way, Jimmy told me about Saint Heinrich the Divine's Wewelsburg Castle—"

"I'm having trouble believing any of that," Fortin put in.

"Well, I'm very interested in getting a look at it," McGrath said. "And, second, I'm here because Mrs. Cronley—Jimmy's mother—made me promise to hold him to **his** promise to look in on the widow of her recently deceased nephew, Jimmy's cousin."

"I presume you're talking about the late SS-Sturmführer Luther Stauffer," Fortin said, but it sounded like a question.

"Correct. And, third, Jimmy wants to ask you—"

"You have a cousin who was in the SS?" Ginger asked Cronley, incredulously.

"I did until Odessa got him to bite on a cyanide capsule in the Tribunal Prison."

There was again a look of disbelief in her eyes, followed by a look of horrified acceptance.

It hurts seeing her react this way. Maybe I wasn't thinking with my dick, which means I am in love with her . . .

If that's true, I've got to get her away from me.

Get her and the baby away from me.

"What about his widow?" Ginger asked. "Do you know where she is? I'd like to see her."

"I'm afraid that's impossible, madame," Fortin said. "She's in the Sainte-Marguerite Prison."

"Why?" Ginger said, her tone on the edge of unpleasantness.

"The Ministry of Justice is in the process of deciding whether she is to be tried for collaboration or turned over to the Americans for trial on charges of crimes against humanity. At the Nuremberg Tribunal. And when that decision is made, I'm going to inquire into her connection with Odessa."

"She's a Nazi?"

"There seems little question about that," Fortin said. "She and her husband were given the privilege of being married in that castle, Wewelsburg, that James describes as the Church of Saint Heinrich the Divine. In a Nazi ceremony in accordance with the rituals of this new Nazi religion."

"Jean-Paul," Cronley said, "as much as I hate to leave this delightful subject, how about we bring you and Pierre up to date on the prison break, and then you tell us what you know, suspect, or have heard about said subject?"

"I was about to suggest that," DuPres said.

"Oh, were you?" Fortin challenged. "And have you any other brilliant suggestions?"

"As a matter of fact, **mon colonel**, I do indeed. If you would buy us a bottle of **good** cognac, it might help to erase the opinion that James's lady and the good Father must have evolved to your

being, vis-à-vis good manners, the French equivalent of an SS-Unterscharführer."

"That's a corporal, Ginger," Cronley said.

"So far as manners are concerned," Fortin
snapped, "I wonder how the hell someone as
impertinent as you, DuPres, ever managed to
graduate from Saint-Cyr, much less hold a commission for more than two weeks."

"That's the French West Point," Cronley added,
helpfully.

"Apparently," DuPres said with a shrug, "they
desperately needed junior officers to explain big
words with multiple syllables to its colonels."

"You may find this hard to believe, Father
McGrath," Cronley said, "but they're really quite
fond of each other."

"You could have fooled me."

Fortin glared at everybody, then asked, "Would
you honor me with your presence at the bar,
Madame Moriarty? For some decent cognac?"

[FOUR]

"When I heard about the breakout from James,"
Fortin said, draining the cognac bottle into his
snifter while waving for the bartender to bring
another to the table, "I told my people to start
looking for them here."

"You think they're coming here?" Cronley said, surprised.

"I think they're headed for Spain, and then, more than likely, for South America."

"And leave Odessa's money behind?"

"I'm surprised Mr. Justice Jackson calls you Super Spook. You haven't figured this out, have you?"

"Please, enlighten me."

"For a price, the Vatican will provide documents that will get these bastards out of Spain."

"Really?" Father McGrath said. "I heard that rumored, but . . ."

"It's no rumor, Father," Fortin said.

Cronley said, "You think that von Dietelburg and Burgdorf picked up money—enough to pay off the Vatican—from the Odessa guys who got them out and are now headed here?"

"No. I think they're gone from here, and, if not in Spain, they will be shortly."

"Then looking for them is a waste of time?"

Fortin ignored the question, and said, "Turning to scenario two: Serov, the NKGB, arranged the escape. It was a professional job, so probably the AVO was deeply involved."

"Why would Serov want to bust them out?" Ginger asked.

"Money, primarily. He gets them to Budapest, and the AVO gets them to tell Serov where the money is. He grabs the money, then kills both of them as they try to escape. He brings the bodies back to Nuremberg and says, 'Look what a good guy I am!'"

"How much money does Odessa have?" Father McGrath asked.

"Estimates range from a hundred million in currency to maybe five, ten times that much. And that doesn't include the gold and jewels."

"Where did they get it?" Ginger asked.

"The currency that they have—that they stole—came from banks. Most of the gold the same way. But some of the gold is—or was—from teeth . . ."

"From teeth?" Ginger parroted.

"Once they had gassed the **Untermenschen** in the shower rooms . . ."

"What are you talking about?" Ginger said. "Gassed? Shower rooms?"

"You don't want to know," Cronley said.

"Yes, damn it, I do!"

Cronley raised his eyebrows, then said, "Okay. In Dachau, for example, when the trains arrived—not passenger cars but boxcars packed with prisoners—they were greeted by SS officers holding the leashes of vicious German shepherds. The men were separated from the women and children, and the old from the young, and the healthy from the sick. The healthy were marched off to work as slave labor in the factories, et cetera.

"Everybody else was told they were to take a shower, after which they would be issued prison uniforms and taken to their barracks. This group then took off their clothes and went naked into the next room, which had a sign identifying it as a shower room. The doors closed. That was the cue for the SS men on the roof to pour a pesticide—it's called Zyklon B—into the room. Depending on conditions, death came anywhere from five to fifteen minutes later."

"Five to fifteen? How . . . How did they know?"

"They knew they were all dead when all the screaming stopped." He saw the look in her eyes. "You want more, Ginger?"

"Finish," she said.

"Next, after waiting a half hour before opening the death chamber doors, other inmates entered and started loading the corpses in wheelbarrows and on tables with wheels and rolled them out of the showers. Just outside were other inmates who were forced to inspect the corpses. They removed any jewelry, such as wedding rings. Then another team of specialists went to work. They pried open the mouths of the corpses. If they found gold false teeth, or gold bridgework, or fillings, they took a hammer and chisel . . ."

Ginger gasped involuntarily, covering her mouth with her hand. Her eyes glistened.

". . . and removed the gold. I'm sorry, baby. You wanted to hear."

She motioned for him to continue.

"You sure?"

She nodded.

"Okay. The wedding rings and the jewelry were put in one basket, the gold teeth in another. The idea was to melt down the rings and the dental work to make gold bars, which were then to be deposited in the Deutsche Bank.

"That sometimes—in fact, often—didn't happen, as called for. Some clever SS officer reasoned that since the Deutsche Bank didn't know how many wedding bands, say, had been minted as gold bars, some rings could be set aside and later converted and distributed among deserving SS officers. Or smuggled into Switzerland and sold, the cash from that again distributed among the deserving.

"From its beginning, the SS was corrupt to the core—criminally corrupt. One of the original big shots, right under Himmler, was a man named Reinhard Heydrich. He had been cashiered from the Navy for moral turpitude."

"Was?" Ginger said. "What happened to him?"

"Heydrich was taken out in Prague by Czech agents when he was 'protector' of what had been Czechoslovakia. To avenge his death, the Nazis, among other despicable acts, rounded up all the citizens—men, women, and children—of a village called Lidice. The bastards put them in a church and burned the church down with them in it. They then burned down the rest of the town and leveled it with bulldozers, sowing what was left with salt."

Tears rolled down her cheeks.

"That's so terrible, it's hard to believe."

"It's true," Cronley said. "But we're getting off the subject."

He turned to Fortin, and said, "Your scenario is, Odessa gave them enough money to buy phony papers from the Vatican to get them out of France and into Spain."

Fortin shook his head.

"That's not what I said. I'm saying Odessa gave the Vatican enough data—photographs, **und so weiter**—so that the Vatican can prepare the phony documents. They'll hide somewhere in France until they get the documents and then they're off to Spain, Portugal—wherever—and, ultimately, to South America."

"Jesus," Cronley said.

"No money will change hands. Odessa's credit is good. They've been doing business with the Vatican for a long time. The Vatican will get paid when these bastards are in Buenos Aires or Montevideo."

"I don't think I understand," Father McGrath said.

"To be truthful," Fortin said, "I do not think that Super Spook does either, so I'll walk you through it. This scenario is based on the premise that Odessa staged the prison break. But we don't **know** that. As I said, I think it's entirely possible that the NKGB—specifically, James, your pal Serov—was involved. The breakout was a little too classy for Odessa.

"But for sake of discussion, let us say Odessa was behind it. They wanted to get Brigadeführer Heimstadter and Standartenführer Oskar Müller out of the Tribunal Prison because they're important to Odessa. And then they learned that you bagged von Dietelburg and Burgdorf in Vienna. Those two are more important to Odessa—you will recall that von Dietelburg was Himmler's adjutant—so they decided to let Heimstadter and Müller stay locked up for the time being."

Cronley said, "You think we're wasting time looking for them here, or, for that matter, in Germany?"

"Never underestimate your enemy, James. I'm surprised you don't know that. And now we come to the part where I tell you what you can do for me."

"I'm going to check on Bruce," Ginger said, getting to her feet, "and then get some sleep."

Everyone got to their feet, too.

She nodded at the men, said good night, and walked out of the bar.

"What's on your greedy mind, Jean-Paul?" Cronley said.

"I'd like to see this castle you're always talking about."

"As would I," Father McGrath said.

"You have access to a light airplane?" Cronley said to Fortin.

"I have a Fieseler Storch."

"That figures," Cronley said. "I'll talk to Cohen. But if I call, you'll have to come right then."

"Fair enough," Fortin said, who then offered his hand to Father McGrath. "Pleasure meeting you."

IV

[ONE]
The Mansion
Offenbach Platz 101
Nuremberg, American Zone of
Occupation, Germany
1205 16 April 1946

"Where are we going?" Father McGrath asked as the lead car pulled off Offenbach and stopped before the twelve-foot-tall, sheet-metal-covered gate in the Compound's fifteen-foot-high wall.

"This place used to belong to the local **Gauleiter**," Cronley replied.

"The governor?" Ginger said.

"Yeah, the Nazi asshole in charge," Cronley said. "Now that he's in the Tribunal Prison, he doesn't need this place anymore, so I took it over."

The gate slid open and the convoy drove inside.

"Very nice," Ginger said as the Mansion came into view.

"The Gauleiter lived well. Twenty-eight rooms, a swimming pool, and a sauna."

"What are we going to do here?" Ginger asked.

"After we pick up fresh bodyguards, and Casey Wagner, we're going to the Tribunal, where I will introduce Father McGrath to Colonel Cohen. He will arrange a tour of the Tribunal for you while he's talking to Father McGrath about Saint Heinrich the Divine and his new religion."

"Welcome back," Tiny Dunwiddie said. "How was Strasbourg?"

"Believe it or not, Fortin actually bought us dinner," Cronley said.

"Will wonders ever cease?"

Cronley looked at Wagner.

"Casey, are you up to speed on the escape?"

"Yes, sir. As soon as I got here, Mr. Justice Jackson sent for Captain Dunwiddie and me and let us read that message—the report of the Prison Escape Committee—that he sent to President Truman."

Cronley nodded. "So, what happens next is, we start talking to people. Starting with SS-Brigadeführer Heimstadter and Standartenführer Müller. I have a gut feeling they're the ones who staged the escape originally planned to get out.

And, in that regard, I got one of my famously brilliant ideas as I walked in here just now."

"Uh-oh," Dunwiddie said.

"Thank you for that expression of confidence, Captain Dunwiddie. But hear me out so you can stop shaking your head in resignation. I'm betting that one of them, probably both, were frequent guests of the Gauleiter here in the Mansion. It might be helpful to have one of them, Brigadeführer Heimstadter, see for himself how things have changed since the glorious days of the Thousand-Year Reich."

"You mean bring them here?" Wagner said.

"I think if the brigadier was taken from his cell without warning by several of our ugliest Polish agents—ones speaking nothing but Polish or maybe Russian—then brought here and installed in my windowless bedroom overnight, all that might serve as an inducement for him to talk to us tomorrow morning."

"You'd have to take all of your furniture out of there," Wagner said after a moment's thought, "and put in a GI bed—a cot would be better—and nothing else, except a bucket for a toilet. Maybe strip him naked and give him a blanket to wear."

"And that is why some people call him Super Spook Junior," Dunwiddie said, drily. "Casey not only agrees with Jim's wild ideas, he's also full of ideas of his own on how to improve them."

"So, what the hell is wrong with my—and Casey's—ideas?"

"Well, for one thing, what makes you think Colonel Cohen is going to let you take Heimstadter out of prison?"

"He didn't become chief of U.S. Counterintelligence for the Tribunal by not recognizing a clever idea when he hears one," Cronley said. "And if he doesn't give me Heimstadter, I'll go to Jackson."

"Who is going to say, especially after he hears Cohen has turned you down, 'No way.'"

"There's one way to find out," Cronley said. "Let's go. You, too, Tiny. I have a task for you that will require all your wisdom and expertise."

"Really? What might that be?"

"I'll tell you later."

[TWO]
Office of Colonel Mortimer Cohen
International Tribunal Compound
Nuremberg, American Zone of
Occupation, Germany
1355 18 April 1946

"Inasmuch as Justice Jackson would be subject to criticism if it came out that he had known Colonel

Rasberry and myself had permitted Super Spook to take Brigadeführer Heimstadter out of the Compound," Colonel Cohen announced after some thought, "I think we have to invoke the Hotshot Billy Principle regarding this problem."

"Two questions, Mort," Colonel Rasberry said, glancing at Captain Cronley before turning to Cohen. "One, do you really think this is a good idea?"

"I'm fresh out of other ideas. How about you?"

"Point taken. Two, who is Hotshot Billy?"

"Lieutenant Colonel William W. Wilson. He is General White's twenty-five-year-old aviation officer. He believes—as does General White—that he became a light bird eighteen months or so ago when his West Point classmates were hoping to make captain before the war was over—"

"He made light colonel at twenty-four?" Rasberry interrupted, his tone one of disbelief.

"Yes, he did. And he attributes this to applying what has become known as the Hotshot Billy Principle. To wit: When you must have permission to do something you know is right and you have good reason to believe that the officer with the power to give you such permission is going to say 'Hell, no,' do it anyway, as success washes away all sins."

"My God! And I. D. White goes along with this?"

"Indeed. He and Billy, without asking the permission they know would be refused, are hard at work trying to establish what they call Army Aviation. Their argument is, light aircraft provide mobility on the battlefield, and when the Army Air Forces becomes a separate service next year, they don't want it to control mobility. **Ergo sum**, the Army needs its own airplanes, its own air force."

"Interesting," Rasberry said.

"So, turning to Super Spook's idea, are you willing to stick your neck out and walk over to the prison with me and tell the OD that Super Spook will be taking Brigadeführer Heimstadter out of the prison overnight?"

Rasberry considered this.

"Okay," he said, finally.

"You heard 'overnight,' right, Jim? You have twenty-four hours from now to get him back in his cell."

"Yes, sir. Thank you, sir. Both of you."

"And when we come back from the prison," Cohen said to Rasberry, "I am going to tell Father McGrath all I know about the new Nazi religion. If you want in on that—let's call it a lecture, for want of a better word—you're welcome."

"Thank you. The more I hear about that, the more it worries me."

"Colonel, could I sit in on that lecture?" Ginger asked.

"Why would you want to?" Cohen said.

"Two reasons. My late husband and I were given a tour of the prison six months ago. And . . ." Her voice trailed off.

"And what?" Cohen said.

She looked at Cronley.

"It's time, Jimmy, that we publicly fess up."

"I was coming to that," Cronley said.

"Confessing to what, for God's sake?" Cohen said, impatiently.

"Colonel, Fat Freddy Hessinger told me how you helped his friend get through all the bullshit the Army gave him to protect him from designing women."

"And so . . . ?"

"I was hoping you'd do the same thing for me . . . For me and Ginger."

After some thought, Cohen asked, "You actually want to marry Super Spook, Mrs. Moriarty? After all you've gone through?"

"Not only marry him but also know what he's up to. Beginning with this Nazi religion Himmler was trying to set up, which I know Jim is very involved in trying to figure out."

Cohen nodded thoughtfully.

"I've been saying all along that the more people

who know about it, the better. So, okay, Mrs. Moriarty, you can sit in."

"Thank you."

"And you, Super Spook, can talk to Sergeant Major Feldman about getting permission to marry. I got the credit for helping Fat Freddy's friend, but Alex did most of the work for me. He's genius at cutting through the damn red tape."

Cohen pushed a button on his phone and almost immediately the door to the outer office opened. A trim, dark-haired male in his early thirties with an earnest face stood in the doorway. He had on a well-pressed uniform bearing the stripes of a sergeant major.

"Yes, sir?"

"Sergeant Major, when we are finished here, Captain Cronley requires your expert assistance, much as you provided Freddy Hessinger, in getting him to the altar as quickly as possible. We don't want him bursting into flames."

"Yes, sir . . . Flames, sir?"

Cohen grinned, then explained, "When I asked Father McGrath what he thought of the impending nuptials, he said Christian scripture tells us it's better to marry than to burn."

"I've heard that, sir," Feldman said, grinning.

"And, Sergeant Major, shortly I'm going to deliver my lecture on Saint Heinrich the Divine. While I'm doing so, (a) I am not available to anyone but Justice Jackson and (b) you will prepare a copy of my notes for Captain Dunwiddie. He will use them to deliver the lecture to everybody at the Mansion."

"Yes, sir."

Cohen turned to Cronley. "And what are your other plans, Super Spook, after speaking with Sergeant Major Feldman?"

"First, to get Heimstadter over to the Mansion, and then I'm going to talk to Standartenführer Müller."

"Good luck with that," Cohen said. "Give Colonel Rasberry and me ten minutes to talk to the OD at the prison and then have at it. You and Ginger can speak with Feldman in the meantime. Meeting over until the lecture."

[THREE]

Twenty minutes later, Colonel Cohen took the chair behind his desk. Father Jack, Ginger, and Tiny Dunwiddie filed back into the office. Cohen motioned for everyone to sit down, and said, "Super Spook on his way to the Tribunal Prison?"

"Yes, sir," Dunwiddie said.

"Did my sergeant major get all he needed, Ginger?"

"Yes, he said he did. Thank you."

Cohen nodded as he pulled a polished wooden box about eighteen inches long and a foot wide from a bottom drawer of his desk. He put it on the desktop and opened it.

"If I use this thing, I will have to sit here during my lecture, but I have decided that the best way to do this is to presume no one knows anything and to start from square one and make a record of what I say."

"What is that thing?" Father McGrath asked.

"Sort of a Dictaphone. But instead of mechanically cutting a groove on a plastic whatchamacallit, it electrically records what's said on a wire."

He held up a reel and then attached it to the device. He then turned in his chair and plugged an electric cord into a wall socket.

"Siemens invented it. One of the technical teams the Army was running found about a hundred of them in a Siemens plant in Hesse. I heard about it, then promptly stole twenty of them."

He flipped several switches, examined several dials, then placed its microphone to his lips.

"Testing, one, two, three . . ."

He then flipped several more switches. With remarkable clarity, his voice came from the speaker: "Testing, one, two, three . . ."

"Amazing!" Father McGrath said.

"The Thousand-Year Reich Lecture at fourteenoh-five hours, 18 April '46," Cohen said into the microphone. "Okay, here we go.

"In 1933, Heinrich Himmler started looking for a castle near Paderborn where, legend had it, a fellow named Hermann der Cherusker had, in 9 A.D., won a decisive battle against the Romans, thus saving the German people from being absorbed into the Roman Empire.

"On November 3, 1933, Himmler visited Wewelsburg Castle and decided that same day to lease it for a hundred years and restore it so that it could be used as an educational and ceremonial center for the SS.

"Sometime around 1936, Joseph Goebbels, the Nazi minister of propaganda, started referring to Germany as the Thousand-Year Reich. And said it was, indeed, going to last a thousand years.

"Most people outside Germany thought it was a ludicrous boast from somebody who worked for a lunatic with a funny mustache who had started calling himself **Der Führer**.

"They were wrong. Hitler and company were dead serious. They intended to make Germany a pure Aryan state—the mission, Himmler said, was 'the extermination of any sub-humans, all over the world, in league against Germany'— which would rule the world for a millennium. To accomplish this, they started by opening the first concentration camp, Dachau, outside Berlin in

1933. In January 1937, Himmler gave a speech in which he said, 'There is no more living proof of hereditary and racial laws than in a concentration camp. You find there hydrocephalics, squinters, deformed individuals, semi-Jews: a considerable number of inferior people.'"

McGrath said, "When did they start—what do I call it?—the Nazi religion?"

"At the moment, Father Jack, I have the pulpit," Cohen said, "which means you sit there and listen while I deliver the lesson for today."

McGrath raised his eyebrows, then nodded.

"In February 1945," Cohen continued, "Roosevelt, Churchill, and Stalin met in Yalta. I was number two on Roosevelt's security detail. My boss ordered me never to let him out of my sight, and I did my best not to. This gave me the opportunity to hear many of their conversations, both public and private.

"In one of these private conversations, between Churchill and the President, the question of what to do with the leaders of Germany came up. I still haven't made up my mind whether they were serious or not, but Churchill proposed shooting all Nazi leaders on the spot when and where found. To which Roosevelt replied, 'Winston, we can't shoot all of them. What about the top forty thousand?'

"That conversation was interrupted by the

arrival of Stalin, and they dropped the subject of how to deal with the Nazis.

"I am Jewish, if I must point that out. I'd already seen photos of what the Nazis had done to my coreligionists and concluded that my relatives in Germany were no more, so I was naturally in support of Churchill's idea.

"I came home from Yalta and, several days later, was promoted to colonel, which rarely happens to Jewish boys with an ROTC commission from the City College of New York who had gone on active duty as second lieutenants in December 1941.

"I also had come to conclude that Franklin Roosevelt was a very sick man and, possibly because of his condition, had given away the store to Joe Stalin, who I had already concluded was one dangerous son of a bitch.

"The day after I was promoted, I was flown to SHAEF—Supreme Headquarters, Allied Expeditionary Force—then in Rheims, France.

"On April 12th, Roosevelt died, and Harry S Truman become President. The same day, I was named chief of CIC Forward, probably because we were already in Germany and I was the only senior Counterintelligence Corps officer who spoke German fluently.

"When, after the surrender, SHAEF moved from Rheims into the I.G. Farben Building in

Frankfurt, my boss, Brigadier General Homer Greene, had me to dinner. As we were having a couple of belts afterward, I said something flippant about Churchill having the right idea. Rather than rounding up the Nazi brass and putting them in cells at Nuremberg to be given a fair trial before hanging them, we could save a lot of money by shooting them when and where we found them.

"He shamed me by saying he was surprised I hadn't figured out Truman's motive in insisting that we try them before we hanged them. 'If we simply shot them,' Greene explained, 'the German people would decide it was vengeance of the victors, and the bastards would be regarded as martyrs of the Thousand-Year Reich.' He went on to say that Truman decided they should be exposed to as much publicity as possible as the common criminals—the murderers—they were.

"I admitted to him I hadn't considered that. And that Truman was right.

"'Good,' Greene said, 'because as of tomorrow morning, you're in charge of security for the Nuremberg Tribunal.'

"I told him that if it were up to me, I'd much rather catch Nazis than be their jailor. He replied (a) it wasn't up to me; (b) the Big Red One—the First Infantry Division—had assigned a regiment to guard the Tribunal Compound, and he wanted me to keep an eye on them; (c) that I was now in charge of running down the big-shot Nazis, not Nazis in general; (d) he wanted me, when I had a spare minute, to run down a probably preposterous rumor he'd heard that Himmler had started a new religion; (e) that to accomplish all this, he had organized a new CIC, the Thirty-first, and named me as its commander; and, finally, (f) as soon as I gave him a list of people I would like to have in the Thirty-first CIC, he would transfer them to me.

"So, I came here to Nuremberg and made up a list of people I wanted and sent it off to General Greene. Before the list got to the Farben Building, I got a call from one Vito Carlucci, a big, fat guy from Jersey City. I thought he was going to ask me again to get him transferred to Italy so he could run down the Italian fascists who had killed his relatives. But that wasn't it.

"He told me, 'Colonel, I've come across something you have to see.'

"'Tell me about it, Vito.'

"'Not only don't I want to talk about this on a nonsecure line, but if I did, you'd accuse me of being drunk or crazy. Or both. Colonel, you have to see this for yourself.'

"So I got in my car, drove to eastern North Rhine–Westphalia, and met Vito in Paderborn. He took me to a battered castle a couple miles outside of town.

"He told me: 'This is Wewelsburg Castle. An SS-Truppführer—sergeant—we caught told me that Himmler ordered it blown up but they couldn't find enough explosives. We're holding him here. Let him tell you the story, then I'll give you a tour of the place.'

"So they bring the SS sergeant into the office. He told me his name—no fooling!—was Johann Strauss. Johann looked a lot like your fiancé, Mrs. Moriarty. Tall, broad-chested, blond, blue-eyed. A real Aryan."

"I don't think that's funny, Colonel," Ginger blurted.

Cohen ignored her.

"Once this six-foot-something, two-hundred-pound SS sergeant got a good look at this five-foot-eight, one-hundred-forty-five-pound Hebrew colonel, his face whitened. And he began to sing like a canary.

"He told me he had been on the staff, as a driver, of SS-Brigadeführer Franz von Dietelburg, Reichsführer Heinrich Himmler's adjutant—"

"That's one of the men who just escaped?" Ginger said.

"He and General der Infanterie Wilhelm Burgdorf," Cohen replied, "formerly SS-Brigadeführer Wilhelm Burgdorf."

"Sir," Dunwiddie said. "I don't understand."

"Toward the end of the war, Tiny, SS bastards

like Burgdorf decided they would rather be treated as POWs than SS when we caught them, so they got themselves discharged from the SS and commissioned at an equivalent rank in the Wehrmacht. When I heard about this, I went to Justice Jackson, told him about it, and suggested he rule from the bench that these phony soldiers be tried as SS officers.

"He turned me down. He explained that it would be illegal because the Nazi government had the same right as we did to commission anyone in any rank they wanted to. He told me, 'A friend of mine, Walker Cisler, the president of Detroit Electric, was recognized as the guy who knew all there was to know about power grids.

" 'Eisenhower wanted him to perform two critical functions. First, to identify the key points in the French and German power grids so they could be bombed. Second, to restore the grids as quickly as possible after we took back the grid area. So he had Cisler directly commissioned as a full colonel. Walker went off to war, knowing so little about the Army that they had to assign a major to teach him how to salute, et cetera.'

"Anyway, the sergeant told me he had been assigned to drive Sturmbannführer Heinz Macher from Berlin to Wewelsburg Castle. They had a truckload of SS troopers with them. They traveled at night because, by then, American fighters were roaming over Germany, shooting up anything on the Autobahn.

"He said he had heard Himmler tell Macher he was to tell SS General Siegfried Taubert, who was in charge of the castle, to remove 'sacred' items and the contents of 'my safe,' then head for the Austrian border and, ultimately, to Italy. Macher would then blow the place up.

"SS-Truppführer Johann Strauss now had my full attention. Despite him looking like Super Spook's brother, Ginger, he wasn't nearly as smart, and I decided he was telling me the truth.

"So, I started asking myself why an SS general-major was guarding an old castle in the middle of nowhere. What was Himmler's safe doing there? What was in the safe? Sacred items? What was the point of blowing up the castle?

"Strauss then told me that when they got to Wewelsburg, General Taubert was long gone, Himmler's safe was empty, and he didn't know anything about sacred items. The place was being ransacked by the locals.

"He said that Macher then told him and the SS troopers that as soon as they blew up the castle, they were on their own. It turned out there weren't enough explosives—all they could find was a bunch of tank mines—so all they managed to do was knock down the southeast tower and the guard and SS buildings. Then they tried, unsuccessfully, to burn down the castle.

"Macher got in his staff car and, driving himself, took off. We caught him at the Italian border. He's now in the Darmstadt SS prisoner enclosure.

"So I asked Johann Strauss how come he was the only SS enlisted man we caught. Why he hadn't taken off with the others.

"He said that he had thought it over and decided (a) that he couldn't get back to Berlin; (b) that because the war was almost over, it would be safer to stay at the castle and wait for the Americans to come; and (c) that he would surrender to them, which he did.

"It was obviously a canned speech, one he had practiced until he was sure he had it right. His eyes told me he was lying.

" 'Johann,' I said, 'the next time you lie to me, I'll have you shot.'

"Blushing like a schoolboy caught with his hand in the cookie jar, Johann finally confessed he was looking for the gold **Totenkopf** rings. He dug in his pocket and came up with one, which he put on his finger and more or less modeled for me. I wasn't sure he did so in arrogant defiance or shame, or neither. But as I looked at the ring and saw the SS skull insignia, I knew it was important.

"At this point, Vito, who hadn't uttered a sound, said, 'Colonel, that's a **Totenkopfring**.'

"I had no idea what it was or its significance. Vito told me that it goes back to the early days of Nazism, when Hitler really needed a bodyguard. The communists weren't the only ones trying to kill him.

"There had been, since 1921, something called the Sturmabteilung—acronym SA—which was an organization of thugs headed by a man named Ernst Röhm, an old buddy of Hitler's. Its primary function was to brawl with the communists, and others, at political rallies.

"They had acquired, on the cheap from war surplus, a large stock of brown shirts, which they wore as uniforms. They wore whatever trousers they had. Understandably, they were called the Brown Shirts.

"Both Hitler and Himmler began to suspect that Röhm wanted to take over the Nazi Party, so they kept an eye on him. Although the SA was supposed to protect Hitler, both at rallies and in his private life, Hitler and Himmler were coming to the conclusion that Röhm didn't have his heart in the latter and, if true, having the SA close to Hitler protecting him also gave Röhm the opportunity to assassinate him.

"So, in 1929, Himmler formed a special bodyguard for Hitler. It was called the Protective

Element—**Schutzstaffel** in German, SS for short. Himmler recruited three hundred men for it. And, from the very beginning, they had to be 'true Germans.' The term 'Aryan' would not come into common use until later.

"In 1933, Hitler and company really started after the Jews, beginning with an official one-day boycott of their shops. Next came a law forbidding kosher butchering. Two years later, the Nuremberg Laws deprived Jews of German citizenship and prohibited Jews from voting in parliamentary elections.

"This pretty much came to a head in 1938. Among other things, a law was passed requiring all Jews to carry identification cards. On October 28th, seventeen thousand Jews of Polish origin, most of whose families had been living in Germany for generations, were arrested with the intention of deporting them to Poland. When the Polish government refused to admit them, they were interned in so-called relocation camps on the Polish frontier.

"And all this came to a head on November 9th, which has become known as **Kristallnacht**, referring to all the broken glass and debris on the streets of Berlin and other cities. Much of it came from storefront windows of some seventy-five hundred Jewish-owned businesses. But some came from the thousand-plus synagogues that they burned.

Thirty thousand Jews were arrested and sent to concentration camps—among them, Dachau.

"And then Hitler and Himmler decided to take advantage of all the hullabaloo that Ernst Röhm's SA thugs were causing to solve another problem they had. They sent the Schutzstaffel all over Germany looking for Röhm. They found him at a country inn—in bed, naked, with a handsome boy. As homosexuality was a real no-no for Nazis, they took photographs of them in flagrante delicto, then shot both lovers on the spot. That ended the problem of Röhm wanting to take over the Nazi Party.

"Himmler then presented those members of the Schutzstaffel who had assassinated Röhm with **Totenkopfrings**, which made them sort of an elite within the elite SS.

"The rings proved so popular that Himmler, expanding this elite corps, awarded them to all three hundred original SS members. The SS by then had grown to about fifty thousand and soon would grow even larger.

"Then Himmler established a new tradition. When Schutzstaffel members who had been given **Totenkopfrings** died, they would take the rings off the corpses and install them in Himmler-provided frames, which then would be given to the families so they proudly could display them on their walls.

"This didn't last long. As the SS grew like Topsy, so did the awards of the **Totenkopfrings**. Himmler was passing them out by the bucketful—about twelve thousand by the end of the war.

"The first thing he did was to order the families who'd received framed rings to send them to Wewelsburg Castle—remember, Himmler leased it for a hundred years in 1933 to serve as an SS educational and ceremonial center—where they would be stored for the ages in a ceremonial chest."

"Twelve thousand rings? Each weighing what?" Dunwiddie asked.

"Depending on who made them, one and a quarter ounces to one and a half ounces," Cohen said.

Dunwiddie said, "That's twelve thousand times one-point-two-five—"

"Just shy of a half ton," Cohen furnished.

"Good God, a thousand pounds of gold rings!" Dunwiddie exclaimed.

"There are at least three theories about what happened to the rings when they reached the castle," Cohen went on. "I don't know which, or any, of them I believe. The one I do tend to believe is that immediately on arrival, General Siegfried Taubert melted them down and sent them with a trusted flunky to Switzerland to quietly sell what were now untraceable bars of gold."

"That had to have been dangerous," Dunwiddie

said. "What if von Dietelburg had found out? Or Himmler himself? They're ruthless."

"An understatement, Tiny. While I don't know about SS-Reichsführer Himmler, I'm certain that if Taubert was selling melted **Totenkopfrings**, then von Dietelburg was getting his percentage. And, for that matter, it seems entirely possible that the whole scheme was von Dietelburg's idea."

"You said that there were three theories," Father McGrath said.

Cohen nodded. "Theory two is that the rings are intact, hidden somewhere in the castle. There are a number of secret places they could be hidden, and I'm sure we haven't found all of them. Theory three is that Taubert, knowing he couldn't transport that much weight, moved them to a cave near here, then blew up the cave's entrance.

"Theory three is what Sergeant Strauss said he believes, which is why he stuck around. So when I got things organized, we started looking for the cave."

"Got things organized?" McGrath said.

"I took over the castle, Father Jack. Before I finished chatting with Johann Strauss that first day, I sent Vito's driver off to find a telephone. Six members of Vito's detachment arrived right after dark. The castle has been under my control ever since, and we have been exploring it steadily. Nobody gets in but my people."

"Sir, I have to ask," Dunwiddie said, "what does Military Government think about the CIC detachment that's in charge of protecting the Tribunal taking over a castle two hundred–odd miles away?"

"They are curious," Cohen replied, a hint of humor in his tone, "and I suspect displeased. But, so far, General Greene has been able to keep the situation under control."

"And what have you found?" McGrath asked. "Anything?"

"This is where it gets interesting. I found—not immediately, but gradually, as I found it hard to believe myself—that Himmler was turning the castle into a holy place, into a Vatican dedicated to a religion he was starting."

"A castle as a holy place?" Ginger said, in disbelief. "That medieval place looks like anything but that."

"A holy place," Cohen confirmed. "And it's a Renaissance castle."

Ginger nodded.

Cohen went on. "This is the point of the lecture, so pay attention. Enter Professor Karl Diebitsch, an artist—and, to be fair, a soldier; he was an Oberführer in the Waffen-SS—who had designed the all-black SS uniform and served as sort of Himmler's artist-in-residence. Diebitsch also designed the gold **Totenkopfrings**.

"Starting in 1934, under Diebitsch's direction, the plaster on the exterior walls of Wewelsburg was removed to make the structure look more castlelike. They opened a blacksmith operation to make wrought-iron interior decorations. The blacksmiths and the plaster removers were concentration camp inmates, mostly Russian POWs. But absolutely no Jews, as Jews would obviously contaminate the place.

"Officially, the castle was supposed to be turned into a meeting place for SS brass. That was bullshit. From the beginning, it was to be the Church of Saint Heinrich the Divine."

"How did you come to that conclusion?" McGrath asked.

"Almost as soon as I got a good look at the castle, I saw that there were major changes to it. At first, I didn't know what, exactly, had been changed, only that clearly there were changes. I later learned that between 1938 and 1943, the Nazis had built two rooms they called the **Obergruppenführersaal**—the 'SS Generals Hall'—and the **Gruft**."

"**Gruft?**" Ginger parroted.

"'Vault,' as in 'burial vault,'" Cohen clarified. "Their ceilings were cast in concrete and faced with natural stone. And they had made plans for another hall on an upper floor. They wanted to turn Castle Wewelsburg into the **Mittelpunkt der Welt**—the 'Center of the World.'

"What I found interesting is that many, if not most all, of the modifications made to the castle had to do with the number twelve. Himmler apparently wanted to reincarnate the Knights of the Round Table."

"As in King Arthur's Knights of the Round Table?" Ginger asked.

"Yes, but a German, or Teutonic, version thereof."

He made a significant pause, collected his thoughts, then continued. "In Nordic mythology, there are twelve **Aesir**—sort of gods—including Odin and Thor. When Himmler re-formed and enlarged the SS, he set it up with twelve departments—SS-Hauptämter. So I began to think that Himmler wanted the castle to serve as the stage for a Nazi version of the Knights of the Round Table.

"In this scenario, Himmler designated twelve senior SS officers as the knights of his round table.

"In the vault, the ceiling is held up by twelve pedestals. In the center of the ceiling there's a huge swastika. A gas line leading to the center of the floor was almost certainly going to fuel an eternal flame.

"In the Hall of the Obergruppenführers, there

are twelve pillars and niches—the latter probably intended for the eventual interment of Himmler's latter-day knights. There is also a sun wheel with twelve spokes. It looks like a wheel with the sun at the center."

"What, exactly, is the purpose of this sun wheel?" Dunwiddie asked.

"In this SS religion they were starting," Cohen explained, "they declared that the sun was the strongest and most visible expression of God.

"If I didn't mention this before, I later learned, credibly, that upper-level SS brass, mostly general officers, would gather secretly at various places in Castle Wewelsburg to conduct religious rites. Or quasi-religious rites."

"Sounds crazy," Ginger said.

"Yes," Cohen said. "Unfortunately, they were dead serious. But speaking of crazy, did you ever hear of the Inner World of Agharti?"

No one replied.

"Edgar Rice Burroughs, the fellow who wrote **Tarzan**," Cohen said, "also wrote about an under-the-earth civilization. He called it Pellucidar."

"But that was fiction, right?" Ginger said. "Fantasy."

Cohen grunted. "Speaking of fantasy, what if I told you that beginning in 1941 the SS began construction of a vertical tunnel in Hungary, sort of a super mine shaft, that would eventually be equipped with an elevator that would take Himmler and his inner circle ten miles downward to the Inner World of Agharti?"

He paused, looked from face to face, then added, "Would you consider that fact or fantasy?"

"Fantasy," Dunwiddie said.

"Insanity," Ginger said.

"Incredible," McGrath said.

"Yes, one would think all that. Yet work on the tunnel continued until November 1944, when the SS ran out of supplies and decided the project would have to wait for the Final Victory. I've been there. You would be astonished at the size of the mounds of evacuated earth and stone created from a hole, say, thirty feet in diameter and two and a half miles deep—that's as far as they got."

"It boggles the mind," Dunwiddie said.

"Let me now turn to what else I learned happened in Castle Wewelsburg," Cohen said. "They began to stage religious rites there. The first official Nazi religion ceremony was the baptism of Obergruppenführer Wolff's son, Thorisman— rough translation, 'Man of Thor' or 'Thor's son.'"

"Thor?" Ginger said.

"The Nordic warrior god of power, strength, lightning, et cetera," McGrath furnished. "That's where we get Thursday—Thor's day."

"I never knew that," Ginger said.

"Present at the baptism," Cohen said, "were

SS-Obergruppenführer und General der Polizei Reinhard Heydrich. Baby Thor got a silver christening cup from Himmler himself."

"Colonel," McGrath said, "I absolutely have to see this place."

"I understand. And I want—"

Cohen's telephone rang. He glared at it.

"And I want your opinion, Father Jack," Cohen went on, "of where my thinking is going wrong."

The phone rang again.

He grabbed the receiver and snapped, "Colonel Cohen."

Moments later, he added, "Good afternoon, Mr. Justice."

Then he said, "I'm on my way, sir," and hung up.

He glanced at the others.

"You'll have to excuse me. I am not sure what's up, but something damn sure is. And this lecture is obviously over." Cohen confirmed that by leaning toward the microphone and formally stating, "The Thousand-Year Reich Lecture interrupted at fourteen-forty-five hours, 18 April 1946."

He looked at the others again.

"It's quarter to three. I suggest you return to Farber Palast and discuss this among you—in the Duchess Suite, not in the bar. I'll try to meet you there about half past five."

He then walked out of his office.

V

[ONE]
International Tribunal Compound
Prison
Nuremberg, American Zone of
Occupation, Germany
1505 18 April 1946

The two enormous black soldiers leading the German prisoner out of the cellblock dwarfed him. Both were well over six feet tall. Their muscled arms and chests strained the OD Ike jackets. The prisoner was restrained with handcuffs, shackles around his ankles, and a chain around his waist. He had a black bag over his head.

As the soldiers and their prisoner passed the guardhouse, Jim Cronley stepped out of it. He made several gestures, first putting an index finger to his lips to indicate silence.

This made one of the huge men smile, revealing several gold teeth.

Cronley then raised his eyebrows, making a question of his next gesture, a back-and-forth movement of his right hand.

The man, smiling, nodded.

Cronley finally made a thumbs-up gesture and pointed to an Army 6×6 truck that had been backed up to the guardhouse.

The man smiled, saluted, and then prodded his prisoner into movement. He stopped him at the truck.

Another huge man standing on the bed of the truck reached down to take the prisoner's hands, then pulled him onto the tailgate, causing the prisoner to grunt. Next, he reached down, grabbed the prisoner by his shoulders and lifted him deeper into the truck bed.

The other man, remaining on the ground, put the tailgate in place and then trotted to the cab and climbed in beside the driver.

The truck horn sounded twice, and the 6×6 began to drive away. As it did, a staff car pulled in behind it and followed.

Cronley turned and walked into the guardhouse. He took a leather folder from his pocket, showed it to the officer of the day—a first lieutenant of the 1st "Big Red One" Infantry Division—and formally announced, "CIC Special Agent Cronley to see SS-Standartenführer Müller."

"Yes, sir," the lieutenant said. "Sir, I have to ask if you are armed."

Cronley hoisted the left side of his Ike jacket, revealing a holstered Model 1911A1 Colt .45 caliber pistol.

"That question was pro forma," the lieutenant confessed. "I didn't notice your holster."

"That's the idea of the Secret Service cross-draw holster," Cronley said as he took the pistol out. "You're not supposed to notice."

He handed the pistol to the lieutenant.

"Safety on," he announced, "a round in the chamber."

"You always carry it locked and loaded?"

"Only when I think I may have to shoot somebody."

The lieutenant laughed.

He removed the pistol's magazine and then racked the action, which caused the chambered cartridge to eject and land on the floor. He picked it up and then turned to the staff sergeant standing behind him.

"Escort Mr. Cronley to Müller's cell. Second tier, Cell 11-R."

"Yes, sir."

———

The guard posted at the cell was a corporal whom Cronley guessed had yet to see his nineteenth birthday. He was wearing a white helmet liner and a white Sam Browne belt. Like the staff sergeant, he was unarmed except for a white police baton.

"Open it up," the staff sergeant ordered, tapping the iron bars with his baton.

The corporal slid a two-by-ten-inch plank out of the way, then put an eight-inch-long key in the iron keyhole and turned it. Finally, with a grunt, he pushed the heavy door open.

A stocky, nearly bald fifty-year-old male was sitting on a GI bed. He looked up with annoyance mingled with curiosity as Cronley entered the cell.

"**Guten tag, Herr Standartenführer,**" Cronley said, cheerfully.

"Who the hell are you?" Müller demanded, in German. "And that's **Generalmajor** Müller."

"That's one of the things I wanted to talk to you about."

"Who the hell are you?" he repeated.

"My name is Feibleman," Cronley said. "James Feibleman. I'm the prisoner morale officer."

"In other words, Biddle or Jackson—probably the latter—sent a Jew to remind me who won the war?"

Well, he knows who Biddle and Jackson are.

And I think he'd challenge me, if he knew who I am. Interesting.

"This Jew was sent to evaluate your morale, your mental condition, to see how depressed you are. We don't want you to try to hang yourself before your trial."

"How could I possibly be depressed in such surroundings?" Müller made a sweeping gesture around the cell, then added, "Waiting to be hanged?"

"That's the point, Herr SS-Standartenführer. We—"

"I've already told you that my rank is general-major."

"Not any longer," Cronley lied. "That's one of the things we thought might depress you. The Tribunal has decided once an SS officer, always an SS officer. In other words, the Tribunal does not recognize those late-in-the-war commission-ings of SS officers in the Wehrmacht. You will be tried, and almost certainly hanged, as SS-Standartenführer Müller."

Müller didn't reply.

"We also thought that learning you're not as important to Odessa as you thought you were might depress you somewhat. Has it?"

"I have no idea what you're talking about."

"Let me paint the picture for you. You're still here while your friends General der Infanterie

Wilhelm Burgdorf and SS-Brigadeführer Franz von Dietelburg are off somewhere enjoying the hospitality of the Organisation der Ehemaligen SS-Angehörigen. Didn't that suggest to you that Burgdorf and von Dietelburg are considered by Odessa to be more important than you are?"

"As I keep telling you, Feibleman, I have no idea what or who you're talking about."

They locked eyes, and then Cronley said, "Well, it's been nice chatting with you, Herr Standartenführer, but now I must have a chat with SS-Brigadeführer Heimstadter to see how his morale is holding up."

He turned and left the cell. He heard Müller mutter something bitterly but couldn't understand what it was.

Well, I managed to upset the bastard.

And when—tomorrow—he gets together with Heimstadter and asks him what we talked about and Heimstadter tells him he never talked with anybody named Feibleman, that will upset both of them.

So, what I do now is go to the Mansion and tell my guys to tell Heimstadter that Müller is singing like a canary.

And then I'll go out to the Farber Palast and have a well-deserved drink.

And then I'll go find Ginger and maybe get lucky.

[TWO]
Farber Palast
Stein, near Nuremberg, American
Zone of Occupation, Germany
1645 18 April 1946

Colonel Ivan Serov was sitting in one of the armchairs in the lobby when Cronley walked in. He stood up, holding a bottle of Haig & Haig scotch by the neck, when he saw Cronley.

"Thank you, Ivan, but no thanks. I have plans."

"There are developments you really have to hear."

"If I go in there with you," Cronley said, nodding toward the entrance of the bar, "you will have as long as it takes for me to down one drink."

"We can't discuss what I've come up with in the bar."

Cronley looked at him.

Jesus, Cronley thought, **he's serious!**

Duty, damn it, calls.

Cronley pointed toward the elevator bank.

"This better be good, Ivan. You're interfering with my love life."

There were four DCI bodyguards outside the Duchess Suite. One of them opened the door, and Cronley and Serov walked into the suite.

"Shit," Cronley muttered when he saw that Father McGrath, Tiny Dunwiddie, and Ginger were in the room.

"And hello to you, too," Ginger said.

"I'm sorry, but I have to have a private word with Colonel Serov," Cronley said. "We'll be right back."

"Actually, James," Serov said, "I'd hoped to have a word with Father McGrath. In fact, with everybody. I've been thinking—"

The door opened again, and Colonel Mortimer Cohen entered the suite.

When he saw Serov, Cohen said, "I wonder why the phrase 'fox in the henhouse' suddenly popped into my head."

"Ivan's been thinking, Colonel," Cronley said. "And you're just in time to hear what."

Cohen motioned toward the Haig & Haig. "While I am a devout believer in beware of Russians bearing gifts, if I were offered a taste from that bottle the colonel is holding in a death grip, I might be inclined to listen to what he wants to say."

"How kind of you. James, why don't you find a glass for the colonel?"

"I've been thinking . . ." Serov began when Cronley finished serving the drinks.

"So you keep telling us," Cronley said.

"I was about to go to Budapest . . ."

"Why?" Cohen asked.

"I came into reliable information that Gábor Péter had von Dietelburg and Burgdorf."

"So it was the AVO who handled their escape?" Cohen asked.

"That would be a reasonable conclusion to draw."

Cronley thought, **As if you didn't know.**

"I didn't think I could get Gábor to hand them over to me, but I thought their changed circumstances—and Gábor's interrogation techniques—might get them to tell me who has Odessa's money. If we can get our hands on that, it would put Odessa out of business."

Both Cohen and Cronley nodded in agreement.

"And it might cut Himmler's new religion off at the knees," Serov went on, "which I now regard as God's mission for me in this life."

That sounds like pure bullshit.

But why do I believe him?

"I went from that," Serov said, "to thinking that Burgdorf and von Dietelburg were not going to tell me or Gábor anything. I think they realize that sooner or later—most likely, rather soon—we're going to kill them and that they would rather die, and be remembered, as martyrs to the cause of the Thousand-Year Reich and the heretical religion of Saint Heinrich the Divine.

"And then I had an epiphany. I began to think of the money itself, which I had never done before. I realized that it was millions, perhaps even tens of millions, of dollars, pounds, Swiss francs, plus gold and precious stones.

"It would not fit in fifty trunks. It is not readily transportable, and I don't think it's buried in the basement of some ruin in Berlin or Vienna, or elsewhere."

He paused, then finished. "So where is it stored?"

"Damn good question, Ivan," Cohen said, "one that never occurred to me. Where do you think it is?"

"When one has a fortune that won't fit in one's hip pocket, one puts it in the bank. It's in a bank somewhere."

"Somewhere in Europe," Cohen said, nodding in agreement. "The first place that comes to mind is Switzerland. But the last I heard, we had a hundred FBI agents—probably more—in Switzerland looking for Nazi money. So where else?"

"Father McGrath," Serov said. "Would you please tell us all you can about Pope Pius XII?"

"Seriously?"

"Quite seriously."

"Okay. So, Eugenio Maria Giuseppe Pacelli became Pius XII in March of 1939. Prior to that, he was papal nuncio to Germany and later cardinal secretary of state. You want more?"

"What would you say, Father," Serov asked, "was the cardinal secretary's most significant diplomatic achievement?"

"Oh, I see where you're going," McGrath said.

"I think I do, too," Cohen said. "And it never entered my goddamn mind!"

Cronley thought, **And stupid Super Spook has no idea what the hell they're even talking about.**

"I believe you're talking about the **Reichskonkordat?**" McGrath said.

"Yes, I am," Serov said. "Tell us about it."

"The Pope made a deal with the Nazis," Cohen furnished. "They agreed to leave the Catholic Church alone and the Pope stopped criticizing the Nazis."

"There was a good deal more to the **Reichskonkordat** than that, wasn't there, Father?" Serov said.

"The Vatican State," McGrath replied. "I don't know the details, but Mussolini went along."

"Yes, he did," Cohen said. "He declared the less than a half square kilometer of the Vatican an independent country free of Italy."

"With all the same sovereign rights as the

Soviet Union," Serov added, "and the United States of America, and every other independent country. Correct?"

"When Mark Clarke's Fifth Army took Rome," Cohen said, "they were under strict orders not to enter the Vatican. And as soon as Hotshot Billy landed Clarke next to the Colosseum—"

"Our Hotshot Billy?" Cronley interrupted.

"I know of only one Lieutenant Colonel William Wilson," Cohen replied. "**That** Hotshot Billy. Before being General White's aviation officer, when Clarke took Rome Wilson was Clarke's twenty-one-year-old—maybe twenty-two—personal pilot. Anyway, as soon as Billy dropped Clarke off next to the Colosseum, he flew back to Fifth Army headquarters, where he picked up the Fifth Army's Catholic chaplain and transported him to Rome. The chaplain then got in a jeep and drove to the Vatican, politely asked to be admitted, and then assured the cardinal secretary of state that the Fifth Army and the United States were going to respect the sovereignty of the Vatican."

"I never heard any of this," Father McGrath said. "Fascinating."

"It gets even more interesting," Serov said. "Can any of you students of international affairs tell me what every sovereign state has in common with its peers?"

"A national bank," Cohen said after some consideration. "Christ! Why didn't anyone come up with this?"

"Into which, I suggest," Serov said, "just before the Germans departed Rome, or probably earlier, the disciples of Saint Heinrich the Divine deposited just about all of their worldly goods."

"Why would the Pope—the Vatican—let them do that?" Ginger asked, a second before Cronley was about to ask the same question.

She's about to be told to butt out, Cronley thought, **and not politely.**

She wasn't.

"A very good question, my dear," Serov said. "One to which I have given much thought."

"And what did you come up with?" Cohen asked.

"How about," Cronley said, "quote, the first duty of a Catholic priest is to protect the Holy Mother Church, unquote."

"You want to explain that?" Cohen said.

Cronley nodded. "There was a priest in Strasbourg, a parish priest—more important, the priest from the parish in which our friend Kommandant Jean-Paul Fortin had been raised. When the Germans moved into Strasbourg, the priest promptly began to collaborate with them. That collaboration resulted in the torture, then deaths, of Fortin's family, after which their bodies were thrown into the Rhine. The SS had learned that Fortin was in

England, serving as an intelligence officer on De Gaulle's staff, and the bastards wanted to send him—and Strasbourgers generally—a message.

"After the war, Fortin looked the priest up and demanded to know why he had done absolutely nothing to aid his family. The priest was unrepentant. He told Fortin sorry, his first duty as a priest was to protect the Holy Mother Church. And, as we know, Fortin put .22 caliber rounds in his elbows and knees before throwing him in the Rhine and watching him try to swim."

Serov said, "I think we safely can assume that Pius XII thinks of himself as a priest with a similar first duty."

"You aren't suggesting," Ginger said, more than a little unpleasantly, "that the Pope knowingly went along with hiding the Nazi money?"

"What I'm suggesting is several things, none of which suggests the Pope is anything but a devout servant of God. But I think we have to consider that he was in Germany for many years as papal nuncio, which means 'speaker for the Pope.' He speaks German fluently. During that period, he met many decent Germans who were both devout Catholics and opposed to Nazism. He also met many devout Catholics who were also devout Nazis, some of whom were in the SS.

"All of these people hated communism, as did the Pope. The Pope regarded—regards—

communism as the greatest threat to the Holy Mother Church."

"And it is," Father McGrath said, thoughtfully.

"They thus became allies of the Church, the Vatican," Serov went on. "And by 1945, it became clear to His Holiness that the Germans were about to lose the war. The Vatican has its own intelligence service—"

"Every priest is a Vatican special agent," Cohen put in. "I'd say their intelligence service makes everybody else's, including ours, look like bumbling amateurs."

"That is not an exaggeration," Serov said. "I think we can safely presume that Pius knew all about the mass murders in the extermination camps and, more important, about Odessa. And that as a man of God—now, this is pure conjecture—he was worried about the retribution the Allies— particularly, perhaps, the retribution of the Jews, but even more particularly that of the Soviet Union—were about to wreak on the Thousand-Year Reich."

"If I can go off at a tangent, Colonel," Father McGrath said, "how much do you think the Vatican—the Pope—knew about this heretical religion Himmler was trying to start?"

"**Had** started," Serov corrected. "And, again, this is pure speculation. I'm sure he heard something about it and dismissed it as harmless Nazi nonsense. Like that elevator shaft they were digging to reach the underworld."

"That was really loony tunes, wasn't it?" McGrath said, chuckling.

"Father, with all due respect, if you really believe in something, it's not—what was that charming phrase you just used?—loony tunes. That is what's so dangerous about the religion of Saint Heinrich the Divine. They're true believers, as devout as any monk in one of those mountain-top monasteries in Greece who spend eight hours a day on their knees praying."

"You really believe that, Ivan?" Cronley asked.

"Devoutly," Serov said.

Cronley sighed. "Okay. Let's say your theory is right on the money. What do we do about it?"

"Odessa, like any organization, has routine expenses. They have to make withdrawals from their account at the Vatican Bank to pay them. One way they can do this is to send someone into Rome, into the Vatican. That would pose the problem for them of getting their agent back across the border with a briefcase, or even a suitcase, full of money.

"I think it far more likely that when one of their largest depositors needs to make a withdrawal, the Vatican Bank sends a courier to them with the funds."

"A courier?" Cohen asked, dubiously.

"Perhaps a lowly priest whose luggage is unlikely to be searched by customs officials when he is crossing a border. But I think the courier is most likely to rank higher in the Vatican hierarchy. At first, I was thinking of a monsignor or a bishop, of whom there is a plethora in Rome, and especially within the Vatican bureaucracy. But then, letting my imagination run wild, I thought the couriers are probably red hats."

"What are red hats?" Ginger asked.

"Cardinals," Serov said.

"Cardinals?" Cohen parroted, dubiously.

"Cardinals," Serov repeated. "Let your imagination run free, Colonel, after I propose this scenario: Let us suppose that Odessa needs some cash—say, a million dollars in U.S. or pounds or francs, or a mix thereof. But a briefcaseful? The Vatican Bank is notified, either by Odessa's man in Rome—and I think we can presume they have one—or by other means. They don't want it in Rome, of course, but in Berlin."

"Why Berlin?" Cohen challenged.

"It seems logical to assume that Odessa's leadership is there," Serov said. "There's a lot of places for them to hide. I'm not saying they have a headquarters in the normal sense. I think the head of Odessa at any time is a former senior SS officer. His deputy is the next-senior former SS officer. **Und so weiter.** They hold their staff meetings in the back room of a bar, or a bordello, never twice in the same place."

Cohen looked thoughtfully at him, nodded, then said, "Okay. Go on with your scenario."

"In the American Zone of Berlin," Serov said, "on the Kurfürstendamm, are the ruins of the Protestant church, the Kaiser Wilhelm. The lord mayor of Berlin, Oberbürgermeister Arthur Werner, who enjoys the respect of U.S. High Commissioner John Jay McCloy, has recently announced he thinks that rather than spending all the money it would take to rebuild the church, it should be left as it is as a monument to all the Berliners who died in the war.

"As a general rule of thumb," Serov went on, "whatever the lord mayor wants, McCloy gives him. So there sits the Kaiser Wilhelm Gedächtniskirche on the K'damm. The Vatican hears of this and is not overjoyed. Far better for them to have a usable, functioning Catholic church than a monument for the masses.

"What to do? They decide to make an offer that Werner and McCloy might find hard to refuse. They will pay for the restoration of the Kaiser Wilhelm if they can turn it into a Roman Catholic place of worship."

"Why the hell would Werner or McCloy go along with that?" Cronley asked.

"Agreed. And they almost certainly, politely,

would decline the cardinal's kind offer. One is always polite to a prince of the Church. Especially one with credentials as a diplomatic representative of the Vatican."

"And," Cronley added, "one who travels as a member of the Vatican royalty is expected to travel: on a private railroad car."

"A private railroad car bearing the insignia of the Vatican," Serov said, "with the Vatican flags flapping on the front of the locomotive."

"And the cardinal's entourage," Cronley went on, "at least one archbishop, several bishops, and a platoon of monsignors and priests. All of whom are carrying briefcases to assist them in carrying out their priestly duties. And in one of those brief-cases is the million-dollar withdrawal."

"Mrs. Moriarty," Serov said. "I've heard it said that your fiancé is known in the intelligence com-munity as Super Spook because he figures things out before his superiors."

"So," Cronley said, ignoring that, "all we have to do is keep an eye on the entire entourage to see which one is going to hand the briefcase with the money in it to somebody from Odessa. Which is going to be damned difficult for us."

"Ivan," Cohen said. "Why do I suspect that you already know that a cardinal is going to Berlin?"

"Because I'm NKGB. We know everything."

Cronley grunted.

Serov said, "His Eminence Cardinal Heinrich von Hassburger—"

"He's German?" Cronley asked.

"You see what I mean, Mrs. Moriarty?" Serov said. "Super Spook figured that out before Colonel Cohen did."

"Will you please stop calling me Mrs. Moriarty?" Ginger blurted, bitter anger evident in her voice.

Cronley wondered, **Now, what the hell is that suddenly all about?**

Ginger, her voice rising, went on. "I know—Jimmy told me—that he believes you had my husband killed, thinking he was Jimmy. And here we sit, acting like we're all best friends."

There followed a long, awkward silence.

"Strange bedfellows," Father McGrath then mused aloud.

"And I'm more than a little uncomfortable, frankly, hearing you talk as if the Pope himself is involved with Nazis," Ginger said.

"That must be because you're a Catholic," McGrath said. "His Holiness can do no wrong."

"I'm not Catholic, Father Jack. I'm, like you, an Episcopalian."

McGrath said, "The Jesuits have a saying: 'Give me a child until he is seven and I will give you a man.'"

Dear God, Cronley prayed. *I don't know where this is going, but please don't let it go back to Serov whacking Bonehead, thinking it was me.*

God either answered Cronley's prayer or Bruce Moriarty Jr. independently decided that the world should know that it was time for him to eat or time for his diaper to be changed, or both.

Ginger rushed to deal with the howling infant.

"As I was saying before Super Spook's interruption," Serov said, "His Eminence Cardinal von Hassburger, and his entourage, will depart Rome for Berlin on 25 April. That gives us a week to set things up."

Cronley thought, **You are one cool sonofabitch, Ivan, I'll give you that.**

"What I suggest," Serov said, "is that after we have our breakfast, we drive to the castle. Now, that poses a question for you, James. What about your Polish agents?"

"What about them?"

"We're going to need all the manpower we can put our hands on if we're going to snatch the cardinal's briefcases."

Cronley thought, **What is he talking about now?**

He said, "What do you mean, 'snatch the cardinal's briefcases'?"

"When I was plotting this scenario of trailing

whoever has a briefcase, I considered the possibility that we would fail. That would mean Odessa would get the money. Then I saw a solution to that dilemma. And that was to snatch the briefcases of whomever we suspected of delivering them to Odessa.

"Doing so, I concluded, would have several advantages. It obviously would keep Odessa from getting the money, for one thing. And it would cause consternation both to Odessa and His Eminence Cardinal von Hassburger. He would wonder if the real purpose of his coming to Berlin was about to be exposed."

"And they couldn't call the cops, German or American, could they?" Cronley said. " 'Bishop Frankenstein was walking down the K'damm when some arch criminal snatched his briefcase, which held a million dollars in it.' And the cardinal would have to tell Odessa, 'Oops! Sorry, you ain't getting no money.' And even if we got caught by the cops—German or MPs—while snatching the briefcase, they'd have to explain the million bucks."

"Only if that briefcase contained the million," Cohen said. "But that is a bridge we can wait to cross when we get to it."

"Returning to your Polish DCI agents, James," Serov said, "what about them? God knows we need the manpower. But Poland is a devout Roman

Catholic country, and we all heard what Father McGrath said about what the Jesuits say—"

"I get the point," Cronley interrupted. "Well, there's one way to find out."

Cronley walked to the door and called out, "Max, come in here. We need to talk."

A moment later, Ostrowski entered the room, and said, "What about?"

He was followed by Ginger Moriarty. As she passed Cronley, she thrust Baby Bruce into his arms. The infant began to howl.

Serov began clapping, and others joined in, some of them laughing.

"I don't think he likes you, Super Spook," Father McGrath observed.

Having no other option, Cronley sat down in an armchair and began to bounce the infant up and down, as he had seen Ginger do.

"He's not a martini, Super Spook," Cohen offered. "Try rocking him gently."

Cronley did. Almost immediately, the baby stopped howling, and he seemed to be smiling at Cronley. Without realizing what he was doing, Cronley kissed the infant, which earned him more applause.

"Did I miss anything important?" Ginger asked, innocently.

"Almost," Serov said, then gestured at Cronley. "The floor is yours, James."

Still rocking the baby in his arms, Cronley said, "Max, I may be about to royally piss you off, but I have to get into this. What would your reaction be if I told you Odessa was hiding its money in the Vatican Bank?"

"My reaction? Surprise. I never thought about that possibility . . ."

Because you're a devout Catholic, right? Shit.

". . . I thought the Swedes probably had it. I mean, we're talking about a hell of a lot of money. I didn't think they would be hiding it in the basement of a burned-out building in Leipzig or Frankfurt am Main."

"You never mentioned this to me."

"You never asked," Ostrowski said, simply.

"What would you say if I told you Odessa is making a withdrawal from the Vatican Bank—probably a million dollars—and is sending it by messenger to Berlin?"

"Oh, I see where this is going," Ostrowski said. "And the messenger is a Vatican priest?"

"Actually, a cardinal."

"And you have plans for the cardinal, right? And you're wondering if as a Catholic I'm willing to go along?"

"You and the other guys," Cronley said.

"I'm sorry you had to ask. But the subject never came up before between us, did it?"

"No, it didn't."

"Okay, Jim, let me lay it out for you. I was born and raised a Roman Catholic, and I'm sure you know what the Jesuits say about that. During the war, before I got in my Spitfire and set off to kill as many Germans as I could, I always—whenever I could—found some priest to hear my confession and give me communion.

"And now I confess my sins and go to mass every Sunday. But it's different now. I do it because it helps me remember going to mass in Poland. In our parish church, Saint Luke's. With my mother and father and my sisters and brothers. They're gone, as you know. All I can do is remember them. And try to run down the Nazi bastards responsible." He turned to Serov and added, "And the communist bastards, Colonel, who were just about as responsible."

Serov remained silent.

Ostrowski looked back at Cronley and finished. "The best way I can do this is as a DCI agent. So, Jim, what are our, repeat, our plans vis-à-vis the cardinal?"

"The other guys feel this way, Max?"

"They do, take my word for it. Or hand me a Bible and I'll swear on it."

"Your word is good enough for me."

"Let me add this. The more devout of us, which includes me, have a hard-on . . . My apology, my lady . . ."

Ginger made a **Don't fret** gesture.

". . . for this heathen religion Himmler was trying to start. We figure if we can shut down Odessa, no more money will flow to these disciples of the devil. So, let me ask again, what are **our** plans for the cardinal?"

"His name is von Hassburger," Cohen said. "He'll depart Rome for Berlin by rail, aboard a special Vatican train, on April 25th, a week from today. The ostensible purpose—or his second purpose—is to offer to pay for the reconstruction of the Kaiser Wilhelm Church on the K'damm, providing that the rebuilt church is Catholic."

"I thought Arthur Werner wanted to leave it as is, as a memorial to Berliners who died in the war?"

"He does," Cronley said. "And while His Eminence is trying to talk Werner into changing his mind and accepting his generous offer, the cardinal's flunkies will be trying to hand the briefcase with the 'withdrawal' slip in it to Odessa."

"And you intend to follow the guy with the briefcase to wherever Odessa is?"

"No," Cohen said. "We're going to snatch the briefcase—make that briefcases, plural—until we have the one with the money. That will keep the money from Odessa and cause general consternation for both Odessa and the cardinal. And then we try to identify 'suspicious persons' and get them to lead us to Odessa."

"So, when do we go to Berlin?" Ostrowski asked.

Cronley said, "You just said that your guys have a . . . That your guys don't like the religion of Saint Heinrich the Divine. Which makes me suggest a change to Colonel Cohen and Colonel Serov's scenario."

"Why am I sure I'm not going to like this?" Cohen said.

"The original plan," Cronley went on, "was for Cohen's guys and mine to head for Berlin on the next train out of Nuremberg. And rendezvous at our safe house in Zehlendorf. In the meantime, we were going to tour Wewelsburg Castle, then drive into Frankfurt and catch the aptly named Army train the **Berliner** to Berlin. But now I think we should give a tour of Wewelsburg. I think it would be inspiring."

"So do I," Serov said right away and turned to Cohen. "Colonel, I think we should give everybody a tour."

"Okay, then, that's what we'll do."

"Max," Cronley said, "after setting up protection for Justice Jackson—"

"Does he know what you're—**we're**—up to?"

"No," Cronley said. "We're taking on the

Vatican by stealing their money, and I don't think he'd approve. After setting up his protection—and that's the priority—could you send some of our people to Wewelsburg tonight?"

"Done," Ostrowski said. "And we'll see you there tomorrow morning."

"We'll leave here no later than six," Cohen said.

"I suggest we make that five," Serov said.

Ginger stood up, walked to Cronley, and extended her arms to take the baby.

"That being the case, it's bedtime for us, Super Spook."

Everyone else stood.

Cronley handed her the child and then escorted the others out of the Duchess Suite.

VI

U.S. Army Railroad Spur
Zehlendorf, Berlin, American Zone of
Occupation, Germany
0900 20 April 1946

Two officers, wearing the aiguillettes and lapel insignia of aides-de-camp to a lieutenant general, were standing on the platform of the siding when Colonel Cohen, followed by Cronley, who had Baby Bruce in his arms, and Ginger, disembarked the **Berliner**.

The senior of them, a major, crisply saluted Cohen, and inquired, "Colonel Cohen?"

Cohen nodded.

"General Makamson's compliments, sir. He asks that you attend him at your earliest convenience."

"What's going on?" Cohen asked.

The major looked at Cronley. "Presumably, you're Captain Cronley?"

Cronley nodded.

"I asked, what's going on?" Cohen said.

"If you will please follow me, sir," the major replied. "And Captain Cronley, please follow the colonel."

Cohen looked at Cronley, shrugged, and followed the major toward a line of staff cars. Cronley saw that the first in line was a Buick, and Cohen got in its backseat.

The other aide-de-camp, a captain, then said, "And this is Mrs. Moriarty?"

"What the **hell** is going on?" Cronley said.

"If you'll give the child to its mother, Captain, and come with me, please."

"What happens to Mrs. Moriarty?" Cronley demanded.

"For now, she'll be taken to the Company Grade Visiting Officer Quarters."

Max Ostrowski walked up and stopped beside Cronley.

"What's going on?" he asked.

"I dunno. But take Ginger and the baby to the safe house."

"I'm afraid I can't allow that," the aide-de-camp said.

"Fuck you," Cronley said, then looked at Ostrowski. "Max, if this clown gives you any trouble, shoot him." He met the aide-de-camp's eyes, then said, "Lead on, candy-ass."

The aide-de-camp stared back in disbelief. Then he walked—marched—toward the Chevrolet. Cronley followed. At the car, the captain opened the front passenger door and motioned for Cronley to get in.

The aide-de-camp got in the driver's seat, and followed the Buick as it sped off.

[TWO]
U.S. Military Government Compound
Saargemünder Strasse
Zehlendorf, Berlin, American Zone of
Occupation, Germany
0925 20 April 1946

The OMGUS Compound had been the last headquarters of the Luftwaffe. There was a story going around that it had been spared—as had the I.G. Farben Building in Frankfurt am Main—from the thousand-plane raids that had leveled both cities because the Americans wanted undamaged office space for their use after they won the war.

It was a pleasant collection of one- and two-story buildings that were painted white. The Russians had liberated the Compound and had just about removed the camouflage netting that covered it when tanks of General I. D. White's 2nd Armored Division—**Hell on Wheels**— ushered the Reds out of the American Zone and into the Russian Zone.

The Buick, after being crisply saluted by a half dozen MPs at the entrance, drove down the central road to the headquarters building, followed by the Chevrolet carrying Cronley.

There was a row of flags—American, and then several silver-star-studded red flags, designating the Army general officer headquarters—flying in front of the building.

Cronley decided the four-star flag had to be that of General Lucius D. Clay. He had been the U.S. military governor of the American Sector of Berlin, and of the American Zone in the rest of Germany, since January.

He also decided the three-star flag had to belong to Makamson, who had replaced General Seidel as G-2 of USFET—U.S. Forces European Theater, now renamed EUCOM, the acronym for the European Command. There were half a dozen red flags with one or two stars. Senior headquarters like OMGUS and EUCOM had many general officers.

The Buick and Chevrolet stopped. The aide-de-camp major got out of the front passenger seat of the Buick as the aide-de-camp captain jumped out of the Chevrolet. They opened both rear doors of their respective vehicles.

"Please follow me, Colonel," the major said to Cohen.

Cohen did, and waited for Cronley to approach.

"Into the Valley of Death . . ." Cohen said, quietly, when he was within earshot. "I have the feeling, Super Spook, that we're in the deep shit."

The major led them to a side entrance of the main building, with the captain following them all.

They entered and went down a long corridor until they reached a steel door guarded by two military policemen. While one of the MPs snapped to rigid attention, the other opened the steel door. The aide-de-camp major without a word motioned for Cohen and Cronley to enter.

They did, and found themselves in a large room, the walls of which were lined with map boards and electronic equipment. There was a large conference table in the center of the room at which men were seated.

Cronley immediately recognized Brigadier General Homer P. Greene, chief of ASA Europe CIC-USFET, and Colonel Harold Wallace, chief of DCI-Europe. There was a lieutenant general— **That has to be Makamson,** he thought—and another brigadier general, several colonels, and a master sergeant sitting at a court reporter's steno-type keyboard.

"Take a seat," the three-star ordered, indicating two folding chairs behind a small table facing the conference table. "I am General Makamson."

Cohen and Cronley did so.

"Why don't you start by telling us, Colonel Cohen," Makamson said, "what, exactly, you and Captain Cronley are doing in Berlin when you are supposed to be in Nuremberg protecting Mr. Justice Jackson?"

"Sir, we are chasing Odessa," Cohen said.

"Under what authority?"

"Captain Cronley's. He has been directed by Admiral Souers, the director of the Central Intelligence Directorate, to run Odessa down and eliminate it wherever found. He asked for my help. I'm giving it to him."

"General Makamson," Colonel Wallace announced, "speaking as chief of Central Intelligence–Europe, I have no knowledge of any of this."

"Harry," Colonel Cohen said, conversationally, "the admiral didn't tell you because he thought you'd stick your nose in to show who's boss and then proceed to fuck things up. And they'd be not just fucked up but FUBAR."

"Colonel," General Makamson snapped, "you will address officers by their rank! And respectfully! Understood?"

"Yes, sir," Cohen said, evenly. "We just could

not afford to have what we were doing Fucked Up Beyond All Repair."

"I think we all know what FUBAR means, Colonel. And when I want your opinion, I'll ask for it. Understood?"

"Yes, sir."

Makamson glared at him for ten seconds, then said, "To avoid losing my temper, I think we have to get on with this. So, you think Odessa is in Berlin?"

"We think that it's very likely that its senior officers are, sir," Cohen replied. "Sir, may I start at the beginning?"

"Why not."

"Sir, we know that Odessa has vast sums of money, which they are using both to get Nazis who are on the run out of Germany and to fund the so-called religion that Heinrich Himmler started."

"You believe that Hitler/Himmler religion nonsense, do you?"

"Before we took the **Berliner** last night, we were at Wewelsburg Castle, which is sort of the Vatican of this new religion. We had with us an expert in heretical religions, Father Jack McGrath, whom Admiral Souers found for us. Would you take his word? He's in Berlin, at the DCI safe house in Zehlendorf."

"You're telling me that Admiral Souers also believes in this Nazi religion nonsense?"

"More important, sir, the admiral tells me so does the President. The President regards it as a threat to his intentions to try to hang the people we have in Nuremberg as common criminals rather than martyrs. He ordered the admiral to look into it. The admiral assigned that task to Captain Cronley."

"Cronley is supposed to be protecting Mr. Justice Jackson," Wallace said, coldly. "You expect us to believe Cronley was ordered to chase Odessa at the expense of that? And without telling me, or, more important, Mr. Justice Jackson?"

"Mr. Justice Jackson is in the loop," Cohen said, evenly.

"I find that very hard to believe," Makamson said. "And there's one way to find out."

He picked up the receiver of a red telephone on the desk.

"This is General Makamson. Get me Mr. Justice Jackson at the International Tribunal in Nuremberg on a secure line."

A moment later, the master sergeant at the court reporter's keyboard leapt to his feet, came to attention, and bellowed, **"Ten-hut!"**

Everyone in the room popped to attention.

General Lucius D. Clay had entered the room. He was trim and fit, with a slim, angular face, penetrating dark eyes, and black hair. He wore simple ODs, and had his characteristic Chesterfield cigarette hanging from his lips.

"At ease," Clay said, a trace of his native Georgia accent evident, as he slipped into a chair at the conference table. Then he said, "Hang that up, General. I just got off the horn with Jackson."

"Yes, sir," Makamson said, and then spoke into the red telephone receiver. "Cancel the call."

Clay looked at Cohen and Cronley.

"General Makamson suggested that you two would be dazzled into silence by my august presence. And that it would be best if I listened to his interrogation over the intercom. That obviously hasn't worked, so I'll take over.

"First, let's clear the air vis-à-vis Justice Jackson. He is fully aware that Captain Cronley was ordered to pursue Odessa by Admiral Souers. He also told me that it was he who dubbed you Super Spook, Captain Cronley, because you're so good at what you do. So, Captain Super Spook, why don't you tell us what the hell is going on here?"

"Yes, sir—"

"And start at the beginning, please, keeping in mind that I want the truth, the whole truth, and nothing but the truth, so help **you** God."

"Yes, sir. Sir, General Ivan Serov came to me at the Farber Palast—the press club—in Nuremberg—"

"You're talking about the same Ivan Serov," one of the brigadier generals interrupted, "who is first deputy to Commissar of State Security Nikolaevich Merkulov?"

"I'm conducting this, General," Clay snapped. "But answer the question, Cronley. Is this who you're talking about?"

"Yes, sir."

"I will now ask the question General Wiley would like to ask. The first deputy to Commissar Merkulov sought you out?"

"That's correct, sir. Serov is assigned to Nuremberg as security for the Russian delegation to the Tribunal."

"Had you any previous contact with General Serov?"

"Yes, sir. I had dealt with him when the NKGB kidnapped Colonel Mattingly."

"Go on. What did Serov have on his mind when he sought you out?"

"Several things, sir, the most important of which was that he had found out where Odessa was keeping its money."

"Before we get into the money, why would Serov tell you something like that? So you would pass it on to Admiral Souers?"

"Sir, this is where it gets a little weird. Serov has always been interested in Odessa and what I call Himmler's new religion. During our conversation, he said that he had just lost his wife to cancer, about a month or five weeks ago."

"Frankly, Cronley, I'm finding it . . . a little weird . . . that a high-ranking officer of the NKGB would discuss his private life with a junior American officer."

"He was very emotional, sir. It may be because he knew I'd lost my fiancée—my **bride**—tragically. I'm not sure. Regardless, he told me that during his wife's final hours, her family had been praying, nonstop, on their knees at her bedside. He told me that after she died, he began to wonder that maybe he should have been on his knees beside them.

"He went on to say he suddenly realized that he was alone in the world. His wife's family wanted nothing to do with him because he was an NKGB officer, and he had no children and had no other living relatives."

"My deep condolences for your loss, Captain," General Clay said.

"Thank you, sir."

Clay nodded, then said, "So Serov had quite a yarn. And?"

"The first thing I thought was that it was pure bullsh . . . Sorry, sir."

"I've heard that word before. But?"

"Then I thought maybe it was true, maybe

Serov was out of his mind with grief. So, I asked him, 'What are you going to do now?'"

"He said that he finally realized that God had a purpose in leaving him all alone, and that purpose was for him to destroy Himmler's new religion, which he described as 'an obscene heresy.'"

"And what was your reaction to that?"

"That I was again in over my head in dealing with Serov, sir. The reason he got to be number two to Merkulov is because he's smarter than just about anyone else in the NKGB. And from my previous dealings with him, I knew what a devious sonofabitch he can be—is. And he wanted something from me. I didn't know what. Or what to do. Period."

"So, what did you decide?"

"Sir, I decided to hear him out. That's when he told me the Vatican—the Vatican Bank—was holding Odessa's money. The **Reichskonkordat**—"

"The what?"

"Sir, that's the deal, the concord, the Pope made with the Nazis. He would stop anyone in the Catholic Church from criticizing the Nazis and the Nazis would leave the Catholic Church alone. It was also connected to a secret deal. Hitler—or maybe Himmler—leaned on Mussolini to have him declare the Vatican free of Italy, which made it a sovereign state."

"I remember that," Clay said, thoughtfully. "A

sovereign state—specifically held by the Holy See—with less than half a square kilometer of territory."

"Yes, sir. And he went from that to asking himself, what do all sovereign states have in common? And the answer to that is, a national bank. And neither the FBI nor the NKGB has been going over the books of the Holy Mother Church's bank with a fine-tooth comb.

"Serov's scenario is, just before we took Rome, the SS deposited what we're calling Odessa's money in the Vatican Bank."

"Does General Serov have a scenario as to why the Pope would permit this?"

"Yes, sir."

General Clay took a puff on what was left of his cigarette, then snuffed out the butt in a makeshift ashtray as he exhaled and made an impatient **Let's have it** gesture.

"Sir, the Roman Catholic Church—the Pope—regards communism as its greatest threat, its greatest enemy. So does—did—Nazi Germany."

"And there it is," Clay said, and quoted, " 'The enemy of my enemy is my friend.' "

"Exactly, sir. Serov pointed out that the Pope was papal nuncio—the voice of the Pope—in Berlin for years, that he speaks German fluently, and that he made many friends, even among Himmler's circle.

"So, Serov got one—maybe more—of his people into the Vatican Bank, where they found a numbered account that had to be the Nazi money. It is in excess of one hundred million dollars. And they also found out (a) that Odessa was about to make a withdrawal of approximately a million dollars, (b) that the Vatican Bank was going to deliver the withdrawal by courier, and (c) that the courier is Cardinal von Hassburger."

"Really? That is quite an accusation. His Eminence is here to discuss the fate of the Kaiser Wilhelm Church with John McCloy, Arthur Werner, and me."

"Yes, sir. But it is the truth."

"So you say." Clay took his time lighting another Chesterfield, exhaled, and added, "Giving you—or General Serov—the benefit of the doubt that the cardinal is carrying money for Odessa leads me to this: Did he tell you what he plans to do about it?"

"Yes, sir. Serov has people in the Hotel Am Zoo—"

"I'll bet he does!"

"—who will let us know when anyone in the cardinal's entourage leaves the hotel with a brief-case. We will then follow him—or, if there's more than one possible courier, all of them."

"And you—and Serov—believe the courier

with the briefcase will lead you to Odessa, or at least an Odessa operative?"

"Yes, sir. Not immediately. After he is interrogated by Serov's people, we think we'll have an address, and probably more."

General Clay puffed his cigarette, then looked thoughtfully at Cronley as he exhaled a cloud of smoke toward the ceiling.

"Captain Cronley, you're seriously suggesting that Serov's plan is to kidnap a representative of the Holy See—probably a priest, possibly a monsignor, maybe even a bishop—and turn him over to the NKGB for interrogation? And the NKGB will then do what, kill him?"

"No, sir. Our plan is to send him back to the Am Zoo so that he can report that he was in the hands of the NKGB and that the NKGB has his briefcase."

"And where is this briefcase? And what if the briefcase doesn't have a million dollars in it?"

"Sir, we will still have the briefcase."

"You and General Serov?"

"Yes, sir. In the event there's no money in it, a man will deliver the briefcase that he will say he found at the Hotel Am Zoo. But he won't turn it over to the cardinal's people until he is suitably rewarded for returning it. There will be an argument. Eventually, somebody senior shows, maybe a monsignor or even a bishop. He pays, he gets the briefcase—and we start following him."

"And then what?"

"Sir, if we in fact have the briefcase with the money, and the courier goes back to the Am Zoo and reports that it's gone, what are they going to do? They can't go to the police and report the robbery. How would they explain a simple priest—or monsignor or bishop—running around Berlin with a million dollars in a briefcase? Now, we're presuming that they will want to tell Odessa about the loss. That means they'll tell somebody to deal with Odessa. Not a simple priest, somebody senior. Anybody senior leaving the Am Zoo is tailed."

Clay looked at Cronley, glanced around the table, then came back to Cronley.

"Is that about it, Captain?"

"Sir, we just got here."

Clay ignored the answer and instead announced, "We will now get everyone's opinion, hopefully brief, about Captain Cronley's tale. We will start with the junior among us. With the exception of Colonel Cohen, whom we will hear last, who's junior?"

The opinions offered were not flattering.

One major general said, "Bullshit, absolute pure bullshit. I kept wondering why you didn't shut the arrogant little bastard up."

He was followed by General Makamson, who said, "I think that Colonel Cohen and Captain Cronley should be escorted from here to the psychiatric ward of the One Hundred Thirty-fourth Station Hospital for a thorough mental evaluation."

When all had finished, General Clay looked at Cohen.

"And now we'll hear, probably for the defense, so to speak, from the Counterintelligence Corps. The floor is yours, Colonel."

Cohen stood up.

"General Clay, sir, what you have seen in Captain Cronley's presentation was why Mr. Justice Jackson calls him Super Spook. And, for the record, I'm happy to take orders from him, sir."

He sat down.

Clay glanced from face to face as he said, "From the beginning of this, the thought that there must be a reason why Captain Cronley has been given the authority to deal with Odessa kept running through my mind. Then that eventually drove me to the conclusion that I'm not going to pit my evaluation of Captain Cronley against that of Admiral Souers. Not that my evaluation would in any way be negative. Quite the contrary.

"So, gentlemen, here's what we're going to do. We're going to pretend (a) that we didn't know Cohen and Cronley are in Berlin and (b) that this meeting never took place. If we don't know of

Cronley and Cohen's plans, how can we interfere with them? That said, there is one exception to this. Colonel Switzer?"

"Yes, sir?" Switzer said.

"As the chief, CIC Berlin," Clay went on, "if the chief, CIC, Nuremberg Tribunal, came to ask for your support in connection with something he said he couldn't talk about, what would be your reaction? Would you help him or not?"

"I'd be inclined to help him, sir."

"Good. Now, I don't know this, but I wouldn't be surprised if Colonel Cohen came to you and asked for support. If you can't give him what he asks for, tell me. Understand?"

"Yes, sir."

"I now declare this conference, which never took place, to be closed. General Makamson's driver will take you, Colonel Cohen and Captain Cronley, wherever you want to go."

"Thank you, sir," Cohen and Cronley said, almost in unison.

"If you come across a bit of information you think would be of interest to me, I'd be grateful for it. I will not share it with anyone."

"Yes, sir," they said.

"Good luck to you," Clay said, then snuffed out his cigarette.

"Thank you, sir," Cohen and Cronley said again in chorus.

They stood up and walked to the door.

Makamson's senior aide-de-camp, the major, was waiting for them.

"If you'll follow me, please, gentlemen."

[THREE]
44-46 Beerenstrasse
Zehlendorf, Berlin, American Zone of
Occupation, Germany
1105 20 April 1946

General Makamson's driver, after taking a circuitous route, dropped off Cohen and Cronley in an alley a block from the safe house and immediately drove away. Before they were halfway to the next alley, headed for the back door of the house, an unmarked Chevrolet staff car stopped near where they had been dropped off. Two men stepped out of passenger doors.

Cronley saw that one was Colonel Switzer, the Berlin CIC chief, and was not surprised. Switzer's boss, Brigadier General Greene, had provided a cover for the safe house. Officially, it was the living quarters for South American Airlines personnel, including flight crews.

Switzer had with him a trim, dark-haired lieutenant colonel, who Cronley didn't recognize.

Cohen seemed unconcerned and continued up the alley, then into the house. Cronley quickly followed, passing the DCI agent guarding the back door.

Ginger, holding the baby, came into the foyer.

"After that ambush at the train station, Jimmy, I wasn't sure I'd ever see you again when they drove you away."

"Sorry to disappoint you, but here I am, if somewhat battered and bloody."

The DCI agent at the door called out, "A Colonel Switzer to see you, Colonel."

"Let him in. He's one of the good guys," Cohen said, then added in a loud stage voice, "Unless you're here, Lou, to tell me what a disgrace I am to the CIC and to the Army in general."

Switzer entered the room, trailed by the lieutenant colonel. Cronley thought he looked to be in his early thirties.

Switzer and Cohen shook hands, then embraced, patting each other on the back.

"Morty," Switzer said, "this is my deputy, Frank Williams."

"Colonel," Cohen said to Williams.

As they shook hands, Cohen added, "This is Captain Cronley, in case you don't know. And this is his fiancée, Virginia Moriarty."

"It's a pleasure to meet you, ma'am," Switzer said, taking her hand.

"And mine," Williams then said, and shook her now free hand.

"Now that we're all friends, Morty," Switzer said, "why don't we have something alcoholic to celebrate your miraculous escape from spending the rest of your life in Leavenworth, the psychiatric wing thereof?"

Cohen chuckled.

"The bar would be this way," Cohen said, making a sweeping gesture with his arm toward its door.

"So that's where we've been and what we've been doing," Cohen concluded his report to everyone in the safe house of what had happened.

Switzer cleared his throat. "If I may, Morty. I want everybody to understand that when General Makamson said he wanted Colonel Cohen and Captain Cronley taken to the lunatic ward for a thorough examination, he was damn dead serious."

"I can understand that," Ginger said.

"Thank you so kindly, my love," Cronley said.

"I have a question for you, Captain Cronley," Colonel Switzer said.

"Sir?"

"Do you also go along with Mort's nutty idea that Himmler was starting a new religion?"

"Colonel, Himmler **has** started a Nazi religion," Cronley said.

Ginger put in: "We were in Wewelsburg Castle yesterday. What I saw there convinced me that Himmler has indeed started something terrible. I have never felt such evil in my life. I wanted to scream and grab my baby and run for our lives."

Switzer was silent, deep in thought.

Finally, he said, "Well, I'm going to be on Makamson's shit list if I loan you so much as a lined pad and a pencil. So, I might as well go whole hog. What do you need, Mort?"

"We need people to sit on this place while our guys are out stealing briefcases. Can I have four of your agents? Preferably with radio-equipped cars."

"Frank?"

"Done," Williams said.

"Thank you," Cohen said. "This one may not be so easy, so feel free to say 'Hell, no.' If I had one of your radio-equipped cars, one with sirens and flashing lights, Cronley and I could hang around the K'damm without drawing too much attention."

Switzer nodded. "It would be useful, wouldn't it, Morty, if my agent knew what was going on? Then if you jumped in the back with a briefcase, he could turn on the lights and siren and get you the hell out of there. I don't mind sticking my neck out, but I don't like to put my guys at risk."

"I'll drive the car," Williams said.

"Why would you want to do that?" Switzer asked.

"Boss, I know you're skeptical, but I think Colonel Cohen is onto something, and I don't want to remember in a couple of years—or maybe even next Friday—that I turned down a chance to be in on it."

"Understood," Switzer said, nodding.

"What I'd like to do, then," Cohen said, "is send at least two guys over to the Am Zoo."

"I think we have to wait until we hear from Serov," Cronley said.

Cohen met his eyes and, after a pause, said, "I think you're right."

"And while we're waiting, I'll summon the reinforcements," Williams said. "Where's the secure phone?"

They didn't have to wait long. At 1215, there came a knock at the front door of the safe house. A scrawny, middle-aged German on a bicycle handed the plainclothes DCI agent who answered the door an envelope. It bore no return address. There was only block lettering handwritten in black ink, the penmanship impeccable: HERR J. CRONLEY.

The agent delivered it to Cronley, and, when

he opened it, he found it contained a plain sheet of paper with more block lettering: KEMPINSKI BRISTOL HOTEL BAR, KURFÜRSTENDAMM 25 1300-1430.

It was unsigned. But there was no question in Cronley's mind that it came from Ivan Serov.

[FOUR]
Kempinski Bristol Hotel
Kurfürstendamm 25
Berlin, International Zone of
Occupation, Germany
1350 20 April 1946

Serov, wearing the uniform of an NKGB general officer, was sitting at a booth in the bar with another man, who was wearing the uniform of an NKGB colonel. Cronley recognized him as Sergei Alekseevich. He had met him while negotiating with Serov to get the kidnapped Colonel Mattingly back from the NKGB. Alekseevich then had been wearing the uniform of an NKGB major.

"What a pleasant surprise!" Cronley said, in German, as he walked up to the booth.

He sat down—without being invited and without shaking Serov's outstretched hand—and switched to English. "How they hanging, Sergei?"

After a bit, Alekseevich grunted, "Herr Cronley."

"You came alone," Serov said.

"Not exactly, Ivan. Everybody but Colonel Cohen is in the lobby, waiting to hear what's going on with you."

"Everybody?"

"Father J-for-Jack McGrath, Max Ostrowski, and Lieutenant Colonel Frank Williams. Plus, of course, Ginger and the baby."

"Who is this Colonel Williams?"

"I'm surprised you don't know. More than once I thought I'd been reliably informed that the NKGB knew all."

That earned him a glare from Serov.

Cronley went on. "Actually, he's a lieutenant colonel. He's number two in Berlin CIC."

"Sergei," Serov ordered, "go to the maître d'hôtel, tell them we have unexpected guests, and then ask James's people to join you in the dining room. I need a moment alone with James."

Alekseevich stood up, acknowledged the order with a curt nod of his head, and left the bar.

"I have two tidbits of new information," Serov then said. "Burgdorf and von Dietelburg have escaped from the AVO."

"Jesus Christ!"

"What is it you're always saying, James? Money talks? Colonel Alekseevich was able to get the

Hungarians to turn them loose with a remarkably small gift."

"What the hell was the purpose of turning them loose?"

"Both were prepared to die as martyrs to the Church of Saint Heinrich the Divine rather than give up Odessa. I confess I was sorely tempted to let them, but then I thought they just might interpret getting free of AVO as an act of God and run right to Odessa, or at least to some high-ranking member of Odessa."

"You are a really devious bastard, Ivan. I say that with all due admiration."

"They sneaked across the Hungarian border into Austria and then across the Austrian border into Germany. They made no attempt to contact anyone during their journey. They're now in Wiesbaden, in Hesse. My people tell me they will probably make their way to the Autobahn at Helmstedt, on the American–Russian Zone border, where they will bribe a truck driver to carry them through East Germany to Berlin."

"Bribe a truck driver? Where did they get the money to do that?"

"I can only assume they stole it from the AVO guard they overpowered when he went unaccompanied into their cell, reeking of Slivovitz. It will take them at least three days, possibly as many as five, to make it to Berlin. So, we'll have that much time in case our plans during that time bear no fruit."

"And what are our plans?"

"His Eminence Cardinal von Hassburger, under the aegis of either John Jay McCloy or General Clay, possibly both, is to tour the Kaiser Wilhelm Church at ten-hundred hours tomorrow, which will give him, or a member of his entourage, at least the chance to meet with someone from Odessa, if not pass a briefcase to him.

"I think we should be there, don't you, James? By we, I mean your people and mine."

"Let me see if I can fit it into our schedule."

"Wonderful! Now let's go to lunch. They serve a marvelous sauerbraten here."

VII

[ONE]
The Adler Room
Kempinski Bristol Hotel
Kurfürstendamm 25
Berlin, International Zone of
Occupation, Germany
1410 20 April 1946

"Apfelstrudel is the appropriate finish for a meal like this," Serov said. "And that strudel was marvelous."

There were murmurs of agreement from all at the table.

"And now duty calls," Serov said, "unless there's something someone wishes to say."

"The only complaint I have," Father McGrath said, "is that we have to call this luncheon off for the call of duty, which means I can't get General Serov—"

"Please, Father, Ivan," Serov interrupted.

McGrath nodded, and said, "On the condition you start calling me Jack."

"Very well," Serov said. "What is it you were saying, Jack?"

"I realized, when you were discussing Heinrich Himmler, how little I know about the man. I was about to say that high among the reasons I'm sorry lunch is over is because I can't ask the general—**Ivan**—more about him."

"We'll find time sooner or later, Jack, to have a long talk about Saint Heinrich the Divine. In the meantime, perhaps I could suggest a book on the subject you could read?"

"How can there be a book?"

Serov smiled, then said, "A book about Saint Heinrich written with impeccable historical accuracy and great literary flair. The author has been compared to Shakespeare."

He snapped his fingers.

Colonel Alekseevich dug into his briefcase and came out with what looked like three small leather-bound notebooks held together with a thick rubber band. He handed them to Serov, who then took off the rubber band and handed one to Ginger.

"With the compliments of the author," he said, and then handed one to Father McGrath and then one to Cronley.

The cover of what he had thought was a notebook held a legend in gold:

A BRIEF BIOGRAPHY OF
REICHSFÜHRER-SS HEINRICH HIMMLER
By General Ivan Serov

Cronley opened the book and saw the text was in English.

"What the hell is this?" Cronley said.

"As I said, James, 'A book about Saint Heinrich written with impeccable historical accuracy and great literary flair.'"

"And aside from that?"

Looking very pleased with himself, Serov explained. "It's sort of a textbook in our agent training system. The students are given one of these to read overnight. The next morning, they are required to write—in English—their own biography of Saint Heinrich."

"Clever . . ." Cronley said. "But in English?"

"Before they reach that part of their instruction, the students are required to speak English. Merkulov—Commissar of State Security Nikolaevich Merkulov—believes that the greatest threat to the Soviet Union is posed by people whose native language is English."

"You mean the United States."

"And England."

Cronley considered that, then said, "Very

clever. As you probably know, since the NKGB knows all, we train our agents first and then send them to the Army Language School at the Presidio, the Army base in San Francisco, to teach them the language they will need. I think the way you do it makes more sense."

"How kind of you to say so," Serov said, beginning to stand. "But now Sergei and I must go. Until what? Eight thirty, in the Kaiser Wilhelm Church."

"I'll be there."

"If you can find the time overnight to read my literary opus, I'd be interested to hear what you think of it."

"If there aren't too many big words in it, I'll give it a shot."

[TWO]
44-46 Beerenstrasse
Zehlendorf, Berlin, American Zone of
Occupation,
Germany
1605 20 April 1946

Cronley made himself a drink, sat down on the couch in the bar, and put his feet on the coffee table. Ginger immediately sat very close to him.

"This will probably do great damage to your ego, my love," he said, taking Serov's book from his jacket pocket. "But right now, I'm more interested in this book than I am in romantic cuddling."

"Actually, so am I, Jimmy. But since I gave my copy to Max, I'll have to share yours. You have my word that I won't try to arouse you sexually."

Cronley opened the book. Their eyes went to the opening page, and they read to the end without uttering a word.

Reichsführer-SS Heinrich Himmler—head of the Gestapo; the Waffen-SS; Minister of the Interior, and organizer of the mass murder of Jews in the Third Reich—was born in Munich, Kingdom of Bavaria, on 7 October 1900.

His father, a devout Roman Catholic who had once been tutor to the Crown Prince of Bavaria, had become headmaster of a Catholic school.

For some reason, young Himmler was not given his elementary and intermediate education in his father's school, but rather in a Catholic school in Landshut.

Himmler served briefly as an officer cadet in the 11th Bavarian Regiment in the last days of the First World War. On separation from the service, he enrolled in the Munich

Technical High School, which, in 1922, granted him a diploma in Agriculture.

He then worked briefly as a fertilizer salesman. It is not known why he left this employment. Soon afterward, he joined what was then an insignificant political organization known as the Nationalsozialistische Deutsche Arbeiterpartei—the National Socialist German Workers' Party—acronym: Nazi.

The Nazi Party was headed by Adolf Hitler, an Austro-German. Hitler had served as a corporal in the trenches in Belgium, where he was gassed and temporarily blinded.

There is an interesting, though unverifiable, story that while serving as a messenger in the trenches, Hitler was attacked by a large herding dog, a Bouvier des Flandres, which bit him in the crotch, causing him eventually to lose one of his testicles. It is known that when Hitler returned to Belgium in World War II, he ordered the complete eradication of the breed, which turned out unsuccessful.

In November of 1923, during the infamous Munich Beer Hall Putsch, Himmler served as the "standard-bearer" to Ernst Röhm. Röhm, then serving as the unpaid secretary to Gregor Strasser, the grandiosely named district leader for Bavaria, Swabia, and the Palatinate. Surprising many, Röhm later acquired enough power to seriously threaten to take Hitler's place as **Führer**—"leader"—of the Nazi Party.

In 1927, Himmler married, and briefly returned to poultry farming. Probably because he was spending so much time on Nazi affairs at low—or no—pay, he again went bankrupt.

Hitler came to his rescue. He named him as head of his personal black-shirted bodyguard, which then consisted of approximately two hundred men. Himmler promptly named these bodyguards the **Schutzstaffel**—acronym: SS—and immediately began to recruit "pure Germans" for it.

In 1930, Himmler was elected to the Reichstag. By then, both Hitler and Himmler were growing increasingly wary of Ernst Röhm, whom they suspected was trying to take over the Nazi Party. Their first step was to make the Schutzstaffel independent of Röhm's SA. By 1933, the SS had fifty-two thousand members.

Himmler then formed the Security Service, the **Sicherheitsdienst**—acronym: SD—under Reinhard Heydrich, a former Naval Reserve officer who had been removed from service for base and vile acts of depravity.

Himmler and Heydrich then worked together to ensure the Nazi Party's influence in Bavaria grew.

In March 1933, Hitler took the first step in increasing Himmler's and the SS's power by naming him Munich police president.

Step two was naming Himmler commander of all the political police throughout Bavaria.

In September 1933, Hitler made him commander of all political police units outside Prussia and, though technically under Hermann Göring, Hitler's deputy, he on 20 April 1934 became head of the Prussian police and the **Geheime Staatspolizei**—the secret state police, known as the Gestapo.

Two months later, on 30 June, Hitler's and Himmler's increasing rant against the Jewish people came to a head on what became known as **Krystallnacht**. This "crystal night" was a callous, mocking reference to the glass fragments from the thousands of windows of Jewish shops and hundreds of synagogues looted and then set afire by mobs under the control of the SS.

The SS also used the tempest to deal with another problem. They burst into Ernst Röhm's room in a country inn, the Gast Haus, found him naked in bed in the act of copulating with a young male, and shot both on the spot.

They photographed the scene of the double

crime—homosexuality and murder—and saw that images were widely circulated.

Thus ended the Röhm threat to take over the Nazi Party.

By 17 June 1936, Himmler had successfully completed his bid to win control of the political and criminal police throughout the Third Reich. His official title became Reichsführer-SS.

Possibly because of his father, Himmler had been interested in ancient German history since his youth, and this had evolved into a fascination with the occult.

In 1933, when the Nazis came to power in Germany, Himmler began searching for a castle in the area where, in 9 A.D., Hermann der Cherusker had fought a decisive battle against the Romans, saving the German people from being conquered. As a result, the German tribes retained their culture and identity long after other tribes had been absorbed into the Roman Empire.

Thus, on 3 November 1933, Himmler visited Wewelsburg Castle and decided that day to lease it for one hundred years and to restore it so that it could be used as an educational and ceremonial center for the SS.

It was his intent to imbue the SS with a sense of racial superiority with the virtues of loyalty, camaraderie, duty, truth, diligence, honesty, and knighthood. His SS was to be the elite of the party, the elite of the German people, and, thus, the elite of the entire world.

By using the castle to indoctrinate SS members in his ideals, he hoped to breed a new man who was, in his words, "far finer and more valuable than the world had yet seen."

Himmler's romantic dream of a race of blue-eyed, blond heroes was to be achieved by cultivating an elite according to "laws of selection" based on criteria of physiognomy, mental and physical tests, character, and spirit. His aristocratic concept of leadership was aimed at consciously breeding a racially organized order which would combine charismatic authority with bureaucratic discipline.

The SS man would represent a new human type—scholar, warrior, administrator, leader—whose messianic mission was to undertake a vast colonization of the East. This synthetic aristocracy, trained in a semiclosed society and superimposed on the Nazi system as a whole, would demonstrate the value of its blood through "creative action" and achievement.

From the outset of his career as Reichsführer of the SS, Himmler had introduced the principle of racial selection and special marriage laws that would ensure the systematic coupling of people of "high value."

Himmler was obsessed with creating a race of supermen by means of breeding. To accomplish this, he established state-registered human stud farms, known as **Lebensborn**, where young girls selected for their perfect Nordic traits could procreate with SS men. Their offspring were better cared for than "common" babies in maternity homes for married mothers.

On 28 October 1939, he proclaimed to the entire SS that "it will be the sublime task of German women and girls of good blood, acting not frivolously but from a profound moral seriousness, to become the mothers of children of soldiers setting off to battle." He next decreed that "war heroes" should be allowed a second marriage.

Personally, he suffered from psychosomatic illness—severe headaches and intestinal spasms. It was reported that he had almost fainted at the sight of a hundred Eastern Jews, including women, being executed for his benefit on the Russian front. As a result of this, he ordered a "more humane means" of execution. This resulted in the use of poison gas—

Zyklon B, an insecticide—to eradicate **Unter-menschen** in gas chambers.

Himmler was determined that: the SS was to be the resurrection of the ancient Order of the Teutonic Knights, with himself as grand master; the breeding of a new **Herrenvolk** aristocracy was to be based on traditional values of honor, obedience, courage, and loyalty; and the SS was to be the instrument of a vast experiment in modern racial engineering.

In October 1939, Hitler appointed Himmler as Reichskommissar für die Festigung deutschen Volkstums—Reich Commissar for the Strengthening of Germandom—and he was given absolute control over the newly annexed slice of Poland.

Responsible for bringing people of German descent back from outside the Reich into its borders, he set out to replace Poles and Jews with **Volksdeutsche** from the Baltic lands and various outlying parts of Poland.

Within a year, more than a million Poles and three hundred thousand Jews had been uprooted and driven eastward. With the characteristic self-pitying and ascetic ethos of self-abnegation that he inculcated into the SS, Himmler informed the SS-Leibstandarte Adolf Hitler Regiment, "Gentlemen, it is much easier in many cases to go into combat with a company than to suppress an obstructive population of low cultural level, or to carry out executions or to haul away people or to evict crying and hysterical women."

It was Himmler's success in indoctrinating the SS with an apocalyptic "idealism" beyond all guilt and responsibility, which rationalized mass murder as a form of martyrdom and harshness toward oneself.

In a speech to SS group leaders in Poznan on 4 October 1943, he said, "One principle must be absolute for the SS man: We must be honest, decent, loyal, and comradely to members of our own blood and to no one else. What happens to the Russians, what happens to the Czechs, is a matter of utter indifference to me.

"Such good blood of our own kind as there may be among the nations we shall acquire for ourselves, if necessary, by taking away the children and bringing them up among us. Whether the other peoples live in comfort or perish of hunger interests me only insofar as we need them as slaves for our **Kultur**. Whether or not ten thousand Russian women collapse from exhaustion while digging a tank ditch interests me only insofar as the tank ditch is completed for Germany.

"We shall never be rough or heartless where it is not necessary; that is clear. We Germans, who are the only people in the world who have a decent attitude to animals, will also adopt a decent attitude to these human animals, but it is a crime against our own blood to worry about them and to bring them ideals.

"I speak to you here with all frankness of a very grave matter. Among ourselves it should be mentioned quite frankly, and yet we will never speak of it publicly. I mean the evacuation of the Jews, the extermination of the Jewish people.

"Most of you know what it means to see a hundred corpses lying together, five hundred, or a thousand. To have stuck it out and at the same time—apart from exceptions caused by human weakness—to have remained decent fellows, that is what has made us hard.

"This is a page of glory in our history which has never been written and shall never be written."

In May 1945, Himmler finally faced the fact that the war was lost. He shaved off his mustache and took off his SS uniform, replacing it with that of a Wehrmacht sergeant. He acquired forged Wehrmacht credentials, identifying him as Sergeant Heinrich Hitzinger, and, with a small group of aides, left Berlin and headed west.

Hitzinger was arrested on 21 May at an informal checkpoint. It had been set up by recently released Russian prisoners of war near Neuhaus, in territory occupied by the British. Two days later, the Russians turned over Hitzinger to the British.

Himmler confessed his true identity to the British duty officer, Captain Thomas Selvester, who didn't believe him but nevertheless sent him to British 2nd Army Headquarters in Lüneburg. There, an intelligence officer confirmed his identity and ordered an immediate body cavity search by a medical officer.

When a physician named Wells put his finger in Himmler's mouth, Himmler bit him. When the doctor removed his finger, Himmler turned his head and bit on a cyanide capsule. After fifteen minutes of agony, Himmler died.

He was buried that day in an unmarked grave in a farmer's field. The burial detail was unaware of who they were burying, and the only person who knows where Heinrich Himmler is buried is the intelligence officer who confirmed his identity.

—END—

"How much of this is true?" Ginger then said, very softly, her voice breaking.

"Just about all of it."

"Those . . . breeding farms?"

"Yeah. And the NKGB had agents in the British Second Army Headquarters. Otherwise he couldn't know about the freed Russians who grabbed Himmler first. Or the names of the British officers. Or Himmler's burial in some farmer's field."

Ginger stood up and ordered, "Come on."

"Where are we going?"

"To the room. Where I'm going to lay down, holding Bruce as tight as I can. And then you're going to lay down and hold the both of us as tight as you can."

Cronley stood up and followed her out of the room.

As he passed through the door, he put his arm around her shoulders.

In the corridor, she turned into his arms, and he held her as tight as he could.

[THREE]
44-46 Beerenstrasse
Zehlendorf, Berlin, American Zone of Occupation, Germany
0745 21 April 1946

Cronley was dipping pieces of steak into the yolk of one of his fried eggs. Ginger, visibly deep in thought and holding Baby Bruce to her shoulder, was moving a piece of toast around her plate with a fork. Father McGrath, his plate clean, held a cup of coffee in one hand and a freshly lit eight-inch cigar in the other.

Max Ostrowski came into the dining room and took a seat at the table.

"I hope everybody else slept well," Ostrowski said, gesturing with Serov's book. "This goddamn thing kept me awake all night, after I read it twice."

He tossed it on the table. Ginger raised her eyes to look at him but didn't say anything.

Ostrowski broke the silence: "Any reason you're wearing your railroad tracks, Captain Cronley?"

"In the hope that when Cardinal von Hassburger, or members of his ecclesiastic staff, sees me in the Kaiser Wilhelm Church, they will think I am a sightseeing captain, and as such, not important. However, when they see your triangles, Max, they will immediately decide that someone should keep an eye on you."

"You want me to get rid of my triangles?"

"Absolutely not. That's the point: If they're watching you, they likely won't be watching me." He paused, and as an afterthought added, "Unless you happen to have civilian clothing?"

"I wish we had this conversation last night. Before I told all my guys to wear civvies."

"Well, your call. You can swap clothes with

one of your guys, if you want, and let him be the subject of intense Vatican curiosity."

"How much time do I have before the CIC comes?"

"Lieutenant Colonel Frank Williams is expected any minute," Cronley said.

Ostrowski hastily went off to change clothes. He had been gone not much more than a minute when Williams and Colonel Cohen walked into the dining room.

"Good morning," Williams said. "Everybody ready to spy on the cardinal's minions?"

"No," Cronley said. "One of us is changing his clothes. You're welcome to have some breakfast."

"We've eaten, thank you," Cohen said. "But how about a cup of coffee?"

"Sit," Cronley said, and made a royal gesture.

Williams saw Serov's book on the table and picked it up.

"What's this?" he said, reading the cover. "A brief biography of Saint Heinrich the Divine? By Serov?"

"Let the record show that nothing gets past CIC Berlin," Cronley said.

Williams opened the book, and said, "Well, let's see what Serov knows about that son of a bitch that I don't."

He then rapidly ran his finger down the first

page and almost immediately turned it and repeated his finger-down-the-page scan.

The fourth time he did it, Cronley said, "Fascinating. I've never seen a real-life speed-reader in operation before."

Williams raised his eyes to Cronley, smiled, and said, "It's convenient, I admit. But it's only one of the character traits contributing to my genius."

Soon, Williams closed the book and gently placed it back on the table.

"You see anything you didn't know before while zipping through that?" Cohen asked.

"I didn't know how well the NKGB had infiltrated the Brits' Second Army. They had to be all over, otherwise Serov wouldn't know that released Russians were the first to grab Himmler. Or the names of the British officers there. Or how he died and where they buried him."

"You know what I didn't see in there?" Ginger said, her tone furious. "Not one mention of Himmler's number two."

"Von Dietelburg?" Cronley asked.

"SS-Brigadeführer Franz von Dietelburg," she said, practically spitting out the name.

"She's right," Williams said. "And now that it has come up, I find that very interesting."

"So do I," Cohen said.

"What should be considered more important," Ginger demanded, "Himmler's heir or the Vatican's money?"

She waited for an answer and, when none was offered, went on. "Since I don't think the Vatican is any happier with Saint Heinrich and his new religion than we are, you should be working with them, not stealing their money."

"What would you suggest we do," Williams asked, his tone sarcastic, "go to the Pope and say, 'Your Holiness, we're on the same page vis-à-vis von Dietelburg'?"

Ginger glared at him.

"Maybe not the Pope," she said, "but the cardinal. Let the cardinal go to the Pope."

"I think Ginger is onto something," Father McGrath said.

There was a long silence.

"Facts bearing on the problem," Cronley then said, formally, using the phase that begins every U.S. Army staff study. "One, Father Jack knows more about Holy Mother Church than any one of us, and we're going to take his advice—"

"Well, I'm glad that he agrees with me," Ginger said. "But I am going to mention in passing that making friends with the Vatican, instead of royally pissing them off, is my idea."

After a long pause, Cronley went on, "Fact two:

Serov told me he arranged for von Dietelburg and Burgdorf to escape from the AVO in Budapest and that he has had people on them. He said yesterday they were headed for Helmstedt, on the Autobahn crossing between the Russian Zone and ours, where they intended to bribe a truck driver to smuggle them into Berlin."

"How about this for fact three?" Williams put in. "We have an ongoing investigation into those Berlin-bound truck drivers. A lot of paperless people are using them to get across the Russian Zone into Berlin. We have heard, credibly, that once the truck gets into a relatively empty area in East Germany, the smuggled passengers are killed and their bodies left a hundred yards or so from the Autobahn. The truck then proceeds to Berlin with their luggage."

"Is this organized," Cohen said, "or random?"

"I don't think a truck driver is going to be able to successfully take on von Dietelburg and Burgdorf," Cronley said. "So, by now, they're in Berlin. But where? Serov's people couldn't get on a truck with them."

"But they could get word to Serov," Cohen said, "with the truck's description and license plate. And have his people meet it here."

"I don't know if this qualifies as one of your facts, Jim," McGrath said, "but if we're going to go to His Holiness with this, we should apply some real pressure. Tell him (a) that it's going to be rumored in the world press that they have many millions of Nazi dollars in their vault, (b) that they had better get rid of it, and (c) that we know they know of many places where all that money can be put to good use."

"The press wouldn't touch a story like that," Williams said. "Attacking the Vatican is number one on their no-no list."

"Janice would touch it," Ginger said. "Janice would love a story like that."

"Who's Janice?" Williams asked.

"My fiancé's former girlfriend," Ginger said.

"Miss Janice Johansen of the Associated Press," Cronley said. "We were—are—just friends. Nothing more. When Serov kidnapped Colonel—"

"Friends? Pinocchio, your nose is growing," Ginger said, her tone mock sweet.

"Kidnapped who?" Williams asked.

"Colonel Robert Mattingly, chief of DCI-Europe," Cohen furnished. "Super Spook had turned Colonel Sergei Likharev. Serov wanted him back. Wanted him and his wife, Natalia, and their two boys."

"I never heard about that," Williams said. "There was nothing in the papers. I didn't even hear about it back-channel."

"You weren't supposed to hear about it,"

Cronley said. "I came up with a Russian who Serov wanted even more than Likharev. We made the swap. In exchange for going onto the Glienicke Bridge with me, to take pictures, Janice filed a story that the exchange was of a Russian officer who had been arrested for public drunkenness in West Germany, and an American officer who had been arrested for drunken driving in East Germany."

"I saw that in **Stars and Stripes**," Williams said. "My reaction was that our colonel could forget becoming a general."

"It is to be devoutly hoped," Cronley said. "Anyway, Janice would love to have this Vatican story. I think we should drop her name into our conversation but keep her out of it for now."

"You're not really serious about kidnapping an archbishop?" Williams asked.

Colonel Cohen stood up, and said, "Let's go."

"For a moment, I was actually worried," Williams said.

Cohen shrugged. "Where I'm going, Colonel, is to see what advice General Serov can offer vis-à-vis kidnapping a senior member of the Vatican hierarchy with as little fuss as possible. If you don't want to come, give me the keys to your car."

Williams took the keys from his pocket and handed them to Cohen.

"Colonel," McGrath said. "Ginger, because of

the baby, obviously can't go. But I can. And I might be useful."

Cohen looked at him.

"Maybe and maybe not," he said, finally. "But the bottom line is, Father Jack, none of this is any of your business. So, thanks but no thanks."

"Hey, that's my call, Mort," Cronley protested.

"I planned to get into this in the car," Cohen said. "But, what the hell, now's as good a time as any. The next time you address me, Captain Cronley, you will call me Colonel and preface your comments with 'sir.' Say 'Yes, sir.'"

When Cronley did not immediately reply, Cohen went on. "I may very possibly land in Leavenworth because of this operation, but if that happens, it will be because I'm calling the shots, not taking orders from a twenty-two-year-old captain. Now say 'Yes, sir,' Captain, or consider yourself under arrest."

After deciding this was not the time or place to get into a who's-in-charge war, Cronley said, "Yes, sir."

"Go get Ostrowski," Cohen ordered, and walked out of the room.

Colonel Williams was left alone in the dining room with Father McGrath and Ginger and her baby.

Then he hurried out of the room.

"I'm coming," he called.

VIII

[ONE]
Kaiser Wilhelm Church
Berlin, International Zone of
Occupation, Germany
0845 21 April 1946

Cronley had driven or walked past the ruined church often but never been inside. When he, Cohen, Ostrowski, and Williams walked inside now, he was first impressed by the enormous size of the building, and then the damage to it.

It was just an empty hulk.

The altar was a fire-scarred marble oblong. A cross—with what was left of Christ nailed to it, the head and legs were missing—hung behind the altar. The windows were gone except for a few remnants of stained glass. The only thing that seemed intact was the inlaid marble floor, which had been swept clean.

There were perhaps forty people in the church. Neither General Serov nor his deputy, Sergei Alekseevich, were among them, and Cronley couldn't pick out among the other people in the church who might be NKGB agents.

"Let's wait for Serov outside," Cronley said.

As they passed through what had been the vestibule, three Polish DCI agents in battered civilian clothing passed them. They showed no sign of recognition.

A minute or so later, a battered Opel Kapitän with Berlin civilian license plates pulled into the parking area. Alekseevich was behind the wheel.

Cohen trotted to the parked car, arriving at it as Serov, with some difficulty, opened the passenger-side door.

"We have to talk," Cohen said.

"No time. The cardinal is about to arrive."

"Now. It's important."

Serov considered that, then said, "Why don't we walk over to the Kempinski while Sergei keeps an eye on the church?"

[TWO]
Coffee Shop
Kempinski Bristol Hotel
Kurfürstendamm 25
Berlin, International Zone of
Occupation, Germany
0905 21 April 1946

Serov, with a cup of tea, and Cohen and Cronley, with cups of coffee, took their seats at a small, round table.

"What's so important, Mort?"

"We have an idea that will probably solve a lot of our problems."

Serov gestured anxiously. "In as few words as possible?"

Cohen locked eyes. "Instead of snatching a briefcase that may or may not have a million dollars in it, we snatch an archbishop—"

Serov, sipping his tea, pulled the cup from his lips. "And I suppose you suggest we hold him for ransom?" he said, sarcastically.

"—to enlist him in our noble cause."

"Think about it, Ivan," Cronley said. "What do you think are numbers three and four, after the Soviet Union and the United States, on the Vatican's worry list?"

Serov considered that for a minute. "You tell me."

"We think it's Himmler's heretic religion, then getting their bank exposed as the depository for the Nazis' money."

"You and Super Spook came up with this all by yourselves, did you, Colonel Cohen?"

"Actually, it was Ginger's idea," Cronley said.

"Well, they say that when one is faced with a problem, one should seek the counsel of the most experienced person one knows."

"Fuck you, Ivan," Cronley said.

"That's what we're doing, Ivan," Cohen said. "We hoped the most experienced person we know in this area of expertise would counsel us vis-à-vis the kidnapping of a Vatican prelate."

Serov shook his head in disgust. "In one word: Don't."

Cohen placed his cup on the table and stood up.

"Oh, have I hurt your feelings?" Serov said, taking a casual sip of tea, before adding, "I am so sorry."

"That's good to know. See you around, Ivan."

"You don't have to go," Serov said.

"How am I going to kidnap an archbishop if I sit here watching you drinking tea?"

Cohen turned away. "Ready, Captain Cronley?"

"Yes, sir."

"We'll keep you posted, Serov . . . But, on reflection, I don't see why we should."

Serov shook his head as he watched them walk out of the coffee shop.

Cronley and Cohen were just about to enter the vestibule of the church when Serov caught up with them. He was a bit short of breath, suggesting that he had been running to catch up to them.

"Let's talk," Serov said. "I've had second thoughts."

"Such as?" Cohen asked.

"If you two persist, as I am very afraid you will, our joint plan of operation will be Foo . . . What is that vulgar phrase of yours, James?"

"FUBAR?"

"Precisely. 'Fouled Up Beyond All Repair.'"

"That's **Fucked Up**, Ivan," Cronley said.

"Vulgarity is something a young officer such as yourself should really try to avoid."

"So, what are you thinking, Serov?" Cohen asked.

"That I have no choice but to lend my expertise to your crazy plan."

"And how do you plan to do that? Kidnap an archbishop yourself?" Cronley said.

"No offense, but I frankly don't think you two could carry it off without attracting a lot of attention."

"I'm crushed," Cronley said. "The last time you kidnapped somebody—one Colonel Mattingly—I seem to recall his bullet-ridden car attracted a lot of attention."

"I really don't expect an archbishop to pull a pistol from under his priestly robes."

"Do I gather you don't want Super Spook's and my assistance in your snatch?" Cohen asked.

Serov took a notebook from his pocket. As he scrawled in it, he said, "What I want you to do is go inside the church and tell your men to stand down from snatching anyone's briefcase. Then get in a taxi and go here. You'll be expected."

He tore out a page from his notebook, handed it to Cohen, who read it and then handed it to Cronley. On it Serov had written "Hotel Majestic, Zillenstrasse 104, Charlottenburg."

"May I ask a question, Ivan?" Cronley said.

"Of course."

"Where's von Dietelburg and Burgdorf?"

After a time, Serov said, "In the next hours, and days, we're going to have to trust each other. As proof of my intentions, I'm going to tell you the truth about that. The bastards got away from us. My men found the truck with the driver dead—slit throat—right off the Autobahn. I have no idea where they are."

"Shit," Cohen and Cronley said, on top of each other.

"We are, of course, looking for them," Serov said. "I'm going inside now. Wait sixty seconds before you go in."

They watched Serov enter the church.

"I'll go in," Cohen said. "You stay here and keep your eyes and ears open."

Cohen was inside for five minutes before he came out. Max Ostrowski was with him.

"What did you tell your guys?" Cronley asked.

"They're going to stay and keep their eyes on Serov's people," Ostrowski said.

"They know who they are?"

Ostrowski snorted. "Jim, we have been keeping eyes on NKGB agents since we were in knickers. We're pretty good at it."

"Let's get a cab," Cohen said. "You come with us, Ostrowski."

[THREE]
Hotel Majestic
Zillenstrasse 104
Charlottenburg, Berlin, Russian Zone
of Occupation, Germany
1010 21 April 1946

The hotel doorman wore a once elegant, now tattered greatcoat with a gold aiguillette draped from his left shoulder. Behind him stood a bellboy in an equally elegant, equally battered uniform.

"Oh, good," Ostrowski quipped, "a Russian whorehouse."

As the bellboy rushed to open the door, a well-dressed man came down the shallow flight of stairs and walked quickly to the taxi. He popped to attention and bobbed his head.

"Major Pietr Rodinski at your orders, Colonel Cohen. If you would be so kind, gentlemen, please follow me."

He spoke in accentless American English.

They followed him up the stairs and into the hotel. It took Cronley about five seconds to decide they were in the Berlin version of Vienna's Hotel Viktoria, a combination gambling palace and brothel catering to the most successful black marketeers.

Confirmation came quickly as they passed through a corridor off the lobby. Doors, fully or partially open, revealed a bar, a card room, a room with vingt-et-un and roulette tables, and a living room. In the latter were ten scantily clad hookers, all obviously sleepy.

At the end of the corridor, there was a steel door. Major Rodinski unlocked it, opened it, waved them toward a flight of stairs, and then locked the door behind them. At the foot of the stairs was a tunnel, and, at the end of the tunnel, another staircase leading upward. Then they came to a final door, which Rodinski waved them through with a bow.

They found themselves in what Cronley thought could be the sitting room of one of the better suites in a five-star hotel.

"There's coffee and pastry," Major Rodinski said, pointing toward a bar attended by a white-jacketed waiter. "And, of course, spirits. If there is anything else that would give you pleasure while you're waiting, just ask."

Cronley thought, **Is he talking about the hookers?**

"What or who are waiting for?" Cronley asked.

There was a flicker of hesitation on Rodinski's face, before he replied, "Why, the general, of course. I thought you understood."

Gotcha!

"You mean General Alekseevich?"

"No, General Serov."

"I thought Polkóvnik Serov was General Alekseevich's deputy."

As if speaking to a backward child, Rodinski said, slowly, "No, Captain Cronley, it's **General** Serov and **Polkóvnik** Alekseevich. Polkóvnik Alekseevich is General Serov's deputy."

"I guess I've been misinformed. That often happens, I've noticed, whenever I deal with the NKGB."

Rodinski's face tensed, but he didn't reply.

A buzzer sounded somewhere behind the bar. It stopped buzzing, started again, and then buzzed a third time.

That's more than just buzzing, Cronley decided. **That's a signal, a message of some kind.**

Proof of this came immediately. The bartender reached under his counter and came out with a German Schmeisser submachine gun. He quickly worked the action, chambering a cartridge, and then put the weapon back where it had been.

Rodinski went quickly to the door, put his back to the wall beside it, and took a Tokarev TT-33 pistol from a shoulder holster under his jacket.

Without thinking about it, Cronley hoisted his Ike jacket out of the way, drew his .45 from its holster, and thumbed the safety off.

The door opened, and two burly men, in somewhat ragged-looking civilian clothing, led a third man into the room. He had a bag on his head, and his hands were tied in front.

Rodinski put his pistol back in his holster as a third man in ragged clothing entered the room carrying a tan leather briefcase. Cronley thumbed the safety back on and holstered his .45 as he walked over to the man.

Without asking, Cronley snatched the briefcase and carried it to the bar and opened it.

Rodinski, his face showing his anger, walked quickly to him. Cronley shoved the opened case over to him. It was stuffed with currency—English pounds, Swiss francs, and American dollar bills.

"Bingo, Pietr!" Cronley said. "Your guys have hit the mother lode."

"I will take the suitcase, please, Captain Cronley," Rodinski said, icily.

"Help yourself, Pietr, as long as you don't try to take it out of this room."

Cronley turned to Ostrowski. "Max, see who's under the hood."

"I will remind you, Captain Cronley, that I'm in charge here," Rodinski said.

"No you're not, Pietr. Until General Serov shows up, he is." Cronley pointed at Colonel Cohen. "Colonels rank the hell out of majors."

The door opened, and Serov entered the room.

"Problem solved. Here's the good general now. How they hanging, Ivan?"

Serov gave him a cold look, then walked up to the hooded man.

"Who the hell is he?" Serov demanded. "God-damn it, James, I thought we understood each other."

"We don't know who he is, Ivan," Cronley said. "Ask your guys. They brought him in. And look what he had with him."

He held the briefcase open for Serov's inspection.

Serov's eyes widened, and he turned to the men

who had grabbed the hooded man. They bolted to attention.

"I don't know if I should put you in for a decoration or have you shot for disobeying orders."

Then Serov turned and jerked the hood off the man. He was nearly bald, short, and pudgy. He wore a black business suit, with a clerical collar at his neck. Rope bound his hands in front of him, and there was a cloth stuffed in his mouth.

The man glared at Serov.

"Take that gag off," Serov ordered. "Untie his hands."

His men quickly complied.

"I am General Serov of the NKGB," he said, his tone cold. "And that is Colonel Cohen of the American Counterintelligence Corps. Who are you, Father?"

The man didn't reply.

"Search him," Serov ordered.

One of his men said, "We have already done that, sir."

He handed Serov what looked like a wallet and a rosary. Serov went through the wallet.

"Well, Monsignor Rosetti," Serov then said. "While I regret the circumstances, it is a genuine pleasure to meet a papal chamberlain. Have you ever met a papal chamberlain, Colonel Cohen?"

"Can't say that I have. As a matter of fact, I don't know what a papal chamberlain is. And now that I think about it, I don't know what a monsignor is either."

"The level of your ignorance vis-à-vis the Holy Mother Church is utterly shocking," Serov said, with mock contempt. "I suggest you take notes, Colonel, as there will be an examination."

The monsignor looked in disbelief and/or confusion between the two.

"I shall start with basics," Serov went on. "A monsignor is a priest who has been honored with that title for his services above and beyond the call of duty."

"Okay," Cohen said.

"Do I have that right, Monsignor?" Serov asked.

"That is correct," the monsignor said, with some hesitation.

That's the first time he's said anything, Cronley thought.

"And a chamberlain?" Cohen asked.

"A **papal** chamberlain is a title bestowed by the Pope. It usually goes to high-ranking clergy—bishops and archbishops—but sometimes to others. Members of the Italian nobility . . . Is that the case with you, Monsignor?"

The monsignor didn't reply at first, but then said, "I am a member of the Rosetti family."

"Thank you," Serov said.

"The Pope sometimes awards them to laymen," Serov went on. "Franz von Papen was so honored."

"The German diplomat?" Cronley asked, surprised.

"The German diplomat," Serov confirmed. "The story going around at the time was that when His Holiness was papal nuncio in Berlin, von Papen was very useful to the Vatican. What about that, Monsignor?"

"Who are you people?" the monsignor blurted. "What is going on here?"

"I told you who we are," Serov said. "And what we're doing right now is waiting. May I offer you a cup of coffee and a pastry?"

That the monsignor had recovered his composure now became apparent.

"Do you have any idea who it is that you have kidnapped? Are you aware that I'm in Berlin at the invitation of the Honorable John Jay McCloy?"

"We know you're in Berlin to pass a million-plus dollars of Odessa's money to Odessa," Cohen said.

That put the monsignor back in his indignation mode.

"I have no idea what you're talking about," he said.

"Shocking!" Cronley offered. "I never thought I would see a monsignor and a papal chamberlain lying through his teeth!"

"I'll tell you this, young man!" the monsignor said, clearly losing his temper. "In this life, and the next, you are going to regret ever having laid eyes on me!"

The telephone rang. They heard one of Serov's men answer it, then announce, "General, the archbishop is ten minutes out."

"I guess Cardinal von Hassburger wasn't available," Serov said, to no one in particular. "Not a problem."

"While we're waiting," Cronley said, "why don't we count the money and see exactly how much of a withdrawal Odessa was making from the Vatican Bank?"

Cronley turned the briefcase over on the bar, dumping the contents onto it. He began stacking the Swiss francs with other Swiss francs, the English pounds with other English pounds. He held up a thick stack of American five-hundred-dollar bills to Serov.

"Ivan, since the NKGB knows everything, how much are pounds and francs worth in real money?"

"Call somebody and find out," Serov ordered.

One of his men hurried to pick up the telephone.

[FOUR]

Fifteen minutes later, just after they determined the currency in the briefcase was worth $2,010,458 in U.S. dollars, the bound, gagged, and bagged archbishop was led into the room.

Cronley was surprised and a little disappointed even before Rodinski pulled the black bag from his head. The archbishop was smaller than, though not as pudgy as, the monsignor. And when the bag was removed from his head, his face was that of a pale, visibly frightened sixty-odd-year-old.

The archbishop's eyes darted from man to man, then grew wider when he saw Monsignor Rosetti.

Serov waited until Rodinski had removed the cloth from his mouth and untied his hands before addressing him.

"Relax, Your Grace. We're not going to burn you at the stake. All we want you to do is carry a message to Cardinal von Hassburger."

The archbishop ignored him, instead demanding of the monsignor, "What's going on here, Rosetti?"

"Your Grace, I was . . . kidnapped . . . by these people off the street. And they have the briefcase."

The archbishop looked around the room and spotted the open case and the stacks of currency beside it.

"That briefcase and its contents," the archbishop declared, indignant, "are the property of the Papal Delegation to the United States Military Government of Germany. I demand its immediate return and our immediate release."

"Duly noted, Your Grace," Serov said. "Do you have any further demands before we get to the reason why I asked that you join us here?"

"Just who are you, sir?"

"I am General Ivan Serov of the Soviet Union's NKGB, Your Grace. Please forgive me for not introducing myself upon your arrival. And these gentlemen are Captain James D. Cronley, of the American Central Intelligence Directorate, and Colonel Mortimer Cohen, of the U.S. Army Counterintelligence Corps."

The archbishop's eyes darted toward Cohen and Cronley, then stared at them as if he wanted to memorize their faces. The look of fear was no longer on his face.

"Now," Serov said, "as for the message we want you to deliver to His Eminence Cardinal von Hassburger. The . . . How much was it, Super Spook?"

"A little over two million U.S., General."

"Ah, yes. The two-million-dollar-plus withdrawal of illicit funds from the Vatican Bank that Monsignor Rosetti was in the process of delivering to representatives of Odessa has been seized by the United States DCI working in conjunction with the Soviet NKGB."

"I have no idea what you're talking about!"

"I'm disappointed. I was led to believe you enjoy His Eminence's confidence. But no matter. When you relay our message to him, His Eminence will understand. Please assure him that neither the NKGB nor the DCI has any intention of trying to embarrass the Holy See in this matter—for example, to have it spread all over the world by the press. Quite the contrary. We are hoping that he—the Holy See—will work with us to eliminate a truly unholy mutual threat."

"I will say again, General Whatever-your-name-is, I have no idea what you're talking about."

"And once again, no matter. What is important is, His Eminence does. I'm going to give you a telephone number at which His Eminence, if he so desires, can reach me to arrange for a meeting. Got the message straight, Your Grace?"

"I heard what you said."

"Now, insofar as returning you is concerned, will you give me your word not to make a fuss while you're being moved? In order to avoid the gag and the tied hands?"

"And the bag on my head?"

"That, unfortunately, I consider necessary. Well?"

"You have my word."

"Put the bags on them," Serov ordered.

From under his bag, the archbishop said, "This will not end here, General!"

"I certainly hope not, Your Grace. I await His Eminence's call."

Rodinski opened the door, and Serov's men guided the monsignor and the archbishop through it.

When the door closed. Cronley looked at Serov.

"Now what?"

"They will be released near the Kaiser Wilhelm Church. I am confident that as soon as he can, the archbishop will let the cardinal know all is not well. But because he cannot tell him while General Clay is showing him around the church, he will have to do it later. That gives us plenty of time to go to your safe house in Zehlendorf."

Serov made a **Follow me** gesture. He led them down the stairs, back through the tunnel, and then down another flight of stairs. There was no door this time, and Cronley saw that they were in a garage.

Half a dozen Soviet soldiers armed with submachine guns bolted to attention when they saw Serov. There was a line of midsize Mercedes touring cars parked nose out against the wall. One of the soldiers ran to the largest and shiniest of them and opened the rear door.

"James, you and Ostrowski ride with Aleksee-vich," Serov ordered, then walked to the open door and got in.

As Cronley and Ostrowski entered Alekseevich's vehicle, Cronley in front and Ostrowski in back, two soldiers ran with their submachine guns to a third car, which then immediately drove to a ramp and stopped, obviously preparing to head up what was to be a convoy.

Serov's car pulled behind the first Mercedes, and then Alekseevich's car, with Cronley and Os-trowski, did the same. A fourth vehicle pulled in behind them.

Cronley thought, **That first car is painted a sort of flat black, including its chrome.**

Serov's car is shiny black, and its chrome gleams. This car is the same, but smaller than Serov's, yet larger than the lead and tail cars.

And they're all Mercedeses, "liberated" from the defeated enemy. The war's been over almost a year, and they're still riding around in German cars? An NKGB general officer in a small Benz?

Why? Because that's all they have.

The Soviet Union is broke.

People and governments that are broke are desperate, and desperate means dangerous.

I'll have to keep that in mind.

[FIVE]
44-46 Beerenstrasse
Zehlendorf, Berlin, American Zone of
Occupation, Germany
1135 21 April 1946

When the four-vehicle convoy tried to turn onto Beerenstrasse, a German policeman was standing in the middle of the street, blocking their way.

"Now what?" Cronley wondered aloud.

"Looks like a fire or something down the street," Ostrowski called from the rear seat.

Beyond the policeman, three-quarters of the way down the next block, there was a gaggle of police and fire vehicles in the street. All were German except for a single American MP jeep.

Cronley made the quick judgment that if the activity wasn't concentrated in front of 44-46, it damn sure was close enough to be of concern.

"Let's go, Max," Cronley ordered, opening the car door.

Cronley started running down the middle of the street. He heard a siren, an American one, screaming behind him, and glanced over his shoulder. Beyond Ostrowski, who was running right behind him, Cronley saw that it belonged to a Buick staff car that was turning onto Beerenstrasse, its red lights flashing and tires squealing.

As they moved to run on the sidewalk, Cronley heard another MP jeep, also with lights flashing and siren roaring, flying up behind the Buick.

A moment later, Cronley muttered, "Oh, shit!"

They were now close enough to be able to see that 44-46 was the center of attention. Water filled the street from fire hoses that were snaked inside the house. Then he saw smoke, a wispy strand of white, escaping into the air above the open front door.

The Buick roared past and stopped at the house, its nose against the fence. Three men bolted from the car and ran toward the building.

That's Homer Greene in front!

Cronley wondered what the chief of Army Security Agency, Europe, CIC-USFET, was doing here, then remembered that Oscar Schultz had talked Brigadier General Greene into providing the safe house cover of being living quarters for South American Airlines personnel.

Cronley, panting from his run, finally reached the door of 44-46 Beerenstrasse a minute later.

He was intercepted by the two men who had arrived with Greene. Standing shoulder to shoulder, they acted as a wall, preventing Cronley from entering the house. Greene, his face weary, came to the doorway.

"What the hell happened here, General?" Cronley said.

"We are working at figuring that out, Jim."

Max Ostrowski came up, breathing heavy from his exertion, took a quick look past them, and muttered something in Polish.

Cronley then looked beyond Greene and the men barring his way. There were two male bodies on the floor of the foyer. One, partially and inadequately covered by a bloody tablecloth, Cronley recognized as Pavel Dumlovski, one of his DCI agents.

"Ginger?" Cronley asked, quickly. "Mrs. Moriarty?"

"You don't want to go in there," Greene said.

Cronley turned and pushed his shoulder past Greene's men, bolting into the house. Ostrowski followed, in the process knocking one of the men off his feet. Greene stepped back.

Cronley then saw that the foyer held a third body, another Polish DCI agent. Cronley ran toward the dining room door, where smoke flowed out the door.

Father Jack McGrath was laying on his back, his chest bloody and his unseeing eyes wide open. The dining room table was on its side.

Cronley entered the room and walked around the table.

And then he saw her.

Ginger was laying on her back, her legs twisted in a grotesque way, her midsection torn open, the left side of her face gone.

"Jesus Christ, no!" Cronley wailed.

He knelt beside her, his right knee in the pool of blood from her head. He reached out and caressed the right side of her face.

And then he jumped to his feet.

"Bruce!" he yelled, rapidly scanning the room. "Where the fuck is the baby?"

Ostrowski went to Cronley, wrapped his arms around him, then half dragged, half carried him out of the dining room into the foyer.

Greene's men hurried to help Ostrowski control Cronley.

The sound of an indignant infant crying came from somewhere nearby.

Cronley turned to the sound and saw a German fireman in black rubber coveralls coming down the stairway holding the infant, wrapped in a blanket, in his arms.

"Oh, Jesus!" Cronley groaned, shook free of Ostrowski's grip, and went to the fireman. "Give him to me. He's mine."

The fireman, more than a little reluctantly, gently handed over the infant.

Cronley automatically held Baby Bruce in his arms, as Ginger had taught him, then rocked him gently. The baby stopped howling.

Cronley said, his voice breaking, "Looks like it's just you and me from now on, little man."

Greene walked to him. "Is he all right?"

"Hungry, I'm sure. He's always hungry. And he smells like he needs his diaper changed."

"My people tell me he's the . . . sole survivor."

Cronley nodded but didn't trust his voice to reply.

Cohen, Serov, and Alekseevich walked up to them. Cronley saw that they weren't out of breath and that Serov was carrying the briefcase with the money in it. Cronley reasoned that the credentials of one of them had been good enough to get past the policeman.

"This place looks like a slaughterhouse," Serov declared.

"And among the slaughtered are Father Jack and Ginger," Cronley said.

"Dear God!" Cohen exclaimed. "Jim, I'm so sorry!"

Serov crossed himself and went to Cronley. He gingerly embraced him and then kissed his cheek. Greene's face betrayed his surprise at the gesture of affection, but he quickly recovered.

"Colonel Cohen," Greene ordered, "I'm going to ask you to hold the fort until the cavalry arrives. They're on the way."

"Where are you going, sir?" Cohen said.

"I do not wish to deliver my report to General Clay over the phone."

"If you're going to see General Clay," Cronley announced, "I'm going with you."

"Out of the question," Greene snapped. "With an infant in your arms and in a blood-soaked uniform? You will stay here, Captain, until we find time to deal with your problems."

"Somehow, General Greene," Serov said, "I think General Clay, when we walk into his office, would prefer to hear from Captain Cronley himself why he had a baby in his arms and a blood-soaked uniform."

"We?" Greene said. He stared at Serov, then softened and nodded.

Serov turned to Cohen.

"When the cardinal calls, Colonel, tell him I'll get back to him as soon as I can. Let's go, Alekseevich."

IX

[ONE]
Office of the Commander in Chief
United States Forces European
Theater
Berlin, American Zone of Occupation,
Germany
1255 21 April 1946

"General Clay, forgive us for bursting in this way," Serov said as he entered Clay's office carrying the Vatican briefcase, "but this is a matter of some urgency."

Cronley, with Baby Bruce, was just steps ahead of two of Clay's aides-de-camp and his sergeant major, who were rushing after them with the obvious intention of throwing them out.

General Lucius D. Clay rose from behind his desk and made a **Stop!** gesture to his men.

"It's always a pleasure to welcome a distinguished Soviet officer to USFET headquarters, General," Clay replied, then said, "My God, Cronley! What's going on? You're covered in blood! And . . . whose baby?"

"Sir," Cronley announced. "Odessa just hit our safe house in Zehlendorf—"

"General Greene is aware of the situation, General," Serov interrupted him. "He was at the scene when Colonel Cohen, Captain Cronley, and I arrived. He was on his way to report to you when there was a problem."

"What kind of a problem?"

"General Greene was involved in a car crash."

"Is he all right? What kind of a car crash?"

"Apparently quite all right—some fender damage, is all," Serov said. "The driver of my escort car thought that the driver of General Greene's car was trying to force me off the road and felt it was his duty to keep him from doing so."

Clay's raised eyebrows showed how little he believed that story. But he didn't challenge it.

"Cronley, how much damage did the attack on your safe house cause?" Clay said.

"This infant is the sole survivor, sir. All of my DCI agents are down—all seven—and Father McGrath and Mrs. Moriarty, the child's mother. The sonsofbitches used Schmeissers and hand grenades."

"By down, you mean dead?"

"Yes, sir."

"Son of a bitch! Do we have people there?"

"On our way here, sir, it looked like every MP in Berlin was headed for Beerenstrasse," Cronley said.

Clay looked around the room, then at his men.

"Okay, so this is what we're going to do. Sergeant Major, call the ops room and tell the SIGABA operator I want Mr. Justice Jackson and Admiral Souers on the line by the time we get there. When you've done that, call the hospital and tell them I want a pediatric nurse and a pediatric physician and whatever it takes to sustain an infant for forty-eight hours sent here by ambulance. Likewise, I want a second ambulance with a trauma physician and a trauma nurse."

"Sir," Cronley said, "I'm not wounded—"

"Button your lip, Cronley! In your frame of mind, you wouldn't notice if you were missing an arm."

He pointed toward one of his aides.

"Find General Makamson and ask him to join me in the ops room. General Makamson only."

"Yes, sir."

"And then call Mrs. Clay and tell her I need her right now. When she and the medics get here, send them to the ops room. Same with General Greene, when and if he shows up here."

"Yes, sir."

"And when you've done that, go by the officers' sales store and get Captain Cronley a pair of trousers. Size, Cronley?"

"Thirty-four/thirty-eight, sir."

[TWO]
Operations Room
Office of the Commander in Chief
United States Forces European Theater
Berlin, American Zone of Occupation, Germany
1305 21 April 1946

"What's going on, General?" Lieutenant General Makamson asked as he came into the ops room.

Clay responded by putting his index finger to his lips and then using it as a pointer, indicating where he wanted Makamson to sit.

The voice of Justice Jackson came loudly over the SIGABA speakers. "I got to the SIGABA as soon as I could, Lucius. What's the urgency?"

Clay said, "General Serov, this is General Makamson, my G-2."

"Did I hear that correctly, Lucius? General Serov?"

"Yes, Mr. Justice Jackson," Serov called out.

Cronley then announced, "Odessa hit the safe house, sir—"

"Odessa did what, Jimmy?" Cletus Frade's voice came over the speaker.

"—Nine KIA," Cronley went on, his voice breaking. "Including Father McGrath and Ginger."

"Jesus H. Christ," Frade said.

"Who's that?" General Clay demanded.

"Cletus Frade. Who you?"

"Lucius Clay."

"I'd say, 'Good morning, General,' but that somehow doesn't seem appropriate, does it?"

"I had hoped to speak with Admiral Souers."

"He should be here in a couple of minutes," Frade said. "Jimmy, what about Ginger's baby?"

"I've got him on my lap. He's the only survivor."

"Well, thank God for that."

"I'm a little confused, Mr. Frade," Clay said. "What, exactly, is your role within the DCI?"

"Well, at the moment, with the admiral out strolling with the President, and Oscar Schultz looking for them, I suppose I'm the DCI."

Makamson snapped: "Even for a Marine colonel, Colonel, isn't that a bit presumptuous?"

"Who you?"

"I am General Makamson."

"Be advised, General, that having just been told that two people very dear to me have been murdered, I'm in no mood for any of your chickenshit observations."

General Clay slapped his hand on the table.

"Enough!" he barked. "Both of you, say 'Yes, sir.'"

Both officers said, "Yes, sir."

"What we're going to do now," Clay went on, "is lay out this incident chronologically and then try to fill in the blanks. Understood?"

[THREE]

Fifteen minutes later, Admiral Souers's voice came over the SIGABA speakers. "This is Souers. Frade just told me we have nine KIA?"

"Odessa hit the safe house, sir," Cronley said. "The nine KIA include Mrs. Moriarty and Father McGrath."

"How do you know it was Odessa?" Souers asked.

"What we've been doing, Admiral," General Clay said, "is trying to lay out a time line and then come back and fill in the blanks."

"That hasn't been going well," Mr. Justice Jackson said. "What I was about to suggest to General Clay, Sid, is that when you came online, we start over, with Cronley telling us what happened. How does that sound?"

"So far as I'm concerned," Clay said, "the floor is yours, Captain Cronley."

"Begin, Cronley," Souers said.

"Yes, sir. I'd say it began when General Serov determined that the Odessa money we've been looking for was in the Vatican Bank."

"In **where**?" Souers asked.

"May I suggest," Clay said, "that we hold our questions until Cronley finishes?"

"Get it out, Cronley," Souers said.

"Yes, sir. In the Vatican Bank. And we have the proof. We caught Cardinal von Hassburger trying to deliver just over two million dollars to Odessa."

"Who the hell is Cardinal von Hassburger?" Souers asked.

"May I suggest, again," Clay asked, impatiently, "that we hold our questions until Cronley is finished?"

"Some questions won't wait, Lucius," Justice Jackson said. "Starting with the press. There has been an obvious explosion. Since we can't afford to have it get out what really happened at the safe house, what are we going to say?"

"I suggest the following," Oscar Shultz said. "That two Americans were among the nine people found dead in the transient hotel of South American Airways in the Berlin suburb of Zehlendorf today. German police believe their deaths were the result of a botched burglary of the often empty villa, and the subsequent fire was meant to cover up any evidence. The victims were tentatively identified as Mrs. Virginia Moriarty, from Texas, and the Reverend J. R. McGrath, D.D., a professor of religion at the University of the South. Et cetera, et cetera."

"That'll do it," Clay said. "Especially if we can sell it to that American reporter . . . What's her name?"

"The AP's Janice Johansen, sir," Cronley said. "She has been very cooperative."

"General Makamson," Clay said, "get with the PIO, locate Miss Johansen, and bring her here. No. To the hospital."

"The hospital, sir?" Cronley asked. "Why the hospital?"

"Because, Captain Cronley, that's where you're going to be. This conference will resume at seventeen-hundred hours. Let's go, Makamson."

Clay and Makamson stood up and walked out of the Operations Room.

"Admiral Souers, sir?" Cronley said. "Oscar?"

There was no answer, and he realized they had broken down the SIGABA connection.

Cronley was looking at the closed door, wondering what was going to happen next, when it opened. Two men wearing doctor smocks entered, followed by a pair of nurses and three burly hospital corpsmen.

Then a middle-aged, gray-haired woman came into the room. She headed right for Cronley. She put her face nose to nose to the infant.

"Hello, beautiful boy," she said.

Then she looked up at Cronley.

"I'm Alice Clay. Can I hold him while they fix you up?"

Cronley neither replied nor even reacted.

"James," Serov said, "give her the infant. You cannot hold him forever. And he is in dire need of a change of diaper."

After some hesitation, he handed the infant to her.

"Thank you, Mrs. Clay."

"Of course, Captain. And my deep condolences at the loss of your fiancée."

He nodded.

She forced a small smile, then quickly left the room with the infant, followed by the pediatric team.

Cronley's throat tightened, his eyes watered, and he had an almost irresistible urge to weep.

He was brought back when one of the doctors asked, "How bad's your leg, Captain?"

"There's nothing wrong with my leg."

"Where'd all the blood come from?"

"Fuck you," Cronley said.

"Captain, we can do this the easy way or we can do this the hard way. Are you going to get on my stretcher, or am I going to have to stick a needle in you?"

Serov said, "Captain Cronley will go with you, Doctor. He doesn't need a stretcher. And if you attempt to stick a needle in him, I will shoot you."

"Who the hell are you?"

"General Ivan Serov. And I will accompany you and Captain Cronley to the hospital."

"I'm afraid that's not possible, General Serov."

"Then he doesn't go to the hospital. Look around you, Doctor. Do you see anyone in a position to order a Soviet general officer to do, or not do, anything?"

The doctor gestured toward the door. "Captain, your ambulance awaits."

[FOUR]
Room 234-C
1512th Field Hospital
Berlin, American Zone of Occupation,
Germany
1505 21 April 1946

The small room was furnished with a hospital bed, a white bedside table, on which sat a telephone that didn't work, two white, straight-backed chairs, and a wastebasket.

When Serov walked into the room, Cronley was sitting in one of the chairs and resting his feet on the bed. Lying at the foot of the bed were his bloody trousers, sloppily folded. The trousers he now wore still had the tags that come with new garments attached.

"Well?" Cronley greeted him.

"Alekseevich is outside with my car," Serov said.

"And what about . . . Bruce?"

"You heard what General Clay's wife said, that she would see to his care while you are, well, being cared for."

"That's it?" Cronley said, and shook his head. "Ivan, I'm not going to leave here without him."

"I have no suggestions. And you cannot wander around this enormous hospital looking for him. If he's even here. Also, if I didn't already mention this, there are now two very large military policemen in the corridor who are probably charged with keeping you in here."

"I'm under arrest?"

"The MP sergeant said they were your protection detail."

"So, what do you think I should do?"

"If nothing happens in the next half hour, I will call the **Kommandatura** and tell them I am being held against my will. Or, better, I'll go have a chat with General Clay and threaten him with my making the call. Presuming the MPs will let me out of here. Relax, James, something will happen."

Fifteen minutes later, the MP sergeant stuck his head in the door and politely said, "Captain Cronley, sir, you have visitors."

"See, James?" Serov said, somewhat smug.

"I'm not good at relaxing."

A trim, mustachioed lieutenant colonel, in pink and green, entered. Cronley didn't recognize the light bird. Without thinking about it, he checked the lapel insignia. It was that of the Judge Advocate Corps.

Great, Cronley thought. **Just what I need. An Army lawyer.**

On his heels was Janice Johansen. She was in her late twenties and attractive, nicely filling out her pink-and-green uniform, the sleeves of which at the shoulder bore gold-thread-embroidered patches reading U.S. WAR CORRESPONDENT. She carried herself with extreme confidence.

"Jesus Christ, sweetie," Janice greeted him. "What the hell happened to you?"

She crossed the room to him, bent over, and kissed him wetly on the cheek.

Then she saw the bloody trousers on the bed.

"God, you took a bullet? Two bullets? What the hell happened?"

"I'll tell you in a minute."

Cronley then asked, "Who are you, Colonel?"

"My name is Waldron, Captain. General Clay sent me to see you—"

"That sounds like a threat. What are you, my defense counsel?"

"—at the request of Mr. Justice Jackson," Waldron went on, "and bearing a suggestion from Colonel Frade—"

"What kind of a suggestion?"

"Quote, shut your mouth, Jimmy, and listen to what Tom Waldron has to say, unquote."

"You know Cletus?"

"He and my little brother were classmates before Cletus changed to Tulane to play tennis."

"You mean at A&M?"

"We are all products of that noble institution. I'm Class of 1937. Now, before we go any further, are you going to listen to Colonel Frade's advice concerning closing your mouth?"

"Okay," Cronley said, chuckling.

"That being the case, the proper response to that question is 'Yes, sir.'"

Cronley nodded.

"Say it."

"Yes, sir."

Waldron turned to Serov.

"I presume, sir, that you are General Ivan Serov?"

"Yes, I am."

"General Clay said he thought you might be here, sir."

Serov nodded but didn't reply.

"What I have to discuss with Captain Cronley is of an extremely personal nature. Both Mr. Justice Jackson and General Clay have told me that Captain Cronley considers you all close personal friends. And because of that, he might be reluctant to ask you to leave us while we are having our talk. But I'll deal with that. So to spare him any possible awkwardness, I'll ask you and Miss Johansen to please step outside."

"They stay, Colonel," Cronley said, flatly. "That is not open for discussion."

"Okay, that's **your** position, Cronley, but I haven't heard from either of them."

Serov said, "Colonel, if Captain Cronley wants me to stay, I will stay."

"Ditto," Janice said.

Waldron nodded. "Very well, then, so be it. We now turn to the subject of Captain Cronley's relationship with Bruce J. Moriarty III, the orphan infant son of the late Virginia Calhoun Moriarty and the late Lieutenant Bruce J. Moriarty Jr. . . ."

Waldron paused, frowned, and twice shook his head in what could have signified frustration.

"I had hoped to avoid this, but obviously that's not going to be possible. I'm going to have to start at the beginning. And since this meeting never took place, which means that nothing said today in here will ever leave this room, and, further, that the normal protocols about classified material do not apply, I can speak freely."

"Speak," Cronley said, impatiently.

"Okay, starting with the announcement that the villain, so to speak, in all of this is Harry S (no period) Truman.

"I had enough service so as to be released within days of the surrender ceremony in Tokyo Bay. I returned to the practice of corporate law in Washington. One of the firm's major clients was Midwest Insurance, whose prewar CEO was one Sidney W. Souers.

"My friend Bob Jackson came to me the day that Truman named him chief prosecutor for the Nuremberg Tribunal and told me the reason Truman wanted the Nazis properly tried, then hanged, was to avoid making them martyrs. He asked me what I thought and I told him I thought it was a stroke of genius. History would show that Truman was much smarter than many thought. I also said that if there was anything I could do to help, et cetera.

"Two days later, Bob was back. This time he had Eisenhower, then chief of staff of the Army, with him. They had been talking. What Bob needed in Germany was a high-placed friend no one knew about who would protect Bob not only from the Nazis still running loose, including but not limited to those in Odessa, who obviously would try to harm him, both physically and politically, but also from certain personnel in the Army and Military Government and from the sometimes rash ideas and actions of the commander in chief.

"The only person in Germany who would know of my role in this was General Clay. Later, High Commissioner McCloy was brought into the loop. In Washington, of course, the only cognoscenti were Admiral Souers, Oscar Schultz, and Cletus Frade. And, of course, Dwight Eisenhower.

"The wisdom of the plan became almost immediately apparent when the President had two ideas, one immediately following the other.

"Idea one was that Bob was actually in physical danger and needed protection, especially since Truman—idea two—had decided that Jackson was going to have enough idle time on his hands to run to earth the large number of senior Nazis who we had so far been unable to locate.

"To protect Bob, Truman didn't want to use the military police or the Counterintelligence Corps or the FBI. That would be too visible and those agents would immediately report to their respective superiors anything they learned about Justice Jackson in which they thought their superiors would be interested. This was especially true of the FBI. Admiral Souers once told me with a straight face that he wasn't sure whom the President loathed more, Joseph Stalin or John Edgar Hoover."

Cronley and Serov both grunted simultaneously.

"Can I quote you on that, Colonel?" Janice said.

"Absolutely not," Waldron said, making a thin smile. "And if you do, I'll deny it. Anyway, the President said he knew of a young officer who could fill the roll. He had met Second Lieutenant James D. Cronley Jr. and promoted him to captain and pinned the Distinguished Service Medal on him for his role in shooting the captain of the German submarine U-590 in Patagonia as he prepared to sell five hundred and sixty kilograms of Nazi uranium-235 to the Soviets."

"I didn't know until this moment that that was you, James," Serov blurted.

"For obvious reasons, General," Waldron said, drily, "there followed no press conference call to trumpet Cronley's exploits."

Serov's face showed his obvious displeasure.

"Truman got on the SIGABA," Waldron went on, "and told Jackson he was getting a DCI protection detail headed by Captain Cronley, whom he knew personally and who would also be useful in helping Jackson track down the at-large Nazis who Truman wanted in the cells of the Tribunal Prison awaiting trial.

"The next thing the President heard was, things had gone better than he had hoped. He was told that Cronley had captured von Dietelburg and Burgdorf in Vienna."

"You know that didn't come without a steep price," Cronley said.

Waldron nodded. "About forty-five minutes after the President was told the good news, General Clay came into my office and announced that the Austrian government had issued a warrant for the arrest of one of Cronley's men on a charge of murder and one for Cronley himself on a charge of being an accessory before and after the fact. They also charged him and his people with violating Austrian airspace and customs regulations by flying unmarked aircraft across the border on several occasions."

"Nice work, Jimmy," Janice said.

"I feel obligated to state that this is all off the record, Miss Johansen."

"Worry not, Colonel," Cronley said. "We have an understanding."

Waldron looked at him. "Right. Anyway, there was a long list of other charges, including from the U.S. Army Air Force and the Office of Military Government. Cronley, surprising no one, had an explanation for his actions. When planning the capture of von Dietelburg and Burgdorf with Austrian authorities, he had decided that the Austrians' true intention was to incarcerate the two Nazis in an Austrian prison for trial by the Austrian government at a later date.

"He decided (a) that this was a bad idea since von Dietelburg and Burgdorf would be killed in prison long before any trial, (b) that his duty was to the President and his orders that the Nazis be tried, then hanged, and (c) the only way Cronley could ensure that those orders were carried out was to personally deliver the Nazis to the Tribunal's cells in Nuremberg.

"He had the means to do so—specifically, two German Fieseler Storch aircraft, which he had spared from the Air Force's ordered destruction. He needed these illegal aircraft to fly into Austria, Italy, France, and elsewhere while Nazi hunting. Justice Jackson agreed with Cronley's argument and arranged for the airplanes to be stored in a guarded hangar at Nuremberg.

"After seeing Burgdorf and von Dietelburg behind Tribunal bars, Cronley and company were put on ice at Cletus Frade's Argentina estancia while Oscar Shultz plied the Austrians with money to make the criminal charges associated with the capture go away."

Waldron paused and glanced around the room.

"I will now turn to the escape itself," he continued, then stopped and looked at Serov, and said, "There are those, General—frankly, including me—who believe that you were up to your eyeballs in said escape. Would you care to comment, sir?"

Serov, stone-faced, said, "I absolutely and categorically deny any connection with the escape of those scum from the Tribunal Prison—"

"Bullshit," Cronley blurted. "Come on, Ivan!"

Serov locked eyes with Cronley. After a minute, he said, somewhat casually, "But, hypothetically speaking, I can imagine a situation where a senior NKGB officer with a certain influence over the Államvédelmi Osztálya might enlist the services of the AVO in getting those two godless sons of bitches out of the Tribunal Prison so that they might be interrogated."

Waldron's eyebrows went up. "Why wouldn't your so-called hypothetical NKGB general just go to the Tribunal Prison and interrogate them there?"

"He would be concerned that Mr. Justice Jackson might disapprove of his interrogation techniques."

"And—hypothetically speaking, of course—once the AVO had Burgdorf and von Dietelburg in hand, did they learn what they wanted to know? And what, exactly, did they want to know?"

Serov nodded. "They wanted the location of

Odessa's funds, estimated to be at least between fifty and one hundred million dollars, and almost certainly more. These are the funds von Dietelburg and Burgdorf intend to use to nurture the heretical religion started by Himmler."

"And did the AVO learn where these funds were being held?"

"Unfortunately, no. Both von Dietelburg and Burgdorf were perfectly willing to die as martyrs to their faith. Frankly, one has to admire their dedication."

"They were killed?"

"No. At this point, I became involved. As you know, James and I were also looking into the matter, and I had learned where those funds were being kept."

"And where was that?"

"To coin a phrase, they were 'hidden in plain sight.' In the Vatican Bank."

"No shit?" Janice said, then added, "Pardon my French. That's **some** story."

"Which, Janice, we will discuss," Cronley said. "As I just told the colonel here, we have an understanding."

Janice gave him the finger.

Waldron shook his head. "Would you be surprised if many people, including me, would find that hard—in fact impossible—to believe?"

"I'm a former NKGB officer, Colonel, nothing

surprises me, including the proclivity of many senior officials to disbelieve what is uncomfortable for them to accept. But, like it or not, that's where the funds of the Nazi religion are, in the Vatican Bank."

"It's true," Cronley said.

Waldron looked at him. "You're in on this, too?"

"Up to my ears." He then gestured toward the foot of his bed. "And my bloody clothing. That's why Odessa hit the DCI safe house."

"I don't suppose you have any proof to substantiate this notion?"

Serov picked up the briefcase from the floor and handed it to Waldron.

"There's two million dollars and change in various currencies in there, Colonel. We took it away this morning from an archbishop who, acting for Cardinal von Hassburger, was in the process of delivering it to Odessa. We have reason to believe there are far more illicit funds—well over a hundred million—being held by the Vatican."

Waldron was unable to resist the temptation to look in the briefcase.

"Jesus!" he said, shaking his head and sighing. "You realize, I hope, that you have just forced the United States to declare war on the Catholic Church, the Vatican?"

"Not necessarily," Serov said.

"We . . . The government has to respond to this," Waldron insisted.

"What Cronley and I are hoping to do is enlist the Vatican in our noble cause."

"What?"

"Think about it, Colonel," Serov said. "The reason they've been hiding Odessa's money is because they see themselves as allies of Odessa—the Nazis—in a holy war against godless communism. The enemy of my enemy, so to speak."

"That's probably true, but so what?"

"We hope to convince the Vatican first that we have no intention yet of broadcasting their connivance with Odessa to the world—" He glanced at Janice Johansen. "Key word 'yet.' Then we tell them what we have learned about the religion Saint Heinrich the Divine has started . . ."

"What makes you sure they don't already know?"

"I don't know that, but I am convinced that if they did, they would have considered the Church of Saint Heinrich the Divine a far greater threat to them than even godless communism and would have really gone after them."

There was a pause, and then Waldron said, "I hate to admit this, but maybe you're onto something. Big question: What makes you think they'll even listen to you?"

"We turned the archbishop and the bishop

loose with the message that we're willing to discuss the two million and change with the cardinal. And only the cardinal. We gave him the telephone number of the safe house so we can arrange to meet."

"And you know what happened at the safe house," Cronley said.

"You think he'll call?"

"If only about the two million alone," Cronley said. "Why don't we go there and see if he has?"

"Ordinarily, that would be a no-brainer," Waldron said, "but . . ."

"But what?"

"But that brings us back to the real—perhaps I should say original—reason for this meeting."

"Which is?" Serov said.

Waldron looked at Cronley. "There is considerable concern on the part of several people about your mental health."

"Oh, bullshit!" Cronley blurted.

"Not only do you have a well-deserved reputation for being a legendary loose cannon, you also have a dangerous friend in Colonel Serov."

"I repeat: Oh, bullshit!"

"This concern is shared by General Clay, Mr. Justice Jackson, and, perhaps most important, by Colonel Frade, who knows you better than anyone else."

"What . . ." Cronley began.

"You agreed to Cletus's message, so remain silent until I'm finished," Waldron said. "Say 'Yes, sir.'"

After a pause, Cronley was about to reply but instead said, "Yes, sir."

"Various solutions to the problem were suggested even before this potential war with the Catholic Church came up and the risk of your involvement for the President and the DCI. These ranged from placing you in a psychiatric institution to sending you to stack snowballs in the Aleutian Islands—"

"How the hell can I defend myself from this **He's bonkers** charge?"

Waldron looked annoyed at the interruption but allowed it. "One definition of bonkers is an individual's inability to face unpleasant facts."

"Such as?"

"The love of your life has just been murdered, leaving behind an orphan infant whom you love. You have delusions about assuming the role of his father."

"So what?"

"You can't have him, now or ever. Can you face that fact?"

"I don't consider it a fact."

"You were not married to Mrs. Moriarty. Fact?"

"Yeah."

"You have no legal rights at all with regard to the baby. Exactly who becomes his guardian will be decided in court between the Moriartys and the Calhouns. Colonel Frade said you've already traveled a rocky road with the Moriartys. True?"

"Okay."

"They are going to press hard for custody of the child because he is the sole heir of his mother, who, Colonel Frade tells me, was a wealthy woman. Still with me?"

"I'm hardly penniless. But go on."

"Colonel Frade tells me that the Calhouns—Mrs. Moriarty's parents—would, in the best interests of the child, be reluctant to engage in a long and bitter court battle for his custody because they know that if they lost the battle, the Moriartys would probably refuse to let them have a meaningful relationship with the child, or any relationship at all. Do you think that's true?"

"Now that I think about it, yes."

"So, are you able to face the fact that when you passed the child to Mrs. Clay, that was the last contact you will have with him until he's an adult?"

Cronley didn't immediately reply.

A minute later, a tear slipped down his cheek.

"Well?" Waldron challenged.

Cronley cleared his throat. "I was thinking maybe if the fucking Moriartys let the Calhouns have Bruce overnight sometime, I could sneak in and see him. But that wouldn't work, would it?

They'd just keep the Calhouns from ever having him. I guess I'm fucked."

"You guess you're fucked?"

"I'm fucked. Period."

They stared at each other, then Waldron said, "Captain Cronley, you have just passed the Waldron Psychiatric Test, having proven to me that you can think rationally under the most stressful and painful conditions."

"Whoopee!"

"Why don't we get out of here and see if the cardinal has called the safe house?" Waldron asked. "Assuming the phone still works."

[ONE]
44-46 Beerenstrasse
Zehlendorf, Berlin, American Zone of
Occupation, Germany
1614 21 April 1946

When they had left for the OMGUS Compound, the street had been jammed with German police vehicles. Now the only Germans in sight were two policemen standing in the street, keeping people away from the safe house.

Beerenstrasse was half jammed with American vehicles, many of them olive drab with military markings, others were Fords and Chevrolets bearing Army of Occupation civilian license plates.

"Ivan, why do I suspect the presence of the Counterintelligence Corps?" Cronley quipped.

They entered the building and found Colonel Mortimer Cohen, Colonel Louis Switzer, and

Lieutenant Colonel Frank Williams sitting side by side on a couch that had obviously been moved to the foyer from elsewhere in the damaged house.

Switzer stood and looked from Serov to Janice Johansen to Waldron. He stopped on Cronley and immediately moved into CIC mode.

"Captain, we're in the middle of an investigation here, and while I'm unsure if you're authorized to be in here—"

"That's bullshit, Colonel, sir."

"—I know unequivocally that it's off-limits to the press and the NKGB and probably to this officer. Who are you, Colonel?"

"Is that working?" Waldron asked, pointing to a telephone on a small table to one side of the sofa. "May I use it?"

"I asked who you are, Colonel."

"And I asked to use the phone. You grant my request and I will grant yours."

Cronley sighed. "Give him the goddamn phone."

Switzer locked eyes, then impatiently gestured toward the phone. Waldron picked up the receiver and dialed.

"Sorry to bother you, sir," Waldron then said, "but your CIC chief doesn't want me in the safe house."

There was a reply, and then Waldron extended the phone to Switzer.

"He wishes to speak with you, Colonel."

"Who is that?" Switzer demanded.

Waldron didn't answer.

Switzer took the extended phone and snarled into it, "This is Colonel Switzer. Who am I talking to?"

The man on the phone told him, and the rest of the conversation consisted of Colonel Switzer saying "Yes, sir" at least ten times.

Cohen laughed after the fifth one, and when Switzer had hung up, Cohen said, "In law school, Lou, they teach you never to ask a question unless you're sure of what the answer is going to be."

Switzer glared at Waldron, and said, "You sandbagged me, Colonel."

"Regretfully, Colonel, you left me no choice."

"The general and Janice stay, too," Cronley said, then turned to Cohen. "Colonel, have we heard from the cardinal?"

"Somebody called and left a number," Cohen said. "I called the hospital and was told you were on your way here. I've been waiting for you and General Serov, especially since you have the briefcase."

Cohen consulted his notebook and dialed a number. Cronley went to him and put his head close to the handset.

After the second ring, a male voice recited the number in German.

"My name is Cohen," Cohen announced.

The voice, changing to accentless English, then said, "You, the Russian, and one other—no more than one other—may find it interesting to be at Platform 12 of the Am Zoo Bahnhof at twenty-thirty hours. Be in civilian clothing and unarmed."

Cohen replied, "Platform 12—"

"I say again," the voice interrupted, then repeated his original message verbatim.

The line went dead.

"He was reading that," Cohen said as he replaced the receiver.

"And he spoke with authority," Serov said. "A senior officer carefully following the orders of someone even more senior."

"I don't have any civvies," Cohen said. "But I suspect that civvies order was to show us who's boss. Fuck him. He called us first. We're in charge."

"I vote for playing nice," Cronley said. "I have—or I used to have—civvies upstairs in my room."

"You still do," Ostrowski said as he came from the staircase into the foyer.

"I vote with Cronley," Serov said.

"I wondered where you were, Max," Cronley said.

"Packing up the stuff of the guys we lost. And on that subject, what do I do with it?"

"Send it to the Mansion. Maybe somebody can use it. We can't send it to family in Poland, even if we had an address." He gestured toward Serov and Cohen. "But first, Max, anything that'll fit these gentlemen?"

"I have no intention of wearing a dead man's clothing," Serov said.

Cronley raised his eyebrows. "Well okay, then, Ivan, but I thought you just voted for making nice. When Colonel Cohen and I get back, we'll tell you what happened at the Bahnhof." Cronley turned to Ostrowski. "Let's show Colonel Cohen where this stuff is."

Cronley started up the stairs. The others followed.

Upstairs, Cronley walked into the two-room suite that he had briefly shared with Ginger and the baby.

"Shit," he said.

Ostrowski took his meaning.

"The CIC packed what little of her stuff was here and in the Duchess Suite. They got Father McGrath's, too."

"I would have liked something of hers," he said, then seemed somewhat surprised he'd said it aloud.

"Sweetie," Janice said, "that would only make things worse."

"Former love of my life, nothing could possibly make things worse."

"Why don't you have Max pack up your stuff

and move it to the Press Club? It's right across the park."

"Except that would be moving into the Press Club with you."

"I'm available, Janice," Ostrowski said.

Janice gave both of them the finger.

"If you should happen to see me at the Zoo Bahnhof, pretend not to recognize me," she said, and walked out of the room.

[TWO]
Platform 12
Bahnhof Zoologischer Garten
Berlin, American Zone of Occupation,
Germany
2035 21 April 1946

As they walked toward the platform beside the cardinal's train, Cronley did not see Janice but knew she was in the station watching.

What he did see was the locomotive of the cardinal's train. Papal flags flapped on either side of the front of the engine's boiler. There was something wrong with the picture, and it took him a moment to figure it out.

The locomotive usually was detached from the railroad cars that it had brought into the station and the cars were backed in next to the platform, usually by a special locomotive.

There was some reason Cardinal von Hassburger did not want the locomotive detached from his train. And then Cronley saw the first car behind the locomotive was customized, its paint glossy and bearing the papal crest on its sides.

That's probably the cardinal's personal car. Or maybe the Pope's?

There's obviously things inside—maybe a radio or a teletype—that required power from the locomotive.

Or maybe water from the engine's supply to flush a toilet or even provide hot water for the cardinal's shower.

Do cardinals take showers or do they take baths?

Does a cardinal remove that little red hat before stepping into his shower or bath?

Cronley was brought out of his reverie when a very large, very good-looking man in a business suit and clerical collar stepped into their path.

"Good evening, gentlemen," he said in what sounded like American English. "I'm Father Kent. Would you be good enough to follow me?"

The gate to Platform 12 was guarded by two large American MPs and two smaller German policemen.

"These gentlemen are with me," Father Kent announced, first in English to the MPs and then in German to the others.

"Relax, Ivan," Cronley said. "Despite what Morty said, I think you look splendid in your borrowed civvies."

Serov looked pained and shook his head in resignation.

They were passed onto the platform. The MPs eyed them, but without much curiosity.

You should pay better attention, Sergeant, Cronley thought.

You're looking at a Russian general and an American colonel in hand-me-down clothes. Plus, a natty captain in a snazzy Argentine tweed jacket and gray flannel trousers.

Father Kent waved them onto the forward observation platform of the papal car, where a second muscular young priest opened the door to the car, and said, also in American English, this one with a distinctive Bostonian accent, "Make yourselves comfortable, gentlemen. His Grace will be with you momentarily."

When he stepped into the wood-paneled compartment, Cronley sensed there was something fishy about it.

It was obviously a private reception room, a place the cardinal could receive visitors he didn't want to meet in public. It was furnished with a low table, a three-seater leather couch, and a half dozen matching armchairs. The only decoration in the compartment was a large crucifix on the wood-paneled wall separating the compartment from the rest of what Cronley guessed was the other two-thirds of the car.

There were three panels, on each of which were three vents six inches long and two inches wide, equally spaced from top to bottom. He didn't pay much attention to them until he thought he saw a light on the other side of the center vent of the center panel.

Cronley studied it more closely. Then the light was gone—and another came on inside the lower vent on the right panel.

Cronley touched Cohen's arm and discreetly pointed out the panels and the vents. Cohen looked, then nodded but didn't say anything.

As Cronley looked at the paneled wall, the door to the left of the wall opened, and the archbishop he had last seen in the Hotel Majestic stepped into the compartment.

He was wearing a black, ankle-length garment that Cronley remembered was called a cassock.

"Good evening, gentlemen," he said. "Please be seated."

He settled into one of the armchairs.

"I suppose it is too much to hope that you've come to return the stolen property. Yet, as it's said, 'Hope springs eternal in the human breast.'"

"I didn't catch your name, Your Grace, the last time we met," Serov said.

"Dietl, Franz Dietl . . . No comment about the stolen property?"

"I can only hope," Cronley said, "that you weren't holding your breath in anticipation of getting Odessa's money returned."

The archbishop chuckled.

"So, what did you want to talk about?"

"We wanted to talk to the cardinal," Serov said.

"His Eminence, sadly, is not available at this time."

"Pity," Cohen said. "I was hoping to put his mind at rest. But since he's occupied, there's no point in this meeting. We've already talked to you. You have our number if His Eminence can ever find a few minutes for us."

"Enough!" Serov snapped. "Hassburger, if you don't come out from behind those panels right now and stop this bullshit, I will be forced to conclude that you're not interested at all in solving our mutual problem."

"You can't talk to . . . His Emin—" the archbishop began and then cut himself off.

There was no response from behind the panels.

"Let's go," Cronley said, and stood up.

Serov and Cohen rose and followed him to the door through which they had entered the room. They had almost reached it when there was a fresh voice.

"I'm willing to listen to what you have to say."

Cronley had seen Cardinal von Hassburger only once before and then only at a distance. He had not been favorably impressed. And now that he saw him up close, he was even less impressed.

The cardinal was, with the exception of his red skullcap, dressed in a cassock identical to Archbishop Dietl's. He was not quite as tall as Dietl, and nowhere near as heavy, but his eyes were something else. They were large and clear and piercing.

The cardinal, Cronley quickly decided, was no dummy.

"I warned Dietl," the cardinal began, "that you had no intention of returning our money."

"You mean Odessa's money?" Cohen challenged.

"The money in question," the cardinal said.

"And you were right," Cohen said. "Snatched from the hands of the evil and now in the hands of the righteous."

"Actually, you snatched it from our hand."

"If the glove fits, wear it," Serov said.

"You must be Serov," the cardinal said.

"General Ivan Serov at your service, Cardinal."

"I suppose I'm expected to say something like this," the cardinal said, "but it is true: I have a busy schedule. Can we get to the point?"

Cohen said, "We have come, Your Eminence, to enlist the Holy Mother Church in a righteous war against some very evil sons of bitches."

"And who would they be?"

"If this wasn't so important," Cohen said, "I'd tell you to go fuck yourself and walk out of here—"

"You cannot speak that way!" Dietl snapped.

Cohen held his palm out toward Dietl while not breaking eye contact with von Hassburger.

"I'm going to ask you this only once, Cardinal. Are you willing to both listen and talk or are you going to continue to hide under that red yarmulke?"

"You're talking about Odessa?"

"There's more to it than Odessa. For lack of a more precise term, I think of them as the people who worship in the Church of Saint Heinrich the Divine."

"I gather you're one of those who pays credence to this Nazi church fantasy?"

"You are testing my patience, Cardinal," Cohen said, his tone icy. "You damn well know it is no fantasy. What I'm going to try to do is convince you it is more of a threat to the Holy Mother Church than the communists and the Muslims combined."

"To what end?"

"To help us wipe the bastards off the face of the earth."

"Would you be offended, Colonel, if I told you I'm rather surprised at the depth of your vehemence?"

"Meaning what?"

"I was led to believe that you were what every intelligence officer aspired to be. That is to say, logical, analytical, rational, and, above all, emotionless."

"Sorry to disappoint you."

"What is it about these—how did you put it?—these disciples of Saint Heinrich the Divine that so bothers you? That angers you?"

"Cardinal, what's your Christian name?"

"What's that got to do with anything?"

Cohen made a **Let's have it** gesture with both hands, which caused the cardinal to sigh.

"I was christened Helmut."

"So that makes you Helmut Cardinal von Hassburger?" Cohen looked at the others, then said, "Okay, from now on you're Helmut. You can call me Mortimer or Morty. If you can't stand that blow to your dignity and prestige, meeting's over. Agreed, Helmut?"

Von Hassburger held up his hands in a gesture of resignation.

"Good, Helmut. So let's start with mass murder. Mass murder of the Jews. My take on that is, Hitler didn't go down that path just because he didn't like Jews. He needed someone to blame for Germany getting its ass kicked in World War One, and the Jews were a convenient scapegoat.

"I think he was even a little surprised at how easy it was to get the German people to go along with him. What I'm saying here is, the death factories came later, after Saint Heinrich came up with the idea—probably from one or more of the classic German philosophers who'd been pushing the idea for centuries—of exterminating the **Untermenschen**, the people they decided were not as good as Aryans."

Cohen paused as he glanced at the others in the room, then turned back to von Hassburger and continued. "You will recall, I'm sure, that when Hitler started the mass murder business— long before the Final Solution—it was with retarded children. These **Untermenschen** obviously had no future, thus feeding and housing them was an unacceptable drain on the economy. It then advanced, with the same justification, to include retarded adults. Some argued that Hitler was doing them a favor by ending their miserable existences."

He stared at the cardinal, then asked, "You ever think of it that way, Helmut?"

"I've heard that theory."

"I thought you might have. Anyway, before that happened—and about the time Saint Heinrich fell in love with this obscure Austro-German politician named Hitler and joined what was then the German Workers' Party—Himmler began to reason that if there were **Untermenschen**, it followed that there had to be **Übermenschen**. But who would they be? Obviously, the German race—**not** to be confused with the German population as a whole. Hell, there were millions of Jews who believed themselves to be part of the German people.

"The pure Germans were blond and blue-eyed. And, of course, above the **Untermenschen**.

"When Himmler formed a personal bodyguard for Hitler—who now referred to himself as **Der Führer**—he accepted into what he had grandly called the Schutzstaffel only those Germans who could prove their forebearers had been ethnically pure for three or more generations. Thus, no Poles, no Austrians, et cetera.

"The members of this new organization, which quickly became known simply as the SS, swore allegiance not to Germany but instead to Adolf Hitler personally.

"Once Saint Heinrich had decked out members in snazzy black uniforms, featuring lightning-bolt SS insignias and with the skull and crossbones—the **Totenkopf**—on their caps, Hitler immediately grew fond of them. And he authorized Himmler to enlarge the SS 'perhaps to five thousand, or even ten thousand, men.'

"Himmler was swamped with volunteers, a great many of whom, he came to realize, were not exactly enamored of **Der Führer**—few understood even a fraction of what Hitler said in his hours-long tirades. They instead volunteered because there was a certain appeal to wearing a snazzy black uniform and being officially recognized as a member of the **Übermenschen** and thus superior to common folk.

"When that recruiting drive was over, forty thousand men filled the SS ranks, and that number quickly rose to one hundred thousand and then to two hundred thousand, where it stabilized for a while.

"Still with me, Helmut?"

"More or less, but it would be helpful if I knew where you're headed with this narrative."

"Kindly bear with me. Now, the next thing that happened, our first serious mistake, was when Adolf started to call himself **Der Führer**. We mocked him: The 'leader' of what? A small, unimportant political party in Munich whose few members were social misfits and disgruntled ex-soldiers, with a sprinkling of lunatics thrown in? Ridiculous!

"And then it got worse. They renamed their party the National Socialist German Workers'

Party—NSDAP—and started referring to themselves as Nazis and came up with the swastika as their emblem. They also stopped referring to Germany as Germany, or even as the Fatherland, and started calling it the Thousand-Year Reich.

"And we thought that was funny, as absurd as **Der Führer**'s mustache. What delusions of grandeur! What nonsense!

"That was our mistake. Our **grievous** mistake. Hitler and Himmler were dead serious."

"Define 'our,'" the cardinal said.

"We Jews, of course. But also the Western democracies."

"But not the Catholic Church?"

"I have unkind thoughts about what Holy Mother Church was up to during this period. And later."

"Which you are going to share?"

"Helmut, there are many facets of the Church of Rome for which I have profound—both personal and professional—respect. With the possible exception of Mossad, which I am sure you know is the Zionist intelligence organization, Holy Mother Church has—is—the best intelligence organization the world has ever seen."

"How kind of you to say so," von Hassburger said, clearly sarcastic despite his smile. "And what unkind thoughts did you have about us during this period?"

"I was disgusted by, but not surprised at, Pacelli's—Pius XII's—behavior when Hitler started after the Jews. **We** Jews."

"He did what he could, Mortimer."

"That's absolute bullshit, and you know it!" Cohen snapped. He glanced again at the others, then went on. "Unless you mean, Helmut, that he did what he could to benefit Holy Mother Church, in which case we agree. That's what disgusted me."

The cardinal's face whitened. Veins on his temples grew and pulsed. Cronley thought von Hassburger was about to blurt out something in anger, but he didn't.

Cohen wasn't through.

"Correct me if I'm wrong, Helmut, but doesn't Pius XII think that communism—at least the Soviet version of it—poses a greater threat to Holy Mother Church than anything else?"

"The Church faces many threats."

"But which does Pius XII think is the greatest?"

"I really have no idea, but I'm certainly willing to agree that Soviet—communist—atheism is a threat."

"And how much of a threat would you say the Church of Saint Heinrich the Divine poses to Rome?"

"We're back to that nonsense, are we?"

"That's the reason we're having this little chat.

Did you ever wonder, Helmut, why I kept you out of Wewelsburg Castle?"

"I'm not sure what you're talking about."

"Come on, Helmut. Didn't your mother try to teach you that honesty is always the best policy?"

"Sometimes, Mortimer, that's not true."

Cronley thought, **Odd. The cardinal really is starting to enjoy this exchange.**

Cohen said, "My mother lied to me. She said that unless I brushed my teeth twice a day, my teeth would fall out. So for years I brushed them twice a day, sometimes three times. But then, about the time I turned forty, my teeth started to fall out anyway."

The cardinal laughed out loud.

Cohen was quiet, then went on, his tone serious. "I've kept you—your minions—out of Wewelsburg for several reasons. There was no question in my mind that you had heard of Heinrich's new religion, but I didn't know (a) how extensive your knowledge was or (b) what you thought of what you had. In other words, how seriously you were taking it.

"If, in fact, you were taking it very seriously, then the last thing I wanted was for you to search the castle thoroughly before I had a chance to. If, on the other hand, you had already decided—or, after a quick inspection of Wewelsburg, decided— that the Church of Saint Heinrich was just one more nutty—and, thus, nonthreatening—Nazi idea, I thought it entirely likely that, to put the problem behind you once and for all, you would blow up the castle. Reduce it to rubble. I didn't want that to happen, either, and not only because I think there's a half ton of gold hidden there."

The cardinal, clearly in deep thought, looked at Cohen.

"Now, that's interesting," von Hassburger said. "It would lend credence to your and—frankly, if you must know—my theory that something serious was going on in that castle. Mortimer, I really would like my people to examine the castle."

"Ready to deal, Helmut?"

The cardinal made a **Let's hear it** gesture.

"Presuming they will share with us what they develop, including what they think, I'll let your people in the castle. And tell them everything we've learned."

"And then, Mortimer?"

"One step at a time, Helmut."

Von Hassburger shrugged. "My thoughts exactly. What sort of a time frame are we talking about?"

"The sooner, the better."

"With that in mind, did you happen to notice the very large, very young priest who showed you in here? That's Father Francis McKenna. He's a Jesuit, very bright, and I've asked him to familiarize himself with Wewelsburg and all that it represents. How would you feel about him going with you as sort of liaison?"

"Fine."

The cardinal stood up and offered his right hand.

"Unless you have something else, Mortimer?"

Cohen shook his head, and then they shook hands.

After the cardinal left the room, Father Francis X. McKenna, S.J., came in a moment later.

"Colonel," he said, with his Bostonian inflection, "I just spoke with Cardinal von Hassburger. I'll need three minutes to get my bag and then I'm yours."

XI

[ONE]
Aboard *The Blue Danube*
East–West Germany Border
2055 22 April 1946

Colonel Mortimer Cohen, tunic unbuttoned and puffing on a long, dark cigar, was sitting on one of the two small couches in what was somewhat grandly called the Drawing Room of the Senior Officer's Compartment when Father McKenna entered.

Captain James D. Cronley Jr., who was sitting on the opposite couch, greeted him: "Father Francis, time and **The Blue Danube** wait for no man. I thought I told you that."

"I had to wind up several things for the cardinal," McKenna replied.

"He doesn't even wind his own watch?" Cronley asked, innocently.

The priest, ignoring Cronley, set his suitcase on the floor and sat down next to him.

The three of them had spent just about all day aboard a C-47, waiting to depart Tempelhof. Permission to do so had never come.

First it was the weather, then it was the Russians flying dangerously close to American planes on purpose. And then it was the damn weather again, then the damn Russians again, all damn day.

About half past three, the priest had announced that he had promised to check in with the cardinal and that he would catch up to them later. He was out the door of the Gooney Bird before Cohen or Cronley could raise an objection.

Half an hour after that, Cohen had finally given up on flying to Munich and had ordered Cronley to get them berths on **The Blue Danube**, the Army train which ran every night between Berlin and Vienna.

When he tried to get the berths, though, he was told there were none available. Cronley had solved this problem by mumbling he was Colonel [**inaudible**] and telling the RTO that he didn't care who got bumped, Colonel Cohen, Mr. Cronley, and "Archbishop" McKenna would be on **The Blue Danube**.

"Where's General Serov?" the priest asked.

"It's just about nine. I would guess he's at the

Four Seasons in Munich, selecting an appropriate wine to go with his dinner."

"He'd have had to fly to be able to do that," the priest said. It was more of a question than a statement.

"The Soviet aircraft which fly dangerously close to Allied aircraft, Francis, do not fly dangerously close to other Soviet aircraft."

"I suppose I should have thought of that."

A middle-aged, somewhat paunchy chief warrant officer entered the compartment without knocking. He walked to the window and pulled down the shade.

"Colonel," he barked, "you understand that nobody touches that from now on. Got it?"

"Touches what?" Cronley asked. He was wearing ODs with lapel insignia indicating he was a civilian employee of the Army.

"The curtain! Don't touch the goddamn curtain. It stays down. Got it?"

"How'm I going to open the window if I don't open the curtain?" Cronley asked, innocently.

"Jesus, where the hell are you from, Mars? Especially don't open, don't even **touch**, the goddamn window."

"Whatever you say. Ain't that right, Father Francis?"

"Absolutely."

Cronley saw that he had pissed off both the warrant officer and the priest. He was pleased.

"What I would like to do," Cronley announced when the warrant officer had finally left the compartment, "is open the curtain and the window, drop my pants, and ride through East Germany with my ass hanging out the window."

Colonel Cohen chuckled.

"It would be a little chilly," McKenna said.

"Probably," Cronley agreed.

"The cardinal is curious about Reverend McGrath, and, frankly, so am I. What can you tell me about him?"

"A lot," Cohen said, "but I wonder why we should."

"I thought we were agreed to cooperate on this business?"

"Helmut and I agreed to give you access to Castle Wewelsburg. Period. Not to brief you on our friends and associates."

That silenced the young priest. Cronley wondered how long that would last.

Maybe ten minutes later, McKenna asked, "Is General Serov on your list of forbidden subjects?"

"That would depend, Francis, on your questions about him," Cohen said.

"Why did he fly instead of traveling with us?"

"Flying is of course faster. But, more important, don't you think it would arouse curiosity if a Russian general got on **The Blue Danube?**"

"I didn't think about that," McKenna said.

Cronley wondered, **Is this an act or is he really that naïve?**

Cohen said, "He'll meet us at the Four Seasons. Then we'll go to the Pullach Compound."

"What's the Pullach Compound?"

"A top secret intelligence operation run by General Gehlen, who used to run Abwehr Ost for the Germans."

"What will we be doing there?"

"If we told you, Francis," Cohen said, "we'd have to kill you."

"I never know when you're pulling my leg," the priest complained.

"Now you're getting it," Cronley said.

[TWO]
Pullach Compound
Near Munich, American Zone of
Occupation, Germany
1305 23 April 1946

Reinhard Gehlen, as a Wehrmacht generalmajor, had commanded Abwehr Ost, the German espionage operation dealing with the Soviet Union. He now was chief executive of the Süd-Deutsche Industrielle Entwicklungsorganisation, the South German Industrial Development Organization. It had nothing whatever to do with industrial development but rather did much the same thing vis-à-vis the Soviet Union, inside and outside the Russian border, and under the aegis of the United States Directorate of Central Intelligence, from its heavily guarded Compound in the village of Pullach.

Since setting up shop, so to speak, Gehlen had become so close to the head of the DCI, Rear Admiral Sidney W. Souers, that they were on a Sid and Rhiny nickname basis.

Gehlen also habitually called his subordinates by their nicknames or Christian names—while they addressed him as **Herr General**—but he was not that close to any of them at the Compound.

Gehlen attributed this to his service in the Abwehr, both before and during the war. Some of the friends he had made coming up in the German Army had been killed. Those losses hurt.

Others had betrayed him, which had been even more painful.

Nor was Gehlen close to any of the Americans at the Compound—with the notable exception of Captain James D. Cronley Jr.

Gehlen had "inherited" Cronley, as he thought

of it, just as the OSS was being disestablished but the Directorate of Central Intelligence was by no means up and running. The European Command was trying to take advantage of that situation by taking over the Süd-Deutsche Industrielle Entwicklungsorganisation. Gehlen knew he could not do what was expected of him with a U.S. Army intelligence officer looking over his shoulder and offering "helpful" suggestions.

The Pullach Compound was guarded by an oversize company of American Negro soldiers. During the war, they had been in an antitank battalion and had taken pride that they indeed were fighting soldiers and not working as laborers at a quartermaster's depot somewhere or as stevedores in one of the ports.

They originally had had black officers, but recently there had been no black officers available to assign to the duty. The first white officer assigned to it had done a good job, but, inevitably, he had gone home.

When Gehlen took one quick look at the new commanding officer, he saw cause for concern. Cronley was a second lieutenant, for one thing, and looked, despite his size and bulk, like he had just graduated high school.

But Gehlen quickly learned that his usual shrewd snap judgment of people in the case of Cronley was pretty far off the mark. Cronley was nowhere near being a just-about-useless second lieutenant. Gehlen began to realize this when he explained the problems Cronley was about to face with his black soldiers.

"I don't see it as much of a problem, General," Cronley said with monumental self-confidence.

"And why is that, Lieutenant?"

"A very wise man once told me that if a second lieutenant—or, for that matter, a lieutenant colonel—finds himself in a situation where he really doesn't know what to do, he should go find a good sergeant and listen to him."

"That's good advice. Who was this wise man?"

"My father, sir."

"Your father was an officer?"

"In War One, a light colonel, sir, the executive officer of Colonel Donovan—excuse me, **General** Donovan. Between wars, Uncle Bill was the family lawyer. I suppose that had some influence on my winding up in the DCI."

Gehlen routinely ate breakfast, and sometimes lunch, with the officers of his staff, but now dined alone. After his first "chat" with Cronley, he started inviting him to dinner.

As this was out of character for him, he gave it considerable thought and finally concluded it was because the young and very junior officer stimulated him intellectually. And when Gehlen thought about that he was forced to conclude that Cronley's mind was as sharp, perhaps even sharper, than his own.

More as after-dinner entertainment than anything else, Gehlen began to tell Cronley about what he thought of as his personal unsolved puzzles—personal because they had little or nothing to do with his work for the DCI and because most of them dated back to just before the surrender.

One so-called puzzle was Phoenix—Operation Phoenix—meaning that, after some time had passed, the Fourth Reich would rise, phoenixlike, from the ashes of the Third Reich.

Gehlen's Nazis knew many details of Operation Phoenix, and given the choice between sharing those with the Office of Strategic Services or being returned to Germany to face the wrath of the Allies and the Jews, they chose to work with the OSS.

And then an American Jew, Colonel Mortimer Cohen, who provided CIC security for the War Crimes Tribunal in Nuremberg, came up with something.

According to Cohen, Reichsführer-SS Heinrich Himmler had started a new, nameless religion at Castle Wewelsburg. Gehlen had heard only whispered rumors about it and decided to take a closer look. But it was now guarded by Cohen's agents. Within an hour of their first meeting,

Gehlen and Cohen had become fast friends and co-conspirators determined to do away with the Church of Saint Heinrich the Divine.

As soon as Cohen, Cronley, and McKenna had been passed through the outer of three checkpoints of the Compound, Gehlen had been notified. He was waiting for them when they walked into his office.

"Jim, I'm so sorry about Mrs. Moriarty."

Cronley nodded.

"Thank you, General."

"Who he, Morty?" Gehlen asked, pointing to the priest.

"This is Father McKenna," Cohen replied. "He's here to hear your confession and save your soul."

The priest's face showed he was not amused, but he said nothing.

"If it gets back to the Vatican, Father, that you're running around with these two . . ." Gehlen said.

"The Vatican knows," Cohen said. "At least, Cardinal von Hassburger does, and he and Pius XII are pals. We are in the process of establishing one of those 'the enemy of my enemy' relationships with the Holy Mother Church."

"That'll have to wait until after I deal with von

Dietelburg and Burgdorf. Got any idea where they are?"

Gehlen shook his head.

"In the good old days, I could have called upon the Sicherheitsdienst and the Gestapo to find people for me. Now I have to rely on the CIC . . ."

Cohen chuckled. "I feel your pain, General."

"Either of you have any thoughts on why they attacked the safe house?" Gehlen asked.

"Well, I suspect they don't like me," Cronley said.

"If I were those two," Cohen said, "I'd be more concerned with getting my ass out of Dodge than whacking Americans."

"That also occurred to me," Gehlen said.

"Maybe it was staged to impress their own people," Cronley said. " 'Hey, guys, look. We're so sure of ourselves, we can whack Americans.' "

"That's certainly a possibility," Cohen said. "Carrying with it the suggestion that Odessa may be having problems of its own."

"I wouldn't count on that," Gehlen said. "So, tell me about this arrangement you're trying to reach with the Holy Mother Church."

"With my usual eloquence," Cohen said, "I suggested to the cardinal that the Church of Saint Heinrich is as dangerous to him, to the Vatican, as communism. I don't think he was convinced but he sent McKenna to have a look at Wewelsburg.

He admitted that he'd sent people to have a look before, but my people had kept them out."

"I just had an idea," Cronley said.

Cohen turned to him. "That's always dangerous. But let's have it."

"We've been saying those death's-head rings—and God knows what else—may have been put in a cave or a tunnel and then the opening was dynamited. And we haven't been able to find the cave, or whatever. How about having some experts look for it? And, for that matter, have a look at Wewelsburg Castle?"

"Where are we going to get the experts?"

"You know what a Light Engineer company's like?"

Cohen shrugged. "I can only guess that a Light Engineer company paints buildings and a Heavy Engineer company builds buildings. Or blows them up."

"I don't often have this opportunity, so I'm taking great pleasure in being able to say, 'Colonel, sir, your ignorance of the function, the capabilities, of a Light Engineer company is shocking.'"

"Okay, wiseass, enlighten me."

"There are basically three kinds of engineer companies," Cronley said. "Combat engineers are the guys who fix roads, place and remove mines, do the dirty work of digging trenches, maintaining roads at night in the rain during an artillery barrage. Then there are the engineer companies that handle really big jobs, like keeping the Mississippi River navigable. Then there's the third kind, Light Engineer companies."

"Which do what?"

"Everything the other two don't. The opposite of how it sounds, actually—they build airstrips, bridges, et cetera."

"Presumably, there is a point to this lecture?"

"There is a Light Engineer company in the Constabulary. If we can talk General White into loaning us one of its platoons, they can do what we haven't done—take a really close look at Castle Wewelsburg, maybe find hidden rooms, tunnels. Maybe they could even find the cave with the death's-head rings."

"I retract fifty percent of the unkind thoughts I've been having about you, Super Spook. Can we ask White on the telephone?"

"I think we have to do it face-to-face."

"And since you don't dare go see General White before you see Justice Jackson . . ."

"Nuremberg, here we come."

XII

[ONE]
Office of the Chief U.S. Prosecutor
Palace of Justice
Nuremberg, American Zone of
Occupation, Germany
0735 24 April 1946

Executive Officer Kenneth Brewster opened the door to Justice Jackson's office and formally announced, "Mr. Justice, General Serov, Colonel Cohen, Father McKenna, and Captain Cronley."

Justice Jackson's response was far less formal. He came quickly from behind his desk, went to Cronley, and put his hands on the captain's arms.

Then he hugged him.

"Jim, I can't tell you how sorry I am about Mrs. Moriarty. I'm so damn sorry."

"I guess it wasn't meant to be," Cronley said.

Jackson patted Cronley's arms, then turned to the priest.

"I don't believe I've had the pleasure . . ." he said.

"This is Father McKenna," Cronley said. "He's here to hear your confession and save your soul."

"Cronley," the priest snapped, "I've had about all I can stand of you and your so-called wit."

"But you're stuck with me, right? Or can you go to Cardinal von Hassburger and complain I'm not being nice?"

"And who is Cardinal von Hassburger?" Jackson asked.

"A Vatican big shot," Cronley said, "who is worried (a) that the world is about to hear they've been guarding Odessa's money for them and (b) that General Serov, Colonel Cohen, and I are right that the Church of Saint Heinrich the Divine poses a greater threat to Holy Mother Church than does communism."

"The first is a hell of an accusation," Jackson said. "Easy—but dangerous—to make and hard to prove. How're you going to do that?"

"Well, for one thing," Serov said, then paused and dramatically put his briefcase on Jackson's desk, "there's a little over two million dollars in various hard currencies in there. We snatched it from one of von Hassburger's bishops while he was trying to hand it over to Odessa, maybe even to von Dietelburg himself."

"Are you giving me that money?" Jackson asked.

Cronley couldn't tell if Jackson was joking. He was reminded of his observation about Serov and his men using the captured small Mercedes and the fact that the Soviets essentially were broke.

"You jest," Serov said.

"I hope you're not thinking of sending it to Lubyanka Square," Jackson said.

Serov chuckled and shook his head.

"I spoke to the President yesterday," Jackson volunteered. "Surprising me only a little, he had heard from General Clay about the attack on the safe house. For some reason, Clay didn't mention to the President that Mrs. Moriarty was murdered in the attack.

"The President now harbors the opinion that the target of the safe house attack was you, Super Spook. As very well it may have been. And he made it clear that he is holding me responsible for keeping you alive. Get yourself a bodyguard, Cronley. Better yet, get two."

"Yes, sir."

"And yet a better idea than that . . ." Jackson said, pulling his telephone to him and then dialing a number from memory. "Ostrowski, Justice

Jackson. Further on our conversation designating you as Captain Cronley's bodyguard, pick two good men to assist you and bring them to my office prepared to guard Cronley around the clock whither in the wide world his duties may take him."

Visibly pleased with himself, Jackson hung the telephone up, and asked Cronley, "Now tell me when I—and, more important, our commander in chief—can expect you to have von Dietelburg and Burgdorf back in the Tribunal Prison?"

"I have no idea where they are, sir, nor do Colonel Cohen, General Serov, or General Gehlen."

"That's hard to believe."

"I agree. Which made me wonder why. And then on the way over here from the Compound, I had one of my famous epiphanies."

"Oh, really, Super Spook?" Cohen said, sarcastically. "Please do share it with us."

"One of two things is true," Cronley said. "Let me back up a little. This is where my epiphany got started anyway. With the CIC, the Russians, the DCI, and even the German police looking for von Dietelburg and Burgdorf, why haven't we had at least a sighting of either of them?"

When no one answered, Cronley went on. "Because the German people don't want them caught. They don't give a damn what they've done. All the Kraut population wants is to be able to thumb their nose at the Army of Occupation and the Nuremberg Tribunal. And as long as we don't have them, that's what's happening."

"Super Spook may be onto something," Jackson said, thoughtfully.

"So where are they?" Cohen asked.

"Actually," Cronley replied, "the first question is, where **aren't** they? In Hungary? I don't think so, not with the NKGB looking for them. Vienna? I don't think they're there either. That's where they were bagged. Humiliating the Austrians, who wanted—want—to put them on display on trial in Austria. Have they gone to Prague? Or Croatia? France? Spain? I don't think so."

Cohen said, "At the risk of repeating myself, so then where are they?"

"I think in Germany, either Berlin or the American Zone. And I don't think we're going to find them. We're going to have to make them come to us."

"How are we going to do that?" Cohen asked, dubiously.

"My epiphany is, they're still interested in Castle Wewelsburg. When I thought about it, there was something fishy about their attempt to blow it up."

"But they tried, James," Serov said.

"And failed."

"What are you saying?"

"I'm saying that if von Dietelburg, head of the

Church of Saint Heinrich the Divine, wanted the Vatican of said church to be destroyed, all we would have found was rubble. They wanted—want—us to think that it's no longer of any real value to them."

"To what end?" Justice Jackson asked.

"So that after we've had our look around, satisfied our curiosity, and left, they can come back."

"For those golden death's-head rings?" Jackson asked.

"And for the contents of Saint Heinrich's safe, which we haven't found; for the 'holy relics,' and almost certainly for God only knows how much money. Now that I think about it, the only reason they were trying to make a withdrawal from the Vatican Bank is because Cohen's guys are sitting on the castle, where they have day-to-day expenses' money."

No one said anything, and then Cronley continued. "I think—hell, I'm sure—that at this very moment one of von Dietelburg's disciples is watching Wewelsburg to see what we're up to."

"Cut to the chase, Jim," Jackson said.

"I've come up with an idea that will bring them back to Wewelsburg. First of all, we have to convince them we're really leaving. I mean, we can't just drive away. They know that Cohen's people have been sitting on the place since he first became involved."

"Whatever your harebrained epiphany is telling you," Cohen said, "I am not prepared to give up control of the castle even for thirty seconds. There's a hell of a lot we don't know about it."

"It will be impossible for us to get them to think we have really given up and left the castle until we do, in fact, leave the castle."

"Did you hear what I just said?" Cohen snapped.

"If we in fact give up and leave the castle, that would make it available to the rest of the European Command, right?"

Cohen repeated: "Did you just hear—"

"Such as the United States Constabulary, right?" Cronley finished.

"What the hell would the Constab want with Wewelsburg?" Cohen demanded.

"Well, after suitable renovation, of course, it would make a lovely home for the Constabulary Non-Commissioned Officer Academy."

"Oh, Jesus Christ!" Cohen said, disgustedly.

"Let him finish, Mort," Jackson ordered.

"The only way von Dietelburg is going to believe we have left Wewelsburg is if we do, in fact, leave," Cronley said. "Which we can do. The proof of that for von Dietelburg is that the Constabulary then moves in and construction on the NCO Academy begins."

"By whom?" Jackson asked.

"The One Hundred Fourteenth Engineer Company (Light), U.S. Constabulary. Presuming I can talk General White into letting me have it."

Cohen said, "I had to have Jim explain to me what the hell's a Light Engineer company. He did. But I'm still not convinced."

"Colonel, sir, it would be inappropriate for a very young and very junior officer such as myself to question the decisions of officers much senior to myself."

Justice Jackson laughed.

"I'll call I. D. White for you, if you'd like."

"Thank you, sir. I'd rather do it myself. Or, actually, set up Tiny Dunwiddie to ask him. Tiny usually gets what he asks General White for. And I'd like to pick General White's brain about Burgdorf. Ever since the general saw the grave at Peenemünde where Burgdorf buried the slave workers alive, he's had a special place in his heart for him."

Jackson considered that for a minute and then reached for the telephone.

"Get me General White in Sonthofen," he ordered into the receiver, then looked at Cronley, and said, "Bear with me a moment."

"Well?" a gruff voice demanded over the phone seconds later.

White apparently had not only answered his own line but answered it on the first ring.

"I'm sorry your gout is out of control again, General. I'll call later."

He hung up and glanced across his desk at the others.

Thirty seconds after that, his telephone rang.

Surprising no one, it was General White.

"Sorry, Bob," he said. "This is one of those mornings where I'm surrounded by idiots."

"I.D., I need to talk to you, but I don't want to do it over the phone."

"I can't get away right now. Would you consider coming here? I can send Billy Wilson in the C-45."

"I'd like to bring Cohen, Cronley, and Dunwiddie with me."

"You may consider that Hotshot Billy is on the way," White said, and then the line went dead.

"That work, Cronley?" Justice Jackson said.

"Yes, sir."

Serov then said, "I think I would be of more value to our noble cause by encouraging my countrymen to exert more effort in looking for von Dietelburg and Burgdorf than they are. Is there any reason I have to go to Sonthofen?"

"No," Cronley decided. "And I think our spiritual adviser would be in the way. Can you keep him occupied, Ivan?"

"Oh, yes," Serov replied.

For some reason, Cronley thought, **that sounds** menacing.

[TWO]
Office of the Commanding General
United States Constabulary
Sonthofen, American Zone of
Occupation, Germany
1455 24 April 1946

Major General I. D. White signaled for the people in his office doorway to come in.

"Now that I've had time to think it over, why am I worried that you've accepted my gracious invitation?" the stocky, forty-six-year-old White greeted them.

No one saluted, but, in turn, Cohen, Cronley, and Tiny Dunwiddie approached White's desk, came to a stance very much like attention, then shook White's extended hand. When they had finished, Justice Jackson went to the side of the desk and shook hands with him.

"My spies tell me you have been infiltrated by the NKGB," White said. "Where's Serov?"

"I can only conclude he's afraid of you," Jackson said. "I can't imagine why. Anyway, he sends his respects."

"As well he should. And you, Chauncey, has the Texan here managed to completely corrupt you? Or are you still redeemable?"

"Unfortunately, I'm afraid it's the former, Uncle Isaac. I have the strength of zero because in my heart I'm completely corrupted."

"In a manner of speaking? Or is there something specific?"

"I think for once Super Spook is right."

White's eyes went from Dunwiddie to Cronley.

"I'm now afraid, Captain Cronley, to ask what I can do for you. What is it you want from me?"

"Sir, your Fourteenth Light Engineer Company."

White's eyebrows went up.

"Now you have piqued my curiosity. What in the world would you do with it?"

"Would you believe," Jackson said, "that as a token of his admiration for yourself specifically, I.D., and the Constabulary generally, he intends to use it to convert an existing structure into the U.S. Constabulary NCO Academy."

White grunted. "No. I would not."

"Sir," Cronley said, "I would apply its many talents in my unending war to save the world from the Thousand-Year Reich."

White's eyes went back to Dunwiddie.

"Chauncey, can you tell me what Super Spook is talking about?" Then he immediately changed his mind. "No, Cronley, you try—hard—to tell me what you're talking about."

"Yes, sir. Sir, would you be surprised if I told you I forgot one of the basic principles of warfare?"

"I'd be surprised if you remember any of them. Which particular one, pray tell, are you referring to?"

" 'Never underestimate your enemy,' sir."

White lit a cigarette, exhaled, and said, "Okay, this game of Twenty Questions is over. Let's have it, Cronley. Nothing cute."

"Sir, yes, sir. Sir, you're aware that just as the war was ending, Colonel Cohen smelled something was off about Castle Wewelsburg and took it under his wing."

White nodded. "Whereupon he learned that the Nazis had attempted to start a lunatic and/or obscene religion with the castle as its Vatican?"

"Yes, sir. That's correct."

"I also heard the Nazis abandoned it after trying and failing to blow it up?"

"Yes, sir. That's what I'm getting to. I started thinking about that. They had what they thought was a good reason to blow the castle up. That raised two questions. What was the reason? And since they had made the decision to blow it up, why had they failed?

"I began to give that some serious thought. Neither von Dietelburg nor Burgdorf were run-of-the-mill Nazis. Von Dietelburg was Himmler's adjutant. I suspect he was a lot more than that, but I know that if he was Himmler's adjutant, he was privy to ninety-plus percent of Himmler's secrets—including, of course, being up to his eyeballs in the Church of Saint Heinrich the Divine.

"And SS-Brigadeführer Wilhelm Burgdorf wasn't a run-of-the-mill Nazi big shot either. He was dispatched by Himmler himself to Peene-münde to make sure that there was nothing of value left when we got there. I suspect he wasn't sent there until whoever was first sent had failed.

"That gives us two really top-drawer Nazi offi-cials. Which raises the question of how come they failed in blowing up an old castle?

"Answer: Because they—for a number of rea-sons I'll get into later—didn't want to destroy it. They just wanted it to look like they had tried to demolish it."

"Interesting reasoning," White said, thought-fully.

"Once I started down that road, sir, a lot of other things began to fall into place. As Colonel Cohen first found, Sergeant Johann Strauss isn't who he says he is. He was left behind at the castle to tell whichever Americans showed up that all the goodies—the secret relics, the death's-head rings, the contents of Himmler's safe, et cetera—were long gone when he got there.

"It probably would have worked with anyone else, but Colonel Cohen smelled a rat—although he didn't say so out loud—from the beginning."

"What's this got to do with my Fourteenth Engineers?" White asked.

"Sir, the only way von Dietelburg and/or Burgdorf are going to believe Cohen's people have left Wewelsburg is for Cohen's people to actually leave Wewelsburg."

"General," Cohen put in, "I've made it clear that that will happen over my dead body."

White made a gesture which Cohen instantly understood was an order to shut up. Then he gestured for Cronley to continue.

"Sir, in my scenario, as Cohen's people move out, the Fourteenth Engineers move in."

"And do what?" White asked, suspiciously.

"Sir, the first thing they do is prepare signs on four-by-eight sheets of plywood. The one hanging over the main entrance would read 'Welcome to the U.S. Constabulary NCO Academy.'"

"I don't think you are trying to be cute, Cronley," White said, "but it damn sure is starting to sound like it."

"Sir, I'm dead serious. If nothing else works, at the end of this, the Constab will have a first-rate NCO Academy."

"Define 'nothing else,'" White said.

"Yes, sir. If the Fourteenth Engineers are unable

to discover hidden passages and tunnels, and the like, in Castle Wewelsburg as they build this NCO Academy. Or if we're unable to bag some von Dietelburg underling visiting the castle to see what we're up to."

"Why do you think he'll be interested?"

"I think he took—takes—the dignity of the SS seriously. It's like a religion to him. We know Wewelsburg was intended for the SS elite, the SS's Generals Corps. And here we are, turning it into a school that will turn PFCs into corporals. I think that's going to piss them off. All of them."

White abruptly changed the subject.

"Cronley, I know what happened in Berlin. At the safe house. Including what happened to Mrs. Moriarty."

"Yes, sir?"

"My wife thinks that you and Mrs. Moriarty were more than good friends from your college days. That you had something going on. True?"

Cronley felt his anger immediately build.

That's really none of your fucking business, General.

However, I damn sure cannot tell you that.

But neither am I going to lie about it.

"Well?" White pursued.

"Yes, sir. We were going to get married."

"So soon after she lost her husband?"

"Yes, sir."

"What, exactly, was your relationship with Mrs. Moriarty when her husband was still alive?"

"She was the wife of my best friend at A&M, General."

"And nothing more? Am I supposed to believe that?"

Cronley heard himself blurt his reply before he could stop himself. "Sir, with all due respect, I don't give a damn what you or anyone else believes."

There was silence in the room. Cronley could feel the tension of the others.

General White then said, evenly, "We've noticed, Cronley. Haven't we, Mr. Justice? That you don't give a damn what anyone believes, including your superiors."

"Leave him alone, I.D.," Jackson said. "You've been intentionally, for reasons I can't imagine, trying to get him to blow his cork."

"So you've noticed that, Bob, have you? And how would you judge Captain Cronley's response to my provocation?"

"He handled it a helluva lot better than I would or could."

"'Great minds march down similar trails,'" White replied. "You ever hear that, Bob?"

White then reached for his telephone.

"Get me Colonel Dickinson of the Fourteenth Engineers on a secure line. If memory serves, they're in Bad Nauheim."

"Dickinson, this is General White. I've decided that the Constabulary needs an NCO Academy, and, further, that the Fourteenth is going to build it for us."

There was a pause long enough for Colonel Dickinson to say "Yes, sir."

"I'll tell you what happens next," White continued. "My godson is in town, and Mrs. White is going to feed us lunch. After lunch, Colonel Wilson is going to fire up my Gooney Bird and fly to Bad Nauheim, where you and either your S-3 or your executive officer—your choice—will be waiting with your bags packed for, say, five days. Got all that?"

There was again a pause long enough for the colonel to again say "Yes, sir."

"Nice to talk to you, Dickinson," White said, and hung up. Then he stood up. "Let's go to lunch."

[THREE]
Aboard *Constabulary I*
Bad Nauheim, American Zone of
Occupation, Germany
1725 24 April 1946

When Hotshot Billy Wilson landed General White's Gooney Bird at Bad Nauheim, Lieutenant Colonel David P. Dickinson, CE, and another engineer officer, Major Donald G. Lomax, were waiting for them.

Both officers were visibly surprised when they were waved aboard the aircraft and found that the interior, instead of the rows of canvas-and-aluminum-pipe seating they expected, was furnished more like a living room than anything else. It had armchairs and couches affixed to a floor of nice carpet, and against the forward wall of the passenger compartment was a small bar.

"Gentlemen, I'm Justice Jackson," Jackson greeted them, then pointed as he spoke. "That's Colonel Cohen, and those two are Captains Dunwiddie and Cronley."

When Cronley got out of the copilot's position, both engineers were surprised there were no pilot's wings on his tunic chest.

"Captain," Major Lomax offered helpfully, "you seem to have lost your wings."

"Major, you can't lose something you never had," Cronley replied.

The major, his face blank, did not know how to reply.

"This is what happens next, after we take on fuel and stow your gear," Cronley then said. "First, we're going to Wetzlar to pick up Sergeant K. C. Wagner. Then we're going to Castle Wewelsburg, where Colonel Cohen will show our new engineer friends here around. Then Nuremberg. Any questions?"

There were none.

"Colonel Dickinson," Cronley said, "have you got any large—the larger, the better—bulldozers, hole diggers, heavy equipment like that, that you're not going to need, say, for the next three weeks?"

"Why do you want to know, Captain?"

"Well, if you do, I want you to get them on their way to Wewelsburg as soon as possible."

"Is that so, Captain? On whose authority?"

"Mine."

"Colonel," Cohen said, chuckling, "welcome to our world. You will have to get used to the idea that we're all working for Captain Cronley—Lord knows that I have fought that battle and lost. The next person up in his chain of command is Harry S Truman."

Dickinson looked in disbelief at Justice Jackson,

who, smiling, said, "This is the other side of Alice's looking glass: 'Abandon all hope, ye who enter here.'"

[FOUR]
Farber Palast
Stein, near Nuremberg, American
Zone of Occupation, Germany
2005 24 April 1946

Cronley's bodyguard detail, which now consisted of Max Ostrowski and two other Polish DCI agents, hadn't gone with them to Sonthofen, but when they landed at Nuremberg, they found the three waiting for them.

Also waiting were Cronley's Horch touring car, a Chevrolet staff car, and three jeeps.

Cronley offered the Horch to Justice Jackson, who smiled.

"Thanks all the same, Jim. Maybe you can pull it off, but I cannot afford to look like Hitler in a Nazimobile on the way to a rally of the faithful."

Minutes later, preceded by a jeep, and trailed by another, Cronley and Casey Wagner rode to the castle in the backseat of the Horch.

There was a large ex-Wehrmacht Mercedes with Red Army plates sitting in a NO PARKING area in front of the hotel, so when Cronley entered the lobby bar, he was not surprised to see Ivan Serov. But he was surprised that instead of sitting with Father McKenna, Serov was with Miss Janice Johansen. He had last seen her in the hospital in Berlin.

"Where's our friend from the Vatican?" Cronley said. "You were supposed to be watching him, Ivan."

"I passed him to Mortimer, who is giving him a first look at the castle."

"You look a lot better than I expected you to, Jimmy," she greeted him. "Nice to see that you've improved, sweetie. And good to see you, too, Casey."

Wagner made a thin smile and nodded once.

"Thank you, Miss Johansen," Cronley said as he and Casey took their seats. "When your life is FUBAR, and there's nothing you can do about it, you throw yourself into your work. I learned that from Ivan."

"Or turn to drink," Serov said, reaching for a bottle of Haig & Haig and offering it to Cronley.

Cronley took the bottle, then poured two inches of the scotch whisky into one glass and half an inch into a second. The latter he slid over to K. C. Wagner.

"Jimmy," Janice said. "I realize this sounds a little lame, but is there anything I can do for you?"

"Oddly enough, I just thought of something . . . Ivan, did you tell her why I went to see General White?"

Serov shook his head.

"I need your literary talent," Cronley said, turning back to Janice.

"To write about what?"

"The about-to-be-built Constabulary NCO Academy."

"You're fucking kidding me."

"Not at all."

Cronley then told her why he wanted her to craft a story that would appear on the front page of **Stars and Stripes** and possibly even the Paris edition of the **Herald Tribune**.

"You realize, Jimmy, that I couldn't write such a piece without first having seen Castle Wewelsburg?"

"That poses problems." He pointed to the table at which Max Ostrowski and the two Polish DCI agent/bodyguards had taken seats. "Not only them, but Justice Jackson just pointed out that when we ride around in my Horch, we look like Hitler en route to a Nazi rally. I don't want whoever is watching the Wewelsburg to report that someone very important just showed up."

"I can have an unmarked car here in thirty minutes," Serov said. "Providing, of course, that I get to go along."

"Your car, the one in the NO PARKING zone outside, will do just fine," Cronley replied. "Whoever wants to know what's going on at Wewelsburg will be confused by a report that a car of a senior Russian officer arrived at the castle accompanied by two jeeps full of DCI agents."

"And Janice," K. C. Wagner chimed in.

"And Miss Johansen. We leave immediately after breakfast."

[FIVE]
Wewelsburg Castle
Near Paderborn, American Zone of
Occupation, Germany
0915 25 April 1946

They found Cohen, Father McKenna, and the engineer officers in the castle kitchen, drinking coffee with Cohen's CIC agents.

"This is General Serov," Cronley announced to Dickinson and Lomax. "And Miss Janice Johansen of the Associated Press. And, last but not least, Casey Wagner of the DCI. I've promised them all a—"

"Of the what?" Major Lomax interrupted. "Did you say of the DCI?"

"Yes, I did. And, to clear the air, so am I. Of the DCI, I mean. Any other questions?"

"No . . . No, sir," Lomax said.

"As I started to say, I've promised them all a tour of the castle. I was about to ask who's best qualified to be the guide, but I think it would be better if we found our own way, and if Colonel Cohen, our de facto tour guide, should miss something, whoever else knows anything can speak up. Any objections?"

There were none.

The tour took just over two hours.

When they had returned to the kitchen and were all seated around the table, Cronley stood up.

"This question is directed to Lieutenant Colonel Dickinson," he said. "But I want anybody who knows something to chime in. Got it?"

There were nods and murmured "Yes, sir"s.

"Colonel, what do you think the chances are that hidden passages and/or rooms in the castle exist that we haven't found?"

Dickinson, without hesitation, replied, "There's absolutely no question in my mind that there are both. The larger question is, how to find access to them."

"No question at all?" Cronley asked, genuinely surprised.

"None," Dickinson said with finality.

"Can I ask why you're so sure?"

"Castles, fortifications, have always fascinated me. Going back to my days in Boston."

"What's in Boston?"

"The Massachusetts Institute of Technology, and a dozen lesser schools."

"Can you give us a little lecture?" Cronley asked.

"It will be a short one," Dickinson said. "Okay. Starting with the idea that castles like Wewelsburg were built primarily for defense. Not like Buckingham Palace, for example, which was designed to let royalty live high on the hog.

"Because places like this were designed for war, they were always making changes to them. Making a wall thicker, for example. Or higher. So how do you make a wall higher or thicker, or both? You try, of course, to use the existing wall. But often that doesn't work out. So you build a new wall. Where? Most often, inside the old wall. That leaves a space between the walls. Am I getting through?"

"You are, but keep talking," Cronley replied.

"Okay, here you are, about to lay the first stone of the new wall. Your back is to the old wall. So where do you try to lay that stone? At a distance that will allow you to work comfortably when the new wall is, say, three feet tall. Two or three feet inside the old wall. So you lay the first couple of stones.

"And then you have a look. And realize that if the old wall is only three feet distant from the new wall, no one will be able to get past the stonemason. So you move those first stones to five feet and have a look and decide, what the hell, it won't cost any more if I put the new wall ten feet away from the old wall. And that's what you do.

"So when you get the new wall as tall, or taller, than the old wall, you connect them, and no one remembers there's ten feet between the walls." He paused and glanced around at everyone. "Still with me?"

Cronley said, "What about inside the castle? For example, you want to make two small rooms out of a big one."

Dickinson nodded. "Think about it. You're building a new wall. Same rules apply, except you may now be thinking of the space between the walls as a passageway. Get it?"

"Got it," Cronley replied. "So how do you find these hidden walls or passageways—whatever they're called?"

"The easiest way would be to look for them on the original plans for the castle. I don't suppose they've survived the centuries, but a lot of work has been done here. Even partials would be helpful."

"Maybe we could find some of those," Colonel Cohen said.

"Johann Strauss," Cronley blurted. "If we can find him, and put the fear of God in him, that would probably help us find the plans. And a lot else."

Cohen met his eyes, and said, "Yeah, but that's a big if. I've got my people looking for him. About the only thing we've learned is that there was no SS-Truppführer Johann Strauss anywhere near either Himmler's or von Dietelburg's offices in Berlin."

"Okay," Cronley said, "but he doesn't know you've learned that. When he sees the activity around here, he's likely to walk right in."

"I'm not holding my breath," Cohen said.

"Then tell your guys to look harder."

"Actually, Super Spook," Cohen said, thickly sarcastic, "that thought occurred to me."

Cronley turned to Dickinson.

"Without a floor plan, is there another way?"

"Sure. Tape measure."

"Excuse me?"

"You measure a room. Then you go outside the castle's wall, outside that room, and measure there. If there's a significant difference—the outside measures twenty-eight feet, say, and the inside is twenty—you know there's eight feet of something missing."

"Dumb question: Do you have a tape measure?"

"Never leave home without it."

"Okay, then you start measuring while Colonel Cohen gets on the telephone."

"Who's Colonel Cohen calling?" Colonel Cohen asked.

"General White."

"And what am I going to say to General White?"

"You're going to talk him out of a troop of Constabulary. We need to really guard this place."

Cohen looked at Dickinson, and said, "The most annoying thing Captain Cronley does, Colonel, is think of something minutes before you do."

XIII

"Good morning, Miss Johansen," Father McKenna greeted her as she strode into the palace dining room.

"I hate people who are cheerful in the morning."

"My apologies. It comes naturally. Occupational hazard, you might say."

"Sure. The Vatican is hiding the Nazis' dirty money and you're a fucking choirboy of cheerfulness."

McKenna, shocked, was speechless.

She turned to Cronley, who looked up at her from his steak-and-eggs breakfast.

"I'm afraid to ask how you slept, Janice. You

should be exhausted after our long day at the castle. Buy you some breakfast?"

She ignored the offer. "Your bright idea ain't going to work, Jimmy."

"To which of my many bright ideas do you refer?"

"This one," she said, and handed him a sheet of paper that had a sheet of carbon paper and another sheet of paper stapled to it."

His eyes went to the top page:

CONSTABULARY TO OPEN NCO ACADEMY
By Janice Johansen
ASSOCIATED PRESS FOREIGN CORRESPONDENT
Berlin, April 6—

Cronley said, "There's nothing here."

"Nothing gets past you, does it?"

"Why won't it work?"

"Because that's all there is."

"A new NCO Academy is not news?"

"If I submitted that to **Stars and Stripes**, they would run it on page seventeen, somewhere buried under the WAC softball tournament highlights. Not that I would submit it to **Stripes**. The best I could do, sweetie, wasn't good enough. It still read like what it was, a bullshit PIO press release, and ol' Janice does not attach her name to bullshit press releases."

"It's important to me, to what we're trying to do here."

"And for that reason I'm off to Sonthofen."

"For what?"

"To see if I can provoke good ol' I. D. White into saying something outrageous onto which I can hang the rest of this lousy yarn."

"If you ask me, that's a really lousy idea."

Janice forced a thin smile. "I don't recall asking you, sweetie . . . See you when Casey and I get back from Sonthofen. He's getting the car as we speak."

"Whoa! You want to take Casey with you? I need him here."

"More than you need that NCO Academy yarn on the front page of **Stripes**?"

After a pause, during which Cronley did not reply, Janice said, "I accept your surrender," and walked out of the dining room.

"Interesting woman," Father McKenna said.

"I thought people in your line of work weren't supposed to notice things like magnificent boobs," Cronley said, mock innocent.

"Why are you so determined to insult me, to pick a fight with me, Cronley?"

"To see what's going on behind that white collar. In my profession, it's called knowing your enemy."

"While I don't think I could claim to be your

friend, even your ally, I most certainly am not your enemy."

"Your primary purpose here, what the cardinal sent you to do, is to find out as much as you can about how much of a threat my organization poses to yours."

"My 'organization,' as you put it, is the Church of Rome. And—I hope this isn't too much of a blow to your ego—I don't think you pose as much of a threat to it as a mosquito does to an elephant by stinging its hindquarters."

"Got to you, haven't I? Where's that well-known **I'm a Jesuit, there's nothing you can say that will bother me** attitude?"

Father McKenna didn't reply.

"By now, Francis, you must understand that I've been spending a lot of time with General Serov and Colonel Cohen . . ."

McKenna nodded.

". . . And I think you will acknowledge that both are senior intelligence officers with a great deal of experience . . ."

McKenna nodded again.

". . . Therefore, as a very junior, inexperienced intelligence officer, I have always paid rapt attention to whatever they had to say."

The priest chuckled and shook his head.

"Many times," Cronley continued, "one or the

other has referred to other intelligence agencies as 'the best in the world.' Better, in other words, than the CIC, the DCI, and the NKGB. Sometimes, one or the other of them so described General Gehlen's organizations over his long career. At other times, they said the Zionist organization's Mossad was not only the best, but vastly superior to ours. And at still other times, both said, separately, that the nameless organization run by your boss, His Holiness Pope Pius XII, was unquestionably the best."

Father McKenna raised his eyebrows. "But the Church does not have an intelligence service like the NKGB or the DCI."

"Hear me out. The entire Church is an intelligence service far more extensive and effective than any other."

"We are agreeing to disagree," the priest said.

"Intelligence is dumped in your lap, Francis, if you think about it. You don't have to look for it. But intelligence is intelligence no matter where it comes from. I speak, of course, of the confessional."

"What is spoken in the confessional remains in the confessional," the priest said, coldly.

Cronley was undeterred. "Okay, fine. Let's leave the confessional out of this. But the fact remains that Holy Mother Church has assets in place around the world, as well as a communications system from bottom to top. I don't know the exact numbers here, but let's say there is no other population in the world where, conservatively, one-third of the citizenry meets regularly with its officials. And the worst sin of all is action contrary to the best interests of Holy Mother Church."

"This conversation is beginning to really offend me."

"I'm simply trying to explain my position. So, let's turn to Mossad. Why are they so efficient? Well, when they go somewhere—anywhere—the Hebrew population is already on their side—"

"Where are you going with this, James?"

"It's quite simple: The reason we can't find von Dietelburg and Burgdorf is because something like ninety-nine percent of the Germans are rooting for them—and against our success in returning them to prison and, ultimately, putting them on trial."

"But it has to be common knowledge among the Germans that those two are really despicable people. And I'm not even getting into the Church of Saint Heinrich."

"Francis, I don't think it's got anything to do with right or wrong."

"What, then?"

"How about humiliation? Maybe even the humiliation of humiliation?"

"Now it sounds like you're babbling again. What is your point?"

"Germany didn't lose the First World War. They lost War Two."

"What is that supposed to mean?"

"Germany didn't surrender in World War One. They came to an armistice with the Allies. The terms of the armistice, and of the Versailles Treaty which followed, were humiliating. They lost territory in Europe. They lost their foreign colonies."

"We know that. Get to your point, if you have one."

"They lost World War Two. They were forced to surrender unconditionally. That was even more humiliating than being forced to seek an armistice."

"I still don't get your point."

"The best way to counter the depression that comes with humiliation is to give whoever is humiliating you the finger."

He demonstrated, making a fist with middle finger extended. McKenna's expression was one of mild displeasure.

"By doing nothing to help us bag von Dietelburg," Cronley went on, dropping his hand, "or, even better, doing something that actually helps them avoid getting bagged, they have the satisfaction of giving the finger to the people that are humiliating them."

"That's possibly, even probably, true. But, so what?"

"The point is, if we want to bag von Dietelburg and Burgdorf, we're going to have to do it ourselves, as no one is going to help us. At least, not help us intentionally."

"Any ideas on how you're going to do that?"

"I'm headed into Nuremberg. Do you want to tag along?"

"What are we going to do in Nuremberg?"

"Try something I admit is desperate."

[TWO]

"This is a magnificent automobile," Father McKenna said as they cruised in the Horch Sport Cabriolet with its canvas top folded down. "I have never been in one."

"I liked it better before Justice Jackson said he doesn't care to ride in it because it makes him look like a Nazi big shot en route to a party rally."

Cronley raised his right hand over his head and rotated it back and forth as if waving to the masses. The priest chuckled.

"That thought occurred to me, too. Where'd you get it?"

"It used to belong to a DCI colonel who got

himself kidnapped by Serov. When I got him back, they sent him to the States, and I grabbed the car."

"Why don't you get rid of it?"

"That would be admitting I made a mistake. Like you Jesuits, I never admit to making a mistake."

The priest ignored that.

"What are we going to do in Nuremberg?"

"**We're** not going to do anything. I'm going to try to talk Justice Jackson into letting me take SS-Standartenführer Oskar Müller and SS-Brigadeführer Wilhelm Heimstadter out of their cells for a few days."

Cronley looked at the priest as if trying to judge his reaction. When there was none, he said nothing.

Three minutes later—which seemed much longer—Father McKenna said, "I'm getting the impression that's all you're going to tell me. Can I get you to change your mind? Curiosity is killing me."

"Okay. I don't think it will work, but I'm going to make clear that their only chance to dodge the hangman—and instead win a trip to Argentina—is if they roll over on von Dietelburg and Burgdorf. I don't expect them to, but I want to judge their reaction. To see if it's as strong as it was the last time I offered them a deal."

"Where are you going to put them when they're out of their cells?"

"One of them I can stash in the Mansion—DCI headquarters—downtown. I don't know about the other. Maybe put him in Strasbourg with my friend Colonel Jean-Paul Fortin."

"Cronley, I've spent a lot of time in prisons."

"I'm shocked! What did they get you for?"

"As a chaplain," McKenna said, tiredly.

"And?"

"Cronley, if I offer an observation and then a suggestion, will you think about it before you immediately issue a withering opinion of it?"

"Have at it."

"Prisoners have nothing to do all day and all night but think. As a result, they are usually able to outwit their guards. I'm not talking about escaping, obviously, but communicating with other prisoners, for example."

"I've heard that, but so what?"

"Another thing I noticed is that prisoners don't trust each other and are thus prone to suspect that prisoner A is a snitch, that prisoner B is getting special treatment for some nefarious reason, et cetera. Still with me?"

Cronley nodded.

"You don't think you're going to get anywhere with these two today because you didn't get very far with them the last time you tried. Correct?"

"Go on. You have my attention."

McKenna patted the back of the front seat.

"If either one of them was seen riding through the streets of Nuremberg in the backseat of your Nazimobile, it would be all over the prison within hours."

"I see where you're going. You are a devious sonofabitch, Father McKenna—I say that with admiration."

"There are a number of other possibilities that I see."

"Such as?"

McKenna told him.

[THREE]
Palace of Justice
Nuremberg, American Zone of
Occupation, Germany
1135 26 April 1946

"You sure you know what to do?" Max Ostrowski, standing next to the Horch, asked of DCI Agent Cyril Kochanski, who was in the front passenger seat, the car's roof still folded down. DCI Agent Basil Frankowski was behind the wheel.

Kochanski nodded. "First, I load the Nazi bastard—"

"SS-Brigadeführer Wilhelm Heimstadter," Ostrowski furnished.

"SS-Brigadeführer Wilhelm Heimstadter," Kochanski dutifully repeated. "First, I load him in the backseat of the Nazimobile, then get in beside him, and we take off. Then, as soon as we're out of sight of the Tribunal, I get out of the backseat and climb up front."

"After telling the general what?"

"That if he even looks like he's thinking of running off, I'm going to shoot him in the knees."

"And then?"

"And then Basil takes us on a fifteen-minute tour of Nuremberg, finally ending up at the Mansion."

"Correct."

"Are you going to tell me what this is all about?"

"If I told you, I'd have to kill you," Ostrowski said, smiling.

Cyril Kochanski gave Max Ostrowski the finger and then signaled Basil Frankowski to get moving.

Forty-five minutes later, the Horch turned off Offenbach Platz and stopped before the twelve-foot-tall gate in the Compound wall. Frankowski tapped the horn to get inside.

Kochanski turned in his seat so that he could

keep an eye on SS-Brigadeführer Wilhelm Heim-stadter. He grunted. Heimstadter, riding alone in back, looked much like a Nazi big shot en route to a rally that Kochanski had heard Captain Cronley mention.

The gate opened inward, and the Horch drove through and up to the front of the large, luxuri-ous house. Kochanski gestured with his fist for Heimstadter to get out. His massive hand almost completely hid the full-size Colt .45 ACP semi-automatic pistol it held.

Then Kochanski got out of the Horch and gestured for Heimstadter to enter the Mansion.

Once inside, he led the German to closed double doors off the foyer.

Kochanski knocked and was told to enter.

Beyond the double doors was the library, a large room with rich, dark leather furniture and book-lined walls. In the center was a heavy wooden table. Seated at it were four men: Colonel Mortimer Cohen, Captain James D. Cronley Jr., Captain Chauncy Dunwiddie, and Father Francis X. McKenna, S.J.

Facing the table were two wooden chairs with arms, and, nearby, four others without arms. Colonel Cohen saw that Heimstadter was trying to survey the luxurious room unnoticed. Then he tried not to stare at Dunwiddie.

"Herr SS-Brigadeführer," Cohen announced,

gesturing at one of the armchairs facing the table. "Please, have a seat."

Then he pointed to Kochanski and directed him to post himself as guard outside the double doors. The big Pole nodded once, turned on his heels, and marched out.

"You're lucky, Herr SS-Brigadeführer," Cohen then said, pushing back his chair. "My august presence and commanding authority are required elsewhere. I had hoped to be part of this interview, as I consider the subject matter of great importance . . . You've got it, Cronley."

Cohen then stood up, as did Cronley and Dunwiddie. Cohen then marched out of the room. Cronley sat back down. Dunwiddie then went to the armless wooden chairs, picked one up using only one hand, then placed it, backward, near Heimstadter. He sat in it, crossing his massive forearms across the top of the chairback.

This bit of theater had been at the suggestion of Father McKenna. He had announced that because Tiny Dunwiddie was not only enormous but also very black, the Germans, not accustomed to such, would be nervous in his presence.

"It therefore follows," McKenna had added, "that they will be even more nervous being in very close proximity of a strange enormous black man with muscular arms crossed and a cold stare."

"That's a very good point," Dunwiddie had replied, and looked at Cronley. "You'd think someone would have thought of that before now."

Cronley, who had made the same observation many times at the Pullach Compound near Munich and here at the Mansion, had chosen to ignore the comment. He noted, however, that the priest now looked rather pleased with his announcement.

"And good morning to you, Herr SS-Brigadeführer," Cronley now began, in fluent German. "How's every little thing in your life?"

"I have reminded you several times, Captain Cronley, that my rank is generalmajor."

"Then we have already agreed to disagree. I've always believed that once an SS-Brigadeführer, always an SS-Brigadeführer."

Heimstadter gave him a look of exasperation.

Cronley, intentionally not introducing Dunwiddie, then said, "Herr SS-Brigadeführer, this gentleman is Father Francis Xavier McKenna, of the Society of Jesus. Somehow, a rumor that we were mistreating former senior Nazi officials, such as yourself, reached the Vatican. Cardinal von Hassburger sent Father McKenna to look into it. So please tell him, Herr SS-Brigadeführer, how we've been abusing you."

"I would prefer, Captain, to have that conversation with the SS-Brigadeführer alone," McKenna said.

"Certainly, Father. Anything to please the Pope's representative."

"That's the purpose of this meeting?" Heimstadter asked. "To hear my complaints about my treatment?"

"That's one of them," Cronley said. "But the major one is to give you a chance to save your sorry ass—specifically, your neck—from the hangman's noose."

"You might want to consider, Captain," McKenna said, "that my report will include a section regarding what I observed about the prison staff's attitude toward its prisoners."

"Well, then, I'll have to watch myself. The last thing I need is to have the Pope pissed off at me."

"I find your attitude toward me approaches intentional discourtesy."

"I'm crushed," Cronley said. "You got any more complaints or can I tell Willi here what this meeting is all about?"

"Do whatever you think you should," McKenna said.

"Okay. So, Willi, the powers that be propose a deal. You tell us either where we can find von Dietelburg and Burgdorf or where Odessa is hiding the money and, quote, other valuables, unquote, it didn't put in the Vatican Bank. For that information, you (a) won't be hanged, (b) will get a new identity, and (c) will be safely transported to Argentina."

"I've already told you, many times, that (a) I have no idea where Burgdorf or von Dietelburg might be and (b) that if I did know, I wouldn't tell you."

"You realize, Willi, that I've been ordered to offer the same deal to your pal Müller?"

"If I were a betting man, Captain Cronley, I'd wager that Standartenführer Müller's reply will be much the same as mine."

"Probably, but not certainly. He's always looking on the bright side. He may decide that the sun shining on him and his family in Argentina is a more attractive prospect than it shining on an unmarked grave here."

"I don't think or expect you will understand this, Captain Cronley, but it's a matter of honor."

"Well, you heard the offer, Willi, and rejected it. I suppose you can change your mind at any time before they drop you through that hole in the gallows. I'm out of here. Father McKenna, when you're through with Willi, raise your voice and call for the guard."

Cronley then raised his voice, called, "Guard," and the door opened. He looked at Dunwiddie. "Let's go."

As Dunwiddie stood, Cronley noticed that it caused Heimstadter discomfort.

Good, you miserable sonofabitch.

McKenna sat quietly for a minute before reaching in his pocket and removing a packet of Chesterfields. He offered it to Heimstadter, who motioned no with his hand, and said, "**Danke.** I gave up smoking."

"I never took it up," the priest said, putting the pack back in his pocket. "Well, Herr Heimstadter, how have they been treating you? Any complaints?"

"I don't know if this qualifies as a complaint, but I was thinking there is something quite perverse in their concern for my health, mental and physical."

"How so perverse?"

"They want to be absolutely sure that when they drop me through that hole in the gallows Cronley was talking about, I'm in perfect health and quite sane."

Heimstadter looked at McKenna as if to determine his reaction to the comment.

"I suppose that could be considered 'gallows humor,' but frankly, Herr Heimstadter, I've never seen much to laugh about in such humor. Actually, I'm just about convinced that what you and others like you and Müller intend to do—bravely face the hangman's noose—is a mortal sin."

"How do you figure that?" Heimstadter flared. "We swore an oath before God! What we are doing is what we swore to do."

"I'd prefer not getting into a philosophical argument with you. I shouldn't have said that. I apologize."

"My experience has been that people apologize only when they know they're wrong," Heimstadter said, smugly.

"You **do** want to argue, don't you? My experience is that people want to argue only when they're not at all sure of the validity of their position."

"I'm absolutely sure of the validity of mine."

"Correct me if I'm wrong, but this oath you took was to follow Adolf Hitler, right? Everybody in the SS took that oath?"

"Follow the Führer's orders unto death, specifically."

"But he's dead, isn't he? By suicide?"

"So?"

"How can you follow the orders of a dead man?"

"His orders, his plans for a Thousand-Year Reich, did not die with him."

"Then this is about this heretical religion he was trying to start?"

"It is not a heretical religion. It is about the Thousand-Year Reich that Adolf Hitler started."

"And you feel your oath to follow Hitler's orders requires you to support the notion of a Thousand-Year Reich?"

"Absolutely."

"Forgive me, but I can't see how your committing suicide by hangman's noose is going to help anything."

"Our deaths on the gallows will serve as an inspiration to those following in our footsteps!"

McKenna was silent for thirty-odd seconds.

The fury was still evident in Heimstadter's facial expression, and McKenna sought to calm it with rational discussion.

"This is what will happen on the day of your execution," he began, in the practiced tone of one who had counseled thousands through the screen of a confessional window. "The date of the execution will not be made public. You will be awakened at the usual hour. If you normally go to mass, you will do so.

"Then, without prior notice and at a random hour, you will be led from your prison cell to the gallows. Your feet and hands will be tied. The sentence of the Tribunal will be read. The hangman will place a black bag over your head, then the noose around your neck. You may well wish to request a cigarette at that point."

Heimstadter, wordless, stared at McKenna.

"Then without warning," the priest went on,

"the door in the floor beneath your feet will fall away, and you will be dropped through the opening. The knot in the noose may—or may not—break your neck and cause instant death.

"Your lifeless body will be taken from the noose and laid on the ground. Your hands will be folded across your chest holding a placard bearing your name, and a photograph taken.

"Your corpse will then be placed in the back of an Army truck. No casket. This procedure will be followed for the next four to six men scheduled for execution that day.

"All of the bodies will be covered by a tarpaulin. The truck will then drive to a crematorium, where the corpses will all be burned.

"At this point, just as soon as the ashes are cool enough to handle, a senior officer whose identity will never be made public will supervise the placement of your ashes into a fifty-five-gallon steel drum along with the ashes of the others executed.

The drum with these comingled ashes will be loaded on a truck carrying other drums holding the ashes of other Nazis, those killed after the liberation of the concentration camps.

"The truck will then be driven to any of the five rivers within a hundred miles of the Tribunal. The senior officer will give the driver directions. A jeep full of MPs will follow the truck.

"Once on a bridge over the river, the truck will stop, and the contents of six of the drums will be dumped onto the bridge. The MPs will then first shovel all the ashes into one pile, which will serve to comingle them, and then shovel the ashes off the bridge into the river. Finally, they will puncture the bottoms of the drums and throw them into the river.

"The point of all this is to make sure that the final resting place, so to speak, of those executed will never be known."

Heimstadter cleared his throat.

"Nice try, Father. But it didn't work."

"Excuse me?"

"Go fuck yourself, papist!"

McKenna nodded slightly and sighed.

"I'll talk with you again when you've regained your composure."

McKenna stood up and went to the door.

"Guard!"

This time, Cyril Kochanski and Basil Frankowski appeared at the double doors, both armed.

"I thought I was getting to him," McKenna said to Cronley five minutes later. "I was wrong."

"You want to try Müller?"

"I will if you insist, but, frankly, my ego isn't up to it."

"Well, then, I think what we should do is send ol' Willi back to his cell at the Tribunal, after another tour of the city, and then when the Horch finally comes back, we head back to Castle Wewelsburg."

[FOUR]
Wewelsburg Castle
Near Paderborn, American Zone of
Occupation, Germany
1830 26 April 1946

Cronley found Lieutenant Colonel David P. Dickinson and Major Donald G. Lomax in what he thought of as King Arthur Hall, but designated as his Court Room, with twelve doors and an enormous, circular wooden table large enough for King Arthur and his twelve Knights of the Round Table.

They went over a stack of huge sheets of parchmentlike paper, making notations on them, after consulting their notebooks.

"What did you find out about our humble home?" Cronley asked.

"It's riddled with secret rooms, passageways, et cetera," Dickinson replied. "What Lomax and I are trying to decide is, when were they added to the castle? In the old days or when the modifications were made ten, twenty years ago?"

"Revealing my ignorance, why does that matter?"

"We don't want a ceiling to fall because we took out a wall. The rule of thumb is, when knocking something down, reverse the steps taken to build the building to take it down."

"How do you know what steps somebody else followed, and in what order, building something ten years—or a hundred years—ago?"

"That's the fun part, Captain Cronley," Colonel Dickinson said. "But not to worry, Lomax and Dickinson, engineers extraordinary, are working on it."

"And when do you think you'll be finished?"

"Some time in this century, if we're lucky," Lomax said, and then saw the look on Cronley's face and felt sorry for him.

"I think we can start to go through a small wall in the big round room tomorrow. One of the possibilities is different from the other eleven. It looks like that might be the place where the project was finished—**ergo sum**, the place to start our reverse construction."

"What time tomorrow?"

"How does oh-nine-hundred grab you?"

"Not as tightly as oh-eight-hundred."

"Oh-eight-hundred it is."

[FIVE]
King Arthur's Court
Wewelsburg Castle
Near Paderborn, American Zone
of Occupation, Germany
0750 27 April 1946

When Cronley arrived, he had expected to find the "destruction" crew setting up in the big round room, with Colonel Dickinson standing at King Arthur's huge round table, perhaps marking up with a pencil parchment sheets showing hidden rooms and passageways in the castle.

What Cronley and Father McKenna found when they entered the room was Dickinson working, but not on any such floor plans.

He was working on King Arthur's round table itself.

Dickinson had somehow managed to get three Dodge three-quarter-ton trucks from what had become the motor pool up onto the second floor and into the room.

Originally designed as an ammo carrier, its three-quarter-ton chassis had been quickly adapted, officially and unofficially, to other tasks. Some, for example, were combat vehicles, with a .50 caliber Browning machine gun mounted on a pedestal in the bed.

Dickinson's trio of three-quarter-tons in the

room had been converted, by the installation of winch-and-cable mechanisms in their beds, into vehicle-recovery trucks. While these winch-and-cables could not lift an enormous GM 6×6 truck, they were more than powerful enough to pick up a jeep.

But what these "jeep wreckers" were doing now, along with an enormous crane that had its end squeezed through one of the windows, was aiding in the disassembly of King Arthur's round table.

"Impressive, Colonel," Cronley said as they approached.

"Don't get too close," Dickinson said. "The damn thing tips the scales at two tons, if it's an ounce. And there's always a chance that, weakened by deconstruction, the son of a bitch could let loose and crush shit out of everyone and anything in its path."

"Duly noted," McKenna said, wide-eyed, taking a couple steps back.

"We got started a little early," Dickinson said to Cronley. "Didn't think you'd mind."

"Dumb question?" Cronley said.

"Shoot."

"Why take apart the table? I thought we were concerned with deconstructing walls, et cetera."

"So did I. Here, let me show you something."

Dickinson led them over to a battered wooden chair against the wall. Leaning against it was a heavy paper tube four feet in length and three inches in diameter. He pulled from the tube a loose roll of parchmentlike papers. When he unrolled them, Cronley saw that they were the engineer's working blueprints showing walls and measurements made the previous day.

The top sheet showed a pencil-sketched outline of what Cronley recognized as King Arthur's Court.

"So, here," Dickinson said, pointing, "you can see this is where we're standing."

"Uh-huh."

"And this is where the round table sat. And this—"

"Oh, shit!" Cronley blurted.

"Yeah. It's not certain, but we won't know till that table . . ."

"Carry on, Colonel. I'm holding you up."

Cronley and McKenna watched from a safe distance as the entire table was lifted six feet off the floor, then tilted enough by one of the three-quarter-ton wreckers so that the other two wreckers, their windshields folded down, could get underneath.

Sturdy ropes were wrapped around the table while half a dozen soldiers, some equipped with air-powered jacks and others with air-powered saws, broke the table into four roughly equal pieces.

One piece remained attached to the crane. The remaining three were held by the wreckers.

Under Dickinson's precise—if profane, even blasphemous—direction, one by one the pieces of the table were inched through the castle wall opening and then lowered onto a waiting 6×6 in the courtyard.

Cronley was about to turn away from watching the activity in the courtyard when there came the sound of a siren, then multiple sirens.

An M8 armored car drove into the courtyard, followed by a second M8, and then three three-quarter-tons in personnel carrier mode. Each held eight Constabulary troopers.

There was the blast of a whistle, and the troopers in the three-quarter-tons leapt out of them, clutching Thompson submachine guns. They acted as if they expected to be attacked at any moment.

And then there was action in the second M8.

Major General I. D. White, wearing a shiny helmet liner with the two silver stars indicating his rank gleaming on its front, leapt nimbly to the ground. Two more Thompson-armed troopers followed him. White tucked a riding crop under his arm and marched regally toward the castle entrance.

Dickinson walked up to Cronley to see the source of the sirens.

"Captain," he said, helpfully, "I wouldn't be at all surprised if the general is looking for you. And I suggest it might be a good idea not to keep him waiting."

Cronley met his eyes, then turned and walked quickly to the door before breaking into a trot.

XIV

Cronley slowed to a walk as he entered the kitchen.
General White was helping himself to a cup of coffee and a doughnut from a tray on the table in the
center of the room. Two Constabulary troopers,
the elder of whom looked as if he required a shave
maybe every other week, eyed Cronley coldly. Both
troopers obviously were prepared to turn their
Thompsons on him if he acted at all suspiciously.
Cronley saluted crisply.

"Good morning, sir. An unexpected pleasure."

General White returned the salute by touching
his riding crop to his gleaming helmet liner.

"I was taking a morning patrol with my troopers and realized we were close to your castle. I thought I'd drop by and pay my respects."

"We're honored to have you, sir."

"You're scared practically shitless, Cronley. I can tell when you are because your military courtesy is impeccable."

Cronley didn't reply.

"In response to your unasked question, Sergeant Casey is sitting—figuratively speaking, of course—on Miss Johansen in Sonthofen. I didn't want her around until I had a good look at what's going on at your castle. I have a number of probing questions for you. Starting with, why is King Arthur's table in pieces and why are they loading said pieces onto that six-by-six?"

"Sir, Colonel Dickinson believes an entry—maybe **the** entry—into the secret passages in the castle is concealed where the table was sitting."

"Now I'm really glad I came," White said, then gestured with his riding crop. "Lead on, Captain Super Spook. Show me the secret passages."

When they walked into the vaulted room, they found Major Lomax on his knees where the table had been. He was gently tapping the stone floor with a ball-peen hammer and then, all of a sudden, raised the hammer over his shoulders and delivered a heavy blow to the floor.

"You're brighter than you look, Lomax," Colonel Dickinson said. "Maybe you should consider a career in the Corps of Engineers."

Lomax ignored him, instead handing the hammer to Technical Sergeant Holmes.

"You see where it's starting to crack, Elwood?"

"Got it, sir," Sergeant Holmes said, taking the hammer and dropping to his knees.

At that point, Dickinson, Lomax, and Father McKenna, who was standing beside Lomax, spotted General White, a natty lieutenant next to him, obviously his aide-de-camp, his bodyguards, and Cronley.

Dickinson called, **"Ten-hut!"** and everybody in the room, which included maybe a dozen soldiers, popped to attention.

"Rest," White ordered, and then pointed his riding crop at Father McKenna. "Who are you, padre? And what are you doing in my castle?"

"I'm Father McKenna, General. I'm on Cardinal von Hassburger's staff. The cardinal sent me here to learn what I can about the Nazi religion Himmler started."

White didn't respond, instead asking, "Sergeant, why are you hammering on the floor?"

"Sir, we think there's a—I don't know—maybe

some sorta trapdoor under here, blocking the entrance to a passage or stairway, or something. Somebody's tried to hide it. And did a damn good job."

The sound of the hammer striking the stone floor took on a new pitch. Then there was a cracking sound.

The sergeant wedged an iron crowbar into a crack and, with a grunt, heaved on it. This caused a section of the floor, almost an inch thick and four feet square, to rise just high enough so that the sergeant could insert a metal wedge.

"There you are, you tough son of a bitch," the sergeant said. "Somebody, quick, get me a length of chain and then move one of the damn jeep wreckers over here. There's no telling how heavy that son of a bitch is going to be."

Ten minutes later, the sergeant had looped the chain through a handle on the underside of the square blocking the hole and then looped the other end through a hook on the jeep wrecker's derrick.

As the sergeant used hand signals to control the derrick, the chain tightened. The truck engine revved as the derrick strained under the weight, then began to lift.

"Here comes the bastard," Dickinson called.

The square slowly cleared the hole, then swung to one side. The sergeant made a slashing motion across his throat, and the derrick operator stopped rising the chain.

The sergeant went to the hole and looked down in it. As he did, Colonel Dickinson got on his knees beside him for a better look.

And then he clutched at his throat with his hand and, gray-faced, turned away from the hole.

The sergeant vomited. Then so did Dickinson.

General White, in his legendary voice of command, ordered, "Everybody out! Now!"

White turned to Cronley.

"You get Dickinson. I'll get the sergeant."

Cronley got a whiff.

"Jesus! Poison gas?" he asked as they hurried toward the hole.

He got another whiff—then vomited.

"No," White said. "That's a mass of human bodies putrefying . . ."

[TWO]

General White cared for, almost parentally, his aide and the two teenage bodyguards, all of whom took longer than almost anyone else to get control of their wrenching stomachs.

Cronley required much the same care—and got it from Father McKenna—before he was able to help anyone else.

Finally, he decided that he had done all he could. He surveyed the chaotic scene and was surprised that everyone was still alive.

Cronley made his way outside, into the cobblestone courtyard, and deeply inhaled the fresh air. He found Father McKenna with Colonel Dickinson and Major Lomax. They were sitting on cobblestones, their backs against the rear tires of the 6×6 truck that held the pieces of the disassembled round table.

Soon, General White approached. "You guys going to be all right?"

Cronley, Lomax, and Dickinson nodded, and, in a chorus, said weak "Yes, sir"s. McKenna made a limp gesture with his right fist, the thumb up.

Cronley saw White's teenage bodyguards more or less stumble out of the castle and come to rest where they could keep an eye on General White.

"If it makes you feel any better," White said, "the first time I smelled that—and what I smelled then wasn't as bad as this—I was hors de combat for six hours."

"Where was that, sir?" Dickinson asked.

"Peenemünde, the German rocket labs. We knew what had been going on there, so we were in a race with the Russians to get there first. The Germans sent SS-Generalmajor Wilhelm Burgdorf—

one of the two bastards Super Spook is looking for—to blow up the place and otherwise make sure that whoever got there first, us or the Reds, would find nothing of value."

"But we did, right?" McKenna said.

"Peenemünde was enormous. There was no way Burgdorf could blow up the whole thing. So he blew up and burned what he could, and then he massacred the slave laborers who had been working there so they couldn't tell us or the Reds what they had seen."

"Massacred, sir?" Dickenson said. "How?"

"He didn't have enough time to shoot all of them—there were hundreds, not counting those who had died from being worked to death—so what he did was bulldoze mass graves, usher the workers into the graves, and, after a perfunctory attempt to shoot them, had the bulldozers bury everybody—dead, or still breathing, or sometimes not even wounded—men, women, and children.

"That's when I smelled this for the first time"—he gestured back toward the castle—"when I opened those mass graves . . . It's a smell that sticks with you a long time. I suspect forever."

He paused and then went on. "So how can we get rid of enough of the stink, Dickinson, and how soon, so that we can have a look in the hole and see what's down there?"

"Exhaust fans are the obvious answer, General," Lomax weakly answered for Dickinson, then suddenly got to his feet and ran twenty feet before bending at the waist and suffering another attack of nausea.

"Where do we get exhaust fans?" White went on.

"The Monuments, Fine Arts, and Archives people, sir," Dickinson said. "They use them to blow air into caves and tunnels and mines where the Krauts stored stolen artwork."

"Do you know for sure where there are such fans?"

"Yes, sir. But I don't know how Monuments is going to like our wanting to take them over."

White nodded. "Can the engineers settle such a dispute or am I going to have to send a couple of Constabulary troops with you?"

Lomax walked back to where they sat by the truck. "We can handle it, General."

"Once you get the fans, how long will it take?"

"I'd run them at least twenty-four hours, sir. But there's always a chance that they could clear it faster."

"Start looking for them," White ordered.

"Yes, sir."

"Super Spook, where's your Nazimobile?"

"It's here, sir, outside by the moat."

"We're going to ride into Nuremberg with the

windshield folded down and see if that'll help in getting the smell out of our nostrils."

"Yes, sir. Why are we going to Nuremberg?"

"To pay our respects to Mr. Justice Jackson."

"Stupid question," Cronley said.

"Yes, it was."

"General, can I hitch a ride with you?" Father McKenna asked.

"You have business with Justice Jackson?"

"No, sir. But I want to send a message to the cardinal."

"What sort of message?"

McKenna paused before replying, then said, "I want to tell him that the situation is even worse than Cronley presented it."

"Castle Wewelsburg got to you, did it?"

"It's made its impression, yes, but not as much as my conversation with Brigadeführer Heimstadter."

"How so?"

"It took me some time, General, to accept that he's perfectly willing, maybe even eager, to be a martyr to this new religion and the Thousand-Year Reich. He's an intelligent man. One would think that after all that's happened—Hitler's suicide, Goebbels and his wife murdering their children before committing suicide themselves, the defect of the Wehrmacht, the unconditional surrender, the utter destruction of Berlin, all of that—that he'd at least begin to question what good his suicide could do the cause. That's what I find really dangerous. How many more are there like him? Intelligent, educated, competent—and clearly out of their minds?"

"More than I like to think, I'm afraid, Father. And you want to tell the cardinal this?"

"I want to get that message to Cardinal von Hassburger soonest. But I don't want to telephone, as I'm convinced Odessa has people listening. So, what I'm going to do is find someone in Nuremberg's Jesuit community who'll carry what I have to say to Rome verbally."

"Sure, you can ride along with us," White said. "Okay, Super Spook, let's go."

As they crossed the courtyard, White's aide and then the two teenage bodyguards struggled to their feet, obviously determined to go where he was going despite their feeling ill.

"Cronley," White ordered, "tell them they're not going."

"With respect, sir, no. I have a rule about not breaking hearts."

"You are one difficult sonofabitch. Did anyone ever tell you that?"

"Yes, sir. But I didn't believe them."

———

Several minutes later, they drove off in the Horch, its top folded down and with both the front and rear seat windshields also folded down.

Cronley was at the wheel. White sat beside him. In the rear, the general's aide and Father McKenna rode regally in the leather-upholstered rear seat, while the general's bodyguards rode uncomfortably in the jump seats.

[THREE]
Office of the Chief U.S. Prosecutor
International Tribunal Compound
Nuremberg, American Zone of
Occupation,
Germany
1710 27 April 1946

"Why do I get the feeling that this isn't a social call?" Justice Jackson said as White, Cronley, and McKenna entered his office. "And what is that sickening smell?"

"First things first, Mr. Justice," White replied. "Father McKenna needs to contact the Jesuit community in Nuremberg and doesn't know the most expeditious manner to find it. I've assured him if anyone knows, you do."

"I don't have a clue," Jackson said as he walked to the window and opened it. He took in a deep breath of the outdoor air.

"That won't work," White said. "The stench clings to you."

Jackson acted as if he hadn't heard.

"Is there anything I can do for you, Father?" he asked. "Aside from having my clerk locate the Jesuits for you?"

"The odor to which you refer," White then said, "is that of the putrefying of what I estimate to be between one hundred and three hundred corpses we have found in a hitherto secret room in Castle Wewelsburg."

"Say that again, I.D.?" Jackson said.

White repeated himself verbatim. He added, "It is not unlike the mass graves I uncovered of slave laborers massacred by the Nazis at Peenemünde."

Jackson walked behind his desk, slumped in his chair, and with both hands gestured **Let's have it**.

White told him what had transpired at Castle Wewelsburg, concluding, "We won't know how many bodies, or who they were, until we can get down there. And we don't know when we can do that. Certainly not until tomorrow."

Jackson wanted an explanation of that, too.

Cronley had just finished providing it when Kenneth Brewster came into the office.

"My God! What smells in here?"

He went to open the window wider.

"I don't smell anything," Cronley said. "Can you, General?"

"The faint smell of roses, perhaps," White replied. "How about you, Father?"

The priest shook his head in disbelief and disapproval but did not reply.

"Ken," Jackson said, "this is Father McKenna, who needs your assistance."

"**That** Father McKenna?"

"I'm afraid I don't follow," the priest said.

"Does the name Heimstadter mean anything to you, Father?"

"We've met."

"Where?"

"In the Tribunal Prison."

"Then that raises the question, what were you doing with Heimstadter?"

"I took him to see Heimstadter," Cronley said, sharply. "Okay, Brewster?"

"And you had Justice Jackson's permission to do that?"

"Because I had his permission to take Heimstadter out of the prison, I damn sure didn't think I needed it."

Jackson said, "Where is your interrogatory taking us, Ken?"

"Sir, there was an incident at lunch. Party or

parties unknown poured boiling water down Heimstadter's back. He's now in the infirmary rather badly burned."

"It wasn't accidental, I gather?" Jackson asked.

"No, sir. And from the moment he got to the infirmary, he's been asking—demanding—to see Father McKenna."

Jackson looked at Cronley. "Jim?"

"How'd you hear about this, Brewster?" Cronley demanded.

"What do you mean?"

"Who told you somebody poured boiling water on Heimstadter? What the hell were you doing, Brewster, hoping to catch me with my hand in the cookie jar?"

"Enough!" Jackson said, softly but angrily. He let that sink in and then turned to Cronley. "Okay, Jim, what were you up to with Heimstadter?"

"I offered him a deal. He gives us Burgdorf, von Dietelburg, and/or the Odessa money and he gets to go to Argentina."

"You had no right to propose such a thing! They're to be properly tried here in court," Brewster said, righteously indignant. Then, realizing he had overstepped his authority, he looked at Jackson and said, "Am I right, sir?"

"Ken," Jackson said, evenly, smiling at his aide who had been top of his class at Yale and who he considered a brilliant lawyer. "Jim was simply following the Hotshot Billy Principle."

Jackson and White exchanged smiles.

"Excuse me, sir?" Brewster asked, confused.

Jackson said, "'If you need permission to do something that you're absolutely sure is right, and know your superior is going to tell you no, do it anyway. Success earns forgiveness.' Or words to that effect."

"I gather Heimstadter rejected your offer?" White said.

"Yes, sir. Cold. But I gave Father McKenna another shot at it."

"And?"

"Cold. Frighteningly cold," McKenna said.

White nodded. "That was, of course, before somebody poured boiling water on him. But if he turned down your offer, Cronley, why would anyone be angry?"

"When we returned him from the Mansion to the prison, we put him alone in the backseat of the Nazimobile and took him on a tour of Nuremberg. Somebody with access to boiling water must have seen him."

"Isn't that dirty pool?" Jackson asked.

"On the contrary, I think it was a fine idea," White said. "I thought so at the time, and now that he's asked for Father McKenna, I believe it a brilliant idea."

White turned to McKenna.

"Father, if your message to the cardinal can wait, how about going to see why Heimstadter wants to talk to you?"

[FOUR]
Prison Dispensary
International Tribunal Compound
Nuremberg, American Zone of
Occupation, Germany
1935 27 April 1946

A prison guard sat uncomfortably in a folding metal chair in a corner of the room, holding his nightstick in both hands. SS-Brigadeführer Ulrich Heimstadter was lying naked on his stomach in a hospital bed. He was swathed in greasy-looking bandages from just below his neck to his upper buttocks.

"I heard what happened," Father McKenna said as he walked into the room. "How are you? How are they treating you?"

"I'm in agony," Heimstadter said.

"Are they giving you anything for the pain?"

"I refused the injection. I wanted my mind clear when I talked to you."

"What's on your mind, Ulrich?"

"You know why those bastards poured the boiling water on me."

"I gather it wasn't an accident."

"When they heard I was riding around Nuremberg in the backseat of that Horch, they concluded that I had betrayed my oath. As that son of a bitch Cronley hoped they would."

"You don't know that, Ulrich."

"Let's cut the bullshit. What I'm wondering now is whether you can be trusted."

"About what?"

"Are you here as a priest? For that matter, are you really a priest? Or are you a DCI agent in a priest's collar?"

"I am not a DCI agent. I am a Jesuit priest assigned to the Vatican."

"Swear to that—swear to God that you're a priest and not an agent of Cronley, or any American!"

"Normally, I wouldn't do that, but these are extraordinary circumstances, aren't they?" He raised his right hand to the level of his shoulder, and said, "I so swear."

"Before God!"

"I so swear before God."

"The first thing I have to do is get out of here alive. If I stay here, the Nazis will kill me as a traitor."

"You don't know that."

"In their shoes, I would regard killing me as a duty."

"What are you asking, Ulrich?"

"If Cronley agreed to have me transferred elsewhere, could I trust him? Would you trust him?"

"You could. I would. But why would he get you transferred out of here?"

"In exchange for information."

"What information? The location of von Dietelburg and Burgdorf?"

"I don't know where they are. But I know where they might be."

"Then why should he trust you?"

"Because, at the very least, the information I have would permit him to arrest three or four—maybe more—of the Odessa people he's looking for. And allow him to recover—steal—some Odessa money."

"And you'd give him all this just to be taken from the prison?"

"I'd give him all that to save my life and to open further conversation about me going to Argentina. Once he learned to trust me. Understand?"

"Ulrich, it is not my business to be your agent in any sort of a discussion. But what I will do, if you like, is tell Cronley what you told me and that you want to talk to him."

"Make that I am **willing** to talk to him."

[FIVE]

Cronley, when Father McKenna had passed Heimstadter's message, marked the time on his wristwatch in order to wait thirty minutes before entering the prison dispensary.

"Herr Brigadeführer," Cronley said as he and the priest approached Heimstadter's bed, "I hate to tell you this, but you look like a beached whale."

When it looked as if McKenna was going to leave the room, Heimstadter called, "Please stay, Father."

"What did you do," Cronley pursued, moving to the head of the bed in order to meet Heimstadter's eyes, "jump into the shower before testing the water?"

"You know very well what happened."

"What's on your mind?"

"If I stay in the prison, I'm going to be killed."

Cronley nodded. "Quite probably."

"If you agree, with Father McKenna as my witness, that you will transfer me some place I'll be safe, I'll give you information you will find valuable."

"First, I get you transferred and then you give me that valuable information? As in the sun will rise tomorrow?"

"The information I will provide will allow you

to arrest four—possibly more—Odessa officers, each of whom almost certainly has far more information regarding the location of von Dietelburg and Burgdorf than you do. You will also be able to seize a considerable amount of Odessa's assets."

"I'm having trouble believing my good fortune," Cronley said. "And believing you."

"Once we get through stage one—once, in other words, that you will be forced to accept that I'm telling the truth—I'd like to go to stage two, revisiting our conversation about Argentina."

Cronley was silent, then said, "Getting you moved to some other place will take at least two or three days. What I will do immediately is post a couple of MPs in here. Okay?"

Heimstadter considered that for a minute, then the whole of his body seemed to go limp, his head dropping to the pillow. He sighed as he nodded.

"Approximately six kilometers to the north of Castle Wewelsburg," he said, "there is a small complex of buildings surrounded by several hundred acres of farmland. It was formerly the Experimental Farm of the Ministry of Agriculture. The complex is currently being run as a farm under the supervision of your military government."

He raised his head, and went on. "Somewhere on that farmland is a building built in secrecy by the SS when the castle was being renovated. The building today appears deserted, damaged in the war. But under it is the complex of rooms originally designed to work with the castle."

This sounds like pure bullshit, Cronley thought, his eyes locked on Heimstadter's.

So why am I believing it?

He said, "And . . . ?"

"And there are at least four—and possibly, probably, as many as six—Odessa officers living there."

"And nobody has seen them? Come on, Heimstadter!"

"They are hiding in plain sight, as the expression goes, working on the farm. Driving tractors, trucks, et cetera. One of your warrant officers—his name is Wynne—is glad to have them. The remote location of the farm makes it difficult to hire the local farmworkers, and these men are good workers."

"Warrant Officer Wynne?"

"He's the American in charge. There are half a dozen other American soldiers on the place."

"How do you know all this?" Cronley said.

Stupid question. He's not going to tell me how he learned.

They pass messages—and other contraband, like cyanide—in and out of this Compound like it's a post office. Even Morty Cohen can't stop it, and God knows he tries hard.

The look on Heimstadter's face showed that he, too, thought it was a stupid question.

He said, "What the farm is, Captain Cronley, is a splendid example of what can happen when the victorious Americans and the defeated Germans put the war behind them and cooperate."

I'd like to kick that flabby white ass of yours from here to Berlin.

"Come on, Father," Cronley said. "Let's go get Ulrich some MPs to protect him. Don't go anywhere, Ulrich. I'll be back."

"I rather thought you would."

[SIX]
Farber Palast
Stein, near Nuremberg, American
Zone of Occupation, Germany
2225 27 April 1946

Jim Cronley entered the dining room and saw that General White was at a table pouring champagne into a crystal stem.

"I was about to give up on you and have my dinner," White said as Cronley approached, "but then Billy Wilson called from the airfield to announce his and Miss Johansen's arrival. They should be here any minute. What happened with Heimstadter?"

"We got lucky, General," Cronley said. "Possibly

very lucky, depending on how much we can trust the bastard."

White made one of his **Let's have it** gestures with both hands, and Cronley started to tell him what had gone on in the prison dispensary.

He had just about finished when Lieutenant Colonel William W. Wilson and Miss Janice Johansen of the Associated Press walked up to the table.

"Ah, there you are," White said, getting to his feet. "We were just about to order dinner. How was your flight?"

Janice stopped at the table, hands on her hips. "You have to the count of ten to tell me about this big story you've got for me, General, before I start throwing things. One . . . two . . ."

"You should know, Miss Johansen, that no one intimidates me. That said, Captain Cronley will explain it all to you. May I offer you a glass of champagne?"

"Only if it comes in a bottle that I can throw at Super Spook if he tries any of his bovine excreta on me."

Cronley grunted. "Calm down, Janice. Sometime after first light tomorrow, Colonel Wilson will take you flying again . . ."

"Over my dead body," she replied. "Better yet, over ol' I.D.'s dead body."

Cronley pretended not to hear her.

". . . This time in a L-19, not in the general's Gooney Bird, so it will be easier for you to take photographs," he went on. "You will fly over a farm complex about six kilometers from Wewelsburg. The farmlands constitute seven hundred hectares. It is currently under the control of the military government. You will first locate the main complex of buildings—"

"What's the sudden interest in a damn farm?" she interrupted.

He ignored her again.

"—And then a second building somewhere on the farm. This will look to the casual observer to be deserted and abandoned because of damage suffered in the recent conflict. To a sharp-eyed observer such as yourself, Janice, there should be obvious evidence of activity. I'm sure Colonel Wilson here will be happy to help, pointing out, say, tire tracks from trucks or tractors, perhaps smoke from a cooking fire—"

"Somewhat repeating myself: What's your interest in this building in the middle of nowhere, Jimmy?"

"Well, Janice, I'm pretty sure it houses five or six Odessa officers, a quantity of Odessa money, and, I dare to hope, von Dietelburg and Burgdorf as well." He paused, then added, "When you return from your flight—and only after we secure the buildings—there may be room in an M8 for you to go with us to find out."

Janice stared at him, then glanced at White, before turning back to Cronley. "And this is my story, Jimmy? No one else knows anything about it?"

"It's yours and yours alone."

Janice's eyebrows went up, and, after some thought, said, "Okay, what's the catch, Super Spook?"

"But only if we still have our understanding."

"Of course we do. Why the hell would we not?"

XV

A Constabulary staff sergeant came into King Arthur's/King Heinrich's Court, walked up to General White, saluted crisply, and announced, "Sir, there's a Russian general at the gate who wants to see Father McKenna."

"I was about to ask who's been running off at the mouth to that goddamn Red," White said, "but I don't have to, do I, Father?"

"He has kept his word, General, and I am now keeping mine," the priest replied, unabashed.

White turned to his aide, who stood next to Colonel Cohen.

"My compliments to General Serov, Russell.

Inform him I would be pleased if he would join us."

"Yes, sir," Lieutenant Russell said, then left the room, followed by the staff sergeant.

Cronley, standing by the opening of an access in the floor, held a length of quarter-inch rope that snaked down into the darkness.

"Wonder if we should go after them?" he said.

"It's been seventeen minutes," Father McKenna furnished. "Any action on the rope?"

Cronley shook his head.

"We'll give them twenty minutes," White ordered. "And then, Cronley, you and the good Father can go down looking for them."

Almost immediately, there was action on Cronley's rope.

"That's three jerks," he announced. "Meaning, reel in the rope!"

He began to pull on it.

Minutes later, a beam of light could be seen in the dark hole, and then a head and shoulders appeared. The head was completely covered with an industrial gas mask. Cronley pulled it off, revealing Major Lomax. Then Cronley bent to hoist Lomax out of the opening, and almost simultaneously so did Serov.

"I'm afraid I recognize that smell," Serov announced. "What the hell is going on here?"

Colonel Dickinson appeared in the opening next, and they repeated the process.

Dickinson finally looked at General White.

He said, "Sir, there's a professionally constructed series of tunnels and passages down there, varying from five to twelve feet in diameter. In one of the side tunnels, which is one of the larger diameter ones, there's a mound of moldering—I should say decomposed—human flesh. I estimate it once was two hundred human beings, give or take."

"Jesus!" White and Cohen said simultaneously.

"And the whole damn thing is wired—professionally wired—for demolition. It's also wired with some light fixtures, but I was cautious turning on any switch in case that would cook off the high explosives."

"Goddamn," White said. "Can you make it safe?"

"I'm thinking about that," Dickinson said, then surveyed Serov with curiosity before adding, "and I just don't know. Maybe. Let me give it some more thought."

"General Serov," White said, "this is Colonel Dickinson and Major Lomax, who I have just decided have more balls than brains."

"If the castle's wired for demolition," Cronley wondered aloud, "why didn't they blow it up?"

After a pause during which no one answered, he answered the question himself. "Because they hoped we would eventually tire of trying to figure out what the hell was happening in this place and leave. Then they could come back for whatever is hidden down there and then really give us the finger again by blowing this sonofabitch up."

General White grunted, then said, "I realize it's categorized as wisdom from the mouth of a babe, but I think Super Spook just nailed it."

[TWO]

The next day, at 0500 hours, everyone waited in the courtyard of Wewelsburg Castle, which now held a fleet of M8 armored cars, their engines idling. There were no chairs. General White, Captain Cronley, Father McKenna, and General Serov were standing near the entrance to the kitchen, sipping coffee.

"I am willing to admit there may be a minor flaw or two in my planning," General White said to Cronley.

"This is no time to shake my boundless confidence in you, General, sir," Cronley said.

"The fact that no one outside can see my M8s does not preclude the likelihood that someone outside has had the castle under surveillance and saw the M8s come in. We very well may have lost the element of surprise."

"I can top that, sir," Colonel Cohen said. "What if the person who has the castle under surveillance and has seen all your M8s come in asks himself, what better time to blow the place up than with all those M8s in it?"

"And," Cronley added, "what if Colonel Dickinson touches the wrong wire, or something, while he's down there trying to deactivate the HE and—**kaaaa-BOOM**?"

White, on the edge of sarcasm, said, "And what do you suggest we do, Super Spook?"

"What you planned from the start, sir: sound Boots and Saddles. I'll go to the military government's building with two M8s. That'll give me—what?—sixteen Constabulary guys. And with the rest of this little army, you surround the other house and block all roads out. And in."

White looked at him, nodded, then put his hand to his mouth and mimicked playing Boots and Saddles, the bugle call for troops to mount up and take their place in line.

"We move out in five minutes," General White then ordered.

"I'd like to come along," General Serov said.

"So would I," Father McKenna said.

"Absolutely not," White said.

"General Serov speaks fluent German, sir," Cronley said.

"I'll go with Cronley," Cohen said.

"No," Cronley said, flatly. "Colonel Cohen goes with General White and General Serov. I'll take Father McKenna with me."

White, silent, glanced at everyone before he said, "I have just successfully resisted the temptation to stand everybody tall while I told you how this is going down. But don't push me any further, Cronley."

"No disrespect was intended, sir," Cronley said.

"Maybe not, but that's the way it came out."

[THREE]
Kilometer 26, Kries Route 33
Kreis Paderborn, American Zone of
Occupation, Germany
0530 29 April 1946

Cronley signaled for the sergeant in charge of Troop "C" 11th Constabulary's M8 light armored car to pull to the side of the road and stop. The sergeant acknowledged the order by nodding his head.

As the first six-wheeled M8 turned off the narrow macadam road, the M8 behind it followed. As soon as the lead M8 stopped, a crisply uniformed lieutenant jumped out of the second vehicle and ran up to the first, then clambered up its side.

"With you there, Lieutenant," Cronley announced, "the sergeant and I are going to have trouble getting out."

"Yes, sir. Sorry, sir."

The lieutenant jumped down, then stood by the side of the road almost at attention, awaiting further orders.

Cronley climbed down from the M8. Father McKenna followed, and then came the sergeant.

"Stand at ease, Lieutenant," Cronley ordered. "We're on the side of a road in rural Germany, not on the parade ground."

"Yes, sir."

The lieutenant shifted positions, this time assuming parade rest.

Curiosity overtook Cronley.

"What's your name, Lieutenant, and where did you get your commission? And when?"

"Lieutenant Freeman, sir, John H. the Third. I'm Norwich, sir. Class of 1945. Is the captain familiar with Norwich, sir?"

If I told this guy I was A&M '45, he'd think I was lying.

And this is not the time or place to get into why I'm a captain, and his First John bars look brand new.

"I have a very good friend, Captain Tiny Dunwiddie, who's Norwich."

"Sir, we had a great big black guy named Dunwiddie in my class, but he can't be the same one. There's no way he could be a captain."

"Maybe a cousin or something," Cronley said, more than a little lamely. "We can talk about it later. Let's talk about what happens next."

"Yes, sir."

"We're going to the—I guess the word is 'headquarters'—of what was an experimental farm of the German Agricultural Ministry. It is now run by Military Government. A warrant officer named Wynne is in charge, and there are half a dozen GIs assigned.

"We have reason to believe that there are four to six—maybe eight—really bad Nazis hiding out on the place, passing themselves off as farmworkers. They're all members of Odessa."

"Of what, sir?"

"It's an organization of ex-SS guys, Lieutenant," the sergeant explained more than a little tolerantly as if speaking to a backward child. "The bastards take care of each other."

"But since they are not locals," Cronley went on, "they can't go home at night. Fortunately for them, when the SS was working on Castle Wewelsburg, they built a house on the farm. They live there. We don't know much about the house—

specifically, its connection with Wewelsburg—but we were reliably informed (a) there is a connection and (b) the house sits on a bunch of rooms and passageways and the like.

"There's probably a connection with the castle, but we can only guess what it is.

"As we speak, General White and the others are approaching—or possibly are already at—the house. They're going to seal off the roads leading to it, cut the telephone wires, and then go inside and see what's there. We hope to catch and identify one of the Odessa guys, thinking that if we do, he just may turn on the others to save his own ass. That may be, and quite probably is, wishful thinking.

"If it comes to this, and it probably will, we're going to tie all the Germans working here to their original homes, check to see that their **Kennkarten** aren't phony, and so on.

"As I said, we hope to get lucky, to catch one Odessa guy and get him to turn on the others. On top of this, we're looking for two really dirty bastards, SS-Brigadeführer von Dietelburg and General der Infanterie Wilhelm Burgdorf. We don't expect them to be here, but we do expect that the Odessa people know where they are and will flip on them to save their own collective skin. Still with me?"

The sergeant nodded. Lieutenant Freeman came to attention, and said, "Yes, sir."

"Now, here's what I'm worried about. Your teenage troopers and their Thompsons."

"Sir?" the lieutenant said. "I'm not sure I follow."

"They all know something unusual is going around, and most of them, having missed seeing combat, might be looking forward to shooting some Nazis. I don't know how this Mr. Wynne is going to react to us showing up, but I suspect he's not going to like it. I certainly do not want him or any of the other Americans shot. And my preference is to keep the Nazis alive and arrest them so that we can collect more information. See my problem?"

"I can handle it, sir," Lieutenant Freeman said, confidently.

"I suggest both of you have a word with them before we go to the headquarters," Cronley said.

"Yes, sir," Lieutenant Freeman and the sergeant said in chorus.

[FOUR]
Headquarters, Detachment 231
Office of Military Government
Kreis Paderborn, American Zone of
Occupation, Germany
0615 29 April 1946

"Hit the siren, Sergeant," Cronley ordered when the main building came into sight.

As they drove up, a paunchy, middle-aged U.S. Army officer in his shirtsleeves came out of the building.

The M8s stopped, and the howl of sirens died.

"What the hell?" the officer growled. "You guys lost?"

"I'm Captain Cronley. And you must be Mr. Wynne."

"I am. What can I do for you?"

"Somebody with enough clout to get me out of my very nice office in the Farben Building has got the idea that there's at least one Nazi hiding out here on your farm."

"Bullshit."

"I'll ignore that, Mr. Wynne. Mostly because I believe you are probably correct. Be that as it may, here I am with my little army. So, please point out the Nazi, or Nazis, to me so that we can go back to civilization."

"No Nazis to point to, Captain. But I can give

you a cup of coffee. And point out the mess hall to your men. Come on in. You, too, Lieutenant."

There was a middle-aged German sitting at a typewriter in Wynne's outer office.

Why do I think I am about to catch my first Nazi? Cronley thought.

He said, "I'm going to have to check your employee's **Kennkarte**."

Cronley noticed that that got the German's attention.

"Can you take my word that they all have one?" Wynne said. "I checked on that personally."

"I'm getting the idea, Mr. Wynne, that you don't know how the system works."

"Please tell me, Captain," Wynne replied, his tone more than a little sarcastic.

Cronley met his eyes, and thought, **I'm within a hairsbreath of standing you tall, you bastard, and reading you the riot act according to Cronley.**

Instead, I'm just going to generalize this so you get my point . . .

Cronley said, "Certainly. In the good old days—that is, during the eleven years of the Thousand-Year Reich—everybody over the age of fifteen had a **Kennkarte**. When you went in the Wehrmacht or the Luftwaffe, they took it away from you and gave you an Army or Air Force identification. Got it, Mr. Wynne?"

"I got it."

"Good. Now, with those exceptions, everyone had one, from the peasant on the farm to the highest levels of Nazi officialdom. If you were in jail—or, worse, a concentration camp—they took away your **Kennkarte**.

"Each **Kennkarte**, printed on hard-to-forge paper, bears a unique number. And every issuing office made a list of who had a **Kennkarte**. And shared that list with at least two, often three, other German offices.

"This made it relatively easy, when the time came, for us to round up the Nazis we want. First, we made a master list of all the **Kennkarten** ever issued, including in what is now the Russian Zone. The Russians shared their **Kennkarte** files with us and we shared ours with them.

"Say we were looking for Hitler, Adolf. The list made it possible for us to check the master files and learn where Adolf's **Kennkarte** had been issued.

"Then we started a list of bad guys' **Kennkarten**. And then started checking everybody's **Kennkarte**. If your name wasn't on the bad guy list, you were home free.

"But if your name was in fact on the bad guy

list, or you didn't have a **Kennkarte**, it was a different story—you're in handcuffs, taken off to whoever wants to try you or hang you, or both.

"Now, if you say you lost your **Kennkarte** and you tell us where it was issued, and provided you're not on the bad guy list, then you can get another one issued.

"If, however, the place you said issued your card reports that you're on the bad guy list, or that they never heard of you, you're in—what is that charming phrase?—'deep shit.'

"So, what we are going to do, Mr. Wynne, is ask each of your employees for a look at their **Kennkarte**. Starting right about now, and for however long it takes. Got it?"

An annoyed Wynne, stone-faced, nodded.

Cronley then held out his right hand to the man at the typewriter and in German said, "May I see your identity card, please?"

Cronley thought, **His expression shows that (a) he is surprised by—and doesn't like—an American who speaks fluent German and (b) doesn't want to show me his Kennkarte.**

The German made an involved pretense of looking for his identity document, then made a frown and confessed that he must have left it at home.

"Not a problem," Cronley said. "You can get it over lunch."

I will graciously offer to give you a ride home.

And if you ever look like you're going to run, arrest you.

[FIVE]
Kreis Paderborn, American Zone of Occupation, Germany
0630 29 April 1946

In the distance, the last of Jim Cronley's M8 sirens died down as General White and his men surveilled the farmhouse in the woods for at least ten minutes. They saw no sign of movement.

Then, with troopers ten feet apart, they formed a line while other troopers went to cover the rear. At a signal from General White, the line closed on the farmhouse.

At the house, White looked through an opening that had once held a window.

He saw nothing and signaled that before signaling two sergeants to rush through the doorway. They did, Thompsons at the ready.

There was no reaction from within the house.

White, holding his General Officer's Model 1911-A1 Colt .45 ACP pistol upright at shoulder height, marched through the door, followed by General Serov and Colonel Cohen.

The sergeants were in what had been the kitchen before being bombed. They had their weapons pointing to the same spot of the floor. They motioned, pointing to evidence of fresh boot prints in the dirt that led to, and under, a tattered rug.

Another sergeant and a very large PFC went to the rug. When they attempted to pull it back, it would not slide. They then yanked on it, in the process tearing it. As it tore, a section of the wooden floor moved up with it—a four-foot square that covered access to below. They realized that the rug had been purposefully attached to the square of wooden flooring.

The large PFC used his foot to remove the square from the opening.

Colonel Cohen walked to the opening and then, in German, shouted down into it. "Come on out! I don't know what's happened, but Wynne's shitting a brick! He wants everybody out of here right now! Did you hear the sirens? There's Constabulary all over the place!"

There was no reply, but a minute later a briefcase came flying out of the opening. Serov moved quickly to it and opened it.

He turned it on its side to show that it was full of currency.

Another briefcase came flying out, and then two battered leather suitcases.

And, finally, a head and shoulders.

"Please, General Burgdorf," General White said, his .45 leveled at the German's face, "give me an excuse to put a couple of rounds in your forehead."

Another voice was heard from behind Burgdorf. **"Gottverdamt, Willi, was ist lost?"**

Burgdorf silently crawled out of the opening. With hands over his head, he sat on the floor cross-legged.

Cohen walked to the opening, and called down in German, "If you've been thinking about suicide, Franz baby, now would be a good time."

Former SS-Brigadeführer Franz von Dietelburg reluctantly joined former General der Infanterie Wilhelm Burgdorf on the floor. They both were wearing ragged civilian clothing.

"Sergeant," General White ordered, "now would be a good time to capture this moment for all of history."

There followed a rapid series of still-camera flashbulbs popping.

"They're all yours, Colonel," White then said to Cohen. "When you're done, load them in separate M8s. And send someone down the tunnel to see if we missed anything, or anyone."

Minutes later, both prisoners found themselves lying naked on the floor.

Cohen had ordered two very large medics to immediately subject them to a search of their body orifices for hidden potassium cyanide capsules. Others searched their clothing for same.

After Himmler had escaped the Tribunal by biting on such a capsule, great care had been taken to make sure no other high-level Nazi escaped his fair trial and subsequent hanging by taking his own life.

The pained look on the faces of Burgdorf and von Dietelburg suggested that the medics who had conducted the search had erred on the side of thoroughness rather than personal comfort.

When they had their clothing back on, one of the sergeants produced a coil of quarter-inch rope and tied them up.

"What now, General White?" Cohen said.

"First, get on the radio and tell Captain Super Spook that he got his men. Then we're all going to Nuremberg to see how Mr. Justice Jackson wants to handle this."

[SIX]
Office of the Chief U.S. Prosecutor
Palace of Justice
Nuremberg, American Zone of
Occupation, Germany
1400 29 April 1946

The convoy of twenty-one M8 armored cars and one Horch touring sedan aroused considerable interest as it entered the Tribunal Compound and then when it stopped at Mr. Justice Jackson's building, blocking all traffic in the area.

Jackson came out of the building, and White said, "Take a look in cars four and five, sir."

Jackson did, and then said, "I feel like Nero welcoming one of my legions home from suppressing the Huns. If I had any, I would drape you in garlands."

"What do I do with the bastards, sir?" White asked.

"Put them in their cells. **Personally** put them in their cells, and then come to the office and we'll spread the good news."

"Mr. Justice, this is Fulda," the SIGABA operator said. "We have the President for you, sir. On a secure line. The conversation will be recorded by a White House stenographer. We have been unable to locate Admiral Souers, but we're working on it."

"Put us through, please," Jackson said.

"Hello, Bob," the President of the United States said. "Sid and I were just talking about you. How's things going?"

"Sid's with you? Someone should tell the ASA. They said they couldn't find him. Anchors aweigh, Admiral."

"You better have some good news for us," Souers said. "Things have gone from bad to worse around here."

"Before we get into that," Truman said, "who's there with you, Bob?"

"General White, Super Spook, Colonel Cohen, Ken Brewster, my clerk. And Miss Janice Johansen of the Associated Press."

"What's she doing there? . . . No offense, Miss Johansen."

"Well, we've decided on the best way to handle this, but I wanted to check with you first."

"Handle what, for God's sake?"

"A couple of minutes ago, General White put von Dietelburg and Burgdorf back in their cells. Personally put them there. I thought I mentioned that."

"No, Bob, you didn't. And you damn well know you didn't!"

"We thought you might be interested."

"Tell me about it. Every damn detail."

"Well, Father McKenna and Super Spook got to Heimstadter, one of the second level—"

"Who is Father McKenna?" the President interrupted.

"A Jesuit priest who works out of the Vatican. They—Cardinal von Hassburger—sent him to evaluate the power of Himmler's new religion. He's now a convert . . . on our side."

"And this Jesuit priest did what?"

"He and Super Spook got Heimstadter to tell them of a house a couple of miles away that the Germans built at the time they were working on Castle Wewelsburg. And suggested that if von Dietelburg and Burgdorf weren't there, the people there would probably know where they were. Cutting to the chase, White and Super Spook went there and bagged both of them."

"Congratulations all around. I really mean that."

"And they discovered the decomposed corpses of about two hundred people in a tunnel under the castle."

"My God!"

"It took the engineers a day, using industrial fans, to get the smell down enough so that people—wearing gas masks—could look around the tunnels. When they did get a look, they discovered the castle has been wired—wired very well—for demolition. The engineers are seeing what they can do about that threat."

Truman was silent, then said, "What do you want from me, Bob? What can I do for you?"

"Well, this is a pretty big story. Von Dietelburg and Burgdorf back in their cells after being captured near another mass murder of some two hundred innocent people. So, with your permission, we'll tell the whole story. Janice is willing to go along, and she has pictures of everything—everything but the bodies, which we have taken for proof. And she'll have it done in a matter of hours. The story could appear on the front page of every newspaper in America. Hell, around the world."

"Which I think is a lousy idea," Cronley blurted out.

"What?" the President and Justice Jackson said on top of each other.

General White said, "Button your lip, Cronley!"

"Well, I'm obviously outnumbered, but I had to say it and I'm glad I did."

"And keep it buttoned," General White said.

"I think we should hear what Super Spook has to say," Truman said.

"Jim," Justice Jackson said, "if you think what we've come up with is a lousy idea, why didn't you say something before?"

Cronley didn't reply.

"Because, Bob," the President said after a brief pause, "you're a justice of the Supreme Court, and I.D. here is a two-star—about to be three-star—general. He would have been wasting his time."

"And he's not now wasting his time, Harry? And ours, too?"

"We won't know that, will we, Bob, until I hear what he doesn't like about your idea? Okay, Super Spook, you have the floor."

"Sir, if we make a big show about recapturing von Dietelburg and Burgdorf, instead of impressing the Krauts—"

"Presumably, you're referring to the German citizenry, Super Spook?"

"Yes, sir.

"Then don't call them Krauts. We're trying to convert them to our way of thinking, not rub defeat in their faces."

"Yes, sir. Sorry. My point is, what the **German citizenry** is going to think a little proudly is, well, it took them a long time, didn't it, even with the entire U.S. Constabulary looking for them."

"Point taken," Truman said. "I.D., Super Spook has enormous balls, but I can't imagine him suggesting to you that the reason we didn't catch these bastards earlier was because your beloved Constabulary wasn't up to the challenge?"

White's face lost all color. Despite his anger, he didn't reply.

"Anything else, Super Spook?" the President asked.

"Yes, sir. We know Odessa is still out there. If the German citizenry is pissed that their guys are back in the bag, and there's any way Odessa can do it, it might occur to them to blow up Castle Wewelsburg. We know it's wired for demolition, and that'd let them give us the finger."

"And how would you handle the press?" the President challenged.

Cronley told him.

Truman fell silent.

"Bob, General," Truman then said. "We do this Super Spook's way. If I have to say this—and I guess I do—that's an order, not a suggestion."

XVI

[ONE]
Kreis Paderborn, American Zone of
Occupation, Germany
0810 30 April 1946

The perimeter of the farmhouse had been secured overnight using a half dozen M8 light armored cars, on the turret of each a Constabulary trooper manning the .50 caliber Browning heavy machine gun. Another ten troopers, each with a Thompson submachine gun in their arms and a holstered Colt .45 ACP pistol on their hip, stood guard.

Inside the perimeter, near a crumbled exterior wall of the bombed house, was one of the jeep wreckers that had been at the castle. Behind it, on the ground but still tethered to the hook of the winch cable, was a gasoline-powered electrical generator. Electrical extension cords snaked into the house.

In the kitchen, Cronley and Serov stood on

opposite sides of the hole in the floor. The extension cords ran down, providing power for the lights that now illuminated the complex of rooms below. The generator, requested at midnight, had been on-site only a little more than an hour.

Major Donald Lomax, of the 14th Engineers, appeared in the opening and looked up at Cronley and Serov.

"Anything in . . . What did you call it, Major?" Cronley said.

"Oh, yeah. Finally. In what looks like a map room or command post that's another level below the bunk rooms. They're dragging them this ay now."

"Them?" Cronley said, then turned his head at the sound of the arrival of a vehicle, its gears grinding and brakes squealing.

He looked out a hole in the wall that once held a window and saw a jeep with Father Francis X. McKenna, S.J., at the wheel.

"Let Father McKenna pass," Cronley called out to the trooper standing outside the window.

A minute later, the priest entered the kitchen. He had a newspaper rolled up and tucked under his arm.

"I didn't know that Holy Mother Church taught her priests to drive," Cronley said by way of greeting. "Judging by your shifts, apparently not too well."

"I learned in Boston, out of necessity."

"How so?"

"If you get in the backseat and there's no driver, you don't get very far."

Cronley snorted.

"They said at the castle you were here," McKenna said, handing Cronley the newspaper. "Today's **Stars and Stripes**."

Cronley unrolled it and saw on the front page a three-column photograph above the fold. It showed Major General I. D. White shaking hands with First Lieutenant John H. Freeman III in front of an M8 armored car. Below it was the news report.

ESCAPED NAZIS SURRENDER

Former Top Deputies to Hitler and Himmler, Exhausted and Starved,

Returned to Nuremburg Tribunal Prison

By Janice Johansen

Associated Press Foreign Correspondent

Munich, April 29—

Former SS-Generalmajor Wilhelm Burgdorf and former SS-Brigadeführer Franz von Dietelburg were today, almost three weeks to the day since their escape on April 5th, put back behind prison bars at the Allied War Crimes Tribunal in Nuremburg.

As members of the Nazi General Staff and

High Command, Burgdorf, a close confident to Adolf Hitler, and von Dietelburg, chief deputy to Reichsführer Heinrich Himmler, have been charged with four counts that include war crimes and crimes against humanity. They are being prosecuted, along with more than two dozen other senior military officers, by the International Military Tribunal in court sessions that began in November 1945.

The pair's short time on the run ended after they crossed paths with U.S. Constabulary First Lieutenant John H. Freeman III. The twenty-two-year-old was commanding a regular patrol of four M8 armored cars near Paderborn when he saw half a dozen men in civilian clothing staggering across a rural road.

"They appeared to be German citizens," Lieutenant Freeman said, "and we stopped to check on their welfare. As we performed a routine review of their **Kennkarten**, the hairs on my neck stood up. Something seemed suspicious."

Two of the identity documents, he said, appeared to be false. And he detected modifications to several of the others.

"All six men looked to be in ill health," the lieutenant said. "But Burgdorf and von Dietelburg were by far the worst. They clearly were malnourished, with unkempt hair and beards, and filthy clothes. And their mental state was unstable. When I started asking more and more questions, they broke down emotionally. They complained that no one in the area would help them. Desperate is what they were, even quick to offer information on hidden valuables in exchange for food."

Freeman said, judging by their condition, that he doubted that they had any valuables. "The probability factor of that was zero to zilch."

But that, he said, didn't matter—it was his duty to take them into custody.

Freeman transported the Germans to Castle Wewelsburg, near Paderborn, which he knew had a small Counterintelligence Corps detachment. With the U.S. Constabulary NCO Academy about to open in the castle, the CIC was on-site screening the many German citizens applying for work.

Constabulary Commanding General I. D. White happened to be at the castle inspecting the school's progress. When he saw the M8 armored cars roll into the courtyard, he went to investigate.

Freeman explained, and then General White ordered that the six men, under armed guard, be given food and drink while the CIC checked their **Kennkarten**.

General White continued questioning Freeman, during which it came out that both are graduates of Norwich University, the nation's oldest private military academy.

The CIC quickly confirmed Freeman's suspicions.

The documents were false. And all six Germans were on at least one list of Nazis wanted by both American and German authorities.

Freeman said Burgdorf and von Dietelburg, after admitting that they were the Tribunal Prison escapees, appeared resigned.

"'It is time we put this all in the past,'" Freeman quoted Burgdorf as saying before transporting them back to Nuremburg.

"I expect no less of a Norwich man," General White joked, quickly adding that he was recommending Freeman for the Army Commendation Medal. "The lieutenant performed an invaluable service for the International Military Tribunal and its mission to provide those accused of heinous crimes against humanity with a fair trial to clear their names, if so able."

"Nice work of fiction," Cronley said, handing the paper back to McKenna. "Lord knows Janice is going to want something in return. But let's hope this helps."

"Prayer always helps," McKenna said, then gestured toward the opening in the kitchen floor. "Finding anything?"

"Only that I'm taking this more and more personally, Father," Serov said. "Forgive me for not wishing you a good morning."

"Under the circumstances, Ivan, understood. But why personal?"

"As I've said, I devoutly believe it's God's mission for me to do everything in my power to stop this heretical religion. It is a main reason that I am now back in my beloved infantry—specifically, serving as adviser to Lieutenant General Roman Andreyevich Rudenko, the Soviet chief prosecutor to the Tribunal."

"Yes. But personal?"

"Over there," Serov said, gesturing in the direction of the castle, "about five kilometers distant, was the labor camp that Himmler named Niederhagen Konzentrationslager. The smallest of all the concentration camps, it held at its height four years ago some twelve hundred prisoners, mostly Soviet prisoners of war. Also imprisoned there were a great many Jehovah's Witness members.

"They shut down Niederhagen KZ in 1943 after more than a thousand died of typhus. We learned through sources that most survivors were transferred to Buchenwald, though an unknown number were imprisoned at Wewelsburg . . ."

"The slave laborers whose bodies we found," Cronley said, making it a question.

"Absolutely, James. Has to be. The state of decomposition is proof their deaths were too recent to be part of the slaves lost to typhus. It is entirely possible, of course, that they could be counted among those summarily executed."

"The monthly Korherr Reports of the SS would show that," Cronley said.

"Perhaps. One would think so, considering the detailed recordkeeping of the SS, although Heinrich Himmler and his SS were unafraid of falsifying anything if necessary to cover their tracks."

Serov looked from Cronley to McKenna.

"Father, if I'm repeating myself, please stop me. Reichsführer-SS Himmler was absolutely ruthless. He feared only one man, Burgdorf, mostly because Burgdorf was unequivocally devoted first to Hitler and, second, to National Socialism. After Claus von Stauffenberg and his conspirators tried, and failed, to assassinate Hitler with the bomb planted at Wolf's Lair, **Der Führer** became even more paranoid about those around him. Especially Rommel and Canaris, but also other Wehrmacht and Navy officers, as well as Himmler, Göring, and others in the Nazi hierarchy.

"The exception was one General der Infanterie Wilhelm Burgdorf. Hitler trusted his personal adjutant mostly because Burgdorf faithfully eliminated threats to **Der Führer**. Ones real or perceived. He had, for example, at Hitler's orders, gone to Irwin Rommel in Stuttgart and seen that the Generalfeldmarschall understood that **Der Führer** felt he should take a quiet death—a cyanide capsule—for his role in the Wolf's Lair debacle.

"This all was not lost on Himmler, and certainly not on his adjutant, von Dietelburg. It's believed that when Hitler sent Burgdorf to sniff around Wewelsburg Castle, von Dietelburg made it known to him that he, too, professed loyalty to Hitler first. Not to Himmler, who von Dietelburg told Burgdorf was planning on escaping Germany through Odessa if it became necessary."

"And he wasn't leaving penniless," Cronley said. "They had more than four million dollars in those two briefcases yesterday, likely part of what Himmler held in his safe. And Lord knows how much else."

There came noises from the hole at their feet—and then Lomax's grunting.

A black canvas duffel devoid of any markings came up through the hole and hit the kitchen floor with a muffled thud.

Lomax said, "This is the first of four we found in the part that served as the command post or map room. They were positioned near its entry, stacked as if staged to be transported somewhere else. The other eight rooms all contained single beds and cots, along with washbasins and toilets."

"That's it?" Cronley said.

"For now, this—I mean, the four duffels—is it. We've been through everything, best I can tell.

We're still looking, using hammers to hunt for hidden passages. But, so far, no tunnels. This place appears to have been a safe house of sorts, a bunker separate from the main complex nearby where that warrant officer had those Nazi farmworkers."

"Wynne," Cronley furnished. "Who devoutly believed he'd cleared the bastards. So far we've identified eleven of them as Nazis. It would surprise me not one bit that they knew about this damn bunker."

"Take a peek in the bag," Lomax said. "It's impressive."

Cronley squatted next to the duffel. He pulled on its heavy brass zipper, and the bag's big mouth slowly spread open wide. Inside was a huge tumble of neat, thick stacks of currency, what appeared to be mostly Swiss francs.

"My God," Serov said. "That easily could be fourfold what the briefcases held yesterday."

"Yeah," Cronley said, nodding. "But what the hell is this?"

He pushed aside the stacks of banknotes. In the middle sat a sack made of crimson velour that Cronley thought could pass as the same material as heavy drapery. It had red-and-black drawstrings with tassels that could be drapery cording. He tugged the sack upright and was surprised at its bulk. He figured that the contents had to weigh at least ten pounds.

He then pulled at the edge of the velour fabric, loosening the drawstrings. The sack slowly opened.

Inside, he found smaller flapped pouches of a black velour, at least twenty of them, each clearly containing an object more or less thumb-sized.

He picked up one, held it over his open palm, and shook the pouch until the flap opened.

"I'll be damned."

"What is it?" Major Lomax said, looking at the heavy ring of gold Cronley rolled in his palm. "A skull ring? What's the significance of that?"

A pair of M8 light armored cars moved into position—one to lead, one to bring up the rear—as Cronley lifted the last of the four black duffel bags into the back of the jeep that Father McKenna had brought.

"I'll drive," Cronley said as he moved in behind the steering wheel.

He signaled the driver of the lead M8 to move out. The trooper at the .50 caliber Browning braced himself as the six-wheeled armored car began rolling.

Serov nimbly jumped up on the jeep's rear bumper and hopped in back with the duffels. Father McKenna stepped into the front passenger seat just as Cronley revved the engine and dumped the clutch. The jeep lurched forward.

"Where to?" the priest said, his voice raised to be heard over the whine of the engine.

"First, the Nazis who worked for Wynne on the farm. Then maybe—probably—Burgdorf and von Dietelburg. They had the briefcases of cash when we caught them. They have to know what happened to the rest of the goddamn death's-head rings, if you'll pardon my French, padre." He paused, then added, "Or they don't. Or won't say. Only thing I know right damn now—and this is not to be disseminated—is that I don't know. But I want the others to come looking. And when they do, we'll be waiting. Our work is not done."

SIX MONTHS LATER

[TWO]
The International Military Tribunal
Nuremberg, American Zone of
Occupation, Germany
23 October 1946

Captain James D. Cronley Jr., Directorate of Central Intelligence, entered the gymnasium through its main double steel doors. The overhead lighting of the enormous space, where only a week earlier the prison guards played basketball games on a regular basis, was significantly less bright than usual.

Ahead, in the middle of the wooden floor, stood three gallows—two for continous operation, the third as a backup—that had been hastily erected. Their ominous silhouettes in the dimmed light stood spare and stark: wooden scaffolds painted black, each with thirteen steps leading up to a platform. Above the platform, suspended by a pair of posts, was a crossbeam dangling a thick rope with a four-coil "cowboy" noose fashioned at its end. The gallows were designed for a five-foot drop through a trapdoor in the platform floor. Wood panels painted black covered the front three sides below the platform, shielding the drop area from view, and a dark canvas curtain covered the fourth on the back side.

Cronley quickly started across the gymnasium floor, coming to a stop at the rear of more than twenty people, standing somber and silent, before the gallows.

"Sorry I'm late, Colonel," he said, softly.

"Sergeant Woods, with his usual efficiency, was about to start without you," Colonel Mortimer Cohen, U.S. Army Counterintelligence Corps, said drily.

Even in silhouette, Cronley could easily recognize the hangman, U.S. Army Master Sergeant John C. Woods. The thirty-five-year-old Kansas native was damn-near infamous. He always wore a dirty and wrinkled uniform, its master sergeant stripes barely attached with a single thread stitch at the corners. He shaved irregulary and never shined his scuffed boots. Cronley, once in passing, had what he considered the misfortune of being introduced to him—the moment made all the more memorable by Woods's crooked yellow teeth and a halitosis that almost triggered Cronley's gag reflex.

Woods bragged that he got away with flaunting anything he wanted because, he said with a foul grin, "I'm the only hangman in the European Theater."

Colonel Cohen told Cronley, "But you haven't missed the grand finale, for want of a better expression. Or perhaps that one is fitting. Burgdorf and von Dietelberg are scheduled as the last two today."

A week earlier, on October 16th, Cronley had stood with Cohen and the twenty-odd other witnesses, an international mix—British, French, American, Soviet—of civilians and military officers who had served during the Tribunal.

When Cohen earlier had asked if he wished to be there, Cronley practically came to attention and replied, "Colonel, I consider it my bounden duty to bear witness to the conclusion of what many have called history's greatest trial."

After nearly a year of trials—which began with an hours-long moving speech by Justice Jackson, the chief prosecutor for the United States—the verdicts finally were handed down.

Those on trial had been charged with four counts: Count 1, participation in a common plan or conspiracy for the accomplishment of a crime against peace; Count 2, planning, initiating, and waging wars of aggression and other crimes against peace; Count 3, war crimes; and Count 4, crimes against humanity.

The majority of those found guilty were sentenced to be hanged, while others faced imprisonment.

Cronley felt particularly compelled to see Reichsmarshall Hermann Göring, who had been found guilty on all four counts, hanged after Colonel Cohen, on the eve of the first executions, had brought up the fact that many of those sentenced to death were complaining.

"How the hell can they complain?" Cronley said. "The court said Göring was—I can almost recite this from memory—'almost always the moving force, second only to his leader' and 'the leading war aggressor, both as political and military leader.' Not only that but he admitted to his heinous crimes. To repeat, how the hell can he complain about his death sentence?"

"Not about the sentence of death," Cohen said. "Rather, the method. Göring wishes to protect his military honor. He said he would have no problem being taken out and shot—a soldier's death—but that to be hanged was, quote, the worst possible thing for a soldier, unquote."

"Seems to me all the more reason to string the bastards up," Cronley said.

There were others, Cohen said. Among them: Field Marshal Wilhelm Keitel—Oberkommando der Wehrmacht chief, guilty on all four counts—and Generaloberst Alfred Jodl—his deputy who signed orders for the summary execution of Allied commandos and was found guilty on all four counts and sentenced to death—had demanded a firing squad. Admiral Erich Raeder—guilty on the first three counts and sentenced to life imprisonment—petitioned the Allied Control Council "to commute this sentence to death by shooting, by way of mercy."

"All have been denied," Cohen announced, looking down at a sheet on his desk and reading from it. "The Tribunal spelled it out: 'They have been a disgrace to the honorable profession of arms.' And 'these men have made a mockery of the soldier's oath of obedience to military orders. When it suits their defense, they say they had to obey; when confronted with Hitler's brutal crimes, which are shown to have been within their general knowledge, they say they disobeyed. The truth is, they actively participated in all these crimes, or sat silent and acquiescent . . .'"

Cohen paused, looked up at Cronley, and then added, "And Göring is scheduled to be hanged first tomorrow."

"And I will be there."

Not an hour later, Cohen answered his ringing office phone.

"Jesus Christ!" he said, slamming the receiver back in its cradle.

He looked at Cronley as he jumped to his feet.

"Some son of a bitch apparently just granted Göring's last wish. That bastard bit a cyanide capsule that had been concealed in a jar of hair pomade . . ."

Early the next morning, at 0100 hours, Cronley stood next to Cohen in the group near the three gallows.

They turned when they noticed that there was some motion at the foot of the wooden steps to the first gallows. Master Sergeant Woods could be seen walking behind it. He soon returned, followed by two soldiers leading another man, who, dressed in black silk pajamas, was almost invisible in the shadows.

Cronley noticed on Woods's hip was a long-bladed knife in a scabbard and wondered if it was one more of the hangman's quirks.

"That's Joachim von Ribbentrop," Cohen said, in a low voice.

Cronley glanced at his watch. It showed eleven minutes past one.

The former foreign minister for Hitler had his hands bound and manacles on his feet.

"He can thank his pal Göring for that," Cohen said. "Before that son of a bitch took the coward's way out, the Tribune was going to allow as a courtesy that they be unbound."

Except for the sound of footfalls on the wooden stairs, the room was eerily silent as von Ribbentrop ascended to the platform and stood with the thick rope dangling before him.

Master Sergeant Woods placed a black hood over the condemned man's head, then slipped the noose over that. He adjusted the rope knot against the neck, then could be heard asking von Ribbentrop something. It was unintelligible. And if there came an answer, it went unheard by Cronley, who then watched as the hangman, forcing himself to walk erect, shuffled to the lever and without ceremony yanked on it.

The door in the floor opened—**BAM!**—which reverberated through the gymnasium, and von Ribbentrop dropped through the opening, his entire body unseen as the hangman's rope snapped taut.

Woods then shuffled to the wooden stairs and down them.

Cronley, without at first realizing it, automatically began silently reciting the Lord's Prayer:

Our Father, Who art in Heaven, Hallowed be Thy name; Thy kingdom come; Thy will be done on earth as it is in Heaven. Give us this day our daily bread; and forgive us our trespasses, as we forgive those who trespass against us; and lead us not into temptation, but deliver us from evil . . .

Cronley heard the heavy footfalls of Woods ascending the steps of the second gallows and raised his head to look as he finished the prayer. **For the kingdom, the power, and the glory are Yours now and for ever. Amen.**

Two minutes later, Field Marshal Wilhelm Keitel entered the gymnasium. The guards escorted him to the second gallows.

Remembering Keitel's cruel crimes, Cronley heard words from the prayer again in his mind: . . . **Deliver us from evil.**

Woods casually double-checked the noose knot

as Keitel, with a look of defiance, stared straight forward. Woods then slipped on the hood and noose.

As the knot was tightened, Keitel loudly declared from beneath the hood, "I call on God Almighty to have mercy on the German people. More than two million German soldiers went to their death for the Fatherland before me. I follow now my sons—all for Germany!"

Without a word, Woods shuffled to the lever.

BAM!

After some ten minutes had passed, there appeared beside the gallows two doctors, an American and a Soviet, who each carried a stethoscope. They disappeared behind the canvas curtains of the separate gallows.

There then came a deep commanding American voice—Cronley didn't see him but recognized that it was that of Brigadier General Homer Greene, chief of Army Security Agency Europe—who announced that it was now permissible to smoke.

A glow grew above the witnesses as at least a dozen flames came from Zippo lighters and wooden matches. Master Sergeant Woods lit a Chesterfield as he came down the wooden stairs.

After a moment, Cronley detected an unexpected but familiar odor above that of the cigarettes and the sulfur of the matches.

He leaned in toward Cohen, and said, "That smell?"

Colonel Cohen nodded, and turned to quietly reply. "Death by hanging causes the spincter muscle to lose its elasticity."

The doctors reappeared, and then each went under the other gallows.

When they had emerged and individually confirmed to Woods that the hanged men were indeed dead, the general ordered smoking to cease.

Woods, taking his time to finish his cigarette, then ascended the steps of the first gallows. At the rope, he pulled the long-bladed knife from its scabbard on his belt and with a smooth swing cut von Ribbentrop free. The rope disappeared through the hole.

Woods then went and tied a new rope with a noose to the crossbeam and then repeated the process for Keitel.

The bodies of von Ribbentrop and Keitel, draped by U.S. Army blankets and the heads still covered by hoods, were then carried by stretchers to a corner of the gym and placed behind a black curtain.

When guards escorted Ernst Kaltenbrunner to the gallows next, Cronley saw by his wristwatch that it was now 1:36. Kaltenbrunner, an Austrian, had been chief of the Reich Security Main Office, where he oversaw the mass murders of the concentration camps. Adolf Eichmann, of the Final Solution, and Rudolf Höss, commandant of Auschwitz, had reported to him.

As Woods readied the noose to be placed over Kaltenbrunner's head, Cronley expected another outburst of anger like Keitel's.

Kaltenbrunner, instead, announced in an even tone, "I have loved my German people and my Fatherland with a warm heart. I have done my duty by the laws of my people and I am sorry my people were led this time by men who were not soldiers and that crimes were committed of which I had no knowledge."

As Woods put on the black hood, Kaltenbrunner added, "Germany, good luck."

Cronley and Cohen had witnessed the trapdoors swinging—**BAM!**—more than two dozen times before, almost a week later, guards escorted former SS-Brigadeführer Franz von Dietelburg and former SS-Generalmajor Wilhelm Burgdorf to the side of the gallows. As all the others, they both wore black silk pajamas, and had their hands bound and feet shackled.

Cohen nudged Cronley to follow him.

"I want our faces to be the last they see."

Cohen and Cronley moved beyond the group

of witnesses. Cohen stopped within ten feet of the wooden steps of the first gallows.

The guard with Burgdorf nudged him forward. Burgdorf, with an icy stare, met Cohen's eyes, then Cronley's.

Before Cronley realized it, he blurted, "Do you have any last words?"

"Captain," Cohen said, coldly.

"Do you?" Cronley pursued.

"I told them!" Burgdorf said, loudly. "I demand an officer's honor—death by firing squad!"

"You, unfortunately, are in no position to demand anything. A firing squad is not an option. I will repeat my question: Do you have any last words?"

"I did nothing wrong!" Burgdorf barked, then came to attention. "May God bless the Thousand-Year Reich!"

Cronley looked at the soldiers. "Carry on."

Cronley watched as the hangman repeated his casual double-check of the noose knot as it dangled before Burgdorf. Then he put on the hood and the noose and then shuffled to the trapdoor lever.

BAM!

Burgdorf's body dropped straight down through the hole, the slack rope quickly becoming taut.

There then came a primal groan as the taut rope continued twitching and turning.

Cronley glanced at the hangman, who revealed a slight grin.

Does that twitch mean Burgdorf is straining?

That his neck didn't snap on the fall?

He's strangling . . .

Cronley then looked at Cohen, who nodded just perceptively.

"It's not the first time," he said, in a whisper. "Some say it's caused by the noose coils being intentionally tied off-center."

The hangman—with what Cronley suspected was a bit of theater, a look of disgust as he stomped down the wooden steps—went behind the gallows and pushed past the black canvas curtain, disappearing behind it.

They watched as the rope continued to twitch and turn, then there came a little slack in it, then it snapped taut again. There was no more movement.

And the hangman just now broke the neck.

That's why he grinned?

He caused the extra suffering on purpose?

When von Dietelburg was marched past Cohen and Cronley, he made eye contact with them. But this time Cronley refrained from saying anything.

As von Dietelburg ascended the wooden stairs, Cronley looked up at the hangman. There was no question in his mind that he detected a trace of a grin. Additional confirmation came when the master sergeant had to repeat going beneath the gallows to complete the execution.

The group of witnesses waited for the doctors to pronounce Franz von Dietelburg and Wilhelm Burgdorf dead, but one by one they began to leave before Master Sergeant Woods cut their ropes free of the gallows.

Jim Cronley knew what would happen now.

Colonel Cohen had explained to him that the bodies of those hanged would be transported—as had been the body of Hermann Göring and those hanged on the 16th of October—to a crematorium. Their ashes would be loaded into a fifty-five-gallon barrel and stirred to comingle them. The barrel of ashes would then be loaded into a three-quarter-ton weapons carrier.

At this point, Brigadier General Homer P. Greene and Colonel Mortimer Cohen would take over. Two more weapons carriers, each carrying a decoy fifty-five-gallon barrel and driven by a senior CIC agent, would be added.

With Colonel Cohen at the wheel and General Greene in the passenger seat of the first weapons carrier, all three vehicles would leave simultaneously. A half dozen MP jeeps mounted with .50 caliber Browning machine guns would follow.

Immediately upon leaving the Compound,

each weapons carrier would drive in a different direction through the streets, passing the city's bombed-out buildings. A pair of MP jeeps would trail each, preventing anyone from following.

Colonel Cohen and General Greene would continue to the center of a bridge crossing one of the five rivers in the area. They would unload the barrel, move it to the edge of the bridge, and remove its lid before pushing it onto its side. After the ashes flowed into the dark green waters of the river, they would shove the barrel over, too.

By a circuitous route that gave no hint where they had been, they then would return to the Tribunal Compound. There, they would go to the office of Mr. Justice Jackson and report what they had done by SIGABA to the President of the United States.

Cronley glanced around the emptying gymnasium. He turned and began walking to the double steel doors to leave.

As he went, he was surprised at his emotional reaction to the hangings.

Actually, he thought, **the damn absence of any emotional reaction.**

The only thing he could compare it to, he decided, was the shooting of a rabid dog by a neighborhood cop. Not pretty, but necessary.

LIKE WHAT YOU'VE READ?

If you enjoyed this large print edition of
THE ENEMY OF MY ENEMY,
here is another one of W.E.B. Griffin's latest
bestsellers also available in large print.

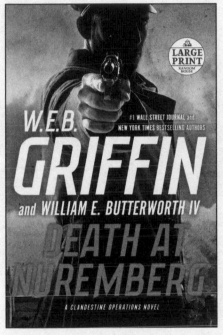